HAINTED

Also by Jordan L. Hawk

HAINTED

Jordan L. Hawk

CHAPTER 1

Dan walked slowly across the uneven backyard toward the lightning-struck oak. Clouds covered the moon and stars, and the rising wind brought with it the scent of rain falling from one mountain over. The only light flickered from the ring of votive candles he'd set out earlier and the lone bulb shining through the kitchen window behind him.

He paused to look back at the house, scanning the windows for any signs of movement. He'd told Bea to take Virgil into the root cellar until it was over, but his brother and sister were at the age where curiosity might get the better of good sense.

Virgil had already seen things no nine-year-old ought to, and Dan didn't intend to add to the list.

There was no sign of life in the house. Bea had brains, for all that she was only a couple years older than Virgil. She'd known what Dan was about, while Virgil just cried and made a fuss.

Virgil cried a lot lately. They all did.

Dan realized he was still staring at the house, putting off what had to be done. His fingers tightened on the wand in his hand, making the charms tied to it jingle and clink. Three feet of solid oak, the wand was cut from the very tree in front of him. Soft deerskin wrapped one end, while the other was capped with an antler, the longer of its two prongs curving to form a vicious hook.

Forcing himself to face the oak, he began to walk again, his steps slow and measured. The tiny light of the candles only illuminated the lowest branches, but he heard the upper ones tossing in the breeze, creaking and rubbing against each other like something alive, the leaves turning the wind into the whisper of a thousand voices.

He'd laid out a circle of salt near sundown, complete except for a gap just wide enough for a single person to pass. Stepping through, he took a handful of salt from the tool belt slung around his hips and used it to close the circle behind him.

"Let nothing cross this line; let the spirits within be contained. So mote it be." The words—and, more importantly, the will behind them—completed the circle. *At least if I fail, Dad—*

No. *The haint.* If he failed, the haint would be confined to the tree for as long as the circle lasted. It would give Bea and Virgil time to get to the neighbors, before the haint could get loose and come looking for them.

The wind picked up, blowing strands of his shoulder-length hair into his face. Holding his wand protectively in front of him, he moved closer to the massive tree, half of which was twisted and dead from a lightning strike. The crow skull tied to the wand rattled, independent of the wind or any tremor in his hand. The other charms started up, too, the sound like a rattlesnake's warning buzz. The mojo bag he always carried in the front pocket of his jeans shifted, like a small animal burrowing close. The silver pentagram around his neck grew ice cold.

The flickering light of the four votive candles, set in each one of the cardinal directions, revealed something in the midst of the low branches. Something large and dark, swinging back and forth in the breeze. There came the creak of a taut rope rubbing against bark, like the soft cry of a child.

Even though he had expected it, the sight of the figure dangling from the tree was like falling into an icy mountain creek, shocking him into numbness. For a minute, he was back on that awful day, before the ambulances had come to take the body away.

Breathe. The memory of Mom's voice comforted him, even as it made his throat tight with grief. *Ground. Center. Shield. Concentrate. Focus on what's in front of you right now, on the job at hand. The rest can sort itself out later.*

The end of the creaking rope was tied into a noose and looped tightly around the neck of the dangling figure. The stink of rot and shit wafted from the haint, accompanied by a teasing whisper of Old Spice. As the wind blew, the body rotated. He saw the face: swollen and purple in death, the tongue protruding between dry lips, the eyes half-sunk back into the head. In each socket glowed a tiny, pale light.

The eyes of the dead.

Thin tendrils of black energy uncoiled from the haint, striking like copperheads at Dan's aura, which flared indigo under the assault. He'd been ready for this, his aura slick and hard as he could make it. Most of the tendrils slipped off like knives against armor.

But he already had part of this haint inside him: in his blood, his bones, his very cells. Where a normal haint might never reach him, this one found the cracks made by loss, by grief, by the tiny little voice whispering: *please,*

Daddy, don't leave me. A few tendrils wriggled through like dark maggots, sinking into him before he could react.

I can't go on. Despair hit him, hard enough it made him dizzy. *I can't do this. Take care of the farm, take care of Bea and Virgil, all by myself? I'm a college sophomore; I don't know how to run a business or be a parent.*

They left me. How could you do that, Mom? How could you?

The grief and loss he'd lived with since Samhain seemed to swell, to become uncontrollable—unbearable. His wand fell from his hand. It felt like too much effort to pick it up again. *What difference does it make? What difference does anything make?*

Something tightened around his neck, cutting off his breath.

Fuck oh fuck oh fuck!

He clawed wildly at the ghostly noose, but it was too late—he'd fallen into the haint's trap and it had him now. His physical fingers encountered only skin, but he could *feel* the rough fibers of the rope, accompanied by the oily slickness of the haint's psychic tendrils.

Black spots danced in front of his eyes. From the shadows of the lightning-struck oak, the haint let out a hollow groan. Dan looked up, but saw only those two burning eyes, lonely and desperate in death, wanting Dan to join him.

Dan tore his gaze away. His dimming sight fell across something near one of the votive candles. Virgil had left his bike laying in the yard, despite being told to put it away earlier, and now the rear reflector caught the candlelight and held it like a steady, red eye.

Virgil. If Dan died here tonight, what would happen to his brother and sister? Maybe he couldn't fill their parents' shoes, but he was still all they had.

His searching fingers found the leather-wrapped end of the wand deep in the overgrown grass. With the very last of his strength, he gripped the wand and surged to his feet. The training Mom had pounded into him year after year took over; his arm swung in an arc with all his weight behind it.

The point of the antler stabbed deep into the haint's forehead, directly between the glowing eyes.

"Hecate, Lady of the Crossroads, Queen of Ghosts, open the way!" he gasped, with what little breath remained in his lungs.

The haint flailed, body jerking and dancing. The psychic tendrils curled back from Dan like the legs of a dying spider. The whole thing began to dissolve into putrid black goo, dripping into a puddle on the ground, until nothing was left.

A dark circle hung in the air, where the antler had pierced the haint's forehead, blacker even than the night sky. It grew larger, seeming to form the mouth of a cave, and Dan heard the baying of hounds in the distance. Something like a mist passed through the opening, pushed by Dan's will and drawn by the hand of the Goddess.

Then there was nothing but the ordinary night, the flickering light of the candles, and the empty, wind-tossed tree.

Dan dropped to his knees, gasping for breath. The tip of the antler dug into the ground.

Fuck. Oh fuck.

I killed him. I killed Dad.

And even though he knew it wasn't right, that what he'd done was give his father peace at last, it still felt like truth.

Wanting to get as far away from the oak as he could, he staggered to his feet and looked down at the black residue, which was all that remained of the haint. He automatically tossed a handful of salt from his pouch onto it. It began to bubble and shrink, the earth absorbing anything he missed. Moving slowly, every joint aching, he went to each quarter and dismissed the energies there, blowing out the votive candles.

When he was done, he stepped back over the line of salt and looked over his shoulder at the tree. *There. It's done.*

He's really gone now. It's just me.

Turning away from the tree, Dan walked slowly back in the direction of the old farmhouse and the life awaiting him there.

CHAPTER 2

Leif Helsvin pulled up at the gas pump and shut off the engine of the black Porsche 911 Turbo. According to the GPS, he'd reached Ransom Gap, North Carolina. From what little he'd seen thus far, it didn't look at all promising.

Still, he went where he had to, not where he wanted to. When you served a Goddess of Death, you learned very quickly there was no arguing, only doing.

There wasn't much to the town—or unincorporated area, as he supposed it was more properly called. A single gas station, seedy-looking garage, library, post office, and diner formed the largest cluster of buildings, with a pharmacy and a grocery store a bit farther along the road. Everything down to the badly-patched road had a shabby air, as if prosperity had passed by the community a long time ago.

An old man wearing overalls and a camouflage cap stared at the Porsche from the next pump over. Most of the vehicles in town matched the older model truck he was busy fueling, which might explain why the sleek sports car was getting even more attention than usual.

The old man's eyes widened even further when Leif climbed out to swipe his credit card at the pump. Leif would bet good money there weren't many men in the area with blond hair worn well below the shoulder, let alone with piercings in his lip, nose, eyebrow, and both ears. The heavy eyeliner and black fingernail polish probably didn't help him blend in with the locals, either.

With any luck, I won't be here long. Rúnar certainly won't spend a second more in this backwater than he has to.

Unless this is it. The end of the chase. Hel's mercy, wouldn't that be wonderful? To sleep in the same bed for more than a week at a time, to stick around somewhere long enough to recognize a few faces and put names to them.

A dull throb at the base of his skull sent little spikes of pain through his head. *That's not going to happen. This only ends when Rúnar decides it ends.*

Leif took three deep, cleansing breaths, trying to push back the headache. Along with the odor of gas fumes and sun-warmed pavement, he caught the faintest whiff of lotus and musk, there and gone. He must have imagined it. The silver piercings in his face, nipples, and scrotum chilled briefly. He felt more than heard a rattle of bones.

I have to try. I owe Alice that much.

Sliding back into the car, he reached into the glove compartment and took out a creased and worn scrap of paper. He'd gotten it from a Walker-Between-Worlds up in Virginia, after the runes and pendulum had pointed him in the direction of Rúnar's next destination.

The other Walker had scribbled a name, address, and phone number on the back of an old envelope. *Simone Miller, Hoary Oak Hill Farm, 28 Oak Hill Rd., Ransom Gap, NC.*

Leif had tried calling first, but the number was disconnected. The Walker in Virginia hadn't talked to Simone Miller in years—nothing unusual in that, but the dead phone meant she might not even be in the area anymore.

Rúnar was here; Leif had to follow, local contact or not. Still, finding out what exactly Rúnar had come here *for* would be a lot easier with the help of someone who knew the resident *draugar*—ghosts.

I'll make do if I have to. Leif brought up the GPS and entered the address. *But I hope I don't.* Because the truth was, he had a bad feeling about this place, although he wasn't sure why.

The pain flared again at the base of his skull, before settling into a low throb. Hoping his intuition was wrong for once, Leif put the car in gear and drove up the road leading deeper into the mountains.

Dan leaned over the guts of the tractor, wishing he had more of a head for machines, or less of a need for one. The accursed thing started making angry noises this morning, while they were pulling trailers of freshly-picked apples from the small orchard down by the creek. At first, Dan pretended not to hear, in hopes the problem might go away on its own. That bit of wishful thinking had gotten him nowhere, except elbow-deep in the recalcitrant engine, covered in grease and the acrid stench of burned oil.

Jimmy, one of the men Dan hired to help bring in the apple harvest and haul it down the mountain to sell, pulled alongside the tract of orchard. "Any luck?" he called, as he set about transferring the crates of apples from the trailer to the bed of his truck.

"No. Might have to load it up and take it to the garage." And spend yet more money they didn't have to spare. "At least it waited until we harvested the last of the apples."

"Ain't that the truth. Anything else you need before I take these?"

"Nah. Come back in the morning and I'll have your check ready."

Jimmy grinned. He was a young guy, big and strapping, who got by on seasonal work like a lot of other folks in Ransom Gap. Cute, in a sunburned farm boy sort of way. "You ought to come out to the Skylight, have a drink with me and the guys."

"Maybe I will," Dan lied. Even if he had been into country music and piss-water beer, he knew the Skylight Lounge wasn't his sort of bar. Carefully situated just over the county line, the place sold cheap beer over the counter and even cheaper moonshine under it, with a side business in meth just to keep things interesting.

Jimmy left with the apples. As he pulled his truck down the narrow dirt driveway, Dan saw him steer over to one side to let another vehicle pass. It took him a moment to recognize the scratched and faded blue sedan. *Corey. What does he want?*

Corey pulled into the driveway and shut off the engine. The passenger door opened, and Virgil jumped out. Corey must have given him a ride up from the school bus stop at the bottom of the hill. Pulling his second-hand backpack out of the car and tossing it over one shoulder, Virgil headed into the house without acknowledging Dan's existence.

Well, that was nothing new. Dan had done his best to raise his siblings over the last six years. Bea was turning out all right, but she'd always been mature for her age. As for Virgil, well, some days he seemed more like an angry stranger than a brother.

Corey shut the sedan's door and sauntered down the slope where Dan waited by the tractor. The autumn sun gleamed on his mahogany-brown skin and tightly-curled black hair. He was a tall man, long and loose-limbed, dressed for work in slacks and a white button-down shirt, although he'd rolled up the sleeves and loosened his tie.

Dan wiped his hand on a rag and held it out. "Corey," he said, trying not to sound guarded. They'd been best friends in high school, but things had never been the same after Dan had come back from college.

Corey shook his hand firmly. "How's it going, Dan?"

Dan shrugged. "Same as always. Apples and goats mostly, and getting the winter crop in the ground."

Corey nodded. Although he worked as an appraiser for the county nowadays, he'd grown up on a farm and knew the rhythms of the seasons. "I hear you. You still seeing Marlene?"

Dan knew Corey was just making friendly small talk, but it took everything he had not to wince. He'd come out to his family just before he'd headed off to college. And he'd meant to come out to Corey eventually, but doing it over the phone hadn't seemed right.

Then his parents died, and he'd had to move back to Ransom Gap, take over the farm, and go right back into the closet, because he couldn't risk the county deciding a gay man shouldn't be raising his younger brother and sister. They didn't have any other family to turn to, and the thought of his brother and sister in foster care scared Dan senseless.

He hated lying to Corey, though. Easier just to avoid his old friend, which meant they were practically strangers these days.

"She brings her little boy over for movie nights with the family now and again," he said lamely, not confirming—or denying—they were an item. "Thanks for giving Virgil a ride up the hill, by the way."

Corey let him change the subject. "Not a problem. Listen, I came over because I have a favor to ask you. Not for me, but for my great-uncle Zach and his wife. They bought a house, but they can't move in because the walls are bleeding."

Dan's fingers tightened, and for a moment he almost felt his wand in his hand again. He had to swallow twice before he could make his voice work. "You know I'm out of the business. I've got two teenagers to look after. If something were to happen to me, they'd end up wards of the state."

Corey held up his hands, and Dan winced, realizing that he'd let more anger leak into his voice than he'd meant. "I understand, my man. But I had to ask. You're the only haint-worker in Ransom County, and Zach's been after me for a week to see if you'd be willing to help out."

Mom would've done it. Would've said it's a haint-worker's responsibility to help bring peace to the dead and living.

Yeah, and look where that got her.

"I'm sorry I can't help," he said. This time, his voice came out minus the anger, at least.

"No problem. I'll let Zach know." Corey hesitated, looking suddenly uncomfortable. "Listen, Dan, I know it's none of my business, but I'm worried about you. You're not doing your haint-work, you're not really seeing Marlene, and you barely even leave the farm unless it's to get groceries."

"I've got a lot of work to do," Dan said. A part of him was unexpectedly glad Corey still cared enough about him to worry, but the rest...

I can't. He wished there was some way to make Corey understand.

"I know, but you have to live a little." The expression on Corey's dark face became even more uncomfortable. "When we were in high school, all you could talk about was getting out of Ransom Gap. Now you act like this farm is the center of universe. I know what happened to your folks was hard on you, but—"

Dan cut him off. "What am I supposed to do, just leave Bea and Virgil to fend for themselves?"

"I'm not saying that! But Bea will be off to college next fall, and Virgil's fifteen, old enough to be left on his own for the evening while you go out. I'm just saying you have to think about yourself some, too."

I did. I thought about myself and look what happened.

It took an effort of will not to glance in the direction of the great oak in the back yard. "I appreciate it. But I'm fine."

"If you say so." Corey started back in the direction of his car. "Just don't get stuck in the past and miss out on your future."

Easy for you to say. Corey didn't understand. To be fair, maybe he couldn't. There were too many things he didn't know, too many details no one outside the family *could* know.

Still, he wished he could've said yes. He been called to haint-work when he was just a boy, and some days he felt like the gift was just rotting inside him, like the decaying pulp of a bad tooth.

He remembered the night on the mountainside: the pain, the fear, the desperation. And if that wasn't reminder enough, he had only to look at the lightning-struck oak.

Trying to put all thoughts of haints and Walking out of his mind, he picked up a wrench and turned back to the exposed engine of the tractor.

Even with the GPS, Leif almost missed the driveway. The narrow, rutted dirt road, half-hidden by the tall grass of the berm, didn't catch his eye until he was almost past it, forcing him to stand hard on the brakes. Fortunately, there was no one behind him; he reversed and pulled even with the drive.

There was no sign of a house from the road, just a long, winding drive heading up a steep hill. *Must be murder to navigate when it snows.* An open field to one side had been abandoned and looked like it was in the process of reverting back into wilderness. The land on the other side was crowded with tall trees shedding leaves of gold and orange on the wind. A mailbox bearing the scars of BBs and paintballs stood to one side of the drive; he could just make out the name "Miller" in faded letters on the side. Opposite the mailbox, a sign in desperate need of repainting declared this to be Hoary Oak Hill Organic Farm.

Sweet death, I feel like an extra in a bad horror movie. On the other hand, the fact the farm was organic suggested he was more likely to encounter aging hippies than crazed hillbillies.

Hillbillies or hippies, I'll take whatever help they can give me.

He navigated the Porsche slowly up the steep drive, listening to gravel hit the undercarriage as he bumped through potholes. A cloud of dust plumed behind him, obscuring everything through his rearview mirror and turning the Porsche's shiny black finish to dull gray.

The house finally came into view as he crested the slope. The ancient, two-story farmhouse had paint peeling everywhere except for the front door, which was an incongruously cheerful shade of blue. A battered truck combining primer gray with rust brown sat near the screened porch. A few goats wandered around in a field, and a handful of chickens scratched in the dirt. The barns and outbuildings looked as if they'd never seen a single coat of paint, their tin roofs red with rust.

Looming behind the house was what must be the hoary oak itself. The oak was truly massive; any given branch would have dwarfed the entirety of a normal tree. One side was alive and covered with golden-red leaves; the other was dead, its bark scored and twisted from a lightning strike.

The oak loomed over everything around it, including the house, and he wondered how old the thing must be. *It looks like I always imagined Yggdrasil, with its branches holding up Asgard and its roots cradling Helheim.* The *landvaettir* associated with it would be powerful, and he made a mental note to leave a small offering if the chance arose. Keeping the local wights happy was always a good idea.

A young man came off the porch as Leif pulled up. A kid really, no more than fifteen, and as unsuited to his surroundings as possible. The teen looked like a walking Gap ad, complete with polo shirt, khaki slacks, and short, styled hair.

Leif powered down the window as he approached. "Can I help you?" the boy asked warily. Although his look was junior-GQ, his country accent marked him as a local.

Leif tried a friendly smile, although the kid seemed far more interested in the car than in him. "Maybe. I'm looking for Simone Miller."

That got the boy's attention fast enough. The fascination with the Porsche vanished, leaving behind surly anger. "Wait here," the kid said. Stuffing his hands in his pockets, he slouched around the side of the house. "Dan! Somebody's here about a haint!"

Not sure what to do—what was a haint, anyway?—Leif got out of the car and waited beside it. The kid went into the house, now studiously ignoring Leif's presence.

While he waited, Leif glanced around at the beautiful view, with the valley falling away below on one side and the mountains rising up on the other. He inhaled deeply; the air was fresh and clean, like fallen leaves and apple cider, wood smoke trailing on the breeze. There was something almost otherworldly about the area; although he'd seen plenty of mountain ranges with more grandeur, these were among the oldest in the world, and their power had seeped into the air and water and earth. No wonder a Walker had taken up residence here. *This whole county is probably thick with psychics and mediums.* He'd already seen a number of barns with protective hex signs painted on them, which meant this was one of those sheltered communities where the old ways had never entirely died out.

Just as Leif began to wonder if he should approach the cheerful blue door, a man walked around the corner of the house. He was of average height, which put him several inches shorter than Leif. His t-shirt strained across broad shoulders and showed off the lean muscles of someone who performed hard physical labor rather than pump iron at the gym. Thick brown hair hung to his shoulders, and eyes dark to the point of black stared intensely from a face with a hawk nose, high cheekbones, and a small, sensual mouth. Even though the day was cool, a light sheen of sweat showed on olive skin tanned from working outdoors.

If I'd known country boys were this hot, I'd have left the city a long time ago.

"Can I help you?" the man asked.

Leif gave him his most engaging smile and held out a hand. "Leif Helsvin. I'm looking for Simone Miller."

The man didn't return the smile, although he did clasp Leif's hand in a brief, firm handshake. Up close, he exuded the aroma of male sweat mixed with bay rum aftershave, a wonderfully masculine combination, which practically made Leif's mouth water. His aura was the smooth indigo of a trained Walker.

"Dan Miller," he said by way of introduction. "I guess you better come inside."

CHAPTER 3

Dan led the way into the house, trying to pretend his palms weren't sweating. He wasn't sure if his nervousness came from the fact two people in one day had shown up asking for haint-work...or the fact this stranger was absolutely gorgeous.

Leif Helsvin. The name suited; he had the looks of a Nordic supermodel, all sculpted cheekbones and pouting lips, with ivory skin fair enough to trace the veins beneath. His long hair was the palest yellow of corn silk, and his eyes a clear shade of icy blue, made all the more startling by the thick eyeliner around them. His tall, thin body was clad in black: comfortable jeans, t-shirt, and high boots with abundant straps and buckles. He wore a black cuff around one wrist, studded with silver, and his belt also sported silver studs. Both ears were pierced multiple times, and silver hoops gleamed from his lower lip, right eyebrow, and left nostril.

Dan had always had a weakness for goth boys, and after six years without a date, his cock was definitely sitting up and taking notice.

Which was just too fucking bad. This Leif was here for haint-work. The best thing—the only thing—to do would be to give him the bad news and show him the door.

Dan led the way into the kitchen, where Bea sat at the table, hunched over a textbook. Virgil slouched on the sagging couch in the living room, playing a video game on an outdated system.

"Leif, this is Beatrice," he said. "The lump in the living room is Virgil."

"I heard that!" Virgil shouted over the explosions and gunfire of his game.

A bemused expression touched Leif's handsome face. "Beatrice and Virgil?"

Dan had wondered if he'd pick up on that. Most people didn't. "Yeah. And I go by Dan, but it's really Dante. Mom had an awful sense of humor for a haint-worker. A Walker," he added, seeing Leif's confusion.

Leif's eyes cleared, but his fair brows pulled down. "I notice you said 'had.'"

Cute and sharp. "You're about six years too late if you needed something from her." Turning to the refrigerator to avoid seeing the look of sympathy on Leif's face, he asked, "You want something to drink? We've got water, cider made from our own apples, and an ale from one of the breweries over in Asheville."

"I'll take the beer, please." Leif spoke with a flat, Midwestern accent; Dan wondered where he hailed from, and what had brought him to a place like Ransom Gap.

Dan pulled out two beers, uncapped them, and handed one to Leif, before indicating they should sit at the table. Bea pretended to be absorbed in her math homework, but Dan figured she was listening intently.

Leif took a sip of the beer and nodded appreciatively. Resting his knobby wrists on the table, he said, "A Walker in Virginia gave me your mother's name and phone number. When I couldn't reach her, I thought I'd stop by. It's important, otherwise I wouldn't have come."

He seemed earnest, his blue eyes wide and hopeful. Dan dropped his gaze and noticed a series of small, white scars on both of Leif's arms, barely visible against the pale skin. He wondered how Leif had gotten them, then remembered he didn't need to be wondering about anything besides how to get rid of the other man. He probably shouldn't have invited him inside in the first place, but it wasn't every day a hot guy crackling with the otherworldly aura of a Walker showed up on the doorstep.

"I understand. I was Mom's apprentice," he said, feeling as if he were admitting to something shameful. "After she died, somebody had to take care of Virgil and Bea, and there wasn't anyone else. I gave it up."

Sounded simple, didn't it? As if there'd never been any pain, or tears, or wrenching choices. As if there'd never been any spring night in the shadow of the lightning-struck oak.

The corners of Leif's shapely mouth pinched in sympathy. "That must have been difficult." He was another Walker; maybe he guessed what it had been like. Maybe he'd even lost his teacher himself and knew for sure, or as much as anyone could.

Dan only shrugged. *Not something I want to talk about.*

"I understand you're not in the business anymore," Leif said carefully, "but I need information, and if you could help me with that, I would appreciate it. I need to know if there are any particularly powerful *draugar* in the area. The one I'm looking for may not be aggressive, other than to protect its land or its family, just unusually strong."

"I'm guessing you mean a haint," Dan said. Haint, ghost, *yurei*, it all meant the same: the unquiet dead. "We've got a few nasty ones around here,

I suppose, although not as many as places without a family of Walkers in residence for the last hundred years. Can you be more specific?"

Leif's mouth thinned; he glanced away, out the window in the direction of the big oak. "I'm tracking a necromancer," he said at last. "And I don't mean the sort who approaches the entrance of the Underworld and politely requests an oracle. Rúnar Ingmarsson is a powerful sorcerer, able to conjure up the souls of the dead to bind them to his will."

Despite the relative warmth of the fall day, Dan shivered. Walkers were meant to help the dead pass on, in peace if possible, but by force if they were intent on harming the living. Binding them to this world was against everything he'd ever been taught.

Leif noticed his shiver and nodded. "Yeah. It's not pretty. He's been traveling all over the country—all over the world, really—seeking out hauntings caused by particularly powerful ghosts. When he finds one, he binds it."

"Why?" Bea asked quietly, and Dan started. He'd forgotten she was even there.

"Greed. Power. Revenge." Leif's eyes were shadowed, and Dan wondered if one of the dead this necromancer had disturbed had been a relative or a friend. "He forces some of them to prophesy, or to tell him where their treasures are hidden. The treasure he sells on the black market. Some *draugar* are sent to kill his enemies, of which he has many. Powerful people always do."

Dan chewed on his lip unhappily. This didn't sound like a situation in which he had any business getting involved. Still, Walkers helped each other out, and even if he'd retired, the impulse to lend a hand was still there.

Not to mention Leif's awfully cute. Which was a terrible reason to do anything, really, although he wasn't sure he could quite help himself.

Maybe he could compromise. "I'm not certain which haint the necromancer might be looking for, not off the top of my head," he said slowly. Bea's dark eyes darted to him, and he felt a stab of guilt for getting involved at all. "I can ask around, though—some of the old folks might have an idea. But, you have to understand, if this Rúnar is as bad as you say, I can't do anything more than that. I've got the farm to run, and Bea and Virgil to look after."

"I can look after myself!" Virgil yelled from the other room.

Dan resisted the urge to ask Virgil if he *wanted* to end up in foster care. Virgil would say yes, just to spite Dan, and the whole conversation would go south from there.

At least Leif didn't look at him like he was some sort of coward. "I understand."

His acceptance made Dan feel even worse. If Leif had been angry, or tried to convince him to do more, he would have defended his decision. Now he *did* feel like a coward.

Maybe there was another way he could help. "Do you have a place to stay?" he blurted, before he could reconsider.

"Not yet. The GPS has a hotel listed nearby. I thought I'd stay there."

Bea screwed up her face. "The Skylight?" she asked doubtfully.

The Skylight Hotel was a ramshackle place next to the Skylight Lounge. Dan had never been inside, but from the look of the building, he doubted clean sheets were much of a priority. Most customers paid by the hour instead of the night, and didn't get much sleeping done between the drugs and prostitution from what he'd heard. Not to mention a guy wearing eyeliner was sure to get harassed by the drunk assholes at the Lounge.

"I wouldn't recommend that place to a cockroach," he said. "Why don't you stay here? You can have Virgil's room."

"What?" Virgil shouted. "Where am I supposed to sleep?"

"The couch. You spend all your time there anyway."

Leif winced at the argument. "No, really, it isn't necessary."

"I can't help you with this necromancer, but I can do this," Dan said firmly. "Mom would be shamed if we didn't have you stay—and made sure you had a proper bed," he added, directing the last bit at Virgil.

Invoking the dead, especially one who'd been a teacher, carried weight with Walkers. Dan saw the shift in Leif's eyes even before a tentative smile formed on his mouth. "Thank you," he said. "And in return, I'm willing to help you out with anything you need."

Although there was nothing flirtatious in Leif's tone, Dan felt his heart beat faster. He could think of all sorts of things he'd like the other man's "help" with.

Stop it. He'd spent years ruthlessly suppressing his libido, but Leif seemed to have woken it up with a vengeance. *I don't know if he would be interested. Even if he was, I'm not out. I can't take the risk.*

"There is something," he said slowly. "One of the local families is having problems with a haint. Nothing too serious, I don't think, but I didn't want to take a look into it without anyone to back me up. If you're willing, we could go out there and take care of it." And surely two Walkers could handle a simple case of bleeding walls.

"Of course," Leif said immediately. "My kit is in my car."

Dan rose to his feet. "I'll get my things and meet you outside. Bea, give Corey a call and let him know we're on our way."

Leif lowered the truck's visor to block the rays of the setting sun. He'd rolled the window down a half-inch, and the air flowing inside was cool and crisp, perfumed by fall leaves and smoke. The narrow road was a series of curves and switchbacks winding across the mountain, with seas of green, yellow, and orange leaves on one side, and bare stone weeping moisture on the other.

It was beautiful country, if a bit too far out of the city for his tastes. He could see why people might put down roots here. If one was the sort to put down roots, that is, which he most definitely was not.

Dan, on the other hand, practically needed a shovel to dig himself free. And that was just to leave the farm.

He glanced at the other Walker, who steered the beat-up old truck with a practiced hand. They'd left the Porsche behind, even though Leif had offered to burn his gas instead; Dan hadn't been sure the low-slung vehicle would make it up the driveway to their destination.

"Thanks again for letting me stay with you," Leif said.

Dan didn't take his eyes off the road, but the corners of his mouth turned up marginally. He had a nice smile, yet it seemed guarded, as if he were always holding something back. "Least I could do."

Leif suppressed a sigh. Dan was a Good Guy, which made him absolutely off limits. Leif preferred his hook-ups to be quick and impersonal; he never fucked anyone he hadn't picked up in a club and he never came back for a second round. It was easier that way for everyone. Because Leif was most certainly *not* a Good Guy and never would be.

Some stains never come out.

Still, there was no harm in just looking. He studied Dan's profile while they drove. The wind blew Dan's brown hair wildly around, scattering strands across his high cheekbones and tickling the corner of his mouth. The dark eyes were as intent on the road as they had been on Leif earlier, as if Dan put every ounce of concentration into whatever task lay in front of him. The hands gripping the steering wheel showed grease ground in beneath the fingernails, and sported calluses, nicks, and scars as witnesses to a living made from manual labor.

It was easy to imagine those strong hands touching him, to picture what it would be like to see those intense eyes light up in pleasure.

No. No, no, no. Time to think about something else.

The truck slowed sharply, and Dan put on the turn signal. *And I thought Dan's driveway was bad. Good thing he talked me out of bringing the Porsche.*

The drive wound back through the woods, before exiting into a small clearing. Four other cars were parked around in the tall grass, and a group of people, most of them of African-American descent, stood around the vehicles talking or sat in lawn chairs. Behind them lurked an abandoned house, its dirt-coated windows like idiot, staring eyes. Even from a distance, Leif could perceive the etheric miasma hanging around it, like a bruise on the fabric of the world.

Dan shut off the engine; he wore a grim look on his face, like a man getting ready to do battle. Which they were, but somehow Leif didn't think it was the *draugr* worrying him. *What's your story, Dan Miller?*

Not my business, remember? No getting involved.

Leif grabbed his bag from between his feet on the floorboards and his prized possession from the back seat. Dan looked surprised earlier, when Leif pulled the sword out of the Porsche's trunk. "You use that for haint-work?"

"When I need to," Leif had told him. He'd removed a shorter staff from his bag and displayed it. "I use this when I can, to help along the nonviolent dead. As for the sword, well, I've found that you can stop just about anything if you cut off its head." He hadn't mentioned his boot knife, his weapon of last resort.

"Never go anywhere without some protection at hand," Rúnar had once told him. *"We have many enemies, my dear."*

A flash of pain through his skull accompanied the memory of whispered words, although at least it didn't erupt into a full-blown migraine.

Leif climbed out of the truck and slung on the baldric; the sword's hilt jutted over his right shoulder. The rest of his tools he left in the black bag for now. Dan kept most of his supplies in an old tool belt, except for an oak-and-antler wand he hung from a loop.

"Damn, dude has a *sword*," one of the men said as they approached. Leif couldn't tell if he was impressed or just incredulous.

Another of the waiting men came forward; his clothing was neat and bordered on something Virgil would wear. Leif assumed he worked in a cube farm somewhere. "Dan. Thanks for coming. I couldn't believe it when Bea called." He shot Leif a curious look.

Dan shrugged, staring uncomfortably down at the dirt. *An ex-boyfriend, maybe?* "Turns out I got some help. This is Leif Helsvin. Leif, Corey Myers."

Corey didn't look entirely sure about Leif, but he put his hand out anyway. "Pleased to meet you."

"Likewise. Dan says you've got a haunting of some sort here?"

"Uncle Zach can tell you," Corey said, nodding in the direction of an older man with a balding head. "It's his house."

"Should've listened to Momma when she said never own a house that doesn't have a haint-blue door." Zach shook his head dolefully. "With the kids moved out, the wife and I were thinking about getting a smaller place. The house here had been foreclosed. Plenty cheap and just the right size. We came over with the realtor and took a look. It needed some work, but nothing too bad. Problem is, we'd only ever been here in daylight."

"What do you know about the history of the house?" Leif asked.

"Not much. I did some asking around, and the neighbors said that a couple lived here when it was new, maybe forty years ago. The husband ran off, and his wife got crazy-mean afterward. Once she died, a cousin took out a second mortgage and started renting out the place. Nobody stayed for long, and eventually he gave up and just stopped making payments."

"What problems have you been having?" Dan asked.

Zach looked uncomfortable. One of the younger women in the group said, "Tell him, Daddy."

"I was here by myself, doing some repairs," Zach said, a defensive note creeping into his voice. "The place hadn't been properly taken care of in a long time. I'd always felt a mite uncomfortable in it, like somebody was watching me, but didn't figure it was anything more than nerves at taking on a mortgage at my age. A few little things happened: tools disappearing, then showing up somewhere I knew I didn't leave them; creaks sounding like footsteps, but might have just been the beams settling.

"I ought to mention that the walls in the back room are painted plain white. Well, the night I stayed late, I happened to walk past the room, and when I looked inside, they were red. At first I thought it was a trick of the light, then I noticed they looked wet. That was right before the smell hit me —it was blood, sure enough. I took right off, and I guess anybody else would have, too!" he added defiantly.

"I guess you're right about that," Dan agreed with a nod. "Leif, what do you think?"

"The missing husband?" he hazarded. "That is, it could be the wife, but bleeding walls sounds more like foul play. If she killed him and hid the body, it could explain a lot—including why her own mental state degenerated after he 'ran off.'"

"Lord help us," Zach said with a shake of his head. "Can you get rid of it?"

Leif and Dan exchanged a glance, and for a moment, Leif wondered if Dan would back out.

Dan's fingers tightened on the leather grip of his sturdy wand. "The two of us should be able to handle it," he said.

That seemed to reassure the extended family. "Thanks, Dan," Corey said. "We really appreciate it."

Dan's mouth thinned. "I'm only doing haint-work while Leif is here," he said gruffly. Turning to Leif, he asked, "You ready?"

Leif nodded and picked up his bag from where he'd set it by his feet. "Let's go."

CHAPTER 4

"How do you want to do this?" Dan asked, as they approached the porch.

The very last rays of the setting sun touched Leif's pale hair, making it blaze in the twilight. His tall, lanky body exuded confidence as they approached the house, and his blue eyes sharpened as he studied the windows.

Nervousness fluttered in Dan's belly—and not just because this would be the first haint he'd faced since that spring night under the oak. Leif was so sophisticated, with his fancy car and his sword, and his talk of traveling around hunting necromancers that Dan felt like a kid or a country bumpkin beside him. Way out of Dan's league, both personally and professionally, but somehow, it made it even more important he not screw this up. He wanted to prove himself, to show Leif he could handle a haint.

Leif stepped onto the porch, the heavy soles of his boots thumping softly against the weathered wood. "We should probably seal the doorways with salt as we go through the house. It'll keep the spirit from slipping past us."

Dan nodded. "I'll go ahead and seal up the windows with salt, too, before we go inside."

Leif gave him a smile, making Dan feel weak in the knees. "Good idea."

Don't get distracted. He walked to the first window. The bushes in front of it hadn't been trimmed in years, and the glass was too smeared with grime to see inside. *We're here to do a job. This is dangerous enough without thinking with my cock instead of my head.*

He'd told himself the risk was minimal because there were two of them, but he didn't *know* that, did he? *If something happens to me, like it did to Mom...*

She'd been soloing the night she died. Dan had been off at college, and there was no one to watch her back.

The intense training a Walker endured inevitably forged a psychic bond between teacher and student, even for those who weren't blood kin. In theory, it allowed the apprentice to pull strength from the teacher if he ended up in a situation he couldn't handle by himself, but it went both ways.

That night, Mom had reached out to him. It was Halloween night, and one minute he'd been partying and laughing with his friends in the dorm, and the next—

The next he'd been with her, dying on the mountainside. She'd reached out for help, but he'd been useless. He'd failed to save her.

The memory felt like a deep burn; he flinched away from the slightest inadvertent brush against it. He tried not to remember the particulars, just focusing on the fact he'd failed her, just like he'd failed Dad later. And if he screwed up tonight and got himself killed, he'd fail Bea and Virgil, too.

It was too late to back out now, though. He'd only known Leif for a couple of hours, but he had the feeling the other Walker would just go in alone if Dan suddenly decided he didn't want to face the haint after all. And if things went south, and Leif died while Dan stood around and did nothing…

I don't think I could take it.

Dan took a handful of salt out of his pouch and sprinkled it over the windowsill. "Hecate, Lady of the Crossroads, close this path," he said aloud, investing every word and movement with his will, because intent meant everything in magic.

He repeated the process at each window on the ground floor. When he worked back around to the porch, he found Leif had opened the black bag and taken out a box of lancets and a long wand with a thick, boxy head, etched with runes and banded with brass.

Leif glanced up as Dan approached. "Hopefully I won't need these," he said ruefully, and tucked a lancet into a front pocket of his jeans. "And hopefully I *will* need the staff and not the sword."

"And I hope a plane flies over and drops a big bag of money at my feet," Dan said wryly.

Leif laughed. "It's unlikely," he allowed. He undid the snaps holding his wrist cuff in place, revealing a tattoo beneath. Two parallel lines mimicked a narrower version of the cuff, with what looked like Viking runes inscribed in a band between them.

"Nice ink," Dan said.

Leif smiled, but it didn't quite reach his eyes. "Thanks. Ready?"

"Yep."

Dan took three deep, cleansing breaths. Leif did the same thing at the exact same instant and tempo, and Dan hoped the synchronization was a good sign. Leif's indigo aura flared, settling into a hardened, armor-like shell around him. His energy was palpable, brightening his eyes from ice-blue to neon. He all but glowed in the shadows, beautiful as something carved from ivory and aged for a thousand years in the darkness.

Dan concentrated on his own shielding, felt it slip into place around him, as if he'd last done this just yesterday and not years ago. When he was ready, he nodded to Leif, and they turned to the house.

Dan pushed open the front door. Zach hadn't bothered to lock it in his hasty flight, and the hinges shrieked like dying men. The air inside tasted close and stale: dust underlain with mildew. Once Leif followed him in, Dan paused long enough to pour salt across the threshold. "Hecate, close this path."

A flash of light passed over the salt in his astral sight, signaling the exit was sealed against the dead. Although people thought of ghosts as passing through walls, the truth was they mostly used doors, even if it meant sliding through one that was shut. When they did walk through walls, it usually indicated a door was present during the time the haint had lived, even if it was bricked up later.

"Do you feel it?" Leif asked. The close, heavy air flattened his voice; the words died unnaturally fast, with not even the hint of an echo.

"Yeah." The sense of being watched was palpable. Which by itself didn't mean the haint bore any ill intent, but in this case the sensation was accompanied by a definite malice. Whatever lurked in these walls, it was angry, and it didn't appreciate their intrusion one bit.

The front door opened into a hall running the length of the house. What had probably been a formal dining room, at least going by the small chandelier, opened off to the left. To the right appeared to be a parlor or formal living room, now bare of furniture and draped in cobwebs and dust.

"I'll go right, you go left?" Leif suggested.

Dan nodded and turned into the dining room. Although he still felt watched, there was no intensification of the sensation. As an experiment, he hit the light switch for the chandelier. The light came on, flickering a few times before dying to the level of a candle's glow. *Good thing Walkers can see in the dark.*

Satisfied the room was more or less clear, Dan backed out and sealed the doorway with salt. A moment later, Leif joined him. Exchanging a look, they continued down the hall without comment.

The kitchen and a bathroom received the same treatment as the dining and living rooms. At the very back of the house, two more rooms opened off the hall once again: a bedroom and a den.

A single glance into the den told Dan everything he needed to know. The shadows there were deeper, somehow, as if there was something more to them than the simple absence of light. The sensation of being watched intensified, and the small hairs on his arms prickled.

"There," Leif murmured.

"Yep." Dan turned and sealed off the bedroom without bothering to go inside. "Ready?"

Leif entered the den first. Dan followed, pausing to seal the doorway with yet another line of salt, to prevent the haint from escaping.

The air in the room was ice-cold, as if they'd walked into a freezer. Currents of energy twisted and turned restlessly in the air, their color bruised and dark as rotting fruit. The atmosphere felt oppressive despite the chill. The mojo bag in Dan's front pocket trembled in response to the menace, like a mouse catching a whiff of cat.

Leif warily slid along the back wall, his long legs and quick movements reminding Dan of a wading heron. By unspoken agreement, Dan stayed near the door, hoping to catch the haint between them.

Before Leif had even reached the other side of the room, the white walls began to flush scarlet. The plain gypsum wallboard grew steadily redder and redder, taking on a wet look. The stench of blood filled the air, as if they'd stepped into a slaughterhouse instead of a home, thick enough for the tang of iron to coat the back of Dan's throat.

Leif unhooked the staff from his belt. "In the name of Hel, Half-dead, I would speak with you, spirit," he declared.

Yeah, Leif was optimistic, all right. And, as the world seemed to hold its breath for a moment, it even seemed like he might be right in this case. Maybe the haint would communicate instead of trying to hurt them.

The boards in the center of the uncarpeted floor rattled loudly. The charms bound around Dan's wand shivered in response, and a deep, bell-like sound came from the blade of Leif's sheathed sword.

"Shit," Leif muttered, even as he tucked his staff into his belt. With his free hand, he drew his sword in a hiss of metal and leather.

The wooden floorboards gave one final groan—and something exploded out of the floor on a wave of corrupted energy and furious hate.

"Dan, look out!" Leif shouted as the *draugr* heaved itself free of its makeshift grave and hurled itself at the other Walker.

The poisonous energy of the hateful ghost formed an abomination of bloody bones and flayed limbs, dripping with gore and stinking of all the secret fluids of mortality. Blind rage radiated outward; this was no ghost to be coaxed into the light, but rather a soul twisted by pain and hate until it wanted only to destroy everything in its path.

Dan swore and dropped back to the very edge of the salt line, which he couldn't cross without breaking the charm. He swung his wand at the ghost, the wicked hook of antler aiming for what might have been its head.

The *draugr* skittered out of the way, and the blow missed. As far as Leif could tell, the entity was nothing but a collection of rat-gnawed bones, slick and wet with plasma, its ligaments and tendons flapping obscenely loose. The bones jumbled together: a humerus here; grasping fingers there; ribs flared like wings one moment, before snapping shut the next. A skull lurked in the center of the maelstrom, the cold light of the restless dead shining in its empty sockets.

His sword was a comforting solidity in his hands, the blade infused with psychic energy and glowing to otherworldly sight. As the *draugr* went after Dan, Leif slipped silently behind it, raising the sword in preparation for the blow to send it to Helheim's gates whether it wanted to move on or not.

The thing twisted like a snake, avoiding the descending blade. A set of claws made from the jagged ends of rat-chewed ribs swiped at Leif's belly; it would have disemboweled him had it connected. He pivoted on one foot, body contorting through instinct honed by years of training. The ragged bones missed flesh, snagging only the cotton of his t-shirt and ripping it open.

Dan took another swipe at the *draugr* while it was distracted, but the thing was terrifyingly fast, its jumble of bones shifting about, disassembling and reassembling quicker than either of them could track. Dan flung a scattering of salt mixed with rosemary and garlic with his off hand. The *draugr* let out a howl of rage when the salt struck it, and its movements slowed perceptibly.

Sweet death, thank you!

Leif didn't waste the opportunity. With all the strength of his will as well as his arms, he swung the sword down and into the maelstrom of shifting bone. "Mordgud, Mistress of the Gate, guide this spirit to heal in Helheim!"

The blade sank into what felt more like cold, thick mud than bone. A rattling gasp escaped the *draugr*—then its form dissolved, reverting to the black ichor of corrupted ectoplasm. The world unfolded in Leif's astral sight; he saw a confused impression of a monumental bridge and a woman in ebony armor, holding out her hands in welcome.

It was over. He and Dan stood in an ordinary room with white walls and a solid, if dusty, floor. The unnatural cold had vanished, and Leif felt no sensation of being watched.

"Not too bad," he said as he drew out a lavender-scented cloth and cleaned off the blade of his sword.

"Are you all right?" Dan asked. "Did it get you?"

"No." He pulled up his shredded t-shirt, revealing the pale skin of his torso. "I'm fine, see?"

Dan's gaze lingered on the exposed skin. A slight flush tinted his cheeks before he glanced aside. "Um, yeah. You're fast—I figured it had gutted you for sure."

Leif shrugged and let his shirt fall back into place. "Just lucky. What about you? Are you okay?"

Dan shrugged. "Yeah. I'm fine. Let's give Zach the good news."

CHAPTER 5

The sun was just cresting the horizon when Leif stepped out into the backyard. Mountains blocked the earliest rays, but the light touched the underside of the clouds, turning them red, blue, and gold. The cold air hardened his nipples around their piercings. The smoke from the wood stove in the farmhouse's living room was oddly sweet, different from the stink of the burning trash he'd used to keep warm when he'd lived on the streets.

He still dreamed about it, distorted nightmares where the tricks he picked up turned into his foster father, Nick, who was the reason he'd taken to the streets in the first place. Or of that freezing winter night in a haunted warehouse, where Rúnar had saved him from a fast death at the hands of a murderous *draugr*, as well as the slower death from drugs or disease which would have been his fate otherwise.

Maybe I should tell Dan I was Rúnar's apprentice. But if he had, Dan would never have let him in the front door, let alone spend the night.

They'd gotten back to the farmhouse after midnight, and he'd woken well before dawn, a headache radiating out from the base of his skull. While everyone else still slept, he'd taken advantage of the house's sole bathroom to shower and shave.

The bathroom had told him a little more about his hosts. The freesia shampoo must belong to Bea; it seemed far too girly for either Virgil or Dan. The body spray marketed to teen boys, on the other hand, could only belong to Virgil. Dan's bay rum aftershave was placed neatly beside a shaving kit which looked old enough to have been passed down from a grandfather. The medicine cabinet held aspirin, cold remedies, and assorted herbs, but nothing stronger.

The house was old and well lived-in; he imagined generations of Millers wresting life out of the rocky land around it. Like Dan's truck, it had seen its share of wear, suggesting money was tight enough for only essential repairs to be carried out. The energy inside felt clean, yet underneath he sensed pools of sorrow and frustration threatening to gather into something worse.

There aren't any family photos. No pictures of weddings, graduations, or vacations stood on the mantel or hung from the walls. *As if they're trying to erase the past.*

Dan hadn't said what had happened to Simone, other than she'd died. There'd been no mention of a father; maybe the man had skipped out. Dan couldn't be any older than twenty-five, and was raising his two younger siblings *and* running the farm. Unlike Leif, Dan was solid, and centered, and certain; someone who could be depended on in a pinch.

Not to mention sexy.

Leif shook his head and pulled his jacket more closely around his thin shoulders. Like all of his clothing, the heavy canvas was black. He'd stitched bindrunes into the lining, and the soft thread scraped against the skin of his forearms, below the sleeves of his t-shirt.

He trekked across the back yard to the enormous oak dominating the property, leaving tracks in the dew-coated grass. It was always a good idea to make nice with the local land wights, especially since he might need to call on their help before all this was over.

The oak seemed like the natural place. He felt the energy moving through the tree: clean and pure, slow and strong. It reminded him of Dan himself, which made a certain sort of sense, if his fellow Walker had been born and raised in its shadow.

He expected to find the detritus of past offerings near the base of the tree, but there was nothing. *Odd.*

The Millers followed a different path than his own, of course. Walkers-Between-Worlds came from every tradition on earth, from Catholic exorcists to Vodoun mambos to Inuit shamans, all of them with their own idiosyncratic ways of dealing with both the living and the dead. But no matter what gods they were bound to or what tools they used, they all worked with the energy and spirits of the earth in some form or fashion.

The oak was just too obvious and powerful a locus for any Walker to overlook. Surely Dan would conduct rituals and make offerings here if he did it anywhere.

Why hasn't he? Even if he'd retired, he'd still mark the important days with offerings to his goddess and to the land wights, wouldn't he?

Leif took a deep breath, centering himself, before kneeling between two huge, knotted roots. Whispering words to dedicate his offering to whatever land wight was present, he sprinkled corn meal and pipe tobacco, then took a lancet out of his pocket and pricked his finger. A single drop of blood fell to splash scarlet against the rough bark of the nearest root.

The fine hairs on his arms stood up, as if a small surge of electricity passed across his skin, accompanied by the heavy sweetness of gardenias. *Something* had responded to his offering, though whether a wight, a wandering spirit, or even some fading echo of Simone Miller herself, he didn't know.

Satisfied he'd done what he could to honor the local spirits, he returned to the house. Leif wandered into the kitchen just as Dan entered, yelling over his shoulder at Virgil: "The bus driver doesn't care, and neither do I. Get a move on!"

When Dan caught sight of Leif, he offered a rueful grin. "I feel bad yelling at him—I hated getting up for school when I was fifteen, too."

"Same here," Leif said, although in truth he'd been on the streets by the time he was Virgil's age. And afterward he'd had private tutors, his education sandwiched between trips to whatever part of the world lured Rúnar next with the glint of gold or the promise of power. "Is there anything I can do to help?"

"You can get the coffee going, if you don't mind," Dan said with a nod at the brewer. "Beans and grinder are in the cupboard above. What do you want for breakfast?"

"I don't want to put you out," Leif said as he took the coffee beans out of the cupboard. The rich aroma filled his nose and he breathed deep.

"Not a problem. Just to let you know, we aren't what you'd call traditionalists, but as followers of Hecate, we're all vegetarian. When you believe in reincarnation, it's bad mojo to kill and eat your fellow travelers."

Bea smiled a good morning at Leif and started setting out orange juice and glasses. Dan placed a pot of oatmeal in the center of the table, its warm fragrance filling the air. Gesturing for Leif to sit, he set out bowls, spoons, and napkins as Bea took a seat beside Leif. Virgil appeared, his hair still damp from the shower, and plopped down opposite his sister.

During the whole dance of their morning ritual, not a single one of the Millers ever glanced out the window at the lightning-scarred oak.

Interesting. Maybe it was nothing, except it reminded Leif of behavior he'd seen before, in normal people who had a haunting on their hands but didn't want to believe it.

Which made no sense at all, because he hadn't sensed any of the dead lingering near the great tree. And surely Dan would take care of any unquiet spirits wandering onto the farm, even if he had given up "haint-work" for the most part.

Leif added a generous helping of cinnamon and a sprinkle of sugar to his oatmeal. "I hope it's all right," he said casually, as he stirred the mixture together, "I made an offering to the land wights this morning at the foot of the oak."

Bea's glass of orange juice slipped out her hand and shattered on the table.

Startled, Leif surged to his feet to help, but she'd already grabbed a dishtowel to mop up. "No, no, sit down," she said shakily. "I've got it."

He sank slowly back into his chair, feeling terrible for having said anything. "I'm sorry. Did I overstep my bounds? It seemed a natural focus for the spirits of the land."

"Don't worry about it," Dan said, although his tone was short, clipped. He took a sip of his coffee, not looking directly at Leif.

"I didn't sense anything amiss," Leif said unhappily. *Great, I've managed to screw up again. Why did I have to say anything?* "If I had, I wouldn't have made the offering."

"There's nothing to sense." Dan put down the coffee cup and dug determinedly into his oatmeal. "I did my first solo with a haint there," he added, as if that explained anything.

Leif hid his frown with an effort. Simone lived here for years: there shouldn't have been any haints hanging around that long. Not unless she'd done something not quite ethical, in which case…

In which case, I'm the last person to pry.

"It doesn't sound like a pleasant experience," he said sympathetically.

"No." Dan's voice didn't warm. "It wasn't." *So don't ask any more,* was the obvious, unspoken corollary.

"Well, Leif," Bea said as she slipped into her seat as if nothing happened, "where are you from?"

It was an obvious change of subject, but he took her up on it. Whatever had happened with the haint and the oak wasn't any of his business, after all. "Chicago, originally, but I've traveled all over."

"Really? Where's the nicest place you've been?"

"I loved Italy," he said. "I don't know that I'd want to live there, but I wouldn't mind going back. The worst was probably Siberia, but that was because of the cold. Not to mention how remote it was—I like my comforts, and sleeping in a tent wasn't my idea of a good time."

They all stared at him as if he'd said something crazy. "Italy?" Dan asked faintly.

"It was nice. A lot of history there. And it was warmer than Siberia or Oslo." Leif tried for a smile, but Dan just looked put-off.

"The most exotic place I've ever been is Tennessee," Bea offered with a wistful smile. "Does your girlfriend like to travel?"

Leif hid a grin at her not-very-subtle probe. "I'm single. And gay."

"Great, just what we need, another homo," Virgil muttered, stabbing his spoon into his oatmeal.

"Virgil!" Bea exclaimed, at the same time as Dan snapped, "That's it, you're grounded."

"Grounded?" Virgil glared at his older brother across the table, as if he were the injured party. "You can't do that! You aren't our dad!"

Bea let out a little gasp, but was otherwise silent. The two brothers stared daggers at each other, dark eyes boring into dark eyes. "Virgil Raymond Miller, you are grounded until further notice, unless you apologize to Leif right this instant."

Virgil ground his teeth, but to Leif's surprise, he backed down. "I'm sorry."

"Apology accepted," Leif said, more interested in the family dynamic than a feeble insult from a fifteen-year-old. The gods knew he'd been called a lot worse than anything Virgil could come up with.

Dan shot him an embarrassed glance. "You're going to think we're a bunch of inbred rednecks."

Bea winked at Leif. "Right. We're not rednecks. We're hillbillies. Completely different."

Leif laughed with her, and the tension eased. They finished eating in silence, except for the clink of spoons against the cereal bowls. Leif's mind went back to Virgil's words: not the insult, but his use of "another."

It doesn't matter. Who cares if Dan's gay or not? He's off-limits, remember?

He'd set up rules for himself years ago, even before he'd left Rúnar. The rules insured no one got hurt; there were no messy entanglements leading to misunderstandings. No reason to break the rules now.

No reason at all.

"Any thoughts as to where we might start looking for the *draugr*—the haint, that is?" Leif asked while he and Dan washed up the breakfast dishes.

Virgil and Bea had left for the bus stop at the bottom of the long drive. To Dan's surprise, when he started to clean up, Leif joined him at the sink and started drying. Which was nice of him; plenty of guys would have just sat on their butts instead of helping out.

"I've been pondering it," Dan said slowly. In truth, he'd lain awake half the night wracking his brain, trying to remember any scrap of information which might be of use. "There are a few nasties here and there: shadow-things, mostly. 'Something scared a hiker on this mountain somewhere.' That sort of thing. You have to understand, I was still apprenticed when I went off to college. There was no reason for me to keep a list, since I wasn't planning on setting up shop here. It seemed redundant, anyway, seeing as how Mom had one in her Book of Shadows."

Leif perked up visibly. "Maybe we could look there? You have it, right?"

Shit. He hated dashing Leif's hopes; it made him feel like even more of a failure than usual. "No. Dad insisted on burning it with her. He didn't want me to have it." Afraid Dan would go the same way, most likely.

He remembered the scene in the funeral parlor all too well. The mortician had really done justice to his art, making her look good enough for the viewing. Or at least, so everyone said, but to Dan, the shape revealed by the open half-lid wasn't Mom at all. Just a wax dummy, which happened to look like her, wearing her favorite dress.

Leif dried the final dish and set it carefully aside. "May I ask what happened?"

I failed her. She reached out to me for strength, and I tried to give it to her, but it wasn't enough. She died alone on a mountainside on Samhain-night, and there wasn't a thing I could do but feel it happen.

"Haint got her," he said gruffly, and hoped Leif would leave it at that.

"I'm sorry to hear that," Leif said. His blue eyes were sympathetic, but Dan could only shrug and look away. "She was cremated?"

"After a viewing, right," Dan agreed, relieved Leif didn't seem inclined to ask any more awkward questions. "The book's long gone."

"What do you suggest? A local archive? The library?"

"We can start with the library today," Dan said; he'd spent those long hours of the night thinking about this, too. "Let me get the goats fed—we sell their milk to a lady who makes soap with it—and take care of one or two other chores, and I'm all yours."

As soon as the words were out, Dan realized they could be taken as flirting. And maybe a part of him had even meant them that way.

Leif didn't seem to notice. "Thanks," he said. "I know you have other responsibilities. I can give you a hand, if you want."

Dan tried to image Leif feeding goats and mucking out stalls, and failed. "Not necessary—you're our guest," he said. "It won't take long. Oh, and if Jimmy—he's a hired hand—shows up looking for his check while I'm around back, just send him out."

"All right. While you're busy, I'll get out my laptop and see if I can find anything online."

Yeah, Leif didn't get out of the city much. "You can try, but it's dial-up only out here."

Leif's look of horror was almost comical, especially when he tried to recover. "That's all right. I'll just use my cell phone as a hotspot." He trailed off at Dan's wince. "No cell service, huh?"

"You must think we really are a bunch of hillbillies."

"Not at all." Dan gave him a skeptical look; Leif shrugged and flashed a winsome smile. "Just, er, used to roughing it."

Dan shook his head and pulled on a heavy jacket of khaki denim. "I'll be back as quick as I can."

As he was heading out the door, the phone rang. He paused, waiting for the machine to get it; if it turned out to be urgent, he'd pick up.

After a few rings, the old answering machine clicked on, and his own voice came out of the tinny speaker: "You've reached Hoary Oak Hill Organic Farm. Leave a message."

There came a moment of silence, as if the caller was collecting his thoughts. His voice when he finally spoke shook painfully. "Uh, Mr. Miller? This is George White. I'm Jimmy's uncle. He…I just wanted to let you know he's been murdered."

CHAPTER 6

"Shit," Dan said succinctly, as he climbed up the hill to where Leif waited.

Leif lowered the binoculars through which he'd studied the graveyard in the valley below. They stood on a low rise overlooking the Ransom Gap First Baptist Church cemetery, which happened to be the oldest burial ground in the area, according to Dan.

While Dan was on the phone with the uncle of the murdered man—Jimmy, was it?—Leif resigned himself to the horrors of dial-up and borrowed the family computer, as his laptop was too new to be equipped with a phone jack. He'd gone to a local news site, hoping to find more details for Dan, only to have his attention caught by the headline: FIRST BAPTIST CHURCH CEMETERY VANDALIZED.

He'd clicked through, and after an interminable wait, read over the article. Apparently, one of the older graves in the cemetery had been disturbed overnight. The sheriff and pastor were interviewed; both of them pointed out Halloween was less than two weeks away, blaming the crime on Satanists, rock music, and video games.

When Dan hung up the phone, Leif pointed out the story to him. Looking shaken, Dan fetched a map from the glove compartment of his truck.

Jimmy died behind the Skylight Lounge according to his uncle, which Leif assumed abutted the infamous Skylight Hotel. Although the winding road between the lounge and the graveyard probably represented a good ten or fifteen minute drive, the map showed they were in fact less than a mile apart, on either side of a ridge. Not far for someone to walk.

Or for something to shamble, as the case might be.

They'd split up after that, with Leif going to the cemetery and Dan to the Lounge. Although Dan hadn't exactly come out and said it, he implied that the bar was the sort of place that a fey-looking man in eyeliner could expect to receive a beating instead of information. Leif hadn't minded. It had given him the chance to take stock and think things over on his own.

When he'd arrived at the cemetery, it was to see a small contingent of news vans parked on the shoulder of the road, slowing traffic while solemn-faced correspondents recorded segments on the vandalism for the evening news. A couple of sheriff's deputies were being interviewed, along with the pastor of the adjacent church, which meant Leif had to watch from afar. He could only imagine what his reception from the police would be if he walked up dressed all in black, pierced, and wearing eyeliner and nail polish. No doubt he fit their image of a crazed, graveyard-vandalizing Satanist.

He always carried a pair of binoculars in his kit, just in case. They came in handy now, and the damage was easy to see. The southern end of the graveyard was clearly much older than the northern, the headstones worn down by decades of rain and snow. One of these graves, marked only by an almost-shapeless nub of stone, had been defiled. Stumps of black candles poked up here and there amidst the grass, and a patch of ground directly above the grave had been cleared of vegetation altogether, although there had been no actual digging into the soil. Black chalk inscribed runes on the headstone, and blood traced patterns in the raw earth.

Rúnar.

The temperature was warm, but the wind on the exposed rise set a chill in Leif's bones. As Dan walked up to him, leaves crunching under heavy work boots, Leif pulled his black jacket more tightly around his thin frame and suppressed a shiver.

"I take it you found out what happened," Leif said by way of greeting.

Dan nodded. He looked grim, his mouth set, his eyes darkened to black. It reminded Leif that this was no faceless victim to him, but a man Dan had known and worked beside.

"Yeah." Dan brushed his loose, brown hair out of his eyes. "The bartender wasn't part of the search party, but he was sure happy to gossip about what they found."

"What happened, exactly?"

"Jimmy went out drinking with some of his friends last night." Dan let out a dry bark of laughter. "He'd even invited me to go with him."

"But you didn't because I showed up," Leif guessed.

Dan shook his head. "I wouldn't have gone anyway. Had to make sure Bea and Virgil got their homework done and were up for the bus. Hard to do that with a hangover."

It was a convenient excuse, but Leif had the feeling Dan had a different one to use if he'd had to. "They went to the bar?" Leif prompted.

"Yeah. Did some drinking, and Jimmy went outside for a smoke. He didn't come back, but his friends figured he'd found something else to do. His truck was still in the lot, but the hotel next door rents rooms by the hour more than by the day, if you know what I mean."

All too fucking well.

"The rest of the guys went home," Dan continued, "but early this morn-ing, Jimmy's mom started calling around to find out where he was when he didn't show up for breakfast. People got worried, especially when it turned out he hadn't rented a room at the hotel. They started to look in the woods out back, in case he'd been drunk enough to wander out there by accident and fall into a ravine."

"And they found him."

"The bartender says it must have been a bear got him, because nothing else could have torn him apart like that."

Shit. No wonder Dan was upset. "You don't think it was a bear."

"No. His uncle said *murdered*, and some other things besides. The po-lice are probably trying to keep it under wraps until they have a chance to in-vestigate, but it sure didn't sound like he died from a bear attack."

There must have been bite marks. If the *draugr* had mauled Jimmy with its mouth while ripping him apart, it would have been obvious his killer was no wild animal.

Leif put his hand tentatively on Dan's shoulder. He couldn't feel the other man's warmth through the thickness of denim jacket, so he squeezed gently, conscious of the arch of bone and firmness of muscle beneath his fin-gers. "I'm sorry," he said. "This can't be easy for you."

Dan shrugged. "I'm a Walker."

He was accustomed to death, in other words. Except that no one ever re-ally was.

Alice. There hadn't been much left of her once the *draugar* were done, either.

"You knew him," Leif said, trying to banish the memory of blood, the noisome odor of the secret places of the body not meant to be exposed to air. "That makes it different."

"What about you?" Dan asked, nodding at the cemetery. "Anything in-teresting here?"

Leif accepted the change of subject and let his hand fall back to his side. "Yes. Take a look."

He handed over the Zeiss binoculars. After using them to study the graveyard for a few minutes, Dan lowered them with a worried expression. "What do you think?"

Leif pulled his gaze away from those intense eyes and stared off across the valley at the ridge on the other side. Autumn had turned the trees into a blaze of orange, crimson, and yellow, and he smelled desiccated leaves and the occasional whiff of exhaust from the news vans below. He tried to focus on the beauty of nature instead of picturing what he knew had happened here the night before.

And the gods knew he could picture it with pinpoint accuracy. Hadn't he seen—and done it—a hundred times before?

"How much do you know about necromancy?" he asked.

"Raising the dead to ask questions about the future isn't really my area of expertise," Dan said. "I figure we're supposed to send them on, not bring them back."

"That we are, but not all of us live up to that standard. This was necromancy, although probably not of the sort meant to predict the future—that's chancy at best. No, this was meant to learn about the past."

Peripherally, he was aware of Dan studying him, but he kept his gaze on the ridgeline, trying not to give anything away. "Want to fill me in as to why you think that?" Dan asked.

"This is Rúnar's work. I recognize his style." *Please don't ask me how. Just assume it's because I've been tracking him for a long time.* "He came here last night and raised a *draugr.*"

"Was this the haint he came to North Carolina for?"

Leif started to answer, but something stopped him. *"Presumably,"* he'd meant to say, but it didn't feel right. His gut twisted, and the base of his skull ached like an old, rotted tooth, every instinct telling him this had only been a step along the way and not the destination.

"I don't think it was," he said slowly.

"Really? Why not?" Dan asked, not sounding too happy. *He must have hoped by tomorrow I'd have Ransom Gap in my rearview mirror and he could get back to his normal life.*

"Intuition," Leif said with a helpless shrug.

Dan nodded slowly, obviously mulling it over. The psychic training they went through meant a Walker's intuition was as much a finely-honed tool as any wand or staff. *But we can be wrong, too.*

"I'll consult the runes," Leif said. "See if they verify my feeling or not."

Dan looked at him curiously. "Runes? Like the symbols on your arm?"

"Something like." Leif bent down to his bag and fished through it until he came up with a sturdy leather pouch. He didn't have time to do a full reading at the moment; instead he simply slipped his hand into the pouch and felt around.

Inside were thirty-three bits of antler, cut crosswise into round disks, each inscribed with a single rune. As he concentrated on his dilemma, he ran his fingers through the runes, until one seemed almost to leap between his fingers and stick there. Pulling out the disk, he saw it bore nothing but a single line.

"What does that mean?" Dan asked, peering over his shoulder.

"The rune is *isa*. Ice." Leif's mouth quirked into a rueful smile. "It signifies a standstill. A time to wait or to seek clarity."

"Meaning this probably wasn't the only thing Rúnar came here to find, and the rune is telling you not to move on but to stay and figure it out."

"That's the interpretation I'd put on it."

Dan sighed. "Why is Jimmy dead, if this wasn't the haint Rúnar was after?"

"Rúnar doesn't take good care of his toys," Leif said, and thought he succeeded in keeping the bitterness out of his voice. Maybe. "He raised the *draugr*, called it up through the earth like a mist, then forced it into a more solid form. It probably had information he needed to help him with his true goal. When he had taken all he could, he simply walked away. Why go to the effort to lay it again, after all? He left it here, mindless with pain and rage, ready to lash out at anyone who crossed its path."

"Jimmy," Dan said, and his voice was rough with suppressed grief.

"Yes." Leif picked up the rune bag and replaced the disk of antler, keeping his hands too busy to give into the impulse to touch Dan again.

"What happened to the haint after it killed Jimmy?" Dan asked, sticking to the practical. "Most of them don't like to stray too far. Would it have come back here at dawn?"

"Probably."

"And tonight, it'll be wandering around again, won't it?"

"I imagine it will."

Dan nodded. "I guess that means we better head home, grab something to eat, and be back here at sundown."

Surprised, Leif turned to face him. He'd expected to return alone; after all, hadn't Dan already said he wouldn't help beyond a certain point?

But he was learning that wasn't Dan's style. Dan might be retired, but with a friend dead and others in danger, he wouldn't just sit on the couch and wait for someone else to deal with it.

And sweet death, it felt good not to be alone in this. After having no one to watch his back, no one to talk to except the voices in his head, Dan was like a gift from the gods. "Thank you," Leif said.

"That's what I'm here for," Dan replied with a lop-sided smile. "Come on—let's get back to the cars before the police spot us up here and start asking questions."

They approached the cemetery via the ridgeline a few hours after sunset, even though it was a rough hike. Dan had a feeling that either the police or the pastor—or maybe both—would be keeping an eye on the place from the road.

What they'd do if they got caught, he wasn't entirely sure. There was no way he'd be able to explain why he needed to visit the cemetery at night, especially not in the company of someone who looked and dressed like Leif. If

Dan ended up in jail, Child Protective Services would start looking long and hard at whether he was fit to raise Bea and Virgil, especially since he'd left them home alone to go wandering around in the dark with another man.

But I couldn't just stay home. Jimmy hadn't been a saint, not by a long shot, but he'd been a good employee, someone willing to work hard and take the initiative. Under other circumstances, maybe he would even have been a friend. He hadn't deserved what happened to him.

People generally don't. Mom surely hadn't deserved to die alone on the side of the mountain, getting colder and colder as the blood poured out of her torn-open body. *Just like Jimmy died.*

But there was no use thinking about it. Bea would do her homework and go to bed without being asked, and would do everything in her power to make sure Virgil did the same. Thank the Goddess for her; Dan figured he would have gone crazy without Bea to help him out and reassure him he wasn't a total screw-up.

Even without the need for flashlights, the walk from the ridge wasn't easy, especially for poor Leif. His boots had heavy soles which kept him from slipping on the leaves, but he didn't know the trick of watching for hidden holes where stumps had rotted away, or briars, or even low branches that would whip back and slap you in the face if you weren't careful. The hilt of the sword jutting up over his shoulder didn't make things easier; it caught constantly on branches and vines, almost yanking him onto his butt more than once.

A series of ravines made the going even harder. They scrambled up a jumble of exposed rock amidst the twisted trunks of rhododendron and mountain laurel. Dan, in the lead, paused at the top and extended a hand to Leif.

"Thanks," Leif said, letting Dan haul him up. His slender fingers were surprisingly strong, their skin soft and smooth.

Embarrassed at the roughness of his callused hands, Dan let go as quickly as he could. He'd figured Leif was way more high-class than him, but he hadn't realized just how much until the other man had started talking about trips to Italy and Sweden the way Dan might talk about driving to Asheville or Charlotte. Although Dan didn't know what Leif did for a living, he clearly wasn't the type who made his money by the sweat on his brow and the strength of his back. *He probably does something brainy, like computer programming.* Way out of Dan's league, in other words. Not that it mattered.

The forest came almost right to the edge of the oldest part of the cemetery, which was probably why the haint had decided to stumble up toward the Skylight instead of out to the road. At the verge of the trees, Dan paused and held up his hand for Leif to stop. For several minutes, they stood and watched in silence, looking for any signs of life in or around the cemetery.

There were none; apparently the pastor had decided against camping out all night in the chilly fall air. The occasional car passed by on the road, but the headlights didn't touch the darkness of the cemetery. Eventually, however, one of the vehicles slowed and turned onto the loop winding through the modern part of the burying ground. The car rolled through slowly, and the driver shone a flashlight out the window. When nothing turned up, the car pulled back out onto the road and kept going.

"Sheriff's department," Dan said softly. "I guess they've got the deputy on patrol checking out things when he passes by."

"How much longer do we have until he comes back?"

"Hard to say. An hour, maybe less."

"We'd better make this quick," Leif said grimly.

"Any last minute suggestions?" Dan asked. He hated to look even more ignorant in front of Leif, but at the same time, he wasn't going to let pride get him killed. "I don't think I've ever tried to take down something brought back by a necromancer, as opposed to the regular sort of haint that just doesn't want to move on."

"There's no real difference," Leif reassured him. If he was wondering why he was stuck with a hick Walker like Dan, he was too well bred to let it show. "There will be a thin slip of wood with a rune carved on it under the *draugr's* tongue; part of the spell Rúnar used to call it back. In theory, you could remove it to loosen the binding. In practice I wouldn't recommend putting any fingers in its mouth that you'd like to get back."

Dan grimaced. "Yeah, I think I'll just stick with stabbing it in the face."

"Good plan."

Another thought occurred to Dan. "Unless—are you sure we can't lay it otherwise? If Rúnar forced it here, it must want to go back, right?" Yes, the thing had killed Jimmy—he wasn't forgetting that. But this was one of the early lessons of haint-work: the dead acted out of fear and anger, out of hate and pure meanness, but you couldn't hold a grudge against them the way you could the living. They'd passed on from this life, and it wasn't ever the Walker's place to judge them, just to do the job.

"Maybe it would even be willing to tell us what Rúnar wanted to know," he added hopefully. "If we knew that, we might be able to get ahead of him."

Leif shook his head sadly. "I wish that were the case," he said. "I've seen this sort of thing before. The unwilling dead are always angry with the person who summons them. They'll try to lay a curse on the summoner, or twist whatever they're forced to tell in order to trick or frighten him. But most of the time, they're barely even human. I was taught only a piece of the spirit can really be brought back to this side. A raised *draugr* isn't a complete person anymore, just a fragment. After the necromancer is done with it, there's nothing left but a creature of pain and rage, lashing out at whatever it comes across."

"Oh," Dan said, feeling dumb. What sort of a Walker didn't know this stuff?

Leif gave him a kind smile, as if he'd read Dan's doubts on his face. "Most Walkers never have to deal with this sort of thing."

"You must've been following Rúnar for a while now." *Poor Leif.* How long had he been dealing with this shit?

Leif glanced quickly away, his lips quirking up into a smile holding more than a touch of self-mockery. "Years," he said. "Come on. Let's get this done."

CHAPTER 7

They traveled as quietly as possible. Dan held his wand loosely in one hand, and kept the other near the pouch on his tool belt holding the salt. The pink crystals came from the Himalayas, or at least that was what the package claimed. Salt from the solid earth instead the shifting sea was best for creating barriers, and what was more solid than a mountain?

Leif moved ahead, his sword in one hand and his staff in the other. His jeans cupped his butt tantalizingly, and the cedar-and-musk scent of his cologne teased Dan's nose.

Concentrate. Easier said than done; Dan's heart wanted to speed up and his breath to quicken, while little sparks of desire sent warmth to his lips and cock.

He had his professional pride, though, and took another series of cleansing breaths, all the while concentrating on making his aura into a shield. Adrenaline and focus altered the world around him, every edge just a little sharper, every color just a few shades more vibrant, every sound exquisitely clear. The crisp evening air prickled his skin, and he felt the stirring of each hair as the breeze drifted across his scalp.

They slipped through the darkness, almost like ghosts themselves, making for the disturbed grave. It wasn't hard to find; residual energy from the summoning pulsed around it in a sickly aura the color of diseased flesh.

The charms on Dan's wand rattled softly, and the mojo bag in his pocket shifted like something alive; even though he'd retired from haint work, he still carried the bag on him everywhere he went. A little bit of protection never hurt, as Mom used to say.

The haint was in the vicinity all right, and Dan spared a moment to thank Hecate it hadn't yet wandered far from its grave. Leif came to a halt at the footstone. The stench of rot rode the wind, and the air grew sharply colder, until frost formed on the weathered lumps, all that remained of footstone and headstone. Leif cast about slowly, his head turning from one side to the other, scenting...

"Leif, look out!" Dan cried.

The haint lurched from the shadows, its spectral form clad in decaying flesh gone black and bloated with death. Its tattered clothing was at least a century out of date, and a clots of matted hair clung to its slimy scalp. The stench of a butcher's dumpster in high summer rolled out from it in a nauseating wave.

Leif moved out of its way with almost uncanny grace. The temperature around the haint plunged, stiffening fingers and joints, and Leif's sword missed as the dead thing surged past him and made for Dan.

Tendrils snapped out from it, seeking to forge a link to drain Dan's energy and infect him with its rage. They hit his aura, sliding off his shields, but he wasn't waiting around for it to attack again. Scooping up a handful of salt, he flung it in the haint's direction.

The haint flinched back, and smoking black pits appeared in its gelid skin, as if it had been blasted with birdshot. Dan pressed his advantage, raising the wand high over his head, hoping to finish it off fast.

It darted under his guard, one heavy arm slamming into his chest with more than human strength. All the air left his body, and he found himself flying back, his shoulder cracking painfully against a tombstone. Stars danced in front of his eyes, and he struggled to draw breath.

Get up! Mom's voice shouted in his memories. *Move or die, Danny!*

You shouldn't say things like that to him, Dad had said later.

I won't lie to him, Harv. This is the way things are for us, and I'd rather be harsh and have a living son, than be kind and have a dead one.

But of course Mom was the one who'd died.

He was already moving, even as the thoughts blipped through his disoriented brain, body remembering even when he couldn't think straight. He rolled instinctively, a moving target, before coming to his feet, the wand still in his hand.

Leif had managed to distract the haint; his sword sheared down, the metal slicing deep into its side. It gave no sign of pain or fear at the hit, instead ramming Leif and knocking him to the ground. An instant later, it straddled him, rotting fingers reaching to strangle.

Dan cleared the space between them with a single leap, his body twisting to bring momentum to bear on the single point of antler arrowing at the haint's skull.

Somehow, it must have known he was there. It lurched off Leif, and Dan's blow missed, almost hitting Leif instead. The haint swung its arm like a club, knocking the wand from Dan's grip.

Shit.

Leif sliced it again, but again the blow was fouled by the haint's terrifying strength. It spun on Leif with a deep growl, and Dan did the only thing he could think to keep it off his companion. With no weapons left but his bare hands, he wrapped both arms around its neck.

The chokehold would have stopped a human opponent, but the haint didn't care, except its head was forced back and away from Leif. Corpse candles danced deep in its sunken eyes, and its preternaturally strong fingers closed around Dan's wrists, jerking his arms loose and tightening agonizingly on the bones.

"Dan! Get down!" Leif shouted.

He went limp, collapsing to his knees, held up only by the haint's grip on his outstretched arms. Leif's sword stabbed through one of the haint's weirdly-glowing eyes, angling out through the top of the skull. The stench of rot burst out, even stronger than before, and Dan shut his mouth and eyes tight as the haint dissolved into black goo on top of him.

Silence fell, except for the far-off hoot of an owl. Dan opened his eyes and saw the stars. Leif's hand touched his arm, light as a feather. "Dan? Are you all right?"

"I'm okay." Dan sat up, wincing as his shoulder throbbed painfully. "You?"

Leif nodded. "Fine," he said, but his blue eyes looked worn in their rings of liner.

It occurred to Dan this was the second haint they'd taken care of together, and Leif had been the one to put both of them down. "Good work," he said, trying not to let his embarrassment show.

"I couldn't have done it without you," Leif replied, and he sounded sincere. "Grabbing it with your bare hands was one of the bravest things I've seen in a long time."

"Well, I was the one dumb enough to lose his only weapon," Dan muttered. He searched the grass until he found his wand. "We should get out of here before the cops come back."

"More hiking," Leif said without enthusiasm.

"Better than sitting in a jail cell."

"Believe me, that's the only reason I'm not heading for the road."

They walked back up the ridge in silence, except for Dan's occasional warnings about hidden holes, low branches, or fallen trees. On the way down, the task ahead of them had occupied Dan's thoughts. With the haint dispatched, his mind turned to Jimmy and to the dead man's family. *He lived with his mom, and it was his uncle who called this morning.* Two people at least were grieving hard tonight. Probably they were having an informal wake for him at the Skylight, since he'd been there a lot and seemed to have been a popular guy from what Dan could tell.

That haint could've killed anybody. Could've wandered out in the road, or down to a house.

It was worse than a regular haunting, somehow. This had been the work of somebody who should've been taking care of the dead, not threatening the living.

"Do you think Rúnar will raise any more haints?" he asked.

Leif's breath came from behind him, ragged with unaccustomed exertion. "That depends on whether he got everything he needed from this one."

Which probably wasn't the case, if Rúnar was sticking around like Leif thought. There might be more of the angry dead running loose, hurting people. Someone else he knew might be next. *Maybe even Virgil or Bea.*

They emerged back onto the gravel road where he'd parked the truck earlier. As Leif started around to the passenger side, Dan stopped him with a touch on the arm.

He observed the thin sheen of sweat clinging to Leif's skin, despite the cool air. Dan noticed the twigs in his hair, sap on his hands, and a thin welt across one cheek where he'd gotten smacked with a branch. Somehow, Leif's disheveled appearance made him even more appealing, like some wild god of the wood, handsome and dangerous.

Dan forced himself to look away and hoped his half-hard cock didn't show through his jeans. "I know I said I'd help you find Rúnar, but not actually help stop him," he said.

"Of course." Leif sounded dejected. "I appreciate your help tonight, but I understand. This isn't really your fight."

"No, you don't understand." Dan glanced back at him, meeting those brilliant eyes with his own. "Tonight made me realize it *is* my fight. The person who did this, who's so fucking careless with both the dead and the living…he's got to be stopped."

"Are you saying you'll come out of retirement?"

"For as long as it takes to finish this, yeah. I'll put everything else on hold, except the basics of keeping the farm running and the animals happy." Ignoring the guilty whispers of his conscience, he managed a small smile. "Until we stop Rúnar, I'm your man."

Leif expression of surprise shifted into a flirtatious look. "I like the sound of that."

Dan glanced away, hoping the heat in his face wasn't obvious. "We should get out of here, in case one of the county mounties decides to drive up," he mumbled.

"Right." Leif immediately sobered and headed around to the passenger side of the truck. Dan went around to his side, climbed in, and started the vehicle. And all the while, he told himself that he was glad Leif had dropped the flirting. He wasn't disappointed. Not at all.

~ * ~

Leif woke from nightmares an hour before dawn. The last one was the worst. He was raising and binding a *draugr* with Rúnar, but Alice had been in the cemetery with them. She'd tried to tell him something, but he couldn't understand, because her lips were stitched shut. Then Rúnar stepped up behind her and cut her throat.

It was a far more merciful death than what Rúnar had actually done to her, but it still brought Leif awake with a scream trapped behind his teeth.

Hoping not to disturb the rest of the house, he showered and went downstairs, only to find Dan in the kitchen ahead of him, sitting alone at the table and sipping coffee. Upon seeing Leif, Dan nodded a greeting. "Morning."

"Almost," Leif replied with a glance at the dark still pressing against the window.

Obviously, he wasn't the only one unable to sleep. Dan didn't mention it, though, only asked, "Want me to show you something?"

I'd like you to show me a lot of things. Trying very hard not to picture Dan naked, he said, "Sure."

Dan poured coffee into a travel mug for each of them, before leading the way out the back door. Frost coated the grass, crackling beneath their boots as they walked across the yard. Fiery red rimmed the eastern sky, but stars still shone bright in the west. A rooster crowed from the chicken coop, and far away a dog barked, but otherwise the world was silent and still.

Dan led the way to the edge of the yard, where a large, flat rock jutted out from the hillside. The outcropping formed a natural overlook; the bottomlands spread out below them, flowing into the valley, until eventually an unobstructed view of the next mountain reared up against the sky.

When they reached the rock, Dan sank down and sat cross-legged on its level surface. "My mom used to do a lot of her thinking out here. It's a good spot to meditate, too, or do a purification spell if that's what you need to clear your head."

Leif sat down beside him. The night's cold radiated out of the stone, soaking through his jeans and chilling his skin. He cradled the travel mug in his hands and breathed deeply of the coffee-scented steam rising from it. "It's a beautiful place."

"You can use it, if you need to get away for a while. I know the house can get noisy, what with Virgil's video games and Bea's music."

"Is that what you use it for?"

Dan smiled slightly. "Sometimes, yeah."

He never smiles completely. Just a little turn of the lips, like he's always holding something back. Dan seemed intense, serious, and so contained he ought to be labeled "Warning: contents under pressure." What would it take to get him to let go, to smile with his whole mouth, his whole being?

"I wanted to thank you," Leif said, trying to concentrate on business.

Dan's interior life was none of his affair—*couldn't* be any of his affair.

He'd felt pathetically grateful last night, when Dan had said he'd help. And not just because of Dan's strength and skill as a Walker, but because it meant Leif wouldn't be completely alone, at least for a little while.

He'll only help you until he learns the truth.

Leif ignored the ugly thought and rubbed at the place where his spine met his skull. "I know it wasn't an easy decision for you to make."

Dan didn't say anything for a long moment. The wind off the ridge stirred his shoulder-length hair, fanning strands over his high cheekbones. "I didn't understand," he said at last. "When you said Rúnar was a necro-mancer, I thought I knew what that meant. But when I saw what he'd done with my own eyes, when I knew Jimmy had paid the price for it, along with that poor haint, I just…I couldn't…"

He trailed off and shrugged, as if he'd run out of words, or fetched up against something he didn't want to say aloud.

Neither of them spoke for a while after that, but the silence was a com-fortable one. A flock of migrating birds streamed across the sky like a dark river, and the cold air stung Leif's nose and made him feel intensely alive. Everything seemed almost painfully clear, and Leif half-fancied he could make out individual leaves on the other side of the valley, even though he knew it wasn't possible.

It was good to just sit and relax. To just *be*, even if only for an hour. Odd how comfortable he'd been around Dan from the beginning; it wasn't something he could remember ever feeling before.

"I've been wondering," Dan said eventually, "how did you figure out you were different?"

Leif arched a brow at the obliqueness of the question. "Are you asking about my being gay, or my being a Walker?"

"Whichever you'd prefer to talk about," Dan said, glancing briefly at Leif. "Or neither—I don't mean to be rude."

"I don't mind." Was Dan asking because of what he'd said last night, when they'd returned to the truck? Leif hadn't even thought, the flirtatious reply out of his mouth before he could take it back.

Leif stared off across the still-shadowed valley. "Even when I was a kid, I knew I wanted to kiss the boys instead of the girls. I don't remember ever *not* knowing. What about you? When did you know you were gay?"

Dan's eyes widened in alarm. "How did you guess?"

It wasn't the reaction he'd expected. "Well," Leif said, uncertain how to handle Dan's sudden nervousness, "for one thing, Virgil looked right at you yesterday when he commented on me being 'another' homo. And Walkers tend not to fit into society's neat categories. A higher percentage of us are homosexual, or transgendered, or bisexual, or genderqueer, or what have you, than the rest of the population."

Dan's broad shoulders relaxed visibly under his denim jacket. "Right. Sorry. It's just that I'm not out. It might be different if we lived in Asheville, but in this area, folks tend to be homophobic. I'd hate for Virgil and Bea to end up in foster care because people found out I'm gay."

The possibly hadn't occurred to Leif. "Would that even be legal?"

Dan's mouth twisted wryly. "Hard to say, but I don't have the money to be the test case. Not to mention a fight in court would land Virgil and Bea in the system in the meantime. Bea will turn eighteen next year, which means at least she'd only have a few months in foster care, but Virgil…" He shook his head. "I can't do that to him."

Leif nodded. "I understand." It was a good thing he'd already decided that Dan was off-limits; he certainly didn't want to cause the family any more trouble. "I, um, spent most of my childhood in foster care myself."

It was something he hadn't meant to admit, in part because of the pity he saw in Dan's eyes. "I'm sorry."

Now it was Leif's turn to shrug and look away. "I never knew my father. My mother was a junkie, and I was three or four when the courts took me away for good. I bounced around the system until I was fourteen, when I decided I'd had enough and ran away."

It sounded simple, stated like that. Clean and impersonal. No mention of Nick, the foster father who'd come into his bedroom at night. No mention of Rúnar, who'd saved Leif from a murderous ghost when he sought shelter in the wrong abandoned warehouse one night.

No mention of the revenge he'd taken, sending a bound ghost to haunt Nick and drive him mad.

"I'm sorry," Dan said again. His kind brown eyes offered more sympathy than Leif would ever deserve, as if he'd sensed there was more to the story.

"It was a long time ago," Leif said with a dismissive wave of his hand. "I only meant I understand why you're trying to keep your family together. I'm just sorry you have to betray yourself to do it."

Dan's tanned cheeks flushed lightly. "It's not about me, but thanks."

They didn't say anything further after that, only sat quietly and watched the day break around them.

CHAPTER 8

After Dan made breakfast and saw the kids off to school, he and Leif visited the Ransom Gap County Library. The library was a small turn-of-the-century building with water-stained plaster ceilings, making Leif wonder if the place was in danger of collapse. Behind the main desk sat an elderly woman who looked as old as the library itself. When she spotted Dan, she gave him a fond smile.

"Are you taking up your mother's genealogical work, dear?" she asked in a voice like two dry branches rubbing together.

"Yeah," Dan said. "I was going through her notes, figuring I'd put a little something together for Bea, before she leaves for college next year. Something to remind her where she comes from. But there were a few gaps from way back. I thought maybe I could fill them in."

The librarian's expression hovered between sympathetic and encouraging. "How thoughtful of you. I'm sure she'll love it. Just let me know if you need any help." She gave Leif a curious glance, but he didn't say anything, and she seemed to lose interest.

Dan led the way to the small library's lower floor. The scent of dust and old paper hung heavy in the still air, and Leif sneezed twice on the way down the stairs.

"Allergies," he said with a rueful smile when Dan glanced back at him. "Nothing I can't handle, although you'll have to put up with me sniffling for the next few hours."

"Are you sure you want to do this?" Dan asked. "I can look, and you can —"

"I'll be fine. Two sets of eyes will be better—and faster—than one. Where do we start?"

The library's records consisted of everything from leather-bound books to microfilm to computer printouts stuffed into binders, depending on the age of the material. "Might as well start with the oldest records we can find," Dan said, surveying the crumbling books, none of which had any sort of lettering on their spines to indicate the contents.

Leif's heart sank. "None of this has been computerized?"

Dan cast him a glance, half-amused and half-embarrassed. "You *have* seen Ransom Gap, right? We might be a lot of things, but rich isn't one of them. Any money spent is going to go to things folks need now, not dusty old records most don't care about."

Leif winced internally at Dan's defensive tone. *Like he thinks I'm judging him because he's poor. Sweet death, if he only knew. I'm in no position to judge anyone.* "That makes sense."

"Just be glad he was buried in a church plot and not in a family burying ground, else we'd really have no hope of finding anything."

"Good point. And it didn't look like the cemetery had been disturbed by any building or roadwork. In theory, the records should still be accurate."

Dan nodded. "There's that, at least." He pulled a heavy tome from the shelf and handed it to Leif. "Might as well get started."

They sat across from one another at the lone table, pouring silently through the accounts. There were no indices, reducing them to a page-by-page search.

"You know," Leif said after a few minutes of reading down the dusty old lists, "we could go upstairs to one of the computers and print out a current satellite photo of the cemetery. That way we could mark off the graves as we find them."

"Good idea," Dan said. "Do you want to do it?"

"I'd prefer not to—the librarian was giving me the evil eye."

"Ms. Simpson? She's harmless." Dan glanced at him, and that small, restrained smile touched his mouth. "Although you're probably not what she's used to seeing around these parts."

"I imagine I'm not," Leif said, mimicking Dan's twang, but with a grin to let the other man know he was just teasing.

Dan jovially flipped him the bird. As he headed up the stairs, Leif listened intently, tracking him up to the first floor. As soon as he was satisfied Dan was safely out of earshot, he stood up and went quickly to the part of the room with the modern records.

I shouldn't be doing this. But here he was anyway, looking for the death records from the year Simone Miller had died. *I should just ask, not sneak around behind Dan's back.*

"Haint got her," Dan had said, brief and brisk and not really telling Leif a thing. As for what happened to his father, and why the family seemed to have scoured away all trace of both parents, Leif didn't know.

Didn't *need* to know, except that he wanted to, and he didn't want to hurt Dan further by prying. What harm would be done by looking up the death certificates and satisfying his curiosity? Dan would never even know.

It didn't take long. The official verdict was a bear had mauled Simone Miller. *Just like Jimmy.* Cause of death was blood loss from multiple lacerations. A police report was referenced; feeling sick, Leif located it quickly.

A press release was clipped to the front of the report. It read:

23:30 on the night of 10/31, dispatch received a call from Harvey Miller of 28 Oak Hill Rd. to report his wife missing. Caller reported Simone Miller was expected home several hours prior and had not returned. Officers on patrol alerted to be on the look out for a blue Honda Acura.

02:30, 11/1 Officer B.H. Taylor stopped to investigate a dark blue Honda Acura pulled off on the left side of Old Litch Creek Rd., two miles north of the intersection with Hoot Owl Rd. The vehicle was empty and locked. A search of the area revealed the body of the victim, later identified as Simone Miller. She was pronounced dead on the scene.

Medical examiner's findings indicate the victim died sometime between the hours of 20:00 10/31 and 00:00 11/1. Cause of death was severe blood loss, accompanied by extensive lacerations and trauma to most major organs. Investigators believe the victim encountered her attacker away from the road, but was able to crawl back to the vehicle.

Results from wound and crime scene analysis are inconclusive, but the most likely scenario is a black bear attack while the victim was out hiking near Old Litch Creek. Residents are highly discouraged from hiking in the area, and should be cautious when approaching any wildlife.

According to US Fish and Wildlife officials, black bears are not usually aggressive unless they are sick or they, or their cubs, are threatened.

This is the first recorded instance of a black bear attack on a human in Ransom County.

Dan would have been, what? Eighteen or nineteen at the time?

Apprentices shared a psychic link with their teacher; it was part of the training. Dan would have felt her die.

Fuck.

Which left the father. Leif put the first set of records back and listened intently. Hearing no sounds to indicate Dan's return, he hurriedly began to scan the death records from that year forward, looking for anyone named "Miller." What he found chilled him even more than Simone's death.

Simone had perished in the line of duty, like countless Walkers before her. It was sad and painful, and knowing the risks probably hadn't made it any easier on her family when she died. But, having known Dan even for a few days, Leif could easily picture Simone dragging her body up the side of the ravine, dark eyes blazing with determination, fighting through agony and injury until the amount of blood in her veins simply became too low to sustain life. The dry facts of the police report couldn't conceal how hard she'd struggled to make it back to the car, to the road, to the chance of getting home to her family.

Harvey Miller was a different story. "Suicide" read the death certificate.

Hoping some mistake had been made and Harvey hadn't died by suicide any more than Simone had died from a bear attack, Leif looked up the police report.

Less than seven months after his wife had died, Harvey Miller hung himself from the lightning-struck tree in the back yard. *"Body found by 9-year-old son after returning from school,"* the report noted.

Fuck. Oh, fuck. Leif closed his eyes against a surge of pity and grief. Harvey had hung himself, and Virgil had found him, and Dan…

Dan had laid his haint to rest, when whatever madness led to the suicide had kept Harvey's soul in this world.

"I did my first solo with a haint there," Dan had said, the spare words like a Band-Aid over a gaping wound.

Leif's heart ached. Had it even occurred to Dan to call in another Walker, or had he believed it his duty to handle it himself? *No wonder he keeps everything bottled up inside.*

Boots sounded on the stairs. Stuffing the report hastily back into place, he closed the cabinet and hurried to the table, dropping into his chair just as Dan entered the room.

"Got it," Dan said, waving the printout in the air.

"Great." Leif straightened and smiled, as if he didn't know anything new. "Let's mark the ones we've already found."

They spent the next half hour going over the cemetery map and the old records. Leif's stomach began to hint it had been a bit too long since breakfast. His sinuses and eyes ached from all the dust, and he had to stop and blow his nose several times.

Dan gave him a sympathetic look over the age-yellowed books. "You sound like me in the spring, when the pine pollen is in the air."

"I didn't think country boys had allergies."

Dan snorted. "Yeah, because of all the clean living. Or the moonshine, I forget which."

"Probably the moonshine." Leif leaned over and compared the record in front of him with the printout. "Hold on—I think I've got him."

Dan pushed his book aside and leaned closer. Leif was suddenly, acutely aware if he turned his head and shifted forward a little, he could find out just how Dan's mouth tasted.

Forcing himself to focus on the matter at hand, he said, "The description of the grave site seems to match up. Jedediah Van Horn, born 18—"

"What?" Dan exclaimed, his olive skin going pale. "Let me see that!"

Startled, Leif passed him the book. Dan stared at the entry. "Hecate's bitches."

"You recognize the name?"

"Yeah." Dan glanced up, his eyes wide with lingering shock. "Jedediah Van Horn was the local haint-worker, back in his day. He was also my great-great-great grandfather."

Dan stood below the trap door into the attic, nerving himself to pull it open. He could barely believe that the thing of rage and hate they'd faced in the graveyard had been one of his own ancestors. *At least there were enough generations between us he couldn't use our shared blood to get through my shielding. That would have been a fucking mess.*

A shiver ran up his spine as the memory of the night under the oak re-played yet again in his mind, as if it had been on a continuous loop deep in his subconscious. The despair the haint had infected him with still gave him nightmares.

And now I've put down another one of my kin. I guess I'm two for two.

"What are we looking for?" Leif prompted him.

Realizing he'd been standing there wit-wandering, Dan reached up and pulled forcefully on the cord. The trapdoor came down, along with a flood of cool air and the odor of mice droppings.

"Mom's Book of Shadows is gone," he said, a little surprised his voice remained steady. "But Dad wasn't a Walker, just a hippy farmer who came to the mountains to find himself, married a local girl, and never left. He respect-ed what Mom did, don't get me wrong, but he didn't *know*. At any rate, I don't think he realized Mom had grandpa's Book of Shadows, and great-grandmom's—not that she called it that—and back even further. Jedediah's diaries are the oldest."

"It's amazing," Leif said, sounding both impressed and faintly envious. "I can't imagine having a link to the past like that."

Dan shrugged. "Our line goes back a lot farther, actually. Jedediah's mother was a Cherokee woman who married a white farmer, but I've got no idea which of them was the haint-worker."

"And you think one of Jedediah's diaries will have the answers Rúnar raised him to find?"

Dan reached up and pulled the folded stairs down. "I surely hope it does. Otherwise, we're probably out of luck."

He climbed up the steep ladder. The attic was finished, and the ancient, dust-laden boards creaked under his boots. The Yule decorations were piled near the trapdoor, where he'd left them last January. Other boxes and assort-ed junk took up much of the remaining space: old furniture which should have been thrown out a generation ago, boxes of the college textbooks Dan had kept even after dropping out, and a couple of stacks of Mom's old photo albums.

Light streamed from the single, round window, its glass panes too filthy to see through. As Leif entered the attic after him, Dan moved aside a few boxes and an old chair to uncover an airtight plastic container.

"Did you ever play up here when you were little?" Leif asked, looking around. "Because I have to say, all this drop-cloth covered furniture would make a great fort."

Dan grinned at the thought of a young Leif at play. "Not really. I think Mom and Dad were afraid we'd fall through the trap door and break our necks. Or damage some family heirloom, such as they are. By the time I was tall enough to reach the trapdoor on my own, coming up here meant work instead of fun."

"That seems a shame." The grayish light from the window fell across Leif's face, washing out his pale color even further, until he was nothing but a figure of silver and black. He'd rubbed his swollen, red eyes at some point, smearing the eyeliner and making him look like a raccoon.

"Here—help me get this down the ladder," Dan said. "Mom always brought me up here to look at them, but I'm not going to make you sit here in the dust."

Leif gave him a rueful grin and sniffled. "I'd appreciate that, thanks."

They wrestled the heavy box down the ladder. The most practical place to open it would be the living room, but Dan's room was closer.

He'd taken the master bedroom after Dad had died, but even after six years it showed little of his personality. The walls bore the same seventies-era wallpaper, the worn rug had never been changed, and the dresser had only a comb, a handful of change, and a bottle of the Florida water he sprinkled nightly on his mojo bag to "feed" it. The door to the closet stood open, revealing a monotonous collection of flannels, ratty old t-shirts, and a lone suit brought out only for weddings and funerals.

Leif glanced around casually. Dan imagined how unspeakably boring the room must look to him.

What the decor really needs is a sexy goth guy sprawled naked on the sheets—

"Um, I guess it'd be easiest to just sit on the floor," Dan stammered, trying not to look in the direction of the bed. Hecate's bitches, he hoped his ears weren't turning pink.

"Sounds good." Leif sat down cross-legged on the rag rug covering most of the hardwood floor between the bed and the dresser. Dan opened the container, revealing a large quantity of leather- and cloth-bound journals. The most recent were on top; as the pile went down, the paper became more yellowed and chewed on by silverfish, the bindings more dried and cracked.

He removed the journals and stacked them to one side, careful to keep them in order. Grandpa's were on top, followed by great-grandma's. She'd had some horrors to tell, having had to lay the victims of a lynching; one of the men had been an ancestor of Corey's, and what was done to him was enough to give anyone nightmares. Other journals followed, a quick look at the first page in each identifying who had written them, until he reached Jedediah's diaries.

There were five of them in all. Five surviving, that is, with the first one taking up as if an older book had existed, now lost to time. *And let's hope that wasn't the one with what we need in it.* Opening up the first to look at the crabbed handwriting with its eccentric, archaic spelling, Dan felt a touch of despair. "We'll never get through these. Wish we knew what we were looking for."

"Anything unusual," Leif said, picking up one of the diaries.

"Because our line of work is the very definition of normal most of the time." As soon as the words were out, Dan winced. *Not "our" line of work, not anymore. Except for this.*

If Leif noticed the slip, he didn't give any indication. "Yeah, well," he said with a wry laugh, "there's strange and there's *strange.*"

"True enough." Dan shifted to lean against the leg of the bed for support. Hoping they'd find what they were looking for before he went blind, he squinted at the terrible handwriting and began to read.

CHAPTER 9

The afternoon dragged painfully on toward evening. When Bea and Virgil came home from school, Virgil retreated to his video game in the living room, but Bea came to see what they were doing, wrapping her arms loosely around Dan's neck while she read over his shoulder. A little twinge of envy surprised Leif; he wondered what it would be like to have such closeness with a sibling. Did he have any brothers or sisters? Had they ended up in the system too?

"Want me to make dinner?" Bea offered.

"Done with your homework?"

"Sort of."

Dan gave her a stern look. "You know better."

She blew a raspberry and left them to their reading.

Leif's eyes had long ago grown tired of deciphering Jedediah's script, and he forced himself not to skim the entries in case he missed something of importance.

The problem with the diaries was that they were just that—diaries. The concept of a Book of Shadows, which recorded only information on rituals, spells, and haints, would have been alien to the time, and apparently Jedediah had never considered his Walking in any way separate from his day-to-day activities. One entry might discuss laying a ghost that had been troubling wagon traffic along the gap after dark, while the next might talk about how many calves the heifers had birthed, or the price of molasses, or which neighbor was sleeping with the parson.

He'd come across various accounts of haints, some mere rumors dutifully recorded, others real but too far away for Jedediah to take care of, especially since by this time he had a wife and three young children. A few local ghosts cropped up here and there, and Jedediah related putting them to rest, but nothing seemed out of the ordinary. Certainly nothing that would catch

Rúnar's interest.

When the sun began to set over the mountain, Leif considered calling it quits for the night. His ass had long ago gone numb, and his neck ached from bending over various books all day. Only the knowledge Rúnar was out there, planning something, kept him from tossing the diary aside in disgust.

Dan straightened slightly, and Leif shot him a curious glance, more than happy to rest his vision for a while. *And Dan is certainly easy on the eyes.* "Got something?"

Dan held up his hand for patience as he scanned the pages. "I think I do. Have you seen any mention of a guy named Ezekiel Goodweather?"

Leif thought back through the archaic names he'd waded through. "Yes. Ezekiel was the local busybody-cum-blackmailer. Jedediah mentioned him in connection with the parson at the Baptist church, who apparently had preached a sermon in reaction to a smear campaign Ezekiel started against another man. The parson shut up pretty soon after, though, and Jedediah seemed to think that Ezekiel must have found some dirt on him."

Dan nodded, looking more grim than the information seemed to warrant. "Makes sense. Listen:

"'May 5,

'I don't like to slander any man, and ain't said half of what I could against Ezekiel G—. But I figure now the rumors are true and he's a conjure man, but one as works only to his own gain and to the ill of others.'"

"A 'conjure man?'" Leif interrupted.

"A Walker. And not necessarily a deathwalker, but someone in touch with the Otherworld and the spirits. Able to cast blessings and curses." Dan shrugged. "They called Jedediah a conjure man, too. I guess it means a haintworker."

"Sounds reasonable. What else does it say?"

Dan cleared his throat and squinted at the cramped handwriting. *"'I heard tell a while back of a strange figure near the graveyards on certain nights. Right after that, Wilbur McGuire dropped his lawsuit against Ezekiel and wouldn't say why to nobody. And nobody can find old Henry Downes, who said Ezekiel swindled him good in a deal*

'On May 1, somebody went to the burying ground of the Methodist church, and dug up some of the graveyard dirt, burned some candles, and wrote on the tombstones. Might have been hex signs, but I never seen any like them. And now Catherine McAfee has gone and thrown over Colonel Monroe in favor of Ezekiel. What sits poorly with me is Colonel Monroe had threatened to shoot any other man who as much as looked at Miss McAfee. But he's just going around with his tail between his legs, like a yellow dog. If this weren't enough, Ezekiel has gone bought up a bunch of cows and chickens, though where he got the money for it I don't like to think. Wasn't from any bank loan, that's for sure.

'I figure he's been calling up the dead and making them tell him what the living ought not to know. Something's got to be done about it, and I guess I'm the one to do it, but I'm afeared what might come of crossing him.'"

A shiver passed through Leif. *Poor Jedediah—he worked to keep the dead from being disturbed, and ended up being dragged back from the Otherworld by a necromancer himself.*

Which was exactly why Leif had instructed his lawyer to cremate him as soon as possible when he died. The idea of being vulnerable to Rúnar's manipulation after death was even more terrifying than the prospect of facing him again in life. Rúnar rewarded those who served him with gifts, money, a sense of worth and belonging: whatever they most desired. Enemies received agony and despair, then death. A betrayal like Leif's? The only limit to Rúnar's cruelty was his imagination. And he had a very, very good imagination.

A ragged ache slid up through Leif's head from the base of his spine. *If Rúnar is the one to kill me, I'll never have the chance to be burned and scattered. I'll be his forever.*

"Anything more?" Leif asked with an effort.

"I'm not sure." Dan thumbed rapidly through the diary, obviously scanning for mentions of Ezekiel's name. "Do you think this could be something?"

"No telling. I'll keep on with this, and you look for any mention of ol' Zeke."

They settled in with a new energy, and it wasn't long before Dan said, "Listen to this: *'June 21 - Went to the Witches Harrow with the Eye of the Uktena, figuring I could do something to keep the dead quiet in their graves, and Ezekiel off of them. Somebody been there before me. If it was him, I hate to think what he might do with the power of that place.'"*

"Oh." Leif sat up sharply, the diary he'd been reading sliding from his grasp. "Yes. That sounds like something Rúnar would be interested in. Where is this place of power?" *And why didn't you mention it to me?*

"Fuck if I know," Dan said, a bit defensively. "I've never heard of it before."

"Sorry—I didn't mean to sound—"

"Don't worry about it. I'm more concerned as to *why* I've never heard of it. A place of power isn't the sort of thing that just gets lost."

"Not with the sort of continuity your family has had," Leif agreed. "Huh. That is odd. Do you know what he meant by the Eye of the Uktena?"

Dan's mouth quirked ruefully. "Not really. All I know is Uktenas are from Cherokee legend. They were supposed to be huge snakes living in the rivers. They had some kind of really bright jewel or crystal embedded in their foreheads they dazzled their prey with, made it just stand there while they gobbled it up."

"It might have been some sort of powerful crystal or gemstone?"

"This whole area is filled with gem mines. They even say there's a giant crystal under Asheville, although I'm not sure if that's true or not."

Leif pondered. "If you're right and the Eye of the Uktena was an object of power, Rúnar would be very interested in it. It's another possibility, besides the Witches Harrow."

Dan nodded. "I'm going to keep looking and see if I can figure out where the Witches Harrow is, or what might have happened to the Eye."

"I'll keep combing through more slowly," Leif said, although he wished he could just jump straight to the last diary and find out what might be in it. But rushing through the only records they had might lead to missing some vital clue. With an effort of will, he forced his thoughts to settle and continued reading.

Dan interrupted every once in a while. "Sounds here like Jedediah put down a haint Ezekiel had raised. Ezekiel didn't like that. They exchanged some words and veiled threats."

Later: "Sounds like their feud got worse. Jedediah found hex signs on his cattle, and some of them sickened and died."

And: "The sheriff disappeared after he went out to Ezekiel's place with Catherine McAfee's father. The father suffered a mysterious accident a few days later, when his horse bolted on a lonely road farther up the gap. He was thrown, hit his head, lingered a little while, and died."

Leif's stomach twisted. It all sounded horribly familiar. Rúnar's enemies had also come to sudden and disturbing ends, none of which could ever be traced directly back to him.

Not just Rúnar. What had been the name of the Ukrainian thief? A hireling, he'd decided to double-cross Leif and Rúnar by killing his fellow guard and making off with a priceless gold torq from the undiscovered tomb they'd looted.

The thief died the next night, when a *draugr* bound and sent by Leif appeared in the back seat of his car on a treacherous stretch of highway. Leif had felt so smug at the time, so righteous, like it was justice and not murder. Like he was strong and powerful and whatever he did was right.

If Dan ever found out—

But he wouldn't. There was no reason for him to even suspect.

"Here we go," Dan said. "Sounds like it all came to a head on Samhain. Halloween. Ezekiel sent out a challenge to Jedediah to face him in the Witches Harrow."

"What happened? That is, Jedediah must have survived, considering this isn't his final diary."

Dan squinted at the page and cleared his throat. *"'Nov. 1 – I like to think I got rid of something evil last night, though I don't know. Don't know about my doing of it, either.*

'As Ezekiel had set the time and place of our 'duel,' as he put it, I had a few days to think on it. I couldn't let him raise the dead of the whole county and sent them on the living, but I didn't see how I could stop him, either.'"

"Is that even possible?" Leif interrupted. "That is, I know places of power can give a boost of energy to most rituals, but what Jedediah is talking about is far beyond that."

Dan's mouth was drawn and grim. "I don't know, but Jedediah sure believed it was. And since he'd actually been to the Witches Harrow, and talked about using it to perform a cleansing on the whole county…"

"Shit."

"Yeah." Dan shifted the book and bent over it again. *"I couldn't risk facing him in a fair fight. I set up the best binding I could, and took my herbs and the Eye, which had been charged three nights in moonlight.*

'When I came to the entrance of the cave—' okay, it sounds like the Harrow is a cave—*'I could feel him inside. I stayed outside and put up a seal, to keep him and his hexes from getting out.'"*

Leif let out a low whistle. "That's pretty bad-ass."

"Is it?"

"He's talking about a working that might be beyond the scope of any sorcerer I've ever heard of, including Rúnar."

"'Even using the Eye, I almost couldn't do it. Before I was finished, Ezekiel realized what I was up to and tried to stop me.

'I can't rightly explain what the battle was like, other than I feel ten years older today. But I managed to beat him, and the Witches Harrow is sealed away, and Ezekiel with it. I guess he's still alive down there right now, screaming and cursing me, but he can't get out, and I guess he'll be a haint himself soon enough.

'I hate to lose the Harrow, but I don't know what else I might've done. But thanks to Ezekiel fighting back, there's a crack in the seal. I figure it'll open every Hallowe'en at sundown and close again dawn, and Lord only know what mischief he might do in those hours. I guess I could take the Eye back and use it to undo the seal, and put him down for good, but I didn't like facing him as a living man. I surely don't want to see his haint.'"

Leif stared down at his hands as Dan's words fell into silence. Distantly, he noted the chipped black paint on his short-chewed nails, but it all seemed far away compared to the cold settling over him.

"This is it," he said quietly. "This has to be what Rúnar came for."

Dan nodded slowly. "Sounds like we'd better keep him from getting it."

"Yes." Because otherwise, every soul in Ransom Gap, both living and dead, would be plunged into nightmare.

The phone rang as Dan was locking up for the night. He hurried through the darkened living room and into the kitchen, scooping up the phone half-way through its second ring. "Hoary Oak Hill Farm."

"Still playing farmer, Dan?" asked a familiar voice.

A laugh of unexpected delight escaped him, which he sorely needed after today. "Taryn? Hecate's bitches, girl, it's good to hear from you!"

"Been a while," she allowed. *Since Mom's funeral.*

"Let me guess: you're calling because you miss hauling hay and mucking out stalls? Or chasing goats around the countryside?"

She snorted. "I thought we agreed not to mention the fucking goat again? And I haven't laid eyes on a hay bale since I was seventeen. Why my teacher thought I had to come up there with him to visit, I don't know."

"Maybe he figured you ought to know another Walker the same age."

"Or he wanted a free vacation where all he had to do was sit around on the porch and drink iced tea while I worked my ass off." She paused, and when she spoke again, her voice had lost all traces of humor. "Listen, I called because I was meditating on my altar, and found myself thinking about that time we got drunk down by the creek and I had to haul your ass back up to the house. Not just remembering it, but like it was actually happening, like you were right there with me. Guess that's a clear enough sign that Anubis wanted me to talk to you. Everything all right up there?"

Dan hesitated just a fraction of a moment too long.

"What is it? You need me to come up?" she asked.

He hated to ask—it was a long drive. "Got a little bit of trouble," he admitted. "A necromancer is in the area. I'm working on it with another haint-worker. Leif Helsvin."

"Huh. Name sounds familiar."

"Tall guy, blond, belongs on a magazine cover."

Taryn laughed. "Or as the centerfold? Maybe I'll come up there just to check him out."

"It'd be worth the drive," he said, then winced. *I can't think of Leif like that.*

She shifted gears, saving him from any further embarrassment. "Seriously, though, do you need me to come up there?"

Dan took a moment to mull it over. But what was there for Taryn to do, really? "Not yet. I'll give you a call if we do, though, all right?"

"All right. Kiss Bea and Virgil for me."

"I'll tell them you called."

"And you watch your ass, Dan. I don't like the vibe I'm getting here."

"Yeah," he muttered as he hung up the phone, "that makes two of us."

CHAPTER 10

Dan stumbled out of bed before the sun had even half-broken the horizon, his head pounding and his eyes full of grit. After spending most of the day and a good part of the night squinting at Jedediah Van Horn's awful handwriting, breathing in the dust of moldering pages, and sitting in an uncomfortable position on the floor, he felt like he was hung over.

And I didn't even have the booze to make it worthwhile.

He showered quickly, trying not to reflect on the fact he had more of the same ahead of him today. He and Leif had set the diaries aside for the night after their final discovery and gone downstairs for a late dinner and more discussion. Today would be spent looking farther through the diaries, trying to figure out where the Harrow was located, and what happened to the Eye of the Uktena.

But for now, breakfast needed cooking and the kids off to school. He rooted through the cupboards for pancake mix and fixings, and started the coffee brewing. *Just another morning.*

Footsteps sounded on the stair, and a moment later Leif emerged into the kitchen. His long hair was pulled into a loose bun, held in place by a pair of bone hair sticks, and he wore the same t-shirt from the day before, with a pair of baggy cotton pants. In one hand, he carried his sheathed sword.

"Good morning," he said with a smile, as if he was genuinely glad to see Dan.

It was a nice change from surly teenaged scowls, Dan had to admit. "Morning. Expecting trouble over breakfast?" he asked, with a nod at the sword.

"I was worried I might have to fight Virgil for my share of pancakes. That boy can eat."

Dan chuckled. "I'll make extra."

"Seriously, I need to do my exercises. I've been slack about practicing my sword forms since I got here. I'd better get back into the habit, or else Mordgud will have something to say about it."

The coffee pot let out one last gurgle. Dan poured himself a cup. "I'm not clear on who Mordgud is, actually."

"She guards the Gjallarbrú—the bridge over the river Gjöll and the entrance to Helheim. I deliver the dead to her, and she takes them on the rest of the way. She's one tough lady, as you might imagine, and she doesn't put up with wasted strength."

"Got it. Have fun."

Leif left. Dan puttered around for a few more minutes, listening for the sounds of his siblings stirring. The water ran in the pipes overhead; Bea must be up and showering.

He set out the ingredients to make apple spice pancakes, humming softly to himself. Leif might want some coffee; he filled a mug and carried it outside.

The sun rose over the mountain, its light bathing the farm and flashing off the bright metal of Leif's sword. He moved like a dancer, his every movement fast and graceful, the sword's blade whistling in the air as he appeared to battle imaginary enemies. Despite the morning chill, he'd stripped off his shirt and tossed it over the seat of the still-broken-down tractor. The early sunlight gilded the sweat clinging to his lean torso, outlining every lithe muscle.

Pale scars tracked his arms here and there, and Dan noticed a black tattoo on his chest, above his heart: a rune Dan didn't recognize. A stylized hound was tattooed on his left shoulder, also in black; a sword on the right. Metal glinted from the silver bars through each pale pink nipple, and a light dusting of golden hair traced the path from navel down, disappearing beneath his loose workout pants.

Dan's fingers tightened convulsively on the coffee mug, heedless of the scalding heat. He could feel warmth gathering in his cock, nipples tightening, lips aching, his whole body *yearning* toward the lissome figure moving with such fluid grace. He wanted to run his hands over the pale skin, wanted to trace the path from navel to groin with his tongue. Wanted to pull loose the bound hair with his hands and sink his fingers into the locks, inhaling and filling his lungs with the scent of male sweat.

He swallowed convulsively, struggling to control his reaction. His erection strained against the fabric of his jeans, easily visible. If Leif saw that, he'd...well, Dan didn't know, exactly.

I could find out.

No. No, bad idea. Leif was way out of his league. He probably wasn't even interested in Dan, at least not beyond some light flirting which didn't mean a thing. And even if he was, Dan couldn't risk it, not for a guy who'd be gone in a week.

He focused his eyes on the broken tractor, forcing himself to think about fighting to repair the piece of shit, until what few mechanical skills he had failed him. He was going to have to take it to the garage, which meant more money down the drain, and he'd better just hope it was fixable and he didn't need to buy a new one.

The unpleasant thought was enough to make him go soft, all right. Maybe the tractor wasn't completely useless after all. Not looking directly at Leif, he walked over to it and set the mug on the hood. "I brought you some coffee."

"Thanks." Leif walked over, grabbed his shirt, and used it to wipe off his face and chest. Dan tried not to stare, but he could smell Leif's sweat, mingled with the remnants of his cedar and rosewood cologne. Heat burned Dan's cheeks.

"I'm just about done," Leif said; if he noticed Dan was having trouble looking directly at him, he didn't let on. "I promise to shower before eating. Don't wait breakfast on me."

"I'll wait. *We'll* wait," Dan correctly hastily. "Virgil's still asleep, any-way."

"Thanks," Leif said again, then laughed. "I say that to you a lot, don't I? I'm not sure how I can repay you for everything you've done."

Dan shrugged awkwardly, certain Leif could see his blush now. "You don't have to. I'm a Walker—it's my job."

"Even if that's true, you've done far more than I could ever have expect-ed." Leif's hand came to rest on Dan's shoulder. He glanced up in surprise. Leif's expression was serious, his winter-sky eyes capturing Dan's gaze ef-fortlessly.

Dan felt as if he couldn't breathe. He wanted to flee, but at the same time, he wanted to lean forward and taste Leif's mouth. He could feel the heat of the other man's fingers through his t-shirt and flannel, and he ached to feel that warmth against his skin.

Leif's fingers tightened slightly, before dropping away. Exertion had left a pink flush on his skin, but Dan thought it deepened before he turned aside and lowered his gaze to the steaming mug. "Anyway, thanks for the coffee."

"No problem," Dan said; the words came out rough, and he cleared his throat self-consciously. "I better go inside and get breakfast going."

Leif nodded, and now he was the one avoiding looking directly at Dan. "I'll, uh, be in soon."

"Take your time." As Dan started away, he heard the dry leaves crunch-ing under Leif's boots, the whistle of the sword as he started up his exercises again. And although he ached to look back and at least let his eyes feast on the other man, he resolutely kept them fixed on the door until he was safely back inside.

~ * ~

As soon as the chores were done, Dan took the truck and headed to the lone grocery store in town. Leif volunteered to stay behind and look through the diaries, something for which Dan was very glad as soon as he walked through the door.

"Dan!" Marlene called from one of the checkout lanes, waving enthusiastically.

His return smile felt like it didn't really fit on his face. But, just like always, no one else seemed to notice.

They'd been a couple for the last two years of high school, even though by then Dan had been pretty sure he was gay. Still, a part of him had hoped for normalcy, for the ease with which everybody else seemed to move through life. No other guy he knew spent the school dances wishing boys could sway as close to each other as mixed-sex couples, or secretly wanted to be the one standing up there with the Homecoming King.

He'd tried to pretend, dating Marlene and doing all the expected things with her, from taking her to prom to getting blowjobs in the back of the car. Instead of making him feel more normal, it had just made him feel worse and worse, until he was ready to crawl out of his skin.

The thing was, he liked Marlene well enough. Always had. She was a nice girl: sweet and kind, the sort of friend who'd be there for you no matter what. He liked being her friend, but he just didn't love her, no matter how many times he told her—and himself—otherwise. He didn't want to hurt her, which he would have if she'd ever found out that he'd spent their backseat encounters with his eyes closed, pretending she was the hot guy on the basketball team.

He'd been glad that she'd moved on when he'd gone off to college. Found a new guy, gotten pregnant, married, and settled down into the life she wanted, the one he couldn't provide. He'd figured they'd remain pleasant memories for each other, nothing more.

Then he'd been forced to come home, and found she'd gotten divorced, and the occasional encounter at the store had turned into lunch dates and movie nights.

We're just friends. She understands that. Didn't she?

There's been no kissing. No nothing. She has to know that I'm not interested in her that way.

There was no reason to feel relieved Leif had stayed back at the house, especially since nothing was actually going on between him and Marlene *or* him and Leif.

Which was pretty pathetic. *All the guilt with none of the fun.*

He waved weakly back at Marlene, grabbed a shopping cart, and hurried into the nearest aisle. Telling himself that he didn't want to leave Leif alone to do all the work, he went down the list and loaded the cart in record time.

Marlene would never let him hear the end of it if he didn't get in her line. He waited impatiently while she checked out the three customers in front of him. When it came his turn, she gave him a brilliant smile. "Dan! You didn't tell me you're doing haint-work again, you bad boy!" She swatted him playfully on the arm.

His smile grew even more fixed. "Sorry. It's just temporary."

"It's true? When Nakesha said you'd helped out Zach, I couldn't believe it."

Nakesha was Corey's wife. "There's another haint-worker staying with me. He did most of the work." Which wasn't exactly true, but Leif *had* been the one to put the haint down.

"Oh, well that makes sense." Marlene chewed on her full lower lip as she rang up his groceries. "You think he'd mind doing some work for me? Well, not me, but Brian says he can't make his child support payments because he can't rent out one of the trailers. Remember when Mike Brown died, and his girlfriend overdosed a week later? That's where it happened. First two times Brian rented it out, people left within a day or two, saying it was haunted. It's been empty ever since. I wouldn't ask as a favor to him, but I could use the money, and I don't want to get the court involved if I don't have to."

Dan doubted Marlene's ex-husband was late with his child support because his trailer park included a haunted single-wide, especially since this was just the latest in a long string of excuses. But their kid surely didn't deserve to be caught in the middle, and maybe if Dan could take care of this, it would shame Brian into coughing up at least some of the money.

"Sure. Leif and I will head out there tonight. Write down the address on the back of the receipt, okay?"

Marlene beamed at him. "Thanks, sweetie! Leif, huh? What kind of name is that?"

Dan only shrugged and dug out his wallet to pay. Marlene scribbled an address on the back of his receipt, winking at him when she handed it over. "I'll have to thank you personally next time I see you."

He mumbled something noncommittal and hurried back to the truck with the groceries.

Dan pushed open the door a bit more forcefully than necessary when he returned to the house. Leif glanced up from the kitchen table, where he sat with Jedediah's diaries stacked up beside him. He'd showered after breakfast and was dressed in yet another black t-shirt and jeans, the ebony eyeliner once more immaculate around his pale eyes.

"How's it going?" Dan asked, nodding to the books before Leif could ask him if anything was wrong.

Leif made a face. "Is it too early to drink?"

Dan carried the groceries over to the fridge and began putting them away. "It's always noon somewhere."

"Thank the gods." Leif scrubbed at his eyes, softening the sharp edge of the liner. "I've been over every page of Jedediah's diaries, and he doesn't say another cursed thing about Ezekiel or the Witches Harrow."

"Maybe he just wanted to put it behind him." Dan could surely sympathize with that, couldn't he? "What about the Eye of the Uktena?"

"That comes up once or twice, by way of using it in ritual context. '*Laid Miss Elsie Brown, as had been set upon by a gang of the local 'gentlemen' and hung herself after being cruelly used by them. The Eye held her calm until I could open the way.*' That sort of thing."

Hecate's bitches, it said something that neither of them was surprised by the nature of that old crime. *We get to see the worst in people, I guess. See the pain left behind, one way or another.*

What had it been like, when Jedediah had laid Elsie Brown? Had he heard the creak of the rope? Felt it tighten around his own neck—

No. He focused on the box of cereal in his hand, opening the cabinet and putting it away where it belonged. Everything nice and orderly. "I guess we move on to his daughter's journals. See what she has to say."

"I suppose." Leif stacked the diaries, then paused and looked up. "Dan? I'm sorry about what happened to Jedediah. I'm sorry Rúnar hurt him. I'm sorry your family got dragged into this accursed business at all."

His clear blue eyes were soft in their rings of liner, and the downward curl of his lips hinted at some pain of his own.

It was all Dan could do not to reach out and smooth the worried frown from Leif's brow. "It's none of your doing," he said. "I'll get Maybel's diaries and look through them, if you want to take a break."

Leif stretched in his chair, his t-shirt riding up to give Dan a tantalizing glimpse of his flat stomach. "That's kind of you, but Rúnar is my responsibility. Not that I'm suggesting I don't want your help, but I can't just sit by and watch, even if it is only for a few hours."

If Leif wanted me to know, he would have already said. But somehow Dan couldn't keep himself from asking: "Why? I mean, it would be the duty of any good Walker to stop Rúnar, I'm not saying that. But you say it's your responsibility like there's something personal between you."

Leif's eyes widened slightly in alarm, before shifting to the hunted, haunted look Dan recognized all too well, having seen it himself a few times in the mirror. *The look of a man who doesn't want to think too hard about the past.*

"I'm sorry," he said quickly. "I shouldn't pry."

"It's all right." Leif sighed and slumped back in his chair, his gaze fixed on the backs of his hands. "Rúnar killed a friend of mine."

Dan winced. "I'm sorry. Was he special to you?" Which was probably the most insensitive question he could possibly have asked; he wanted to kick himself as soon as the words were out of his mouth.

Leif's lips twitched slightly. "*She* was special to me, yes, although not in the way you mean. Her name was Alice. She was a Walker-Between-the-Worlds, but her charge was the living, not the dead."

"Oh," Dan said. He'd heard tell of such Walkers, but he'd never met one. Deathwalkers tended to be clannish, sticking with those whose calling took them to the Underworld and nowhere else. "Was she helping you with a case? I mean, working with the living family or something?"

"No. I was the one she was sent to help."

"You?" he asked, surprised.

"I was pretty screwed up," Leif said ruefully. "How doesn't really matter right now. Alice showed up one day when I was in college, walking back to my apartment from classes. She told me Loki had sent her to me."

Dan searched his memory; he had enough trouble keeping up with the various goddesses of death, let alone the rest of the pantheons Walkers worshipped. "Loki is some kind of trickster god, right? Like coyote or rabbit?"

"Something like that. He's also Hel's father, and when one of Her tools needed repair, He did what any doting parent would do and tried to fix it. He sent Alice to straighten me out, make me into the Walker Hel needed me to be."

Leif looked out the window in the direction of the oak. Shadows seemed to gather behind his eyes, and the corners of his mouth turned down at some dark memory. "To make a long story short, she did. She also crossed Rúnar, and he murdered her. I was the one who found her body."

Dan swallowed against the knot of pain threatening to block his own throat. "May Hecate give her spirit peace. I'm sorry, Leif."

"As am I." The smile Leif cast him was wistful. "Alice died at Rúnar's hands, and I've been chasing after him every day since. But he always stays one step ahead of me, no matter what I do. He can't shake me entirely, but I can never catch him, as if we're locked together in some horrible dance."

Dan sank down into the chair beside Leif and set a hand on the other man's shoulder. The muscle and bone were hard under his fingers, and Leif's heat soaked into his skin, making his heart speed up. "That's because you haven't had help before. You and me, we're going to take Rúnar down."

And, gods, he was in it now, wasn't he? He'd already committed himself to this fight, and yet this felt like a promise. Like a vow.

The light streaming in through the window touched Leif's face, highlighting his perfect cheekbones, making his pale skin and corn silk hair almost glow. His expression softened into something tender, and, gods, Dan didn't think he'd ever seen anything as beautiful. More than anything in the world, he longed to lean forward and press his lips against Leif's, but this wasn't the raw heat he'd felt earlier. He wanted to put his arms around Leif and hold him close, let Leif know he wasn't alone. He wanted to keep Leif safe, and take care of him, and…

Taking a deep breath, Dan forced his fingers to let go one by one and sat back in the chair. The absence of Leif's heat made his hand feel icy, even though the kitchen was warm. "We should look at those diaries."

"Yes." Leif looked away and down, his gaze betraying nothing. "We should. I'll meet you upstairs in a minute."

Dan nodded, not questioning, only glad to have a few minutes to get his reactions under control. Still, it took an effort of will to get to his feet and head for the stairs.

I'm just horny, that's all. It isn't anything more than that. I like Leif as a friend, and he's gorgeous. Of course I'm going have intense feelings around him.

If that's all it is, why wasn't I hard?

It wasn't a question he could afford to answer. He walked the rest of the way up the stair and went to his bedroom, to begin sorting through the journals.

CHAPTER 11

T hank Hel, it didn't take long for them to discover what had become of the Eye of the Uktena—or at least, how it had passed out of the hands of Dan's family.

"He gave it away?" Dan asked, gaping openly.

They sat cross-legged on the bedroom floor once again, pouring over the diaries of Jedediah's daughter—and the next Walker—Maybel. Unlike the five thick volumes the long-lived Jedediah had left behind, hers were sadly slim, as she had died in childbirth not long after training her eldest son as her apprentice.

They also held the only account of the last years of Jedediah's life, once he'd grown too absent-minded and feeble to keep a journal.

"He didn't give it away," Leif corrected. "Well, not exactly. Seems like he owed money to a lot of people, and in the end, the creditors basically seized whatever they felt like taking. Maybel was heartbroken. She writes: *'Gerrald Oglesby took with him the Eye of the Uktena. I begged him to leave it, but he refused. Everybody says he's the worst miser in the state, and there ain't no hope of getting it back from him.'* It sounds like the crystal was set in an amulet of some kind," he added, in a weak attempt to make something positive out of the news.

Dan gave him a look that said he saw through Leif's attempt. "Right. Well. Back to the library tomorrow to see if we can track him. Wonderful."

"Maybe not," Leif said, trying to be optimistic even though he doubted the truth of his own words. "Let's go through the rest of these. Perhaps Maybel underestimated Mr. Oglesby's font of human kindness."

"Sure she did," Dan muttered, but did as he suggested.

And maybe there had been some Walker intuition behind his suggestion, because before long Dan paled horribly, his face going the color of old cheese. "Oh, fuck me. He's the miser in Saddle Creek Park."

"From the sound of your voice, I'm going to guess that's bad news."

"It was a story Mom told me once, about a haint down by Saddle Creek. Nobody's seen it for a long time now, since the place it haunted is part of a park that closes at dusk. Way the story went, an old miser was supposed to have a store of gold hidden out in the woods behind his cabin. A bunch of thieves heard the rumors and went out there one clear night when the moon was up, thinking to make him tell them where his treasure was buried."

"By force if necessary, I take it."

"Yeah. They tortured him. Maybe he would have given up the treasure eventually, but he was an old guy, and he died. The thieves got scared and buried him out the woods. His haint is supposed to chase people in the woods on clear nights, once the moon is up." He held up the diary. "According to Maybel, Oglesby died just as the story goes. It can't be a coincidence."

"All right. The thieves wouldn't have put up a marker, which means Rúnar doesn't know where the miser's body is buried. He can't just call him up whenever he wants to."

"He'll have to wait for the ghost to come to him?"

"Yes. Do you have any idea what the weather is supposed to be for the next few days?"

Dan shrugged. "I'm a farmer. Of course I know what the weather report says. Mixed clouds and sun for the next few days, but it's supposed to clear up by Saturday night…oh fuck."

"What now?"

"Normally the park doesn't have anything going on after dark, but that's going to change this coming weekend. Ransom Gap is holding its first annual Apple Days festival there to, what was it? 'Celebrate mountain culture, crafts, and stroke our own egos,' something like that."

"And this celebration will last until after dark."

"Got it in one."

"Shit. Maybe the forecast is wrong. I mean, since when do the weathermen get anything right?"

Dan shook his head slowly. "I surely hope you're right. Because unless we get more luck than anyone in Ransom Gap has ever had, half the county will be living it up in the adjacent field, while the haint is prowling the woods along with Rúnar."

Leif steered the low-slung Porsche through the entrance to the Shadyside Homes trailer park. Although some of the inhabitants had made an effort to brighten up their surroundings with neat pots of flowers, cheerful welcome signs, and colorful mailboxes, there was no disguising the age of the trailers. The vinyl sides of most showed algal growth near the ground and on the northern sides, and a few sported overgrown lawns with abandoned toys or rusted cars out front.

"That ought to be it," Dan said, pointing at the most decrepit-looking of all the trailers. The tall grass in front was unkempt, and paint peeled from the wooden stairs leading up to the sun-faded door. Broken blinds hung crookedly over the windows.

Leif had been surprised earlier, when Dan said a friend had a haint needing their attention. News spread fast in Ransom Gap, it seemed.

He didn't mind. After everything he'd seen and done with Rúnar, this sort of work felt almost like a vacation. Something clean, after so many tainted years.

Leif pulled onto the cracked pavement of the drive. A streetlight shed a sullen amber glow on the trailer, but the only other light in the overcast night came from the neighboring trailers.

Dan strapped his tool belt around his narrow hips and picked up his wand from the passenger side floor. "Ready?"

"Ready."

They climbed out of the car and walked up the creaking steps. The door opened at a touch. It looked as if the lock had been broken, maybe by someone hoping for a place to squat. Any trespassers probably hadn't stayed long, though. Hauntings were better than any security system when it came to keeping out the living.

The trailer's interior stank of mildew, stale air, and mouse droppings. The electricity was turned off; the only illumination came from the sulfurous glow of the street light out the window. Leif's night-sharp eyes picked out a few bits of cheap furniture, a kitchen with vintage appliances, and a vinyl-covered recliner. An etheric stain clung to the thin carpet, forming the rough outline of a fallen body.

The floor creaked as Dan joined him inside. A moment later, the scents of garlic and rosemary freshened the air as he laid a line of salt and herbs across the doorstop and windows.

Leif crossed to the back door and did the same thing with a handful of salt, then marked off the boundaries of the living room where the girl had died. The feeling of watching eyes crackled along Leif's skin, raising all the fine hairs on his arms and neck as he worked. Something cold brushed against his face, like trailing fingers; he ignored it. A moment later, the fingers touched his arm—and gave him a vicious pinch.

"She touched me," he said calmly, as he finished the last line of salt.

The charms on Dan's wand rattled in warning. Leif took his staff out and held it in his left hand, in case he needed to draw his sword with the right. For now, though, the blade stayed put; although the haint wasn't happy to have them there, Leif hadn't yet sensed any true malice in it.

The air thickened and shimmered near Leif, strobing through the colors of grief before taking on the aspect of the dead girl. Her bare feet were bloated, and the vomit which had choked her clung to the front of her thin night-gown. Tears streamed down her mottled cheeks from eyes burning with the unearthly fire of the dead. She moaned, her thick tongue no longer able to form words, only articulate sounds of utter misery.

That could have been my fate. Was the fate of a lot of the people I knew on the streets.

The staff glowed in his hand, sending a flush of warmth up his arm, even as the silver in his body flashed cold. "It's all right," Leif told her, holding out his free hand.

She flinched back, but the salt barriers around the room sparked with blue fire, pinning her in. Leif moved closer to her, projecting calm.

"It's all right," he repeated. "I understand. You've been lost and sad, but I've come to help you."

She wanted help, but even without words she conveyed her despair, her fierce loneliness, her grief for the boy she'd loved, strong enough to hold her to this world.

"I know," Leif said gently. "I do. But he's waiting for you in the Other-world. He sits at dinner in a beautiful castle with a golden roof, waiting for you to join him."

She drifted closer, radiating tentative hope.

"It's true," he assured her, and felt the tension in the air shift. The girl put her hand into his, and he curled his fingers tenderly over her stiff, mold-caked ones.

"Mighty Mordgud, guardian of the Gjallarbrú, open the long road for this lost one," he said.

The air seemed to fold back—or dissolve and reveal what had always been there, perhaps. The great bridge leapt the raging river guarding Hel-heim, and he saw Mordgud in her black armor, taller and stronger than any mere human, with laugh lines around her eyes and mouth.

Leif sometimes wondered what the dead saw when he took them across; he doubted it matched his own vision. "She will take you the rest of the way," he told the girl, and passed her hand to Mordgud.

The girl started to leave with Mordgud, and reality condensed around them. Before she was entirely gone, she glanced over her shoulder; restored lips and tongue formed the words: "Thank you."

When they were on the road again, with Shadyside disappearing in the rear view mirror, Dan glanced over at Leif. "You do good work," he said.

The dashboard lights outlined Leif's face, spreading a greenish glow over his fair skin. He kept his eyes on the road, but gave a short nod of acknowledgement. "I try."

"I mean it. You've got a-a good manner," Dan said awkwardly, not sure how else to describe the gentle way Leif had given peace to the troubled haint.

"Just doing my job," Leif said lightly.

Dan watched him for a few more moments, wondering if he ought to push it or just let it lie. "That's not it," he said at last. "You're amazing. Look, just take the compliment, all right?"

Leif's shoulders hunched in slightly, as though he half-expected to be hit instead of praised. "I'm glad you think I'm good, but I'm nothing special. Far from it."

Dan wondered what had happened to make him unable to hear anything positive about himself. "I think you are," he said. "Something special, that is."

Leif glanced at him, black-lined eyes going wide with surprise. Then his expression softened, and he returned his gaze to the road. "Thanks. You're pretty special yourself."

Dan looked at the road, too, at the patch of pavement illuminated by the headlights. Warmth curled through him, and a grin tugged at his mouth. It felt odd, as if he exercised muscles he hadn't used in years.

"Thanks."

They didn't speak again, only drove through the night in a silence which didn't need words to communicate.

Later that night, Dan lay in bed, staring at the ceiling and willing himself not to think.

He could worry: that was fine. Normal, even. Worry about the haint, worry about the Apple Days Festival, worry about Virgil staying out until almost midnight and sassing him when he asked where the boy had been. Worry was a familiar companion, one with which he'd spent many a long night.

What he couldn't do was remember how utterly edible Leif had looked this morning while practicing with the sword. How warm his shoulder felt when Dan touched him. How badly Dan wanted to lean forward and kiss away his look of concern when they talked about the haint and the upcoming festival, and what sort of mischief Rúnar might try to make. How kind he'd been to the haint in the trailer, how gentle and open, and you couldn't help but feel you could tell him anything and he wouldn't judge you. Like he understood, somehow.

Would he? If he knew just how bad I failed everyone, would he understand?

"You're pretty special yourself." The words didn't feel deserved, but they made Dan's blood tingle with a fire he'd suppressed for too long.

He wanted Leif to think he was special. He wanted Leif to like him.

He wanted Leif to look at him the way he'd looked at Leif that morning in the yard.

I want him to want me.

I want...

Dan bit his lip, telling himself he shouldn't think about it, even though his cock was hard and straining against the loose sweatpants he wore to bed. Anonymous fantasies were fine; they didn't mean anything. Imagining he was having sex with his friend who was just across the hall, sound asleep in Virgil's borrowed bed, was something else altogether.

He tried to think of someone else, anyone else, but all his body could remember was Leif's graceful form, his sensual mouth, and his soft hair.

His right hand glided idly cross his skin, making him shiver in reaction as he traced a lazy pattern on the vulnerable skin of his abdomen. He pictured Leif touching him instead, his hands soft but strong, the black-painted nails scraping teasingly. His hand drifted higher, circling in across his chest, closer and closer to one nipple. Leif would crouch over him, loose hair like silk against Dan's skin, as his teeth closed hard—

Dan gasped, shuddering as his nails tweaked hard on the tight bud, sending a jolt of pure pleasure straight to his balls. Fuck, he loved having his nipples played with: licked and bitten and teased. He thought he'd caught a glimpse of a tongue piercing on Leif; what would it feel like?

Panting and flushed with heat, he tossed back the covers and shoved down the waistband of his pants, freeing his cock. His mind went back to this morning, with Leif half-naked in the sunlight, gleaming with sweat. If Leif had touched him first, it was his turn to slide his hands over those lean, taut muscles. He'd follow with his mouth, licking sweat off his skin, biting the pierced nipples and making Leif whimper and moan. Would the silver be cool, or as warm as Leif's fevered skin?

He'd make his way down, licking and nipping and feasting on Leif's body until he reached the trail of hair on his lower belly. Once he reached the edge of the cloth, he'd straighten and pull Leif close, sliding his hands under the workout pants to grip those tight buttocks.

"Gods, you're hard," he'd whisper, feeling Leif's erection push against his own through their clothes.

"Because I want you."

Dan wrapped his hand around his cock, swallowing back a whimper as he began to stroke himself. Moisture beaded at the tip of his aching member, and he gathered it on his palm, using it to slick the hard length.

What would Leif's cock be like, when Dan finally shoved the workout pants down? Long and slender like the rest of him? It would stand out against his pale skin, flushed deep purple-red with desire. And Dan would satisfy that desire, happily, as many times as Leif wanted. But first, Leif would touch him, ivory hands against Dan's darker skin.

Dan tweaked a nipple with his free hand, imagining Leif's mouth on him again, the scrape of teeth against tender flesh. His skin ached to feel

Leif's; gods, it would be fantastic to hold him with nothing in between.

Once they were both naked, Leif would work his way down, nibbling and kissing, until he wrapped those gorgeous lips around Dan's swollen shaft.

Dan bit back a moan, hips thrusting helplessly as he pumped himself faster. The vision of Leif's mouth wrapped around the head of his cock was enough to send him almost to the edge. What about the tongue piercing? Would he use it to work Dan's slit, before sliding down and taking his entire shaft at once—

Ecstasy boiled up from Dan's tightened balls, his whole body going stiff as he came, sticky and wet in his hand. He twisted, biting the pillow, not crying out, not shouting Leif's name in passion as his body shuddered hard, spurting again and again.

After a timeless space of white-out, he rolled over onto his side and lay still, while his breathing slowly evened. Shame washed over him; what would Leif think if he knew Dan had just jacked off to a fantasy of him?

He'd met plenty of men over the last six years, since he'd resigned himself to a life of celibacy. Some of those men had been cute, or handsome, or even sexy. But none of them had affected him like this. None of them had left him with this helpless longing.

Dan shivered as sweat cooled on his skin, and pulled up the covers. *Samhain. Halloween. I just have to hold out a week and a day. After that, Leif will be on his way, and everything will be back to normal. I'll forget about him, and go back to whacking off to the hot male model on the magazine cover.*

The promise rang hollow, though. Leif had wormed his way into Dan's mind and libido, and Dan had the feeling it wasn't going to be easy to exorcise him again.

CHAPTER 12

Leif spent the night tossing and turning, his infrequent stretches of sleep interrupted by either his standard nightmares or newer dreams of dark eyes and a hidden smile.

Somehow, Dan had managed to crawl inside his head, claiming a space Leif had no intention of surrendering. He respected Dan as a Walker, liked him as a friend, and found him physically attractive. But that was supposed to be the end of the story. There couldn't be any fonder feelings, nothing romantic, because romance wasn't what Leif was about. He was about a quick fuck, leaving everyone happy, with no attachments which would only end in painful complications.

He didn't fall fully asleep until near dawn, which meant he dozed through the noise of the household waking up and getting ready for the day. By the time he finally made his way downstairs, breakfast was long over, although Dan had left a pot of coffee on for him.

The phone rang as Leif entered the kitchen; he scooped it up as he passed by. "Hoary Oak Hill Farm," he answered, having heard Dan use the greeting a few times.

There came a brief hesitation. "Hello?" said a feminine voice with a strong local drawl. "Is Dan there?"

Leif peered out the window, but didn't see the other man. "I'm not sure —he's probably out with the goats. Can I take a message?"

"Sure. Tell him Marlene called to thank him for going over to Shadyside and to see if he wants to do a movie night tonight."

Movie night? As in a date? But that couldn't be right.

Leif's fingers tightened slightly around the cool plastic of the receiver. "Marlene for movie night," he repeated back. "Got it. What number should he call?"

"Oh, he knows it," she said with a little laugh. "I'm his girlfriend."

"I see," Leif said woodenly. "I'll let him know."

He hung up and glared at the phone for a minute, before realizing what he was doing. *Stupid.* There was no reason to be jealous. In fact, this made things far, far easier. Whether Dan was bi or just using this Marlene as part of his straight cover, he was in a relationship. Completely out of bounds, in other words.

He never mentioned her. That's why I'm upset. He thought they were friends, he thought they'd had a moment on the meditation rock, when they talked about being gay. He thought…

He shut the thought down, fast. It was better this way. He ought to be happy about it.

I just need to get laid. He'd been stuck here in hick-town, in the same house with a hot guy. Of course he was going crazy. Some dancing, some drinking, and some fucking, and he'd be back to normal.

Not to mention it would get him out of the house while Dan's girlfriend was over.

Without even pouring a cup of coffee, Leif went back upstairs and started tossing clothes into his black travel bag. When he had all the supplies for a night of good dirty fun, he slung it over his shoulder and headed outside.

He found Dan out in the barn, grabbing a bag of goat feed out of storage. When Dan spotted him, a frown line sprang up between his dark brows. "You going somewhere?"

"Just down to Asheville for the night," Leif said easily. "I'm low on some supplies, and it seems like a good idea to stock up before we brave the Apple Days Festival."

Why he bothered to concoct the lie, he wasn't entirely sure. Why *shouldn't* Dan know he was headed somewhere for an evening of hot, sweaty, anonymous sex?

"Oh. All right," Dan said slowly, as though he thought there might be something more to it.

"Do you need me to pick anything up for you?"

"No." Dan watched him with what seemed like concern.

"Someone named Marlene called," Leif said, as off-handedly as he could manage. "She wants to do movie night tonight."

"Oh. Thanks." Dan didn't seem particularly enthusiastic for a man who'd just found out his girlfriend wanted to see him. "Have a safe trip. Call me if you need anything."

The offer left an unexpected ache in Leif's chest. *I could call him from jail, or broken down on the side of the road, or from a bar too drunk to drive, and he'd come.* Because it was the sort of thing Dan did, even when there was nothing in it for him.

Leif wondered if he'd ever really known anyone decent enough to simply help out another human being, no strings attached. *Alice, maybe.* But even she had come to him because her god sent her, not out of some altruistic impulse of her own.

At first, he'd thought Rúnar was like that. Decent. Good. A savior, even. *Sweet death, I was a fool.*

Dan was the real deal. *Which is even more reason to leave him alone before I fuck up his life.*

"You have my cell number, right?" Leif asked. "If you think of anything you need later on, just call. Leave a message if I don't answer."

"Sure. Sure thing."

Leif gave him a feeble smile. "Right. See you tomorrow."

He left Dan in the barn, went to the car, and threw his bag in the trunk. Pulling out slowly to spare the undercarriage, he concentrated on driving, until he was too far down the road to be tempted to look back.

That evening, Leif sauntered in the door of what the internet advertised as one of the city's better gay bars. The place was a bit kitschier than he preferred, but the atmosphere was welcoming, and it looked like a good place to cruise.

The cinderblock walls were painted black and decorated with Christmas lights, and neon under-lit the bottles behind the bar, making them glow like magic jewels. Through the shifting bodies, he caught sight of a wooden dance floor; a band advertised as the Parking Lot Mastodons was still setting up. In the meantime, the typical techno-industrial dance mix blared from the speakers.

This was familiar territory, and he felt himself relax, a tension he hadn't even noticed until now leaving his shoulders. He might not know much about small town Appalachia, and he might be lost navigating even something as simple as friendship with a decent guy like Dan, but this swirl of sex and booze, this he knew.

He found an empty stool at the end of the bar nearest the dance floor. An androgynous bartender with fantastically pink hair brought him a top-shelf scotch on the rocks, which he nursed slowly. Before he even finished the first round, a man leaned on the bar beside him, body angled toward Leif. "Hi."

Leif glanced at him. "Hi, yourself."

The guy was cute—really cute. Short black hair stood up in messy, gelled spikes, showing off a long neck and ears adorned by heavy-gauge wooden plugs. A spray of freckles across his nose offset his pale skin. He wore canvas high-tops, and his tight jeans and t-shirt hugged a slender body. He looked to be in his early twenties, and Leif pegged him for a student at the local university. His hazel eyes did the same once-over on Leif, and his expression made it clear he also liked what he saw.

"Are you with the band?" Leif asked, nodding at the Parking Lot

Mastodons logo emblazoned across the front of his t-shirt.

"Nah—I picked up the shirt at one of their other gigs, figured I'd wear it tonight since they're playing. I'm Kristian, by the way."

"Leif."

"Cool, like Leif Ericson?"

"Something like that, yeah." The band started their first set, launching into a song blending folk metal with industrial beats. The volume made it difficult to hold a conversation—but talking wasn't really the point of this excursion, was it? "Do you want to dance?"

Kristian's eyes lit up eagerly. He led the way to the dance floor, giving Leif a nice view of the firm ass encased in tight jeans. They wove into the crowd, until bodies pushed in against them from all sides.

I wonder if Dan likes to dance.

Leif silently cursed his traitorous brain. A little desperately, he let the beat of the music drive his body into motion, focusing on the man here in front of him he could have, not the one located an hour away he couldn't.

As they danced, their thighs brushed, at first accidentally, then more deliberately. Leif settled his hands onto Kristian's slender hips, pulling him closer, until they were grinding together. The younger man's eyes were dilated with lust and his lips parted, as if asking for a kiss.

Leif obliged him, sealing his mouth against Kristian's, tasting maleness and cheap beer. Kristian's arms snaked around Leif's waist, his hands cupping Leif's ass. They were both hard inside their jeans, the air thick with sweat and lust.

Kristian leaned forward, his lips at Leif's ear. "I know a place we could go," he said.

Leif shook his head. "I have a hotel room nearby—close enough to walk. Let's go there."

Kristian flashed him an eager grin. "Sounds like fun."

Leif took Kristian's hand and led him out of the club. They stopped once on the way back to the hotel in a discreet alleyway, kissing and groping hungrily for a few minutes, just to keep the tension high.

"I've never been in a penthouse before," Kristian said breathlessly, when they made it back to the room.

Leif shrugged, not interested in small talk. The suite was nice enough, with shining hardwood floors and a spacious living-room area. The bed looked large enough for four people, and the bathroom sported marble tiles. The city lay spread out below, visible on two sides through enormous windows. The lights looked like a delicate net of diamonds; beyond, the mountains bulked up against the stars in inky blackness.

Dan was on the other side of one of those mountains. Watching a movie with his girlfriend, or even fucking her for all Leif knew.

Stop it.

Desperate to get Dan out of his mind, Leif turned to Kristian and pulled him close. Kristian responded eagerly, his hands tugging at Leif's shirt, pulling it free from his jeans and peeling it off over his head.

"Nice ink," he said.

Leif ignored the comment, interested only in getting Kristian out of his shirt as well. He ran his hands greedily over the other man's narrow torso, tweaking the taut nipples with his black painted fingernails.

Kristian panted and leaned forward, kissing Leif's neck, biting lightly. His warm lips went to one nipple and nibbled, just hard enough to ride the edge between pain and pleasure. Leif's hips bucked in response, grinding against Kristian's hip.

Kristian's hands found Leif's belt and undid the heavy buckle, before moving on to the button and zipper on his jeans. Leif's cock sprang free, and he moaned at the feel of a warm hand wrapped around his aching length, tugging back the foreskin.

"Let me get my boots off," he managed to say, with what little coherence he had left.

He raced through the buckles, before kicking the boots off and shucking his jeans and underwear. Kristian took the opportunity to remove the rest of his clothing; when Leif stood up again, the other man pulled him close. Their cocks rubbed together, pre-come slicking their skin.

Leif pulled back. "Hold on. I want to suck you."

Kristian let out a groan of encouragement. Leif pulled condoms and flavored lube from the nearby desk, where he'd stored them earlier.

Kristian fumbled a condom on over his thick, heavy cock. Leif slicked a handful of flavored lube over it, before dropping to his knees and wrapping his lips around the head.

He closed his eyes as he concentrated on teasing the head, rubbing the ball of his tongue piercing against the slit, something Kristian should be able to feel even through the condom. The tart flavor of the raspberry lube went a long way to disguise the taste of the latex.

Kristian moaned, his hips jerking slightly. One hand fisted in Leif's long hair, but didn't push him forward, letting Leif set the pace. Leif sucked slowly, taking another few inches, before sliding back to play with the head more, over and over, until at last he'd swallowed Kristian's entire cock.

"Jesus, that's good. You're amazing."

Not wanting to take him over the edge, Leif leaned back, letting the head slide free of his lips with a soft "pop." Kristian whimpered like an abandoned puppy, and Leif grinned.

Leif grabbed the lube and slicked Kristian again—then turned and bent over the couch, his legs spread as far as they would go, his ass and balls and aching cock all exposed. "Fuck me," he growled.

Kristian groaned appreciatively and retrieved the lube. He spread some along Leif's painfully-hard cock, before circling his entrance and slipping a finger knuckle-deep inside. Leif moaned and pushed back, wanting more.

The other man obliged, adding a second and third finger. Leif groaned at the delicious sensation of being stretched, pressing his face into the couch, his cock aching as Kristian rubbed his prostate. "Fuck me," he repeated, more frantically this time.

Kristian's fingers slipped free, teasing another small groan from him. Strong hands gripped Leif's hips as the blunt head of Kristian's cock breached him. Leif moaned and pushed back, desperate to have more: desperate to be filled, to be ridden, to be fucked into oblivion.

Kristian began to thrust, groaning with every movement of his hips. Leif moaned too, wrapping his hand around his aching cock and matching the strokes to the shaft pounding his ass. The familiar haze of pleasure wrapped itself around his brain, and he gave himself over to it gladly, because it meant he didn't have to think, didn't have to worry, didn't have to remember.

He pressed his face against the back of the couch to muffle his own cries. *Yes, yes,* his brain babbled over and over, words he never actually said aloud during the act. *Yes, more, fuck me, please, open me, fill me.* The cock lodged in him hit his prostate again and again, and he felt his balls tighten and tingle, every thrust pushing him closer to the edge.

"Yes," he moaned into the cloth. "Yes, do it, take me there, fuck me, feels good, Dan, please—arrgh!"

His cock pulsed frantically, come erupting onto the floor, his ass clenching tight around the shaft working it. Kristian moaned in response, his fingers gripping Leif's hips as he jerked forward once, twice, thrice—then stilled, pushed deep inside as his orgasm claimed him.

For a long moment, Leif sagged against the couch, boneless with the afterglow of pleasure. When he felt Kristian feather a kiss across his spine, he knew it was time to move.

"Mmm, that was good," he said sincerely. "Bathroom is over there if you want to clean up before you leave."

Kristian didn't seem too disappointed by the dismissal—or shit, maybe he'd heard Leif moan the wrong name and didn't care to linger. At least he was smiling when he returned from the bathroom and pulled his clothes back on.

"I had a great time," he said as Leif walked him to the door. "Maybe you'd like to get together again some evening?"

Leif put on his most apologetic smile. "I'm sorry, but I'm just here on business. I'm glad we met, though—you made my stay a *lot* nicer."

Once Kristian was gone, Leif went to the bathroom, which came equipped with both a large tub and a truly enormous walk-in shower. He

turned the temperature up to near-scalding, and stood beneath the jets of water, washing away all traces of his encounter with Kristian.

What's wrong with me?

He always closed his eyes while giving head, and he never had sex face-
to-face. Those were the rules. It let him keep whoever he was with at arm's
length, as it were, kept anonymous hookups from becoming too, well, *intimate.*

And yes, sometimes it made fantasizing easier, if the person he ended up
with wasn't quite what he might have chosen otherwise. But the fantasies
were just as anonymous as the hook-ups themselves, merely faces and bodies, without name or personality.

He never fantasized about anyone he knew. Certainly he never accidentally cried out someone else's name, let alone have it trigger his orgasm.

*And who would I have fantasized about before? Whose name would I
have called?*

And, shit, wasn't that pathetic?

By the time he stepped out of the shower, he felt wretched, lonelier by
far now than before he'd gone out to the bar. Pulling on a pair of loose, cotton pants, he went to the couch, remembered what he'd just done there, and
sat on the edge of one of the plush chairs instead. His cell phone lay on the
table, and he picked it up, weighing it in his hand for a moment before giving
in to the impulse to dial.

The phone rang twice, before Dan's familiar southern accent drawled
out: "Hoary Oak Hill Farm."

"Hi. It's me. Uh, Leif."

"Hey, man. Is everything all right?"

"Fine. It's…" Fuck, he hadn't even thought of a plausible excuse for
calling. "I just wanted to see if you'd remembered anything you need for me
to pick up."

"Nope. Hold on a sec." The next words were muffled, as if Dan had put
his hand over the receiver. "Hey, Bea! Can you think of anything we need
from Asheville?"

Her reply didn't make it through the phone. "Nothing," Dan said when
he came back on the line. "Bea says to tell you she hopes you're having a
good time, by the way."

"Thanks. I, uh, shouldn't take you away from the movie."

Dan's rich laugh was like a warm hand, rubbing tension out of Leif's
shoulders. "Don't worry—it's some awful kiddie movie Marlene's son
dragged over."

"She has a child?" Leif asked, surprised. "Sorry—of course it wouldn't
matter to you."

"What do you mean?"

"That your girlfriend has a son." It might even make things easier, Leif supposed.

"Um, Marlene hasn't been my girlfriend since high school."

"Wh-what? But she said—when she called…" He trailed off, too surprised to finish.

"Did she?" Dan said, not sounding very happy. "Look, I don't want to talk about this over the phone."

"Of course not," Leif said hastily, and tried not to grin. *It's nothing to be glad about. It doesn't change anything.*

There came a heavy rapping on the suite's outer door. "Hold on a minute," Leif said. "Somebody's at the door."

Just as he opened the door, he remembered what he should have recalled before, and might have if he hadn't been distracted by Dan's revelation.

He was in a penthouse suite, only accessible with a keycard, and housekeeping surely wouldn't be up here at this time of night.

Kristian stood in the hall outside. One shoe was gone, and there was mud all over his shirt.

"Kristian—" Leif started to say in confusion.

Kristian looked up, the pallid fire of the dead burning in the hollow sockets of his skull.

CHAPTER 13

Details leapt out in that first, frozen moment. A bloody furrow marred the skin of Kristian's throat, where a thin rope had cut off his airflow and his life. Burst vessels turned the whites of his eyes scarlet, vivid against the hazel irises, and gave his slack cheeks a mottled appearance. Blood—not his own—decorated his mouth like a lipstick smear, where a bloodied, rune-carved slip of wood had been forced beneath his dead tongue.

"No," Leif whispered.

"Leif?" Dan's voice rose with concern through the phone. "What's going on?"

With a moan of rage, the *draugr* who had been Kristian lunged into the room.

"Shit!" Leif twisted out of the way, feeling the cold fingers nearly scrape his skin. His foot came down on the steps into the sunken living room, and he fell heavily, the phone flying off in another direction.

The sword—

But it was safely tucked away beneath the bed with the rest of his kit, where a hook-up wouldn't see it and be tempted to ask questions. He had nothing—not his sword, not a shirt, not even a fucking pair of shoes.

Shoes. If I can get to my boot knife—

Kristian let out a deep, hollow sound and darted forward. The white pinpoints of his eyes glowed, cold and compelling as the gaze of a snake.

Leif dodged, scrambling over the couch they'd screwed on, but Kristian was too quick. Inhumanly strong fingers tightened on Leif's ankle, grinding the fragile bones together. Leif bit back a cry of pain and kicked with his free foot as hard as he could.

His bare heel connected with Kristian's face, smashing the nose with a loud crunch of bone. Black blood dripped sluggishly from the wound, smoking as it hit the synthetic material of the upholstery, but the *draugr's* hold didn't weaken.

Shit!

Leif kicked again and again, pain jarring up through his foot and ankle. On the fifth blow, the icy fingers finally loosened enough for him to rip free.

His boots were on the floor behind the couch where he'd left them. He grabbed up the right one, thrusting his fingers inside. The hidden sheath was at the very top on the boot, and he yanked out the thin, flat knife concealed there—

Only to be struck from behind and sent flying into the wall. The knife spun out of his hand, skidding away and under the couch.

He didn't waste time lamenting its loss. Leif ran all-out for the bedroom, left foot slipping on his on own blood. Kristian came over the couch with a snarl, his high-tops thudding heavily over the wooden floor as he broke into a run not a split second behind Leif.

Leif grabbed a heavy lamp from the desk and hurled it blindly behind him, hoping to slow down the dead man. There came a heavy thump and the footsteps faltered, before picking back up again.

Leif burst through the door into the bedroom and hurled himself to the floor, momentum sliding his belly across the polished wood and carrying him half-under the bed. His fingers brushed the canvas bag holding pouches of salt and herbs, then the longer bag concealing his sword.

Kristian grabbed him by the legs, yanking him out from under the bed. Leif's wrist caught in the canvas loop, dragging the sword bag out behind him. He fumbled wildly for the zipper, the cold metal teeth scraping his fin-gers. *Shit, shit, where's the fucking pull?*

An implacable weight settled across his back, heavy enough to make his ribs creak. A stench like blood mixed with the contents of a filthy toilet rolled out from the *draugr* as it leaned forward. Icy fingers closed around Leif's throat just as he found the zipper pull and yanked.

Kristian's dead fingers were hard and relentless as bands of iron. Leif tried to ignore them, tried to ignore the burning in his lungs and the black spots in his vision. The only thing that mattered was finding the hilt of the sword, because the touch of leather and steel meant the difference between life and death.

His groping fingers closed on the hilt. The bag tried to foul the blade, but he managed to pull it free. Leif struck blindly at the thing crouched on his back.

The blow was wild, just a backward flail. The rune-inscribed steel hit something, though, and the iron fingers loosened. Leif heaved back and up, spilling Kristian off of him.

Move, move, move! Don't just lay there and wait to die!

He staggered to his feet, gagging and coughing, a garrote of pain around his throat and his lungs on fire. Kristian crouched a few feet away, his face a wet ruin of broken bone, a flap of skin hanging loose where the blade had sliced him. Black blood pattered sluggishly onto the wooden floor, but it didn't matter—he could lose every drop and it wouldn't even slow him down.

The unholy light burned in his eyes, and the compulsion placed on his ghost rode him without mercy or compassion. He lurched to his feet and stumbled forward.

Leif swung his sword with all his strength behind it. "Mighty Mordgud, help him to the Helgrind!" he screamed, or tried to. What actually came out of his damaged throat was nothing more than a raspy whisper.

Kristian's head parted cleanly from his body, hit the wall, and came to rest against the entertainment center. The *draugr* began to dissolve into corrupted ectoplasm. The stench of an open grave billowed out: rot and corruption and writhing little maggots.

Fuck. Oh, fuck, no. No.

Only an hour ago, those hands now turning to black ooze had touched his body. Those lips had kissed him. One hour, and Kristian had gone from a beautiful young stranger to one of the unquiet dead.

My fault. If I hadn't picked him up, brought him here, he'd still be alive.

Pain pulsed through his skull. *Your fault. You might as well have strangled him yourself.*

Bile clawed at the back of his abused throat, and he couldn't breathe, couldn't get enough air into his lungs.

"Leif! LEIF!"

The tinny sound came from the living room. Leif stared blankly for a long moment, unable to think who would be calling his name.

The phone. *Dan!*

He stumbled into the room, almost falling down the shallow steps. Scooping up the phone, he croaked, "Dan?"

"Leif?" Dan's voice cracked with fear. "What the fuck happened? Are you all right? I heard you yell, then crashes—"

"I'm fine," Leif said quickly.

"Hecate's bitches, I know what I heard! What I'm hearing in your voice now! What happened?"

And, sweet death, he sounded worried. As if he really cared; as if he'd run all the way to Asheville on foot if Leif needed him to.

Leif swallowed against the soreness in his throat. "Rúnar. He sent a *draugr* after me."

"Get out of there. Now."

Adrenaline jittered along his nerves, and his head pounded ferociously, making it hard to think. Leif took a cleansing breath, then another, struggling to center. "No. He knows where I am. If I go outside, he might be waiting with more of the dead under his control. If I hole up here and put barriers over the doors and windows, I can wait him out until dawn."

"I'm coming down there. Where are you?"

"No!" If Dan came charging down here and Rúnar caught him, killed him, turned him into a thing of rage and pain and hate the way he'd turned poor Kristian...

It would destroy me. Bad enough Kristian had died because Leif wanted to get laid, but to have his selfishness get Dan killed as well...

That would be it. The last black mark on my soul. There would be no possibility of redemption after that, no way to ever make things right.

Tendrils of pain bored deeper into his skull. *You're already beyond redemption, and you know it.*

"Stay where you are," Leif continued tightly. "I'll be all right."

"I'm not sitting here in safety when you need backup! Now tell me where you are."

Leif shook his head, wincing at the flare of pain. "I have to secure the room. I'm getting off the phone now."

"Leif, please, call me back. As soon as you can. *Please.*"

He wasn't sure he should agree, but he couldn't say no to Dan. "All right."

Leif hung up and went to his bag. At least the penthouse suite was separate from the rest of the hotel, and no one else had gotten caught up in the fight or called security.

Although I probably won't be able to stay here again, even after paying for damages.

He laid lines of salt and herbs along the door, the windows, and even the fireplace, which was set with gas-fired logs. Once that was done, he took out his staff and went to every corner of each of the three rooms, chanting and scattering salt.

There. The suite was as metaphysically secure as it was possible to make it. *Time for clean up.*

A layer of salt soaked up most of the remaining black ichor. After wiping it up, Leif tried to scrub the stains off the floor with a solution of vervain and lemongrass, which at least lightened the dark splotches. They'd probably never entirely disappear, though, unless the flooring itself was removed.

Will it be enough to make anyone suspicious?

Kristian was gone, his body dissolved into nothingness. The stain was just that; organic, but nothing to test positive for blood or DNA. People had seen them leave the club together, and they'd be on the security footage coming into the hotel. But Kristian would be on those same cameras, leaving...and not coming back.

Even though *draugr* could become solid when it suited them, they could pass insubstantial through doors, walls, even their own graves. There would be no sign of Kristian's horrible return. And in the morning, Leif would be captured on the cameras, leaving a good eight hours later. The alibi was solid.

Gods, what was wrong with him, why he was even worrying about his own safety now, when he'd just gotten a young man killed? *But I can't stop Rúnar from inside a jail cell.*

In the middle of the gooey puddle which had been Kristian's severed head, Leif found the fragile slip of rune inscribed wood, leaving no doubt as to the fact he'd been murdered and summoned back.

Oh, Kristian. I'm sorry.

The weight of guilt seemed to make the very floor creak under him as he went to retrieve the dropped phone.

Dan paced back and forth across the worn linoleum of the kitchen floor, desperately willing the phone to ring. Bea sat at the table, watching him with a worried frown on her face. Marlene and her son had left, and Virgil hadn't yet come back from a night out with his friends.

Call, Leif. Come on, call me back, and let me know you're all right.

Helplessness washed over him, a sick feeling turning his guts inside out. Having to stand there and just listen to Leif's fight over the phone, hearing the cries of pain and the shattering furniture, unable to do a single thing to help—

It had been Mom's death all over again.

He hadn't even realized he was screaming Leif's name over and over again into the receiver, until Bea had grabbed his arm in desperation. "Dan! Goddess, please, what's wrong?!"

"Leif's in trouble," had been the only words he'd been able to summon, but he'd weighted them with pain and fear.

Marlene went pale but hadn't asked questions, just bundled up her son and taken him away, letting Dan get to work.

Except there was no work to be done. Nothing to do but wait and pray Leif called back.

"Do you want me to make some tea?" Bea asked.

"No," Dan said. Then, because she didn't deserve a short answer: "Thanks, but I don't think I could drink it."

The shrill ring of the phone made them both jump. Dan snatched it up. "Leif?"

"It's me."

Thank you. Thank you, Hecate, Lady of the Torches, for leading him safely through this.

Dan took a deep breath, but his voice still trembled on the words: "Are you all right?"

"I'm fine. Just shaken."

"What happened? You said Rúnar found you?"

"Yeah." Leif sounded hoarse, like he had a bad cold, or had been crying his eyes out. "Fuck, Dan, I was stupid. Stupid, and selfish, and…"

Dan closed his eyes, as if that would somehow let him see Leif across the miles. "Leif, whatever happened, it wasn't your fault."

A laugh crackled down the line, but it held no humor. "Sure it was. I've been hunting Rúnar for a long time. He knows my habits as well as I know his. I don't know how he found me, exactly—maybe he just hired someone to watch for me. He has more than enough money to do that."

"Watch for you where?"

"A gay bar. I just thought I'd dance, have a couple of drinks."

"And he had you followed back to your hotel so he could send a haint he had in reserve after you," Dan guessed.

There came a moment of silence, as if the call had dropped, before Leif let out a long exhalation. "Yes. That must have been what happened."

Dan gripped the phone cord, twisting it violently between his fingers. "What if he has more of them? I don't like the idea of you just sitting there alone, waiting for him to attack you. I can be down there in an hour."

"No." Leif's voice was stronger now. "I don't want you to take the risk. I've got the room sealed—as long as I don't step outside before dawn, nothing else can get in to me."

"What if he lures you out somehow?"

"Short of having *draugar* attack the other guests, nothing could get me out of this room. And that's not his style." Leif paused for a moment. "No, scratch that—I might go outside for something."

"What?"

"You." Leif's voice softened. "If Rúnar caught you and used you as a hostage, or set the dead on you, I'd have no choice but to leave the room and try to help. Which is why I'm begging you to please, please stay put."

Me? Despite all the fear and the tension, the words sent warmth curling through Dan's chest, filling up hollow places he hadn't even known existed. "All right. I'll stay here."

"Thank you," Leif said, quiet relief audible in the words. "As for me, I'll hunker down with my back to the wall, my sword in my lap, and a clear line of sight to the door. I don't think I'll need it, but it isn't as if I'll be getting any sleep tonight anyway."

"I'll stay up with you."

A pause, broken by a soft stutter of breath. "You don't have to do that."

"Yes, I do. If you won't let me come down there and help you, the least I can do is keep you company on the phone until dawn."

"Dan—"

"We don't even have to talk." He remembered the heart-clenching moment he'd known Leif was in trouble and there wasn't a thing he could do to help. It had felt like falling into an abyss, like he'd missed a step running downstairs, like all the air had been sucked out of the room.

Like dying alone on a mountainside.

"I just need to know you're okay," he finished hoarsely.

"I'll make some coffee," Bea offered.

"Thanks, Bea. You get on to bed when you're done." He transferred his attention back to Leif, searching for something to lighten the mood. "Besides, staying up with you will give me the chance to tan Virgil's hide when he comes sneaking back in after his curfew."

Leif laughed tiredly, and despite the distance between them, Dan could almost see him smile. "All right. You've got yourself a deal."

CHAPTER 14

When he pulled into the drive at Hoary Oak Hill Farm, Leif almost put his head down on the steering wheel from sheer relief.

His body ached from sitting on the hardwood floor all night. A pillow or chair would have been nice—a nice temptation to get comfortable and go to sleep, something he hadn't been about to do, not with Rúnar nearby.

Rúnar. Gods, he must have been close last night. Maybe he'd even stood on the street outside and watched the lights in the penthouse, waiting for Leif to die.

The memory of the last time they'd been face-to-face remained sharp enough to cut, despite the passage of years. Rúnar had been sad—hurt. Disappointed.

"How could you do this to me?" he asked, his quiet tone a thousand times worse than if he had yelled. "I've given you the world, and this is how you repay me?"

Leif had almost forgiven him. Despite the things they'd done, the pain they'd caused. Rúnar had saved his life, given him a purpose, shown him things he never would have even guessed existed. Rúnar was everything in the world to him: friend, father, lover, savior.

Everything.

He was the only person who'd ever seen anything of value in Leif. Maybe the only one who ever would. And Leif had loved Rúnar for that. A part of him still did.

It had been difficult, but he held firm and walked away, and Rúnar let him go. It was over.

Except, of course it wasn't, because Rúnar killed Alice and left her body in Leif's apartment. And when Leif confronted him, he'd vanished, leaving behind only a note. *"You're mine. You will remember that, one way or an-*

other."

He'd been an idiot to believe Rúnar would just let him go. Leif knew how possessive his teacher was, how driven, and yet he'd foolishly assumed he could just walk away without any consequences. And as a result, all the blood Rúnar spilled since that day was on Leif's hands, including poor Kristian's.

He wasn't certain why he hadn't told Dan the truth. That the *draugr* was some college guy who would still be alive right now if Leif had just kept his pants on. If he hadn't been selfish, thoughtless, stupidly predictable.

I don't want Dan to think...no. I don't want Dan to know what a worthless piece of shit I am.

The haint-blue farmhouse door slammed, and Leif blinked himself out of the exhausted fugue he'd slipped into. Dan strode across the bare dirt between the house and the drive, not quite running, but almost. There were dark circles under his eyes, but improbably, he was smiling, wider than Leif had ever seen.

Maybe their night on the phone had cracked some of Dan's reserve. Not that they'd discussed much—nothing important enough to distract Leif should another *draugr* appear. They'd talked about movies and music, and Dan had related some entertaining stories from his childhood, most of them about the stupid things he and his friends had done in high school. Speeding and drinking, mainly: small time rebellions, but he'd gotten Leif to laugh and forget about his troubles for a while. Taking care of Leif as best he could even from a distance.

Leif climbed out of the car, feeling like an old man. "Hey," he said as Dan approached.

"Hey," Dan replied, before pulling him into a hug.

Leif returned the embrace, struggling to breathe through the sudden tightness in his chest. Dan felt warm and solid, like the stone of the mountain come to life, but infinitely more comforting. The scent of bay rum rose from his skin, mingled with goat musk and sweat, as if he'd just come from tending the animals before the car pulled up. He hadn't shaved, and the stubble on his cheek scraped against the side of Leif's jaw.

I want... Too many things, and none of them right. A couple of hours with Leif had ended in a man's death. He was cursed, tainted, everything in the world Dan most emphatically was not.

But still, it felt incredible, being in Dan's arms. Like coming home.

The hug ended all too soon. "Don't scare me like that again," Dan said, a bit gruffly.

"I'll do my best not to, believe me."

Dan studied him carefully. "You look exhausted. Come on—let's get you to bed."

"I should get my things out of the car," Leif said, although he was tempted to just leave them. But having his weapons locked in the trunk, out of arm's reach, wasn't smart. He'd done everything he could think of to make sure no one followed him out of Asheville this morning, but he couldn't be certain it worked. *Maybe I shouldn't have come back. If Rúnar tracks me here and targets Dan...*

Shit. I'm an idiot. But what was done was done.

"I'll bring them in," Dan said, his fingers curling warm and strong around Leif's upper arm. "Don't worry."

Too tired to think about it any more, Leif let the other man guide him inside and up the creaky stairs. "You should put lines of salt around, just in case," he mumbled as they entered his borrowed bedroom.

"Already taken care of." Dan steered him toward the bed. "Do you want me to make you some chamomile tea to help you relax?"

Leif sat down on the edge of the bed and pulled off his boots. "No. I just want to crawl under the covers and forget everything for a few hours."

"All right." Dan lingered, though, while Leif stripped down to his boxers, holding up the covers for Leif to slide underneath.

The edge of the bed gave under Dan's weight. Barely able to keep his eyes open, Leif looked up at the coffee-brown eyes and the mouth gone small and still with worry. "Thank you," he said.

A smile flickered over Dan's mouth, transforming it. He didn't say anything immediately, only lifted his hand and very, very carefully brushed a lock of hair out of Leif's face. Leif shut his eyes at the touch, savoring the warmth of Dan's fingers against his skin.

He'd never felt safe when he was a child, or if he had, the memory was beyond retrieval. Later on, there had been a sense of security, but at a terrible price.

He felt safe now. Safe, and warm, and cared for. Maybe it was just the exhaustion talking, but he clung to the feeling even as it pierced him like the sharp end of a new-grown shoot, breaking through the cold soil and into the sun.

"Sleep tight," Dan murmured. The bed shifted again as his weight was removed, and it occurred to Leif he ought to open his eyes and thank the other man again, but sleep claimed him before he could even fully form the thought.

Dan carefully closed the door to Virgil's—now Leif's—room and sagged against it.

The hug hadn't been intentional, but after the agonizing wait for Leif to get home, not knowing if anything might be lying in wait for him on those twisty mountain roads between Asheville and Ransom Gap, the relief had just been too great to hold back. From the moment he'd spotted the Porsche pulling up to the moment Leif was in his arms, everything was just a blur of heart-twisting gladness.

The hug had felt good, too. Right, somehow, although maybe it was just a long, sleepless night talking. Their bodies had fit together perfectly. Dan could rest his chin on the taller man's shoulder, his corn silk hair soft against Dan's face and mouth, the scent of cedar and musk rising from warm skin.

Letting go had been surprisingly difficult, although not as hard as looking away when Leif had undressed in front of him a few minutes ago. "Hard" being the operative word in more ways than one. The sight of Leif's long, lean body, clad in nothing but a pair of black silk boxers tantalizingly hinting at the tight butt underneath, had been enough to make his mouth water. Even now, the memory made his cock twitch against the restriction of his jeans.

"Dan?" Bea called from the foot of the stairs.

He jerked himself out of his reverie, feeling a flush rise to his cheeks. Not wanting to risk waking Leif, he went down the stairs and led the way into the kitchen. "Yeah?"

Bea's hands twisted together, and she kept looking down at them, or at the floor, while she chewed on her lip. Not good signs.

"Come on, Bea," he said, rubbing at eyes that felt filled with sand. "Out with it."

"I'm just worried," she confessed, her voice low, as if she were afraid the sleeping Leif might overhear. "This necromancer Leif is chasing is dangerous."

"We've known that from the beginning."

"I know, but last night made it hit home." Her dark eyes finally lifted to his, and it struck him suddenly just how much she looked like Mom these days. "Leif could have been killed, not by some random haint, but by one Rúnar sent to murder him. What if he finds out you're helping Leif? Will you be next?"

And shit, he hated to hear the fear in her voice. "No. I won't," he said firmly.

"You don't know that! I'm scared, Danny."

She sounded like a little girl. Like the eleven year old she'd been when she took Virgil into the root cellar the night—

With an effort, he straightened shoulders wanting to sag with exhaustion. "This is only temporary. You know that. I have to help Leif with this, because if I don't, Rúnar will do who-knows-what to the people of this town, living and dead."

"But it sounds like he's really powerful—"

"Which is why I don't intend to go up against him. All Leif and I have to do is get to the haint at Saddle Creek Park first. Once we've laid it, Rúnar won't be able to find the Eye of the Uktena, which means he won't be able to open the Witches Harrow. He'll have no reason to stay in Ransom Gap, afterward."

And neither will Leif. But that wasn't something he was prepared to think about just yet.

Bea searched his face for a long moment, maybe trying to find the truth of the matter. Whatever she saw made her relax. "All right. Just be careful. Please."

"I will," he promised, and gave her a hug.

She squeezed him tight, then stepped back, waving her hand in front of her face. "Ugh, go take a shower!"

"Ha ha," he said, although he felt a flush of embarrassment. Although he knew she was exaggerating, what if Leif thought he stank? "Fine—I'll take a shower. I'm hitting the bed for a few hours after, if you don't mind making sure Virgil's actually splitting firewood and not goofing off in the woodshed."

It had been after three a.m. by the time Virgil snuck back in that morning. Dan had asked Leif to hold on for a moment, before exchanging a few choice words with his brother, the result of which was Virgil now had a long list of extra chores in addition to being grounded.

Bea grinned wickedly. "Oh, don't you worry. I'll make sure I see some sweat out of him."

She headed out the back door, her work gloves in her hand, and Dan went back upstairs. He paused outside Leif's door for a moment, on the way to his own room. Leif was no doubt curled up under the down comforter, his long hair spread over the pillow, his beautiful mouth relaxed in sleep. What if Dan should slip inside, should bend over, should kiss those lips...

Stop it. He needs sleep, not me drooling over him.

Still, it took Dan several more minutes before he could work up the effort to turn away and shut himself inside his lonely room.

"I'm not sure what to expect here," Leif said that night, as they loaded their things into their respective vehicles, "I've never been to a...what is this again? A hootenanny?"

Dan glanced up from where he was busy stashing his wand and tool belt behind the seat of his truck. "Well," he drawled, "first we make the moonshine, then the jug band plays. I hear tell they might even have a washboard tonight! Next there's a contest to see who's got the most teeth, and finally we end the evening by marrying our first cousins."

"About what I expected."

"You two are such pricks," Bea said, walking up with Virgil. "I'm riding with Leif."

"No fair! I want to ride in the Porsche!" Virgil broke in.

"You're riding with me," Dan said firmly, "where I can keep an eye on you."

Virgil folded his arms aggressively over his chest, creasing the dark blue polo shirt he wore. Between his posture and his pout, he looked like a petulant banker.

"I don't see why I can't just go with my friends anyway," Virgil whined.

Dan shoved his seat back into position with more force than was probably necessary. "Because you're grounded," he said, with far more patience than Leif could have mustered.

"Shouldn't you make me stay home?"

"And have you sneaking out five minutes after we're gone? Do you think I'm stupid?" Dan pointed authoritatively at the passenger seat. "Get in. *Now.*"

Virgil got in and slammed the door. *Well, they're going to have a fun ride.*

Dan ran his hand distractedly through his hair. "Ready?" he asked.

Leif nodded. "I'll follow you."

Dan gave him a crooked grin. "Sure that rust bucket of yours can keep up?"

"I'm certain Bea will give me directions if you lose us," Leif answered dryly.

As they followed Dan's ancient truck along the winding back roads, Bea peppered him with questions about the Porsche. How fast did it go, how much had it cost, did it get good mileage? Leif was happy to answer her questions; if nothing else, it helped keep his mind sharp. Despite a five-hour nap, he still wasn't entirely recovered from the night before.

Have Kristian's friends missed him yet? Has anyone reported his disappearance to the police? What about his parents?

"Are you all right?" Bea asked, and he realized he was clutching the wheel hard enough for the cords to stand out on the backs of his hands.

"Sorry," he said. "Just lost in thought. You're going to college next fall, right?"

"I've got a scholarship." She looked out the window. "You know, there's nothing going on between Marlene and Dan."

Leif came very close to missing a hairpin turn and driving off the side of the road. "I—it's none of my business."

She grinned impishly, obviously delighted at having flustered him. Apparently, Virgil wasn't the only troublemaker in the family. What had Dan been like, before responsibility had weighed him down and stolen his smile?

"I'm just sharing information," she said sweetly. "They dated in high school, but broke up when Dan went to college. She married the first guy who came along, had a baby, and got divorced."

Discussing this with Dan's little sister was absolutely the wrong thing to do. "She told me she's his girlfriend, when she called yesterday morning."

"She wants to be," Bea said. "But they're just friends. She's nice, even if she does keep bugging us to go to church with her, and her son is adorable. I keep telling Dan to come clean with her, but he'd rather pretend there's no reason."

"That's a perceptive analysis," Leif said, not bothering to hide his surprise.

"I'm in high school. It pretty much makes me an expert on relationship drama."

Leif burst out laughing. "Oh really? What about *you?* Got your eye on someone special?"

"No," she said, prim as a school marm. "Not really. I've got college next year, and I'm not making things any more complicated than they already are. I'm not going to be another Marlene, stuck here for the rest of my life, popping out babies and chasing my high school crush."

"You're like seventeen-going-on-seventy, aren't you?"

Bea laughed. "I guess. Maybe things would be different if Mom and Dad were still alive."

"That sort of thing makes you grow up fast, I suppose."

"Yeah. At the time, I thought Dan was *ancient*. But he was only two years older than I am now." She shook her head.

"You're really close, aren't you?" Leif asked. What would it be like, to have such a bond with a sibling or a friend? *Or anyone?*

She picked at the frayed edges of her shorts, which appeared by their ragged cut to have started life as jeans. "I guess. I mean, he can be kind of a pain some times. 'Bea, do your homework. Bea, fill out this scholarship application. Bea, let's have an awkward talk about condoms and birth control.'"

Leif couldn't suppress a snicker. "I'm not sure who I feel more sorry for with that last one."

"Seriously? I thought I was going to die. But, you know, a lot of guys wouldn't have even tried with the girly stuff, just let me figure it out on my own. With Mom gone, he...well. You probably don't want to hear this, but he took me to the store to pick out pads the first time I had my period, and he listened to me bawl my eyes out over this boy who broke my heart when I was in seventh grade, and he had to stand around in the lingerie department while the sales lady helped me try on bras."

Apparently, there was a lot more to raising a girl than Leif had realized. "He's a good man."

"I know. And I know that I'm really lucky, having him be there for me every time I needed it, no matter how weird it probably was for him." She took a deep breath, then added, "I'm really glad you came here."

Leif frowned slightly at the non sequitur. "You are?"

"You've been good for him. I mean it. I don't think I've seem him smile this much since Mom and Dad died."

Warmth crawled across Leif's cheeks, and he hoped she didn't notice in the early evening light. "I didn't realize."

"You're all right, Leif." She settled back the bucket seat. "Whatever you're doing, keep it up."

CHAPTER 15

They drove the rest of the way in silence. Saddle Creek Park was well down in the gap; a historic sign beside the entrance said it had been the site of some civil war battle or other, which no doubt was why it had been chosen for the site of a park.

Leif didn't know how many people actually lived in Ransom Gap, but the grassy parking area was surprisingly packed with vehicles. A few people too lazy to walk idled at the end nearest the festival field, waiting for a spot to open up. Dan steered the truck to an area close to the woods, and Leif followed his lead.

The sun had disappeared behind the shoulder of the mountain, and the space between the trees was dark. As Leif parked the Porsche neatly beside Dan's truck, he thought some of the leaves shivered without any wind to stir them.

"What's the plan?" he asked, when they got out of the vehicles.

Dan chewed on his lip, eyeing the woods distrustfully; he must have seen the unnatural movement as well. "The haint won't be out until moonrise. We've got a little while. I guess we might as well mingle."

"I'm going to meet Freddie," Virgil said shortly, walking away from the truck.

"You be back here when it's time to leave," Dan called after him. "I mean it!"

Virgil ignored him. Bea dug an ancient cell phone out of her pocket. "I told Roxy I'd call her when we got here."

"Have fun. And don't drink!"

She rolled her eyes at him. "I know, Dan, I know. I'm not going to blow my scholarship over a stupid drink."

His face softened. "Sorry. I know you wouldn't."

"Good luck with your haint," she said, and headed off in the direction of the crowd, the phone held to her ear.

"Bea's got a good head on her shoulders," Leif said once she was gone. "She's not going to let you down."

Dan gave him a rueful look. "I know. I just worry about her even more, ever since Virgil got a wild hair up his ass. He and I always had our problems, but lately…" He trailed off and shook his head. "Anyway. You want to hang out here, or head up to the festival?"

"Festival," Leif said, surprising himself a little. "I have to say I'm curious."

Dan led the way through the parking area, across a short bridge over what Leif assumed to be Saddle Creek, and to a series of open fields meant for little league baseball games and soccer tournaments. Tonight, the area was lit up by floodlights and packed with people. Vendors sold pottery, jewelry, wooden spoons, homemade jams and jellies, and fall produce. Children screamed and ran around a play area with an inflatable castle and slide. One entire end of the festival was dedicated to food vendors, all of whom were selling variations on the theme of fried: fried funnel cake, fried Oreos, fried ice cream, fried Twinkies, fried pickles, fried bananas…

"Fried Kool-Aid?" Leif asked in disbelief.

"Now you see why we ate before we left."

"Just looking at the signs is making my arteries harden."

Dan steered them away from the food vendors, past some of the craft tables. Leif lingered here and there, his eye caught by some truly magnificent woodcarvings and pottery. Even though he drew plenty of odd looks—he was absolutely certain most of the festival-goers had never seen a man wearing eyeliner before—he felt oddly relaxed, far more than he would have expected.

It's Dan. On his own, he would probably have hated the festival. Having someone to joke with about the awful food and the men in t-shirts emblazoned with Confederate flags, or to share his appreciation of the delicate wooden vases carved from oak burls, turned it into something fun.

At least, until they got to where the band was playing.

In keeping with the "mountain culture" theme, the county had unearthed a group of octogenarians with fiddles, mandolins, and banjos. Even from a distance, though, Leif could tell these men were the real thing. Old as they might be, they played with fierce heart.

A large group of people had gathered around the players, most listening, but some couples dancing enthusiastically to the reel. As they approached, one of the watchers detached herself from the group, ran up to Dan, and hugged him.

"Dan! I was wondering when you'd get here!"

"Uh, hi, Marlene," Dan said uncomfortably. "I didn't know you were coming."

The infamous Marlene. She was…normal, really. Medium height, blonde hair suspiciously dark at the roots, and a curvy body just beginning to show the effects of a sedentary lifestyle.

Leif wanted to dislike her on principle, petty as it was. But he couldn't deny her brown eyes lit up with genuine happiness when she looked at Dan.

"Of course I came," she said brightly, as if no one in their right mind would stay at home when they could come to the Ransom Gap Apple Days Festival instead. "I even found a sitter for Junior. Figured I deserved to have a night of fun for myself." Her grin turned a little sly. "Want some?" she asked, pulling a mason jar partway from her overlarge purse.

The sight of the jar brought a grin to Dan's face. "You know it." He took it from her, moved his body to block anyone from casually seeing what he was up to, and took a sip.

The liquid in the jar was clear, but Leif saw chunks of cantaloupe floating lazily near the bottom, along with cherries and blueberries. Having downed a small sip, Dan offered it to Leif. "Here. Have some of this."

"What is it?"

"What do you think it is?"

Leif winced, but took the jar anyway. He'd had more than his share of nasty bootleg the world over and didn't particularly look forward to adding moonshine to the list.

He took a sip and almost dropped the jar in shock. "That's *good!*"

Dan laughed. "Leif, if I ever hand you something to drink, you can be sure it's the good stuff."

He took a second sip, savoring the flavors of the fruit. "I stand corrected."

"Marlene's grand-daddy makes it," Dan said, taking the jar and passing it back to Marlene, who put it into her purse.

Marlene eyed Leif uncertainly. "Aren't you going to introduce your friend, Dan?"

Dan winced. "Sorry. Leif, this is Marlene Stoddard. Marlene, this is Leif Helsvin. He's the haint-worker I told you about. He's staying with us at the farm while he takes care of some business."

"Oh, you were the one on the phone yesterday," Marlene said, and some of the wariness disappeared from her eyes. Not all of it, though. *I wonder what she thinks she has to be wary about? Does she suspect Dan's not as straight as he pretends?* "I guess you do the same sort of haint-laying as my Dan?"

Tell her you aren't hers. But that was stupid—Dan wasn't Leif's, either, and was old enough to manage his own affairs.

When Dan didn't say anything, only looked wretchedly uncomfortable, Leif fixed a false smile on his face. "You know Dan's a Walker?"

"It's how we met. I mean, I knew him already at school, but we'd never really talked much. I was a cheerleader, and he was in the band. We saw each other at all the football games, though."

"Marlene had a little trouble with a poltergeist," Dan said, cutting off Marlene's reminiscences. "Her family's been in the area almost as long as mine. Her folks knew to call my mom. Mom let me help out, since I was her apprentice by then."

"It was amazing, how brave he was," Marlene said, watching Dan's face as she spoke. "Before, I thought the boys who played football or basketball were heroes. That night, I saw a real hero."

She really loves him. Of course she did. Who wouldn't?

Dan only shrugged, obviously uncomfortable. "Mom did most of the work," he mumbled in the direction of the ground.

"Always the modest one," she said, rubbing his arm in a familiar fashion. "Hey, Leif, would you mind holding my purse while me and Dan have this next dance?"

"Of course," he said through lips gone suddenly numb.

"Thanks, sweetie. Oh, and help yourself to more of what's in the jar, if you want," she added with a wink, before grabbing Dan's arm and hauling him after her past the ring of listeners. Dan cast a frantic glance over his shoulder as he went, as if he expected Leif to save him.

At least the reel was vigorous, not a slow dance. Even though he really wanted to break out the moonshine, Leif needed to keep his senses sharp and refrained from cracking open the mason jar again. Instead he watched while Dan and Marlene bounced and spun through the moves of the dance.

There was no reason to be jealous. There was no reason to be mad at Dan for not standing up and *telling* the poor girl he was...well, not gay, since he might lose Bea and Virgil over that. But couldn't he at least say he wasn't her fucking boyfriend?

It's none of my business. None of it. One way or another, I'll be gone come November first. That's only a week and a day away. I can't get attached, and I can't get judgmental.

And, gods, judging Dan made him nothing but a hypocrite, considering all the lies he'd told. Was still telling.

But he was glad when the moon crested the horizon, and he had an excuse to cut into the dancers and shove Marlene's purse unceremoniously back in her hands.

"Time to get to work," he told Dan, before turning and walking away.

Dan could tell Leif was pissed, although he wasn't sure why. The other Walker led the way from the festival back to the parking lot, his shoulders a stiff line. Dan waited until they had cleared the bulk of the crowd, before breaking into a trot to catch up with Leif's longer strides.

"Everything all right?" he asked, because he wanted it to be. Marlene's presence had thrown him for a loop, although thinking back on it, he wasn't sure why he'd assumed she wouldn't be here.

Maybe because she never mentioned it last night? But neither had he.

"Fine," Leif shot back, the word snapping like a firecracker.

Dan started to say he was sorry; but just what was he apologizing for? Dancing with Marlene? That wasn't a crime, was it?

She told Leif I'm her boyfriend. The haint attack last night had made him forget that part of the conversation. *Was he relieved when I said I'm not, or am I misremembering? Or just reading too much into it?*

Shit. He didn't know what to think, what might be real and what was surely just wishing.

"Leif," he said, not knowing what to say but unable to just let it lie, "I'm sorry if I've upset you."

"You haven't," Leif said, keeping his blue eyes on the landscape around them and never on Dan. "I'm just jumpy after last night. The sooner we get this *draugr* put to rest, the better."

"That's understandable," Dan said, although he had the feeling Leif wasn't being exactly truthful. "We'll get this done quick, grab Bea and Virgil, and make an early night of it."

"You don't have to cut your fun short because of me."

The weight on his shoulders grew by another fraction. "I'd rather go home with you."

As a peace offering, it wasn't much, but Leif slowed, allowing Dan to walk the rest of the way beside him. While Leif went to retrieve his things from the Porsche, Dan geared up by the truck.

"Do you really think Rúnar will risk coming tonight, with this many people around?" Dan asked. Even in the parking lot, the noise from the crowded festival was loud. "If he doesn't know we're onto his plans, wouldn't it be safer for him to wait until tomorrow, when he could do this without worrying some drunk is going to stumble right into the middle of his spell?"

Leif hesitated as he buckled on his baldric and adjusted the hang of his sword. "I don't know," he admitted. "I thought he'd be here tonight, but Rúnar never liked an audience for his work."

"That would surely be a stroke of luck in our favor, if he stayed home tonight."

"May the goddesses grant it to us."

Dan gave the pouches of his tool belt one last check. "Ready to do this?"

"Ready."

After a quick glance around the parking area to make sure they weren't observed, Dan led the way into the woods. The thick net of branches closed overhead, blotting out the moonlight. A crackle and crunch rose up as his heavy work boots crushed the dry, fallen leaves.

Dan firmed his grip around the wand in his hand. The charms on it rattled softly, and he felt the fine hairs on the back of his neck stand up. The night air held a new chill, and his breath turned to plumes of steam in front of his face.

Something's close.

He kept moving, pressing deeper into the woods. The haint was around here somewhere; the only trick was to get it to notice them and manifest. *Unless it already noticed and is toying with us.*

He took deep breath, focusing on every sense, the way Mom had taught him. The sounds of laughter and music echoed through the woods from the festival, fading in and out like a badly-tuned radio. The clear light of the moon washed over every leaf, edging it in sharp shadows. The cold wind brushed his neck and made his skin tingle, and the rich odor of fresh-turned earth permeated the air.

Wait a minute.

"Dan!" Leif said urgently.

They both came to an abrupt halt. Just in front of them, near the base of an ancient tree, which must surely have been a sapling in the miser's day, was a freshly-dug pit.

"Shit!" Leif drew his sword, swinging around to put his back to Dan, his head turning rapidly as he searched the wood. "Rúnar's here!"

A tremor ran through the surrounding trees, their branches groaning and rubbing against each other.

Dan gulped down air, trying to center. There was something in the woods now, the leaves crunching under dragging footsteps even as the temperature plunged and frost edged the moist dirt beside his boots. The mojo bag stirred in his pocket, fueling his shields with its protective magic.

"I think he's gone," Dan said. "But he left something behind to stop us."

CHAPTER 16

The temperature plummeted; Dan's breath turned instantly to steam, and frost outlined every leaf. His skin buzzed and shivered with etheric energy, the fillings in his teeth aching all the way to the root.

The haint was a thing of shadow and hate, spewing out a reek like spoiled milk and rotting blood. Darkness blurred its features, turning it into a sinister, hunched figure.

It snapped forward, the hissing rattle of disturbed leaves the only warning Dan got. He jerked back, felt ragged nails slash across his arm, tearing a deep gash in his jacket and frosting the skin underneath.

"Fuck!" He twisted aside, his grip loosening involuntarily on his wand as his arm went numb from the haint's touch.

A wet chuckle emanated from what remained of its mouth, accompanied by a belch of rot and mildew.

Leif snarled, his sword like a pure shaft of moonlight slicing the air. The haint ducked and wove, everywhere and nowhere all at once. It let out a sound half scream and half old man's cackle, driving into Dan's eardrums like knitting needles.

Dan darted in with the wand and was driven back again by the slashing claws. Leif took advantage of the distraction Dan provided, his sword a streak of light in the dark forest.

The haint was faster. It ducked under Leif's guard and swung an arm into his chest with all the terrible strength of the dead. Leif went flying back into a tree, crumpled to the ground, and lay there limp.

No!

Dan felt something snap deep inside. An inarticulate howl rose up from the bottom of his lungs, carrying on it all the fear and denial he could muster. Without conscious thought, he hurled himself at the haint, using all the force his coiled muscles could summon to swing the wand in a deadly arc.

The tip of antler smashed into the back of the haint's head, the impact jarring Dan's shoulder in the socket. A terrible shriek rose up from the haint, and the savage nails slashed impotently at the air even as they began to disintegrate into a thick, black tar.

"Hecate of the Keys, Open the Way!" Dan shouted, willing the haint to move on with all the force he could muster.

It shrieked again, even as hounds bayed somewhere on the edge of hearing. The world unfolded, as if a door swung open onto some vast space—then closed again, the dead man gone on to whatever awaited him.

"Leif!" The wand fell unheeded from his hand, and Dan stumbled through the swirl of disturbed leaves, reaching for the other man. *No, no, goddesses of the Underworld, please let him be all right.*

Leif struggled to his knees. "I'm fine," he gasped. "It knocked the wind out of me, and I'll have a pretty good bruise on my back tomorrow, but I'm fine."

Relief shivered through Dan. Leif made it to his feet, leaning against the tree for support. "Thanks. I owe you one."

Dan took a small sip of breath, meaning to say…he didn't even know, exactly. The moonlight cut across Leif's features, revealing every plane of his high cheekbones, the delicate sweep of his brow. His long, pale hair tumbled about his face, tousled and utterly mad, like some fey spirit from the very dawn of time.

Safe. Safe, and relatively unhurt, and yet Dan's hands wouldn't stop shaking. Heat and cold boiled in his chest, until he wasn't even sure where fear ended and relief began. Gods, Leif could have died if he'd hit the tree wrong, and Dan needed to say how fucking glad he was Leif was okay, but he couldn't get the words out past the storm of emotion. He took a step forward, and another, until he could practically feel the heat of Leif's body. Leif's eyes widened slightly, pupils dilating. The tip of his tongue licked his lower lip.

The unconscious gesture snapped the hair-fine thread of Dan's control. He pressed Leif back against the tree, needing to taste those lips just once, to feel Leif's heartbeat, to know they were both warm and alive.

Leif's mouth froze under his, and oh fuck, he'd screwed up. He started to pull away, to apologize, to rebuild whatever his impulsive action might have torn down.

Leif's hands closed on his shoulders, and he returned the kiss with desperation, like this was something he needed just as bad. His lips were firm and supple, and tasted like the moonshine they had drunk and something else, something unique and indisputably masculine. The silver hoop in his lower lip was warm from his heat.

Gods, it was good, just what Dan needed. He leaned in tighter, felt

Leif's body against his, hard and sinewy through the layers of their clothing. Leif's hands threaded through Dan's hair, tugging and gripping, and he drew away just far enough to nip at Dan's lip with his teeth, before diving back into the kiss again.

Gods. This isn't happening. But it was; he could feel not just his own heart pounding, but the shaking of Leif's body against his; not just the tight urgency of his own erection, but the hard length of Leif's cock pressed against his hip.

Leif rubbed him through the denim. He gasped and broke the kiss. "D-Don't."

Leif stilled. His blue eyes had gone dark with desire, and his breathing was ragged. "I want to make you feel good."

Dan fought for control against a body with absolutely no interest in it. "And I want you to. But it's been a long time."

Shame coursed through him, scalding hot. But Leif cocked his head, and his expression shifted from raw hunger to something more controlled. "How long?"

Dan swallowed. "Since I came back from college. Six years."

Leif's eyes widened, and Dan wryly reflected he'd managed to surprise his friend. "Ah." Leif leaned his head against Dan's, foreheads touching and breath mingling without their lips actually making contact. "Let's not make you wait any longer."

A small, involuntary sound tore its way out of Dan's throat. Leif's fingers caught hold of his belt, undoing the buckle before worrying at the button of his jeans.

Yes. He wanted this, wanted it bad enough for his body to shake and his hands to tremble like a virgin's as he fumbled at Leif's belt in return.

"You don't have to," Leif said, his lips brushing against Dan's jaw, feather-light yet still sending a shudder of desire through him.

"I want to," he managed to say. "Please, Leif."

The other man chuckled. "Well, I can hardly say no to such a generous offer."

Somehow, he fumbled loose the button on Leif's jeans, yanked down the zipper, and clumsily pushed the denim down far enough to find the stiff bulge of cock behind the silk boxers. Leif hissed and leaned into him when Dan shaped his length through the silk.

"Feels like I'm not the only one who's eager," he murmured into Leif's ear.

Leif shivered. "You have no idea."

Dan tugged him free of the boxers, and, gods, Leif's cock was every bit as shapely as he'd imagined. He ran his hand appreciatively along its length, feeling the velvet skin slide over the hard shaft, gathering the gleaming pearl of moisture from the tip and slicking it back over the head.

He started to tell Leif he was beautiful, but those long, white fingers freed him from his own clothing. For the first time in years a hand that wasn't his own wrapped firmly around his cock.

Coherent thought fled, escaping along with a groan of sheer, animal pleasure. He leaned his weight against Leif, his hips thrusting involuntarily into the tight tunnel formed by the other man's fingers and palm. Leif moaned and pressed his face against Dan's hair, his own hips moving as he fucked Dan's hand in return.

"Is it as good as you remember?" Leif growled.

Dan whimpered helplessly. Both of them were practically dripping pre-come. He could feel the slickness against his fingers as he pumped Leif's cock, and feel it against his own length as Leif slipped a fingertip over the head with every stroke, gathering the liquid.

"I'll take that as a yes," Leif murmured.

"Y-yes," he managed somehow, because it felt fantastic to finally touch this gorgeous man he'd been longing for, ever since the moment Leif had pulled into the drive. "It feels good; missed this." He swallowed. "Want this. Want you."

Leif turned his head and kissed Dan, plundering his mouth ruthlessly. At the same time, Leif pulled his hand back just enough to run a fingernail along Dan's slit, sending a shockwave through him.

He moaned into Leif's mouth, feeling the tingling build in his balls. Pulling back, he whispered, "Leif, I can't..."

"Don't hold back," Leif said, his blue eyes bright with hunger.

That was all it took. The heat in his balls built toward the inevitable. Dan rocked his hips frantically, thrusting into Leif's tight, slick grip, and oh gods, it had been too long, was too much, sensation building on sensation until he couldn't stand it a second longer.

He body clenched, ecstasy slamming white-hot through him as his cock twitched in Leif's grip, come spilling onto the forest floor. Leif made encouraging sounds deep in his throat, and he rocked his narrow hips once, twice, before coming as well.

For a timeless moment, there was nothing but their ragged breathing. They leaned against one another and the tree, loosely entangled, breath panting, cocks going soft in the cool night air.

Did I—did we—really do that?

But yes, Leif—gorgeous, wonderful Leif—was leaning half-against him, with a smile on his kiss-swollen lips.

"Thank you," Dan said, not entirely sure of the etiquette of the situation.

"My pleasure." Leif drew back a little. "We should get ourselves back in order, before someone comes along."

A chill walked up Dan's spine. *Stupid.* After years of making sure no one outside the family knew he was gay, he'd gone and had a jerk-off session with a hot guy only a few hundred yards away from half the township, in a place where any drunk or horny couple might stumble over them.

Or Rúnar, if he's still lurking about. And wasn't that a terrifying thought?

"You're right. And I guess we should find Bea and Virgil and go home, since we've taken care of things."

Leif gave him a sly grin that said he was reading more into Dan's choice of words than had been intended. Dan's face flushed hotly, but he ducked his head with a grin of his own. "I meant the haint."

"Mmm hmm. Of course you did." Leif squeezed his shoulder, before pulling away to put himself back in order. Dan did the same, stealing a sideways glance at Leif.

Where does this leave us? Was Leif really into him, or had Leif just wanted the comfort of another body after his brush with death? Or did the possibility of getting caught, by revelers or Rúnar, turn him on?

They walked back to the festival together, and even though they neither spoke nor touched, he could feel the connection between them like a live wire. *Maybe it doesn't matter. Maybe I should just enjoy a good thing while it lasts.*

Maybe I should just stop thinking. For once in my life, for a few hours, stop worrying and let it happen.

He could do that. He thought. And if not, well, there was always tomorrow.

Leif lay in bed alone the next morning, his thoughts chasing themselves in useless spirals. Rúnar had beaten them to the miser's haint and the Eye of the Uktena. He and Dan had spent most of the night at the kitchen table, trying to figure out what to do next. Any further discussion—or continuation—of what had happened in the woods had been shelved in the face of this greater priority.

It wasn't supposed to happen this way. I can't get involved with Dan. I have to tell him last night was fun, but a one-time deal only.

It shouldn't have happened in the first place, of course. But when Dan had unexpectedly kissed him, he simply hadn't been able to hold back.

His breath quickened at the memory of the kiss, and his cock stiffened when his thoughts drifted to afterward. Dan's confession of a six-year dry spell had been surprising, but on reflection, quintessentially Dan. It fit perfectly with his reserve, with the sense he kept a hard shell between the world and the vulnerable core of himself.

And I'm the one he wanted to let inside. It stole his breath and made his chest ache. *How can I say no to that?*

All those noble intentions, and I abandon them the first time Dan kisses me.

Dull pain pulsed through his head. *Weak. Faithless. Selfish.*

He threw back the cover and sat up, shivering in the chill of the morning. The room had a space heater, but he didn't bother turning it on, instead grabbing some clothes and padding to the shower.

Maybe I should talk to Dan. Tell him, well, not everything. But let him know people get hurt around me, and I care about him and don't want that to happen.

Maybe we can just keep things cool. Get together if the opportunity presents itself, but otherwise keep our relationship professional.

He could do it, couldn't he? It wasn't as if he'd gotten attached. It wasn't as if he cared about Dan as something more than a friend or even a fuck-buddy.

Right?

He closed his eyes and leaned his head against the old, stained tiles of the shower. The pounding water soothed the ache a little, but did nothing to calm the thoughts ricocheting inside his skull. *I can't. I can't.*

No one will ever love you. Except for Rúnar, of course.

Could I be any more fucked-up?

After showering, he went back to the cold bedroom and finished dressing, using the small mirror on the dresser to apply a thick layer of eyeliner. And if he was a little more careful with it today, and a little bit more fancy, that didn't have anything to do with the man cooking breakfast down in the kitchen, did it?

Fuck, he wasn't even any good at lying to himself.

He headed down the stairs, feeling an odd little flutter in his chest at the prospect of having breakfast with Dan and the rest of the family. As he passed through the living room, a heavy knock sounded at the front door. The voices in the kitchen fell silent, and Dan appeared in the doorway connecting it with the living room, looking puzzled.

"Do you want to me to get it?" Leif asked, but Dan shook his head and brushed past.

The haint-blue door swung open, revealing a tall African-American woman dressed in all black: leather pants, leather trench coat, leather boots, and a cotton top. Her thick ebony curls were drawn back from her face and held with a black hair tie at the crown of her head. A large, silver ankh hung around her neck, reflecting the early morning light. Her indigo aura was firm and hard. Another Walker.

"Dan Miller," she said by way of greeting, her grin brilliant in her dark face.

"Taryn!"

"Taryn!" Bea echoed, and shoved past Leif to throw her arms around the newcomer. "Dan didn't say you were coming!"

"That's because he didn't know, little bird." Her accent was deep southern: Alabama or Mississippi, maybe.

"Glad to have you," Dan said, shaking her hand once Bea was out of the way. "Truth is, we might need your help. Taryn Latiolais, this is Leif Helsvin."

"Hello," Leif said, extending his hand.

She slammed into him like a speeding car. One instant, he was standing with his hand out; the next, he was against the wall, one of her hands fisted in his shirt and the other holding the blade of a knife to his throat.

CHAPTER 17

"Taryn!" Bea shrieked, and Dan shouted: "Stop! What are you doing?"

Hard brown eyes bored into Leif's, and the curve of her full upper lip twisted into a snarl. "What I was sent here to do. I told you his name sounded familiar when we talked on the phone, didn't I? Did a little checking, and found out Anubis wanted me to come here, all right—to save you from this conniving piece of shit."

Oh. No. Fuck, no.

"You don't—" he started, desperate to keep her from saying the damning words.

"Keep your mouth shut, asshole," she warned, applying more pressure to the knife, the first layers of skin parting beneath it. "I don't know what game you're playing, but I'm not letting you drag Dan and his family into it."

"Taryn, *back off!*" Dan shouted, dark eyes snapping with rage. "Let go of him and put that knife away, or I swear I will get the shotgun out of the closet and *make* you. Hear me?"

Her lips pressed together, but she let go and took a step back. Leif watched warily as she slipped her knife back into the sheath. She had a pair of them, one at each hip. The blades looked to be hand-forged Damascus steel, and were set into a pair of handles carved from the matching halves of a bear's lower jaw. No doubt they were what she used to put down the dangerous dead, like his sword or Dan's antler-tipped wand.

Virgil stood frozen in the doorway to the kitchen, his eyes wide and frightened. Bea had retreated to a corner, her hands clasped in front of her mouth and tears on her face. Dan looked worried and angry.

"How about you tell me what the fuck is wrong with you," Dan said to Taryn. "Leif is my friend, and if you think you can just waltz in here and—"

"This bastard isn't your friend," she said, her eyes never leaving Leif's face. "I don't know what lies he's been telling you, but that's all they are. He's a sorcerer and a necromancer of the worst kind, and I aim to make him pay for what he's done."

She knows. All the blood drained out of his face; she noticed and smiled, cold and cruel as an alligator.

"Leif is here because he's *hunting* a necromancer," Dan argued. "Rúnar. We've been working together on this. I don't know what you've heard about Leif, but it's a lie."

"He told you he's *hunting* Rúnar Ingmarsson?" Taryn laughed, a little sound with no humor. "He's not here to stop Rúnar. He's here to help him."

Leif shook his head. How could he make them—make Dan—believe him? "No. That's not true."

"You were his apprentice!" Taryn shouted. "Oh, I've heard about you, boy, things that would make a snake's blood run cold. You bound a ghost into a box and sent it to your own foster-father. It haunted his family for two fucking years: beating on the walls, pinching and screaming, feeding its madness and pain into them, until a boy tried to kill himself just to get away."

Leif wanted to say something. Wanted to deny it, or pretend she was crazy, or it was a trick—something, anything. But he couldn't. He could only stand there and listen to her fury, focusing on that because it meant he didn't have to see the look on Dan's face.

"Leif?" Dan said tentatively, when the silence stretched too long. "Tell her she's got the wrong guy."

He knows now. Oh, sweet death, he knows. Leif felt naked—no, beyond naked, cracked open to his very soul.

And all there is to see inside is corruption.

Taryn grinned like a skull. "Lie to me, necromancer. Tell me you didn't spend years traveling the world with Rúnar, torturing the dead to gain knowledge or power, ripping treasures from the ground that didn't belong to you. Using them to get revenge on those who'd done you wrong, without caring who else got hurt. Tell me you aren't here to distract Dan, to play him, or to make him a pawn in whatever game you're running with your master."

"I'm not." His lips were numb, and it took him two tries to speak. "I'm here to stop Rúnar."

"Your own teacher? I think not." Because, being a Walker, she *knew* the depth of the bond. She knew how vital, how deep-rooted it was, even for normal people like Dan, people who weren't so stained and broken only another monster could love them.

"I swear it, by Hel's left hand. I'm here to stop him, not help him."

The silence that followed was full of the things he hadn't said. "And the rest of it?" Dan asked.

Leif took a deep, shaky breath and forced himself to meet Dan's gaze. "She's...not wrong."

Bea let out a little gasp, but otherwise the house was utterly silent.

"Rúnar saved my life. He taught me everything," he went on, and every word felt like a step further onto an iced-over lake, just waiting for the one to crack the surface and drop him into the depths. "Including necromancy. I've done things. But I swear—*I swear*—I've changed. I've spent years chasing after Rúnar, trying to stop him. Trying to make up for the damage I caused."

For a long, long moment, Dan just stared back at Leif, his dark eyes inscrutable. Then he turned abruptly aside and fixed his gaze on the wood stove.

"Get out of my house."

All the color drained out of the world, taking with it heat and light, leaving behind an icy gray wasteland. Somewhere, in the back of Leif's aching head, there was delighted laughter, and for a minute all he could smell was lotus and musk.

He had to say something, had to do something. Had to reverse time, take them back to last night, or yesterday, or even the night in Asheville. Anything but this, anything but the weight of his lies smashing down around him.

They see your true self, and they hate you. Dan hates you.

No one will ever care for you but Rúnar. No one, not ever. Don't you see? Don't you understand?

"Dan," he said, forcing the words out past the bands tightening around his chest, "please, *please,* let me explain—"

"I said get the fuck out!"

The shout might as well have been a slap. No one moved, except for Taryn, who shifted her weight from one foot to the other. She didn't look gleeful, as Leif might have expected. Instead she just looked pissed. Maybe she thought he was getting off too easy.

Maybe he was.

"I'll just get my things," he said, but the words felt like they came from someone else's lips.

He crossed the living room to the stair. One foot in front of the other, to the second floor and his borrowed room. By the time he reached the bed, his hands were shaking. Gods, if only he could just curl up in the blankets and cry.

I don't deserve that kind of mercy. He'd brought this on himself, after all.

He'd always known he'd have to move on, have to leave Dan behind. Like a fool, he'd thought maybe they could part on good terms, be friends. And even though he'd told himself over and over there couldn't be anything more, he'd still nurtured a seed of hope, tiny and barely alive, but there nonetheless.

But the soil of his soul was hopelessly tainted, and nothing would ever grow there again. There was no redemption, because there was no undoing the past. It was as simple and as bleak as that.

When Bea knocked tentatively on the open door, he found himself standing in front of his bag, a crumpled shirt in his hands, even though he didn't remember getting either out. The shirt was the one he'd worn the night of Kristian's death, and it still reeked of their mingled sweat.

"Where will you go?" Bea asked in a small voice. She was a good person, like Dan. She'd make a real difference in the world, once she got out there and found her place in it.

"Asheville," he said, stuffing the shirt roughly into the bag. "It's close enough to still hunt Rúnar."

"You're going to keep after him?"

"Nothing's changed. Rúnar is still out there, and he's still dangerous." Leif zipped up his bag and slung it over his shoulder. Belatedly, he remembered that his shampoo and conditioner were still in the bathroom, along with his toothbrush, but fuck it. He'd buy more. He had plenty of blood money to go around, after all.

He turned and found Bea staring at him, her teeth worrying her lower lip and her eyes huge. "Taryn means well," she said hesitantly. "I'm not defending what she did, but—"

"Why not? She's told you the truth, which is more than I ever did."

"She and Dan aren't even giving you a chance to explain!"

"Maybe there's nothing *to* explain." He brushed past her, heading for the stairs.

"Leif—"

"Let it go," he said, not looking back. "Even better, forget you ever knew me at all."

He went the rest of the way down the stairs. He could do this; he *had* to do this. But the sight of Dan standing in the living room, arms folded and eyes fixed on some far-off point, undid all his resolve. He stopped at the foot of the stairs, clutching his bag and his sword, and knew he would have given anything, literally anything, just to have Dan smile at him one more time.

But it wasn't going to happen.

The haint-blue door thumped shut behind him. He threw his luggage into the trunk of the Porsche, slammed it closed, and climbed in. For a long moment, he just sat and clutched the steering wheel.

Pathetic. Sitting here, wishing I wasn't a worthless piece of shit. Wishing I could have tricked Dan just a little longer, made him think I'm something other than a weak, selfish coward.

Hate boiled up in him, seeping through the pain radiating out from the base of his skull. *Why don't I ever learn? What's it going to take before I finally get the message and realize I'm nothing?* How many times had life tried to teach him that lesson, from his junkie mother to his foster father, to the tricks he'd blown in alleys while they cursed him, to Alice, who'd at least cared enough to show him where he'd gone wrong?

He cranked the engine and slammed the car into gear, hard enough to bruise his palm on the shifter. The instant the wheels hit the hardtop, he gunned the engine, fishtailing in loose gravel before straightening the car out.

Fuck this, and fuck me.

At the moment, driving was the only outlet for the rage and loathing churning through his veins. He pressed the pedal to the floor and roared off down the narrow road leading out of Ransom Gap.

Dan placed the log on its end, raised the ax high over his head, and brought it down with all his strength. The log split cleanly, pieces flying in every direction. He picked them up, tossed them on the woodpile, and moved on to the next piece.

Sweat ran into his eyes, and his t-shirt was soaked through. His arms ached from a long morning of splitting firewood, and his stomach informed him lunch had been at least a couple of hours ago. He ignored the aches and pains, focusing only on splitting the log in front of him, stacking it, splitting and stacking the next, over and over again.

Maybe if he kept it up long enough, he'd push himself into a numb state of exhaustion where he didn't have even the energy to think. Maybe if his arms ached enough, he wouldn't notice his heart hurting.

Leif lied to me. He'd fooled Dan into thinking they were friends, even into thinking there might be the possibility of something more between them.

I should've known better. He must've had a good laugh at the country bumpkin who actually thought somebody so sophisticated would be interested. How could I have been such an idiot?

He should've thrown Leif out of the kitchen the day he showed up. *I was done with haint-work. Out of it. And I let myself get drawn back in, and for what? A pair of pretty eyes and a slick tongue?*

Leif was sly as old Reynardine from the stories, and just as untrustworthy. Except instead of luring maidens back to his lair, Leif seduced haintworkers for Rúnar, to...what? Keep them busy chasing his tail, while his teacher did whatever he pleased? Get information on local haints worth binding?

But why go through the charade with the haint last night? Leif could have died—getting hurt by that thing was no act. And the night on the phone —I would have sworn it wasn't an act, either.

Well, maybe it just meant Leif could have won a fucking Oscar if he'd gone to Hollywood instead of Helheim. Or Dan was just piss-poor at figuring shit out, especially when his cock was doing his thinking for him.

The back door closed, and Dan realized he'd been standing stock still for several minutes, his hands gripping the ax handle until his fingers had gone numb. The wind blew through his sweat-soaked shirt, and his muscles had cooled down enough for him to starting shivering.

Time to get back to work.

He reached for the next log, but Bea stepped in front of it, blocking him. Her hands were on her hips, and her brows pulled down into a scowl. "Are you going to sulk out here all day?"

"Wood needs chopped," he replied, annoyed by her attitude. Normally Virgil was the one who treated him like an idiot. He didn't think he liked it any better from his sister.

"Make Virgil do it, while you call Leif."

Dan's hands tightened on the ax. "I'm not calling Leif. And neither are you."

"Goddess, you're starting to sound like Taryn!"

"Good! In case you didn't notice, *she's* the one who came in and-and saved us from my mistake!"

Bea rolled her eyes as only a teenager could. "Taryn means well, but she doesn't know the situation. Or do you actually believe the crap coming out of your mouth?"

Dan buried the ax blade in the old stump they used as a chopping block. "I'm not taking that kind of backtalk from you. You get back in the house right now, and don't you dare say another word about-about *him*."

"No."

"You're grounded."

"I don't care!" She clenched her hands into fists, and tears started in her eyes. "Leif was trying to help! Maybe he screwed up in the past, but he's re-ally trying now, I know he is. He's the one person who might actually know enough about Rúnar to stop him, and you threw him out of the house because your feelings are hurt!"

"Leif lied to us, Bea!" Dan shouted, abandoning all pretense of control. "Don't you get it? He *lied.* If he wasn't up to anything, he would have told us up front he was Rúnar's apprentice!"

"Well, gee, given how you took the news, I can't *imagine* why he wouldn't have said anything," she shot back, voice dripping with sarcasm. "I mean, I'm sure *any* Walker would be just *thrilled* to work with an ex-necro-mancer out to stop his teacher."

"And there it is," he said, seizing on her words gratefully. "You don't understand, Bea, and I don't blame you for it. But there's a link between ap-prentice and teacher. There has to be trust and caring, enough for a psychic bond to form between them, or else it just can't be done."

"He can't change?"

"I *felt* Mom die!"

He'd never meant to say that, never meant for anyone else in the family to know. All the color drained out of her face. "I don't understand."

Hecate's bitches, it was a hard thing to say. But she needed to understand. "It felt her die." *Cold and alone, reaching out to me in her hour of need, just to have me fail her. "That's* how close a teacher and apprentice are. You can't shrug off that kind of bond, Bea. You just can't."

Her eyes widened, and now the tears were free and spilling down her cheeks. Before he could say anything, she hugged him, sweaty as he was. "I'm sorry, Dan," she said into his shoulder, her voice cracking on a sob. "But don't you see? Doesn't it make what Leif's done even more special?"

"That's why he has to be lying."

She drew back from him. "Yeah. Because you were just like Mom. Couldn't tell the two of you apart, most days."

"Bea—"

"*Listen* to me. No, screw that—listen to your heart. I *know* Leif's one of the good guys, and I think, deep down, you do too. Since he walked in that door, you've been happier than I've seen you since Mom died."

Fuck. Was it that obvious? Bea had always been a sharp one. An old soul, Mom had called her once, and Dan didn't have any reason to think she'd been wrong.

"Just talk to him," Bea cajoled through her tears. "I'm not saying you should ask him to come back, even. But at least hear his side of the story before you give up on him."

Her last words hit him unexpectedly, an ungentle tap to the chest. Leif had never known his dad, been abandoned by his mom, and shuttled through the foster care system from one family to the next.

In other words, a lot of people had given up on him, right when he needed them the most. And now here Dan was, setting up to be the next in line.

"All right," he said. "I'll go in and call him. Happy?"

"Yeah."

"No promises, though. Hear me? It's just a phone call."

"Yeah, yeah. I get it."

They went inside. Taryn and Virgil were on the couch, playing a video game. The other Walker glanced up at him, her mouth a thin line. "Ready to make a plan?"

"I want to talk to Leif first."

She shook her head, dark curls bouncing. "Shit, Dan, use the brains you were born with."

Virgil looked up in alarm. "Taryn's right—he's dangerous! You can't call him!"

"I can and I will," Dan said stubbornly. "Taryn, listen, I appreciate your warning. I'm not ignoring what you told us, trust me. But you don't know Leif. Whatever he used to be, every instinct I've got tells me he's on our side now."

Taryn locked eyes with him for a long, long moment. She was a Walker; she understood those gut urges, those little whispers in the back of the skull, those half-formed feelings which might be a spirit or a god trying to tell you something.

"The only instincts you're listening to are the ones in your pants," Virgil said nastily.

Taryn cuffed him lightly on the back of the head. "Show your elders some respect, boy. This is Walker business."

Dan went to the phone. He hesitated just a moment before dialing Leif's number. *What am I even going to say to him?*

As it turned out, he didn't have to worry; the call went straight to voice mail. Dan hung up with a sigh. "He's got his phone turned off. Guess he doesn't feel like talking to anyone right now."

"He said he was going to Asheville," Bea offered. "He looked real up-set, too."

Asheville wasn't a big city, but it was plenty big enough to hide a single man who didn't want to be found.

Yes, but Rúnar found him there.

He wouldn't, surely.

But the same gut instinct told him, yes, Leif would.

Dan turned decisively away from the phone. "Taryn, can you keep an eye on Bea and Virgil tonight?" he asked, pleased his voice sounded steady even though his heart beat fast with sudden fear. "I'm going down to the city, before Leif does something stupid."

And hope to all the gods I get there in time.

CHAPTER 18

Leif sat at the bar of the same gay club he'd come to before. The bartender slid a second scotch in front of him, and he took a sip, wondering if he should just start throwing them back until he was well and truly drunk. Sweet death, he wanted to. Maybe if he drank enough, he could forget the look in Dan's eyes, the coldness in his voice.

I can't believe I fucked up this badly.

He'd never meant to bring more pain down on Dan's head, but he'd done it anyway. And, yeah, Taryn had been the one to blow his cover, and he half wanted to hate her for it. But the truth was he had no one to blame but himself.

He was out of options. He'd lost whatever help Dan might have given him. Rúnar had the Eye of the Uktena, and Samhain was less than a week away. He had no idea where the Witches Harrow might be located, or if he had a chance of stopping Rúnar.

Nothing was left but this. To be bait, in the futile hope Rúnar would somehow tip his hand.

Being bait didn't mean dying, though, not without a fight. If he got killed because he was stupid enough to get drunk now, he'd have to explain to Hel why he'd been careless with the job she'd given him.

With a sigh, he set the glass back down, having only tasted a sip. In the background, a DJ spun industrial tunes, and the sharp musk of sweat and lust stained the air. A couple of men had tried to strike up a conversation with him, but he'd shut them down quick. He wasn't endangering anyone else. Rúnar would have to find his own victims.

And he would, probably from one of the many cemeteries in the area. He'd send one after Leif, maybe to attack him on the street, maybe to follow him back to the hotel. It didn't matter. He'd keep coming back, night after night, keep fighting, until Rúnar finally got tired of it and came to take care of him personally.

A hand fell heavily on his shoulder and spun him around. Leif grabbed automatically for a sword that wasn't there, dropped his hand to his boot knife—then stilled and stared.

Dan stood there, his brows drawn down over his dark eyes, his mouth a thin slash of disappointment. "What the fuck are you doing here?

No. No, this was *not* happening. Dan had thrown him out, had repudiated him—he wasn't, *couldn't* be here.

"I should ask you that," Leif managed to say through his shock.

Dan's hand tightened, pressing the thin cover of muscle into bone. "What do you think you're doing? Are you *trying* to get yourself killed?"

"It's called being bait," Leif snapped.

Dan paled sharply. "You can't—"

"Don't fucking tell me what I can do!" And gods, this was too much to ask. *Why is he here?* Was this some final torment, some last dig, just to show Leif everything he couldn't have?

Leif wrenched loose of Dan's hold and tossed money down on the bar, covering the drink and the tip. Shoving past Dan, he forced his way through the crowd of people streaming into the nightclub.

Rain had moved in while he was inside, falling in a solid sheet past the awning. Beyond caring, he lengthened his stride, felt the icy water soak through his t-shirt in seconds.

"Leif!" Dan shouted, but the sound was distant. Hitching back a sob of fury and grief, Leif broke into a blind run.

Shit!

Dan ran as fast as he could after Leif, his shoes slipping on the rain-slick concrete. Hecate's bitches, could he have fucked this up any worse? He'd meant to find Leif and apologize, but he hadn't been able to contain his horror at realizing Leif had actually gone back to the club. He'd lashed out in his fear, but he'd never expected Leif to actually *run* from him.

The sharp tang of wet asphalt and ozone rose from the pavement beneath his feet, and the rain turned into swirling sparks where it reflected the streetlights. The club was on a side street lined with parking lots and loading docks. Leif ran down the sidewalk, his long legs setting a pace Dan couldn't match. The street curved sharply uphill, and Leif disappeared from sight.

Fuck! If he lost track of Leif now, he'd never see him again. Leif wouldn't come back to the club; he'd disappear into the city and either confront Rúnar without Dan to back him up, or…

No. Don't think like that.

Dan ran until his lungs burned. The rain plastered his hair against his face and his t-shirt against his skin, stealing warmth.

Or was the air getting colder?

"It's called being bait."

No!

He put on a last, desperate burst of speed, praying he was even running in the right direction at this point, and Leif hadn't ducked down some side alley. The mojo bag stirred in his pocket, reacting to the presence of the restless dead. The industrial district gave way to downtown, and before him Dan saw the triangular shape of Pritchard Park.

The small park was speckled with trees, their leaves scattering in the wind to stick wetly to every available surface, turning the ground treacherous. A small amphitheater dominated the park, consisting of brick step seating interspersed with tumbled boulders, giving the sunken area a more natural look.

Leif stood in the center of the amphitheater: a tall, still shape like a heron waiting to strike at an incautious fish. He didn't have his sword, of course, but his boot knife was in his hand. He'd pulled off the cuff covering the bindrunes on his left wrist and held up his forearm like a shield in front of him. Steam rose from the icy rain hitting his warm skin, and etheric flame glazed the knife blade and wrapped the bindrunes in a bluish glow.

On the side opposite Dan, the amphitheater opened directly onto the street. A dark shape shambled across the pavement toward Leif, the unholy light of the dead visible in its eyes even from a distance.

All of Leif's attention was focused on the haint in front of him. But from his vantage point, Dan saw a shadow coalesce amidst the tumbled rock behind Leif, its presence masked by that of the first spirit.

Fuck. At least Leif had his boot dagger, but Dan's wand was still back in the truck. Even as he stretched his legs as far as they would go, putting on every ounce of speed, his mind flailed, trying to find something, anything to act as a focus or a weapon.

But there was no time left.

"Leif! Behind you!" Dan shouted.

He leapt from the top step, his body the only weapon he had against the second haint. His aura flashed to hardness just before impact, and the haint crumpled beneath him, both of them slamming into the rocks.

Unfortunately, only one of them could actually be hurt by the fall, and it wasn't the haint. Dan managed to mostly keep it between his body and the rocks, but the impact still knocked the wind out of him and sent a bolt of pain through his right hip.

The sour stink of rotting vomit burst out of the haint beneath him. It growled and heaved, sending him skidding across the rough ground and onto the amphitheater floor. He thought he heard Leif shout his name, but he couldn't take his eyes off the haint long enough to find out.

It staggered to its feet: dressed in a WWI-era uniform, its face dark blue with congested blood and stained with mucus and other fluids. The cold flame in its sunken eyes fixed on Dan's face, and it staggered forward implacably, hands reaching out to strangle.

And, fuck, he had no wand, no weapon, nothing to keep it off—

My mojo bag has salt in it.

He scooted back on the concrete, trying to put distance between himself and the haint while he dug in his pocket for the flannel bag.

It practically sprang into his hand, as if aware of his need. Whispering an apology to it, he ripped it open, dumping the contents into his other hand: two lodestones to ward off evil, two horseshoe nails for luck, and a generous heap of coarse-grained salt mined from the earth.

With all of the strength he could summon, he hurled the contents of the bag straight into the haint's bloated face.

It staggered back, the salt burning holes into its blackened flesh, as surely as if Dan had shot it point-blank with birdshot. Imbued with power from their association with the mojo bag, the nails and lodestones tore angry, smoking creases through its flesh, baring dead, brown bone beneath.

But it wasn't enough. The haint slowed down, but the binding Rúnar had worked didn't unravel.

Dan scrambled to his feet, ignoring the pain in his hip. He poured all of his will into his aura, and it flamed into a wall of protection, even as his hands curled into fists. He'd hold the injured haint off of Leif for as long as he could, and pray to Hecate it would be enough.

"Dan! Get down!" Leif shouted.

He obeyed instantly, as if his nerves were directly wired to Leif's. The haint charged even as his knees hit the ground, its hands groping for his neck, the stench of its decay flooding his senses.

Leif's knife *thocked* cleanly into its skull, directly between its eyes.

"Hecate, Lady of the Keys, open the way!" Dan shouted, throwing all his will behind Leif's.

Hounds bayed, almost in Dan's ear, and he thought he felt the brush of spectral fur. Then the haint was gone, safely delivered back to whatever afterlife from which Rúnar had dragged it.

Silence.

Dan staggered to his feet, aware once again of the rain pelting him, of the cold night air leeching heat from his body through his soaked clothing.

"Dan," Leif said.

Dan turned, and for a long moment they stared at one another. Leif looked wild, his hair hanging in water-logged ropes in his face, his lips parted, his blue eyes practically burning with a mixture of grief and hope.

"I'm sorry," Dan said. He crossed the space between them, until only a bare inch of air separated them, until he could all but feel Leif's heat. "Throwing you out was the worst mistake of my life."

Leif licked his lips nervously. "Don't say that. Not until you know everything I've done."

"I don't need to know what you've done, because I know who you are now. That's what matters to me."

"Don't," Leif whispered, and his voice broke on the word. "What if—what if I tell you, and you hate me?"

"I couldn't hate you." And slipping his arms around Leif, he drew the other man close and kissed him.

Leif made a soft sound deep in his throat, half-sob and half-laugh, before kissing Dan back. And gods, it was as glorious a kiss as Dan had ever imagined. Leif's arms closed tentatively around him: strong and warm and wonderful.

When the kiss finally ended, Dan tightened his hold gently on Leif. "I could see you were hurting," he said softly. His wet hair dripped rain into his eyes, but he didn't want to let go long enough to brush it aside, half-afraid Leif might disappear if he broke contact. "I just didn't know where the pain came from. I'm sorry I threw you out. I'm sorry I let my pride and my hurt get in the way of doing the right thing. I knew better; I knew *you* better. Can you possibly forgive me?"

Leif swallowed, throat working visibly. "Anything. I'd forgive you anything."

The wind gusted, sending wet leaves and rain cascading across them. Leif shivered, his skin pebbling with goose bumps under Dan's hands. "You're freezing," Dan murmured.

"I've got a hotel room. We can go back there. If you want."

The suggestion made his heart speed up and his cock harden. "Yeah. I want."

"Well, uh, here we are," Leif said, unlocking the door to his room. It was a different hotel from the one he'd stayed in before: older and not quite as upscale. The suite was much smaller, with a single room serving as bedroom and sitting area, and a tiny bathroom with a combination shower and tub. Still, the restored building gave off the impression of grand old luxury, with hardwood floors softened by area rugs, nineteenth-century bath tiles, a huge antique bed, and a beautiful view through the expansive window.

"It's a sight better than the Motel 6," Dan said with a wry twist of his lips. "Are we going to get in trouble for dripping on the rugs?" Both of them were utterly sodden from the rain, water pooling on the floor around their shoes.

"It'll be fine," Leif said, ushering Dan in, then closing and locking the door behind them. "I'll have the laundry service take care of our clothes. Then we can seal up the room."

Dan glanced nervously between Leif and the bed. "I should change before I get water everywhere," he said, hefting the overnight bag he'd grabbed from his truck.

Leif swallowed, feeling unaccountably nervous himself. Which was ridiculous, of course; he'd brought any number of men back to hotel rooms before.

But none of those times ever mattered. Not like this.

He didn't really understand what had brought Dan down to Asheville after him. But the sight of Dan standing between him and the *draugr*, not a weapon on him except for his determination, had seared itself into Leif. It wasn't the act of someone who despised him.

He cares about me. Even knowing I lied.

Of course, Dan didn't know the particulars, but he was a Walker. He knew the score; he could imagine what Leif might have done with Rúnar.

"All right," Leif said, and Dan headed for the bathroom with his overnight bag in his hand.

While he was gone, Leif sealed the windows with lines of salt, then added another line around the hearth. While he was there, he lit the gas fireplace. It wasn't quite the same as a cheerful wood fire, but the flickering yellow flames spread gentle light through the room. There were extra pillows and blankets in the closet; Leif piled them on the area rug in front of the fireplace. Turning down the lights help set the mood further. After a moment of thought, he put in a call to room service.

Dan came out just as Leif hung up. Dan had toweled off and changed into a pair of battered jeans and a plain red t-shirt, which looked amazing with his dark hair and eyes, and was tight enough to show off the breadth of his shoulders nicely.

"Can I borrow your cell phone?" he asked. "I need to call Taryn and let her know I'm staying the night."

"Sure," Leif said, although he wasn't pleased to hear Taryn was still at the farm. On the other hand, she probably wouldn't be at all happy to hear he was coming back. "I'll change while you call."

He left his sodden clothing in a pile on the bathroom floor, quickly toweled off, and pulled on fresh boxers, the loose cotton pants he wore when practicing his sword forms, and an old shirt. Not dressed to kill, that was for certain.

His eyeliner was hopelessly smeared; his reflection in the mirror looked like a raccoon with two black eyes. He washed it off, but hesitated when he reached for the stick to reapply it. The face staring back at him seemed younger and more vulnerable than the one he was used to seeing. He didn't like it, but maybe he owed it to Dan to wear as few masks as possible, at least for tonight.

He put the eyeliner down, scooped up their wet clothing and deposited it into the laundry sack, and exited the bathroom. Someone knocked on the door and called: "Room service!" Dan had obviously finished his conversation with Taryn; now he looked at the door with alarm.

"It's all right," Leif said, although he double-checked through the peephole. He didn't *think* they'd been followed, but he couldn't discount the possibility.

He opened the door, and the server pushed in a small cart, on which sat a bottle of relatively expensive champagne in a silver-plated ice bucket, two fluted glasses, and a large covered tray. "On the table will be fine," Leif said, while Dan stared at the bottle with wide eyes. "And I know it isn't your job, but would you terribly mind taking these down to the laundry?" he added, holding out the sack, a healthy tip tucked discreetly between two fingers.

The server accepted both with aplomb. "Of course, sir. Anything else?"

"Not now, thank you." As soon as the server was gone, he locked the door again and laid a final line of salt across the doorway. It was probably a bit paranoid, but after what had happened earlier, he didn't want to take any chances. Once he'd finished, he put away the pouch of salt and opened the champagne.

"Um, you know, you don't have to seduce me," Dan said.

"Maybe you deserve to be seduced."

Dan flushed adorably and ducked his head. "Room service isn't cheap."

"The money came from my time with Rúnar," Leif said, because Dan deserved his honesty. "For the most part, anyway. When I turned eighteen, he set me up with a nice account, including my cut of the jobs we'd done together. Starter money, he said. It grew from there, and after…well, it isn't like I'm spending very much of it, chasing him around the country. It mostly just sits there and grows into a bigger pile."

He gestured for Dan to take the tray and carried the bottle and glasses over to the pile of pillows. He sank down on one and tucked his legs beneath him comfortably. Dan followed and set the tray on the floor, uncovering it to reveal a spread of strawberries dipped in dark chocolate. Leif poured them each a glass of champagne and handed one to Dan. The firelight caught in the pale yellow liquid, turning the stream of bubbles into tiny sparks.

Dan watched him intently, holding his glass in his large, work-hardened hands. "You don't have to talk about him. Not if you don't want to."

Leif took a sip of the champagne. "I owe it to you to be honest. I've lied too much to be anything less."

"And, truth be told, I appreciate it. But I don't want him in this room with us."

Oh. It tightened Leif's throat and sent a surge of heat straight to his groin. "And what do you want?"

Dan's dark gaze had fastened on Leif's mouth. At the question, though, he took a deep breath and visibly focused on Leif's eyes. "I want to make you happy. I want to do what's best for you. I'll sleep on the floor, if that's what you want. Or just hold you, all night. Whatever you need from me."

It broke something deep inside Leif; split him open and swept away all the lies and the barriers. "What if I need for you to make love to me?" he whispered, and sweet death, he'd never called it that before in his whole life.

Dan leaned in close, his hands gliding up Leif's back before pulling him into an embrace. "Then I'm a lucky man."

CHAPTER 19

The faint perfume of bay rum aftershave teased Leif's senses, along with the scent of Dan's shampoo and soap and skin. He tipped his head back, felt lips against the corner of his mouth, the kiss soft and sweet.

Goddesses. He felt himself trembling with desire as he returned the kiss with interest, deepening it. Dan responded, bodies pressing tight against each other, need and lust swirling in a haze between them.

Leif shifted to straddle Dan's lap. Dark eyes watched him, their intensity shifting from affection and concern to something hotter. The chocolate-sheathed strawberries gleamed in the firelight. Leif plucked one off the tray and fed it to Dan. The chocolate melted on his fingertips; Dan caught Leif's fingers one at a time between his lips, sucking and licking off the sweetness. Leif's heart beat faster, and his cock hardened in response, the boxers and loose cotton pants doing nothing at all to hide his arousal.

He took the next strawberry for himself, watching Dan's face while he tongued the chocolate, sucking suggestively on the fruit like the head of phallus, before popping the whole thing in his mouth. A light flush spread across Dan's cheeks; his lips parted, begging to be kissed again. Warm, callused hands slid down Leif's back, shaped his hips, then slipped around to cup his ass and urge him closer.

Leif grinned. The emotional bits were new territory, but *this* was familiar ground, something he knew, something he could feel confident about. He rocked forward, his erection grinding against the hardness straining against the zipper of Dan's jeans. Snagging another strawberry, he held it between his teeth while leaning over. Dan nibbled at the other end, and they met in a swirl of lips and chocolate and sweet berry.

Dan's hands slid up under Leif's tee, warm against his skin. Leif sat back and stripped off the shirt, letting it fall on the floor. Dan watched him ravenously, fingers gliding up his ribs, making him shiver with need.

"I like your ink," Dan said, voice ragged with lust.

Leif touched the tattoo directly over his heart. "This is the rune *ear*," he said, pronouncing it as in *earth*. "Hel's rune, some call it. I had it done...after." When he'd dedicated himself to his Goddess, his need for atonement making pain the only offering he could give.

Dan nodded, his soft hair brushing the hands Leif had braced on his shoulders. His fingers shaped the rune reverently, tracing it out onto his pecs. From there he moved on to Leif's nipples, toying and tugging on the piercings. Leif arched his back. "Mmm, yes. Harder, please."

Dan did as requested, before sealing his mouth around one nipple, sucking and biting, sending a jolt of pleasure through Leif and straight into his balls. He gasped and jerked his hips against Dan, fingers digging into the other man's shoulders.

"You like that?" Dan whispered, lips brushing teasingly against sensitized skin.

"Sweet death, yes." Leif sat back and tugged impatiently on Dan's shirt. "My turn."

Dan willingly shed his own tee. Leif pushed him back against the pillows and stretched out on top of him, legs intertwined. The feel of bare skin against his was delicious, especially combined with the sensation of muscles hardened from long hours of manual labor on the farm. He kissed Dan deep, exploring the other man's mouth aggressively with his tongue, while running his hands over Dan's chest and sides.

Slowly. Because this wasn't about getting off with some stranger. He worked his way leisurely down Dan's throat. He bit lightly at the join between shoulder and neck—and was rewarded with a whimper and a jerk of the hips—and tongued the hollow where the fragile wings of the clavicles came together. Dan's tight, brown nipples begged for attention, and he lavished it on them, listening to his lover's moans as he licked and sucked.

He brushed his lips against the tight lattice of Dan's belly, traced the line of hair leading down with his tongue. Dan buried the fingers of one hand in Leif's hair. "Feels good," he whispered.

"What does?" Leif murmured.

"Everything. Your hair on my skin, your mouth, your hands. Tell me what you want, sweetheart, please. I want to make you feel good, too."

Am I that? Your sweetheart? Oh, gods, he wanted to be. "You're doing it just by being here. Believe me."

Dan wasn't going to be put off, though; he hooked his fingers in the waistband of Leif's pants, tugging impatiently. Leif shucked off both pants and boxers willingly, expecting Dan to take hold of his aching shaft right away. Instead, Dan leaned back and just looked at him, eyes heavy-lidded with lust.

"Mmm." Dan ran one hand lightly, teasingly, along the side of Leif's cock, making it jump and bob. "I meant to tell you the other night, but you have a gorgeous prick."

Leif laughed breathlessly. "I didn't know you were a connoisseur."

Dan slid his hand back down to the base, lifting Leif's cock slightly while his other hand cupped Leif's balls. "You shave them?" he asked in apparent surprise, even as he tugged and fondled.

It was hard to think straight enough to answer. "I like the way it looks on me."

"And a silver ring, of course," Dan teased, pulling gently on the lorum piercing.

"Do you like it?"

"Mmm hmmm." Dan's work-roughened hand closed around Leif's shaft, drawing out an involuntary whimper. "I want to suck you."

Oh, gods, yes, please. "Condoms and flavored lube are in my bag, by the bed," he managed to say.

Leif rolled onto his side, stroking himself while he watched Dan open the bag and sort through it.

Dark brows lifted. "You do travel prepared," he said dryly. "I've been in sex shops with fewer toys."

Leif grinned. "Grab whatever you want to use. I'm game."

"Maybe next time. Right now, I just want you."

Next time. The thought was oddly intoxicating. This was only the first time of many. *Unless I screw this up. Unless—*

No. Dan wanted him—wanted *him*, not just a cute ass or nice cock. *And I want him.*

I'm pretty fucking sure I'm in love with him.

Maybe he was rushing things; he'd never been in a real relationship before, had no clue what was too soon or too late. He only knew he'd never met anyone like Dan: sexy and sweet and so painfully real he made everything else in Leif's life feel hollow.

Leif's hands shook slightly as he unwrapped the condom Dan handed him. Somehow, he managed to get it on without too much trouble. Dan had chosen the raspberry-flavored lube; he slicked it over Leif's length, making him sigh with pleasure.

"Lean back," Dan murmured.

He did, and a moment later, Dan's lips closed over the head of his cock. And *fuck*, it felt good: warm and soft, the lightest teasing scrape of teeth. Leif whimpered and bucked helplessly, and in return that hot mouth closed over him, sliding down his shaft, sucking hard.

And oh, it was good, the heat and friction and suction. He started to close his eyes, remembered, no, not this time, he *wanted* to see, needed the intimacy.

And what a sight it was: Dan, looking like one of Caravaggio's angels, his skin gilded by the firelight, the tips of his dark hair skimming Leif's pale skin. With his kiss-swollen lips wrapped firmly around Leif's cock, his black gaze darted up and a spark seemed to jump between them.

It was almost too much. "N-No," Leif managed to say, somehow. "Not yet, please."

Someone else might have taken it as a challenge and sucked harder. But this was Dan, who took him at his word and pulled away. His eyes were wild and his lips parted, and he looked utterly, completely fuckable. "Bed?" he asked breathlessly.

"Oh, gods, yes." But first there was the matter of Dan's remaining clothing. Leif grabbed his belt and unbuckled it, and the two of them together managed to get him out of his jeans and briefs.

They stumbled to their feet, skin against skin, their lengths rubbing deliciously together. The bed was big and soft, and they collapsed into it, face-to-face, kissing and thrusting and moaning.

"I need you," Dan growled in his ear. "Will you fuck me?"

"Yes; yes, anything you want." But first he wanted to pay better attention to Dan's cock than he'd been able to the night in the woods. He moved to kneel on the bed between his lover's legs. Dan grabbed a pillow and slid it under his hips.

Leif paused to admire Dan's cock: thick and hard, rising from a nest of dark curls, flushed deep red against the untanned skin of his belly. He started to reach for another condom, but paused before he picked it up. "Did you get tested since the last time you had sex?"

"Yeah," Dan said, a puzzled look briefly breaking through the lust-glazed expression on his face. "I'm clean."

"Good, because I want to taste you."

Dan swallowed heavily. "You don't have to—I mean, it doesn't seem fair—"

"Shh." Leif bent his head and ran his tongue from the base of Dan's shaft all the way to the slit, getting a soft moan in response. Salty-sweet precome beaded at the tip; he sucked it into his mouth, savoring the taste.

One of Dan's hands curled loosely in his hair, and Leif reminded himself again to open his eyes, to look up, to engage. It felt odd and a bit frightening, but the blissful expression on Dan's face made it easier.

His mouth slid down further, reveling in the sensation of the thick cock in his mouth. Drawing back, he rubbed the ball of his tongue piercing against the slit and head, before working his way down again.

"Oh yeah," Dan whispered, the words accompanied by more inarticulate sounds. Leif pulled his mouth away slowly, sucking hard until the head left his lips with a soft, wet pop. Stretching out on his belly, he ran his tongue lightly down from the slit to the base, then sucked one ball into his mouth. He closed his eyes now, inhaling deeply, enjoying the musky scent of his lover.

When he'd finished lavishing attention on Dan's balls, he let his tongue trail down, along the taut line of the perineum, before circling lazily around the puckered flesh of the anus. Dan let out a startled gasp and jerked.

"Everything all right?" Leif asked, pulling back and glancing up in concern.

Dan's face was flushed. "Y-yes, I just haven't, uh, done that before."

"Ah." Leif grinned. "Just relax, and let me know if you want me to stop."

He went back to rimming with gusto, wanting to do something Dan hadn't experienced with anyone else—and have him like it. Which he did, judging by the sounds he was making and the way his fingers clenched in the bedcovers.

The lube had ended up on the floor; Leif paused what he was doing long enough to fetch it. Coating one finger thoroughly, he added it to his tongue, easing it in, feeling the muscles clench and relax.

"Missed this," Dan gasped.

Leif grinned and added a second finger, stretching gently. "I'll bet." He nibbled lightly on Dan's cock and received a whimper.

"Unf, Leif, *please!*"

Leif moved to a kneeling position, still working Dan gently with his fingers, stretching and opening and relaxing. Gods, Dan looked delicious, his dark hair fanned around his face on the pillow, his lips swollen from kisses, his cock red and leaking with need.

"Please what?" Leif teased.

"Fuck me, touch me, let me touch you, *please.*"

"Gladly." His cock ached and throbbed inside the latex sheath; he smeared on more lube and positioned himself, Dan's heels resting lightly on his shoulders.

He pushed in slowly, the tight ring relaxing to give him access. Dan's legs flexed, urging him further inside. "Is this good?" Leif asked, his voice cracking with desire and frantic need.

"Oh, fuck, yes." Dan reached for him; with a groan of pleasure, Leif leaned forward, burying his length deep.

Hot and tight, and it felt like he'd waited too long for this. Dan's hands slid over Leif's chest, tweaking his nipples and sending bolts of ecstasy straight to his cock. Leif began to thrust, varying his rhythm and position until the found the perfect angle to make Dan moan.

It was wonderful, thrusting slickly into the tight heat, watching Dan's face distort with ecstasy. "You feel amazing," he whispered hoarsely, wanting to make sure Dan knew how desperately he needed this, how fantastic it was to touch and be touched. Wanting him to know this *meant* something; it wasn't just two bodies moving together.

Dan's fingers twined through Leif's hair, tugging him down. "You're gorgeous," Dan said, and kissed him.

He'd never kissed while having sex; there was something shockingly intimate about it. Leif whimpered, parting his lips and letting Dan's tongue invade him, fucking his mouth in the same rhythm as he fucked Dan's ass.

He kept it up until he had to pull back for a breath. Dan slipped one hand between them, wrapping it around his unattended cock and tugging frantically. A moment later, his skin pebbled with goose bumps; his back arched and his eyes squeezed shut. *"Leif,"* he moaned, cock twitching and body clenching as come spurted between them.

It was too good, too much, to hold back any longer. Leif thrust once, twice, pushing in deep as ecstasy crested into a blinding whiteness behind his eyes.

When he opened his eyes again, he found himself blinking through sweat-mussed hair down at his lover. Dan looked beautifully sated, his skin flushed with effort and slicked with sweat.

"Mmm," Dan murmured, pulling him in for a kiss.

"You seem happy," Leif said, when he was able to form words again.

"I am. You?"

"Oh, yes."

Leif eased out, getting a last whimper from Dan, then padded to the bathroom to dispose of the condom. Grabbing a washcloth, he moistened it with warm water and took it back to the bedroom. Dan reached for the washcloth, but Leif shook his head. "Just relax. You're always taking care of everyone else. Let me take care of you for a while."

Dan's smile bloomed, big enough to reach his eyes at last. And gods, it was everything Leif had imagined, like the sun breaking over the mountains. "All right."

When Leif was done, he tossed the washcloth into bathroom and crawled into bed. Dan rolled to face him, brushing his hair back and kissing him tenderly. "You're amazing."

"Hardly," Leif said, even though it was impossible not to feel pleased at Dan's praise.

And this was good, too, curling up together, little touches and kisses, expressions of affection making his heart ache. "I've never spent the night with anyone," Leif admitted. "Not, you know, like this. Cuddling. Sleeping."

Dan's eyes widened slightly. His callused fingertips traced Leif's face gently. "I'm glad you're doing it with me."

"Yeah. Me too." Leif closed his eyes and snuggled in closer. "Thank you."

"For what?"
"Everything, baby. Everything."

CHAPTER 20

Dan opened his eyes to find the morning light streaming in through gauzy white curtains. The air against his face was chilly, but the covers were warm…though not as warm as the bare skin pressed against his.

Leif watched him from the other pillow, blue eyes bright through a tumble of flaxen hair. Without the eyeliner, he looked younger and far more vulnerable. Dan wondered if Leif meant it to be a shield between him and the world.

After they'd made love—and, although Dan had never called it that with his fuck-buddies in college, this experience was totally different—they'd cuddled under the blankets and just talked. Leif had told him everything, from the abuse he'd undergone from his foster father, to what Rúnar had done for—and to—him, to his own mistakes and the price Alice had paid.

And, Great Goddess, it had been everything he could do not to cry, to stay strong for Leif, who'd had tears of his own to shed. Leif had just been a kid when Rúnar had found him; small wonder he hadn't judged the necromancer, given what Rúnar had saved him from. And not just the haint in the warehouse, but the rest of it: starving on the street, selling his body, with drugs the only relief he could find.

But what really broke his heart was the way Leif's shoulders had hunched together, and how he'd drawn into himself as he'd spoken, as if waiting for a blow of some kind, either physical or emotional. Expecting to be rejected.

"I understand," Dan had whispered, wrapping his arms as tight as he could around Leif's thin body. "Oh, sweetheart, I understand. Anyone who says they'd have done different hasn't ever really hurt."

Leif had cried afterward: wrenching sobs, as if his frame would shake apart. But it had been a cleansing storm; after, he'd lain quietly in Dan's arms, his blue eyes more at peace than Dan had yet seen them.

Now, Leif smiled, and the sweetness of it made Dan's heart ache.

"Hey," Leif said.

"Hey yourself. How did you like spending the night with someone?"

"I liked having you by me," Leif said, and Dan didn't miss the fact he'd specified. Leif snuggled in closer, wrapping his lanky frame around Dan's more compact body, his erection pushing against Dan's hip. "And you're definitely nice to wake up to."

"That's because you haven't caught a whiff of my morning breath, yet."

Leif laughed and kissed him. "There. Now we've had to deal with each other's breath. Want to brush your teeth and hop in the shower with me?"

His morning wood had taken on a new urgency with a naked body in the bed beside him and the memory of all the things they'd done together last night fresh in his mind. The way Leif had looked above him, long hair hanging down, firelight outlining every lean muscle as he thrust…

"A shower sounds good," Dan said, his voice rough with lust.

Leif grinned and trailed a hand down Dan's side, over his hip, and along his cock—then rolled out of bed, leaving him hard and aching.

"Tease," Dan said with a grin.

Leif padded to the bathroom, giving Dan a very nice view of his tight butt and erect cock. He paused in the doorway and cast a playful look back over his shoulder. "Well? Are you coming?"

Steam billowed out of the shower when the hot water hit the cool morning air. They stood and kissed for a moment under the stream, water running down their faces and hair, until Dan pulled away with a laugh. "After the rain last night and now this, I think you're trying to drown me."

"Now that would be a waste," Leif said, and grabbed the bar of soap.

He went slowly, lathering Dan's chest, his shoulders and arms, and his back, before finally turning his attention to Dan's butt, hand sliding teasingly along his crease. They stood face-to-face; Dan sighed happily and leaned against his lover, soapy bodies sliding sensuously against each other, his legs parted slightly.

Leif moved farther down, lathering legs and feet, before sliding up to caress Dan's balls and cock. The combination of slick suds, warm water, and a firm hand sent heat curling through his balls and drew an animalistic groan from deep inside.

He captured Leif's hand and wrapped his fingers around the soap. "My turn."

The hot water made Leif's pale skin flush pink. Dan rubbed lather over it, tracing the stark black lines of the tattoos, tweaking the hardened nipples, then dipping across his flat belly to the soft thatch of golden curls surrounding his cock and shaved balls. Leif arched against him: lids heavy over blue eyes, breath coming in short excited pants.

"Do you like it when I touch you?" Dan asked, watching the pleasure on his lover's face.

"Sweet death, yes. Your hands feel good. All rough and strong and—mmm!" The last words were lost as Dan closed his hands around Leif's cock, forming a tunnel and tugging.

Dan licked his lips, feeling a bit uncertain. But Leif seemed to like what he'd done up until now, and if he was a little rusty, the only cure was more practice, right? "Turn around," he ordered.

Leif braced his hands against the back wall of the shower and spread his legs, like he was about to be patted down by the police. Dan lifted the heavy mass of Leif's wet hair and draped it over his shoulder. Lathering up his shoulders and back, Dan admired the lean muscles, the flare of a scapula, the curve of spine. The taut buttocks deserved attention, soap-slick fingers gliding over skin, drawing a sigh of pleasure in response.

Dan leaned in, his chest against Leif's back, reaching around to wrap his fingers around Leif's cock. This brought his own erection in contact with the crease of Leif's ass, soapy suds letting him slide slickly against it.

"Yes," Leif whispered, pushing back against him. Encouraged, Dan began to stroke his lover while rubbing himself against Leif's butt. It felt fantastic: slippery and hot and firm against his aching cock.

Leif moaned his name, head bowed between his outstretched arms. The curve between neck and shoulder tantalized, and Dan nipped him there lightly.

"Ah!" Leif pushed back, a shudder going through him. "Harder, please!"

His skin was hot against Dan's mouth and body, flushed from the shower. Dan laved the spot with his tongue, then bit harder, hips pushing against Leif's buttocks even as his hand stroked Leif's cock more urgently. Leif's pants spiraled up into groans, each one a spur to keep going, keep rubbing, keep up the friction against his aching member.

Leif's head arched back. "Yes, baby, please, don't stop, please, I'm close," he begged, voice cracking with pleasure, and it sent a jolt of sheer heat straight into Dan's groin.

"I'm not, I won't, want to take you there," he growled, his cock sliding in Leif's crease, everything hot and slick and cresting into scalding waves of pleasure.

He came, muffling his groan against Leif's shoulder, semen slicking Leif's thighs along with the pounding water of the shower.

"Ah! Yes!" Leif shouted, his cock twitching in Dan's fingers, come hitting the shower tiles as his narrow hips thrust helplessly against Dan's grip.

Dan released him, and Leif turned to face him, draping his arms over Dan's shoulders and kissing him softly. "Mmm. Best shower ever," Leif murmured against his lips.

"Yep." Dan kissed him again. "Shall we clean up from our clean up?"

It took a while, but they eventually got out of the shower. The laundry service delivered their cleaned and dried clothes while they were shaving. Leif took twice as long in the bathroom, since he carefully shaved his balls as well as his face, and applied a thick layer of eyeliner around his pale eyes.

"Breakfast?" Leif asked, while they dressed.

Dan hesitated. Conscience nagged at him: he had responsibilities back at the farm. He shouldn't be wasting his time lollygagging around Asheville with his...boyfriend? Lover, certainly.

Taryn will have gotten Bea and Virgil off to school. And Bea would have made sure the goats and chickens were fed. There's nothing that can't wait a few hours.

"I'd like that," he said, trying to drown out the little voice insisting he was being selfish and shirking his responsibilities. "I know a great little place to eat down on Wall Street, if you want."

Leif grinned. "Sounds fantastic."

They drove to a parking garage downtown. It felt odd—in a good way— to watch Leif climb out of the Porsche and saunter over to where he waited by the truck, knowing this gorgeous man was his.

"Why do you want me?" Dan blurted when Leif joined him. "I mean, you've been all over the world, you're handsome, you're experienced. You could have anybody. Why choose some backwoods hick who hadn't been laid in six years? Which sounded way more pathetic out loud than in my head, by the way. And let me tell you, it sounded pretty fucking sad in there."

Leif laughed and leaned in, pinning Dan against the truck's door with his body. "Well," he drawled, trailing his thumb across Dan's lips, "for one thing, you're awfully cute." His fingers slid down to cup Dan's chin, tilting his head back. "Not to mention, you're one of the good guys. I don't think you realize how rare that is."

He kissed Dan, hungry and possessive. Dan kissed back, forcing himself to ignore the same little voice screaming he couldn't do this, not in public.

I can be out here. Asheville isn't Ransom Gap, might as well be another world even if it's only an hour's drive away. No one was going to see, and certainly no one was going to care even if they did.

The narrow street was lined with gingko trees, their fan-shaped leaves gloriously gold against the blue autumn sky. Leif used his cell phone to take pictures of the bronze cats along the wall for which the street was named. The eatery they went to specialized in local ingredients, and works by Asheville artists hung on the walls.

Dan hadn't really had what he would call a boyfriend in college; more like a few good friends who had also been fuck buddies. It was strange to sit across a table from another man and know they were there as a couple. Leif ordered the tofu scramble; Dan had a berry waffle, and they watched each other eat with the intensity reserved for new lovers.

Leif snatched up the check when the tattooed waitress laid it on the table. "I can pay for my half," Dan objected, feeling his face heat slightly. Yeah, Leif had money, but Dan wasn't about to start leeching off him.

Leif's eyes softened in their rings of liner. "I know. But you're always doing things for me—for everyone, really. Let me take care of you for once. Please? I want to feel like a good boyfriend."

Boyfriend. "Well, if you put it that way," Dan said, warm all the way down to his toes.

At Leif's suggestion, they stopped in at the library and spent a fruitless hour looking for any references to either the Eye of the Uktena or the Witches Harrow. Having made this gesture toward duty, they spent the rest of the day wandering through the city together: investigating the little shops, admiring the architecture, enjoying the fall sunlight in the parks. For the first time in years, Dan talked about his time in college: revisiting the double-decker bus turned coffee shop where he'd hung out, the bookstore where a study group had met, and the civic center where he'd gone to see bands play.

"It sounds like you had good friends in college," Leif said, a bit wistfully. They stood beside Vance Monument, a rather phallic column memorializing a civil war governor.

"Yeah." Dan stared across the street at a middle-aged man sitting on the corner, playing a saxophone for tips. "I wonder what happened to them, sometimes."

"You didn't stay in touch with anyone?"

"Nah." Dan sighed and rolled his shoulders in his jacket, trying to shake off the sudden tension stiffening his muscles. "College was like a dream, you know? And Ransom Gap was the real world. The place I had to go back to when I woke up."

He felt Leif just behind him, not quite close enough to touch. "You've been through more things than most people have to face in a lifetime."

It made him want to laugh, although the sound would have been bitter. Given everything Leif had endured, he didn't see where he had any right to complain at all. "Could've been worse."

"It could always be worse. Not really the point. Did you ever intend to go back to Ransom Gap?"

"No." The admission stripped his throat raw, but he couldn't lie to Leif. "I figured I'd leave, go somewhere else. Somewhere I could be out." He shook his head. "Sometimes I wonder what I was thinking."

"What do you mean?"

Dan hesitated, not certain what he wanted to say. Leif believed he was one of the good guys. Would he still think well of Dan if he knew the truth?

Leif had been honest with him last night, even though it had obviously caused him pain. *I owe him that in return. No matter how bad it hurts.*

"I was selfish," he said, staring fixedly at the saxophone player. "I told you Mom died. Haint got her, like I said. I guess she got it back, though."

"You don't know?"

Dan shook his head. "No. I didn't feel that part. I didn't know anything was wrong until she was trying to get herself back up the slope to the car, fighting for her life. She reached out to me, because she needed my help. But I failed her, and she died there alone."

"Dan—"

"Let me finish. I should've come home for good. Given up any thought of moving away. Taken her place as a haint-worker; looked after the family. I should have done my duty."

Leif's hand came to rest on his shoulder, his grip firm through Dan's jacket. "Babe, no. You had the right to your dreams."

"You don't understand." Dan took a deep breath, trying to calm his racing pulse. "I went home for the funeral, but I came back here. Went to class, slept with guys, had fun. It was all about me, about what I wanted. In early March, though, Bea called me. It was one in the morning, and she was crying her eyes out, said she'd been trying, but she and Virgil were hungry, and she couldn't get the fire to light, and she just didn't know what to do." She'd sounded so scared, and the memory still made his chest ache and his eyes burn.

"See, it turned out Dad had been drinking himself into a stupor every day since the funeral. Not taking care of the farm, not making any money, barely even buying groceries. And Bea had been trying to keep it together, keep Virgil and her fed and going to school, but she was only eleven years old."

Leif's fingers tightened. "I'm sorry, Dan. For all of you. But it wasn't your fault."

"If I'd stayed, things would've been different. I'd have held it together. Kept Dad in one piece, yelled at him enough, thrown out the booze. Done something.

"I went home. Dropped out of school and tried to remember everything I could about farming. Thank Demeter the farm was paid for free and clear. A mortgage would've put us under. But it was too late for Dad. I'd waited too long. I failed him, too."

"Dan, please, listen." Leif turned him gently, until they faced each other. "Your father made his own choices. You aren't responsible for what he did."

Dan shook his head miserably, unable to look Leif in the eye. "You don't know. If I'd stayed, taken some of the burden…but I didn't, and Dad couldn't deal, and he…died."

Leif sighed. "I know."

"You know?"

"Yes." Leif winced, and now it was his turn to look away. "The day we were at the Ransom County Library, I looked up the police reports for your parents' deaths. I'm sorry. I shouldn't have pried."

"No. It's all right." And, a little to his own surprise, Dan realized it was. "After all, everybody else in the county knows Dad hung himself from the oak."

Still, saying the words out loud felt wrong. He'd grown up knowing you didn't talk about the bad things. Good things were fair game, and common inconveniences, but the really ugly, painful stuff never got spoken of, even among family.

But somehow talking to Leif about it didn't seem too bad. "I guess you probably figured out he wouldn't move on. Too hurt, too mad at me, too mad at Mom...I don't know why, really. But he became a haint in the tree, and I had to make him go. First and last solo work I ever did."

Leif leaned in closer, his blue eyes serious. "Listen to me. It wasn't your fault. You didn't do anything wrong."

"I should've felt something, when I laid him. I should have felt sad, or guilty, or something. But I didn't. I just felt empty. I'd been mad at him, the last couple of months he was alive, because I had to come back and take over, but even that was gone. There was just nothing left. Tell me, what kind of guy puts a hook of antler through his Dad's forehead and doesn't feel anything? Not a good guy, Leif. Don't get the wrong idea about me."

Leif pulled him in for a hug; the difference in their heights made it easy for Dan to lean his head against Leif's shoulder. "A human being feels that way," Leif said. "A decent human being, who's ashamed because he was *rightfully* pissed, but can't let himself feel it because he doesn't want to disrespect the dead."

"If I had—"

"Your father was wrong." Leif cut him off harshly. "I'm sorry. I know it's hard to hear, but it's the truth. You were only, what, nineteen at the time? The man had a responsibility to his kids, and if he couldn't live up to it, it was his duty to get some help and *not* lay it on you."

"It isn't like that," Dan said, pulling away. "If I'd just come home—"

"Nothing would have changed. You can't force someone to want to live. They have to make the decision on their own." Leif caught one of his hands and drew it close. "It wasn't wrong of you to want something for yourself. It didn't somehow make your father lose his shit. You're entitled to your life, Dan, and it doesn't mean trying to live out the one he gave up as some kind of penance."

Dan winced and looked away. "I owe it to Bea and Virgil. My fault or not, it surely wasn't theirs. I have to do right by them. I have to give them the chance to get out of Ransom Gap. And...I can't risk being out when we're back home."

It hurt to say the words. It had been hard enough to go back into the closet when he'd moved home. Doing it a second time, after glimpsing what he might have had with Leif, was almost unbearable.

"I haven't forgotten what you said the morning you showed me the meditation rock." Leif let go of Dan's hand and stepped back, putting distance between them. "Would it make things easier if I found somewhere else to stay?"

"No!" Dan moved closer, touching Leif's arm lightly. "No, please. Nobody will think anything of you and Taryn staying with us."

And I want to wake up beside you. But it sounded too selfish to say aloud.

"All right." Leif agreed, and it seemed he brightened a little. "What do you say we grab a beer at the place we passed on Patton Ave.?"

CHAPTER 21

L eif steered the Porsche up the bumpy gravel driveway, the clouds of dust thrown up by Dan's truck leaving a tan layer on the black paint. The sun had slid down the sky into the west, and golden light flashed off the windows of the farmhouse as it came into view. The ancient oak formed a black mass against the brighter sky.

Poor Dan—poor all of them—to have such a prominent reminder of their father's death.

His hands tightened on the steering wheel, remembering the raw pain in Dan's voice. Normally, he would have nothing but sympathy for anyone as troubled as Harvey Miller. In this case, seeing the anguish the man's suicide had caused his children made it difficult to muster anything except fury. *And Dan, blaming himself for his father's death as well as his mother's, having to carry that burden alongside the responsibility for keeping the farm going, and raising Virgil and Bea...*

He's amazing. And he doesn't even see it.

The day had been like something out of a dream. He felt oddly light, free almost; even his chronic headaches had stayed away, at least until he was back in the car by himself.

They'd returned with a vengeance on the drive back, accompanied by those whispers of doubt. *He doesn't care about you. He's only using you.* But the doubts lacked any real force; they were too unlike Dan.

Dan parked his truck beside a big, mean-looking 1967 Camaro SS, painted black and tricked out all over in chrome, which must belong to Taryn. *And speak of the devil.*

She came out onto the porch and stood with her hands loose and casual —and near her knives. He could feel her attention on him even before he climbed out of the car. *I'm guessing she isn't here to welcome me back.*

The front door burst open, and a slim figure darted out. "Leif!" Bea shouted, running into the yard to throw her arms around him. "I'm glad Dan found you!"

Startled, he returned the hug. "Me too."

"Here, let me help you with your bag. And don't mind Taryn. She'll come around." Grinning brightly, Bea grabbed his bag out of the trunk and slung it over her shoulder.

Leif glanced at Dan, who shrugged. "Bea might have talked some sense into me, before I came looking for you," he admitted.

"You bet I did. Come on, you're just in time for dinner. I cooked."

"Well, we've still got the number for Poison Control posted by the phone," Dan said resignedly.

Bea stuck her tongue out at him in reply. Leif pulled the rest of his things out of the trunk and followed them to the house. It made him feel oddly warm to think Bea liked him enough to convince Dan to come after him. Like family, almost—except for him, family consisted of a junkie mother, a rapist foster father, and Rúnar.

Not like family at all, then. Or, just maybe, this was a different kind of family: the right kind. The sort he might not even have believed existed, until he'd seen it himself. They had problems, gods knew, but they still cared about each other.

Even Virgil, who looked none too happy when he stuck his head out the door. "Great. *He's* back."

"Be civil," Dan snapped.

"I moved my stuff into my room. I'm done sleeping on the couch!"

"That's fine," Dan said tightly. "Leif doesn't need your room anymore."

Leif tried to look as if the announcement didn't come as a surprise. Even though he knew Dan had come out to his family, he hadn't really expected Dan to acknowledge their relationship to anyone back in Ransom Gap, even within the safety of the farmhouse.

Virgil's eyes narrowed in anger. "I can't believe you're doing this, you fucking faggot!"

The tension was thick enough to be palpable, like a line drawn between the brothers: Virgil in his stylish hair and khakis, and Dan in his battered jacket and jeans, shoulder-length locks blowing on the breeze. They had the same dark eyes, both blazing with fury.

"You and I are going to have a long talk, right now," Dan said, and although his tone was low, the words cut the air like scythes.

Virgil's lower lip trembled slightly, but he pulled himself up. "Screw you. Freddie is going to pick me up at the end of the drive. I'm going somewhere I can breathe."

"Virgil, stop it!" Bea yelled, but her younger brother ignored her, stomping off down the driveway.

For a moment, Leif thought Dan might run after Virgil and try to physically restrain him. Instead the fight seemed to go out of Dan. His broad shoulders slumped and he shook his head. "I don't know what I'm going to do about that boy. I really don't."

"Virgil's a jerk," Bea said with a glance at Leif, as if worried he might leave again. "Don't let him get to you, okay?"

"I won't." Virgil had his issues, but Leif wasn't in much position to judge, given some of the things he'd done at that age.

Dan and Bea went into the house. As Leif followed them, he had to pass Taryn, who didn't seem inclined to get out of his way.

"I'm watching you, motherfucker," she said, her hand closing hard on his arm to stop him. "Dante and Bea say you've changed your ways. But I say a snake who's shed his old skin is still a snake."

His jaw tightened, but he swallowed down the reflexive anger. "I know I've done things I can't ever put entirely right. I'm not asking you to change your mind, or to forgive me. Just let me do the job I came here to do."

She didn't give an inch. "I've been friends with Dan for a long time. My teacher knew Simone from way back, and we came up here for a few weeks every summer. If you break that boy's heart, I promise you I will stick a knife through yours."

"I'll let you," Leif agreed, and pushed past her into the house.

Taryn cornered Dan after dinner, as he'd expected. He'd headed outside to close up the chickens in their coop for the night, and she followed on his heels, soundless as a shadow. She'd put on a long, leather coat against the evening chill, and it flared out behind her as she walked.

"Miss the old days of helping out on the farm?" he asked lightly as he approached the coop. The chickens knew the routine, and as the sun was almost down, they'd already gone inside to roost for the night.

"Yeah, right," she muttered. "You know why I'm out here. Figured we could talk in private."

Dan kept his sigh inside his head. He checked the food and water, before closing up the coop securely to keep out any raccoons or coyotes that might be looking for a chicken dinner. Once he was done, he leaned his shoulder against the side of the coop, hands in his pockets, and met Taryn's gaze. "Talk."

His haint-worker's sight picked her out easily in the growing dark: black curls drawn back from a strong face; fierce, no-nonsense eyes; and the lean, tough build of someone who'd done more than her share of fighting.

"You want me to say it? Fine. You're thinking with your dick. Leif Helsvin is bad news with a pretty face, and you're just letting him lead you around by your balls."

"You're wrong."

"He lied to you about being involved with Rúnar. He tortured the dead to get revenge on the living. A Walker, Alice, died because of him, and maybe he didn't do the deed himself, but it was still his fault. You're just going to let that slide?"

"It's not a matter of me letting it slide. Don't you think we talked about this?"

She folded her arms across her chest and gave him a cold look. "Actually, no. I think he flashed you a nice smile and wiggled his ass, and once you'd fucked him—"

"Stop. Right there." Dan came off the coop and walked toward her. "I'm serious, Taryn. After all those summers your teacher came up here to visit with Mom and dragged you along, all the times we talked on the phone about haints or whined to each other about how hard our apprenticeships were, I'd think you'd know me better than that."

"I figured I did, but I never thought you'd side with a necromancer, either."

"Leif is trying to put things right. Don't act like you've never done anything wrong. You and I have both fucked up, but we did what we could to fix things and learn from our mistakes. Why can't you give Leif the same chance?"

Her lip twisted in obvious disgust. "Listen to yourself! Leif didn't just make a 'mistake.' He didn't just screw up. He deliberately used necromancy to hurt people, the living and the dead."

Dan ground his teeth. "I get that Leif did some bad shit, all right? I probably know more about it than you do, because, yes, we fucking well *talked* about it. Or are you saying I'm the kind of guy who doesn't care what's screwing him, as long as he's getting laid?"

"Shit," she muttered. "I didn't say that."

"I'd fucking hope not."

"Just tell me one thing, and be honest, to yourself if not to me. Would you trust him like this even if he weren't your type? If he were a woman?"

"Yes." No hesitation.

She looked away, obviously not liking his response. "He's going to break your heart, Dan."

Hecate's bitches, what a low blow. "You don't know him."

"Sure I do. His type breeze into town, have a good time, and are gone again just as quick. They don't care what wreckage they leave behind, whether there's ghosts as need laying, or lonely men pining for them."

Leif had told him about Kristian. It had been hard to hear, even though they hadn't had any understanding at the time—the opposite, in fact, since Dan had been trying to convince himself not to get involved with Leif.

Leif had begged forgiveness, whether for the sex, or for calling the boy by Dan's name, or for Kristian's death at Rúnar's hands, Dan didn't know.

All of them, probably.

And he didn't hold any of it against Leif. But he had to admit Taryn was right: the man did have a pattern, and when he left town on the first, Dan would surely be just one more notch on a heavily-whittled bedpost.

Sensing his hesitation, Taryn pressed her advantage. "He doesn't care about you, Dan. You're just a convenient lay."

"That's not true," Leif said tightly.

Shit. Dan and Taryn both turned at the same time, probably looking equally guilty.

"How long have you been sneaking around, snake?" she asked with a curl of her upper lip.

Leif met Taryn's sneer with one of his own. "I wasn't *sneaking.* I came out here because I thought the three of us should discuss how we're going to stop Rúnar. It isn't my fault you were too busy assassinating my character to notice."

"Not sure you have enough character to assassinate."

"Enough," Dan said. Surprisingly, they both fell silent and left off glaring at each other to look at him. "Taryn, I appreciate your concern, but I'm an adult. It's none of your business who I'm sleeping with."

She cut a hard glance in Leif's direction. "Doesn't mean he's trustworthy, either."

"I trust him."

The grateful look on Leif's face warmed him. Taryn, on the other hand, seemed downright pissed. Too bad.

"I trust him," Dan repeated. "I believe he's changed. And you can either accept it or you can go back to Birmingham. Your choice."

Taryn's expression didn't shift, but after a minute, she reluctantly nodded her head. "Fine. Just don't bitch when I get to say 'I told you so.'"

"Fuck you," Leif snapped, his blue eyes going hard and dangerous.

Hecate's bitches. "Can we leave off fighting each other and concentrate on fighting Rúnar?"

"Fine." Taryn folded her arms over her chest, the leather of her long coat creaking. "Give me a rundown on the situation."

Leif remained silent while Dan talked, but he shifted closer, dropping a possessive hand to Dan's waist. Repressing a sigh, Dan pretended not to notice.

"No idea where this place of power might be?" Taryn asked when he was done.

"Nope."

"And you think Rúnar's going to make his move on Halloween?"

"That's about the shape of it."

"Any idea what he might do when he gets there?"

Leif finally spoke up. "Rúnar wants power. Or, no—he wants control, to be more precise."

"What do you mean?" Taryn asked, not bothering to conceal her skepticism.

The corners of Leif's mouth tightened and his eyes darkened with old memories. "Everything around him must be as he's ordered it. Possessions. People. The easiest way to make it happen is by gathering enough money to buy loyalty, or enough power to intimidate."

"Same as Ezekiel," Dan said.

Leif nodded. "At a guess, he wants to use the Harrow to threaten anyone who challenges him. Don't forget, he's a sorcerer as well as a necromancer. With that sort of energy behind his spells, he could crush anyone he perceives to be an enemy."

Taryn's eyes narrowed, but she gave a grudging nod. "Makes sense."

"Wow, thanks for the vote of confidence," Leif said with mock-sweetness.

"What's our plan?" Dan asked hurriedly, before things could get out of hand. "We've got to keep Rúnar from getting to the Harrow with the Eye of the Uktena. But how?"

"If we could find where it is, maybe we could dynamite the entrance to the cave," Taryn speculated.

"You have C4 in your car?" Leif asked archly.

"No, motherfucker, I don't. But there are ways to get things on short notice. Something I'm sure you know."

Leif shrugged. "You're probably right. Fine. We still have the little problem of finding the cave in the first place."

"Spelunking is big around here, right?" Taryn asked Dan.

"Not here." Dan shrugged. "Other counties, yeah. But there aren't any deep caves nearby—or at least, none anybody knows about."

"Of course not. Have you tried a pendulum?"

"Haven't had time to even think of it, but it's a good suggestion."

"All right." She straightened her shoulders, her coat snapping softly around her. "I'll grab my pendulum and hit the roads tomorrow. See if I can find the cave."

Leif looked skeptical. "Surely Jedediah's seal would keep anyone from finding it easily."

"Maybe—be we can't know until we try, right?" Dan asked.

Taryn smirked. "Exactly. Unless you've got a better idea?" she added in Leif's direction.

He let out a small sigh and shook his head. "No. I don't. But I would like to go back over the journals and make certain we haven't missed any clues."

"Good idea," Dan said quickly. *Fuck, this is getting exhausting.*

"All right." Taryn turned and strode back in the direction of the house. "Let's get to it."

CHAPTER 22

"Want some help with your chores?" Leif asked the next morning.

Dan glanced up. He sat on the mud bench by the back door, tying on his heavy work boots. Bea and Virgil were off to school, and Taryn had left to drive around the county with her pendulum.

Leif was fresh out of the shower, his long hair damp across the shoulders of his black shirt, his pale skin still pink from the warm water. He looked absolutely edible, leaning against the doorway, arms folded and his hip cocked sexily to one side.

Down boy. "I don't know," Dan said dubiously. "Maybe you should just go over the diaries and our notes again, in case there's some clue we missed."

Leif shrugged and grinned. "In other words: 'Stay out of the way, city boy.'"

"That isn't it. Entirely," he admitted when Leif shot him a skeptical look. "But the other needs doing, too."

"All right. Do you mind if I bring the books out to the barn while you work and keep you company? I like being near you."

It felt strange—wonderfully strange—to have someone want to be near him, let alone a man like Leif. "That would be great."

Leif fetched his jacket and slung it around his shoulders, while Dan poured coffee into a pair of travel mugs. As Leif passed by on the way to the back door, his arms full of books, he paused and leaned in close.

"By the way," he murmured, "I put in a butt plug. It's in me right now, filling me, stretching me, making me ache for more. Just to give you something to think about this morning."

Dan swallowed against the desire tightening his throat and chest and making his jeans suddenly uncomfortable. "How do you expect me to work with this hard-on?"

Leif chuckled. "Makes things interesting, doesn't it?"

It took Dan a few deep breaths to calm down enough to walk. They went out to the barn; the goats were still out in the pasture, but soon enough they'd need to be under cover at night. Leif found a comfortable seat on a stack of hay bales, while Dan set himself to clearing the old straw out of the goat stalls.

Leif lounged on the hay, reading intently. Whenever Dan's eyes lingered on him, though, he'd shift position with a throaty sigh, or absently rub his cock through his jeans. It kept Dan half-hard all morning, and the only thing he could think of was tearing off Leif's clothes and fucking him senseless.

As Leif had said, it did make things interesting.

He held out until lunch. At noon, though, he called a break. As soon as they were back inside in the house, Dan pounced, grabbing Leif from behind, trapping the other man's arms against his sides.

"Gods, you've been driving me crazy for hours," he growled, nuzzling the back of Leif's neck.

"I thought you wanted lunch," Leif said teasingly, pushing back against Dan.

"Oh, I'm hungry, all right," he murmured, dropping one hand to rub at Leif's erection while grinding against him from behind.

"There's a condom and lube in my front pocket," Leif gasped. "I brought them just in case we got carried away in the barn."

"Bend over the couch. I'm going to fuck you right now."

Leif let out a little moan, seeming to like Dan's commanding tone. He fumbled at his belt and jeans, let them fall to his ankles, and bent obediently over the back of the couch.

And, gods, what a sight that tight ass was. His hands trembling with lust, Dan managed to unzip his fly and pull out his aching cock.

"Please, baby, hurry," Leif begged. "I need you."

The words made his cock even harder, pre-come beading on the tip. Somehow, he managed to retrieve the condom from the puddle of Leif's jeans and get it on, slicking it thoroughly with lube.

Leif moaned when he pulled out the butt plug. "I'm ready for you!"

It was all the encouragement Dan needed. Gripping Leif's hips, he shoved into that tight, welcoming heat. Leif groaned and pushed back against him, wanting more, and it was everything Dan could do to keep from coming on the spot.

He leaned over Leif's back, nipping at him through the thin fabric of the t-shirt. "You feel incredible."

"Oh, gods, you do too. Fuck me, Dan, please!"

Unable to resist such a request, Dan began to move, thrusting slowly. The tight ring of muscle gripped his cock, as if wanting to keep it buried deep inside. Leaning, back, he watched himself disappear into his lover's body. Combined with Leif's whimpers and moans, the sight made his balls tingle and tense, so he picked up the pace. Leif cried out in encouragement, fingers digging into the back of the couch, and gods, it was sexy, having him beg and plead and moan with pleasure while Dan fucked his ass—

The front door swung open. "Dan? You home?" Marlene called cheerfully as she stepped inside. "I brought a pumpkin pie from the store—"

Time froze. Dan's brain flailed, caught between the edge of orgasm and the shock of Marlene's interruption. She seemed equally stunned, her mouth a silent "oh" of shock, her hands clutched around the store-bought pie.

The pie fell from her grasp and hit the floor.

Dan lurched back and away from Leif, frantically stuffing his softening penis into his pants, condom and all. "Shit! Marlene—"

She shook her head slowly, backing away. "How could you?" she whispered, tears springing to her eyes. "How could you do this to me?"

"Marlene," he repeated, reaching for her, "listen, just—let's talk about this—"

"Don't touch me, you sick bastard!" she shouted, and he flinched back.

She ran out, the door banging shut behind her. "Marlene!" Dan yelled, hurrying onto the porch after her. But it was too late; she was already in her car, peeling out in a squeal of tires and flying gravel.

Shit. Oh shit.

Maybe she won't tell anyone. Maybe...

This is Marlene. She's going to tell everyone in the fucking county.

"Dan?" Leif asked uncertainly from behind him.

What am I going to do? Say she's lying? Would anyone believe me over her?

"Dan?" Leif repeated. "Do you want me to leave?"

Startled out of his thoughts, he turned and saw Leif waiting by the door, his jeans up but his belt still unfastened. His skin had gone deathly white, and his blue eyes were wide and vulnerable in their circles of eyeliner.

It was enough to snap Dan out of it. *What was I thinking?* Bad enough he'd asked Leif to be his dirty little secret, but ask him to lie about it when they'd been caught? To pretend it had never happened, to outright deny they were anything more than friends?

"No. No, of course not." Dan pressed his fingers into his eyes. "Hecate's bitches, why did she have to just barge in?"

Because she's Marlene. She'd done this sort of shit ever since the divorce.

No. Be honest. She'd done it since they'd had lunch together a few times, then dinner, and she'd started coming over every couple of weeks for movie night, and they'd done things like dance together at the Apple Days

Festival. Since she'd started acting like his girlfriend, and he hadn't done a single thing to dissuade her from it, because it made his life easier.

Fuck. She must feel like shit right about now.

"I'm sorry," Dan said, running his hand back through his hair. "I'm going to call her."

"I'll clean up," Leif offered, gesturing at the remains of the pie. There was a boot print in the middle of the spill, where Dan had stepped in it on his way out the door.

"Thanks." But Leif still looked uncertain, and if the situation was a fucking mess, it surely wasn't his fault. "I'm sorry, sweetheart. I should've locked the door."

Leif shrugged and gave him a small, sad smile. "I didn't think of it, either. I never meant to cause any trouble for you."

"This isn't your fault," Dan said, and pulled him into a hug. "Please, quit blaming yourself. I can't take it right now, okay?"

"Sorry." Leif hugged him back. "Call her. Maybe you can convince her she didn't see what she thought."

"No. I won't lie. I'm going to apologize for leading her on."

Leif looked uncomfortable. "Yeah."

See? Not such a nice guy after all, am I?

Either she wasn't in range of a cell tower, or she wasn't taking any calls from him, because he ended up in her voice mail. "Marlene, I'm sorry," he said. "I really am. Just give me a call, all right? I need to talk to you."

Hanging up the phone, he leaned his head briefly against the refrigerator. The sounds of Leif cleaning up came from the living room, and for a minute he tried to believe the entire situation could be mopped up as easily. He'd apologize to Marlene, she'd forgive him, and his secret would stay safe.

Sure. That's what will happen. Everything will be fine.

Fuck.

"What next, Danny-boy?" Taryn asked after dinner.

When Bea and Virgil went upstairs to do homework, the three adults headed out to the back yard. Taryn dragged up three folding lawn chairs, Dan started a small fire in a burn barrel, and Leif fetched a beer for each of them from the fridge.

The air was crisp bordering on cold, making Leif glad for his jacket and the warmth coming from the barrel. The apple-wood smoke blended a sweet tang with the breath of the humid mountain air. Overhead, a million stars wheeled through the sky, competing with the glow of the city in the distance. It reminded him of the trip to the steppes, the nights spent sleeping in tents, the nearest artificial lights hundreds of miles distant. There had been more stars visible there than he'd ever dreamed could exist.

I wish I could show those stars to Dan. I bet he'd love to see them.

Leif glanced at Dan, who sat beside him, staring at the flames dancing in the barrel. A dark cloud had hung over him all afternoon. No doubt he'd spent every moment worrying about what might happen now someone else in Ransom Gap knew he was gay. Marlene hadn't returned any of his calls, and while Leif hoped she wouldn't do anything to get back at Dan, he remembered all too well the pain in her voice when she'd caught them together.

Not "how could you do this" but "how could you do this to me." Which meant it had hurt her on a personal level.

Dan hadn't mentioned the incident to anyone else, though, or even spoken much at all. Leif desperately wanted to bring back his smile, to make him feel better, but what could he do when he was part of the problem?

Now Dan roused himself with a shake and looked at Taryn. "What?"

She frowned, shapely brows drawing together. "Are you all right? You've been mighty quiet tonight."

"I'm fine." He took a sip from his beer. "The pendulum didn't turn up anything?" An easy guess, since she'd come back just before sunset, slamming her car door behind her and stalking up to the house as if the universe had personally gone out of its way to annoy her.

"No," she muttered. Her dark eyes flickered to Leif, as if expecting him to deride her for failing. He sipped his beer instead.

"What do we do now?" she asked Dan. "Time's short, in case you've forgotten. We've got three days—less—to figure this shit out."

"Yeah." Dan sighed. "I don't know what to do next. I truly don't." A log shifted in the burn barrel, casting a sudden flare of light across Dan's features. He looked young and vulnerable, and Leif ached to hold him. "We're out of options."

And, gods, Leif hadn't wanted to bring it up. But as usual, he did what he had to, not what he wanted. "I could try necromancy. Not summoning the dead like Rúnar is doing, of course, but going to them and asking for their help."

"You mean world-walking?" Dan asked worriedly.

"Yes."

Taryn took a swing of beer, her dark eyes fixed on him over the bottle, as if trying to figure out what angle he was playing. "Might work," she allowed.

"World-walking isn't like taking a trip down to Asheville, Taryn," Dan said, an edge in his voice, as if he thought she might be encouraging Leif out of spite.

"I know that, Danny," she snapped. "I finished my apprenticeship same as you."

It was the final trial every apprentice went through. In order to properly work with the dead, every deathwalker had to make the journey to the Underworld, whatever form it might take for him or her, whether the gates of Hel-heim, or the barge over the river Styx, or the journey beneath the astral sea to the world of the *ghede.*

Walkers who worked with the living had their own journey to make, Al-ice had said.

The danger came from the simple fact the Otherworld was inhabited, and Walkers were never anything more than tourists. Spirits were sometimes attracted to them—spirits no longer human, if they ever had been. Some of them were friendly and willing to help on the journey. Others devoured wan-derers for snacks. The most dangerous were the ones who seemed helpful, until it was too late for the astral human to escape their snare.

Leif's first Journey through the nine worlds had been frightening. Rúnar had drummed for him, the sound carrying him out of his body at the begin-ning, and drawing him back into it in the end. He'd passed the test, traveling through each of the nine worlds, until he reached the gates of Helheim.

The second Journey had been less guided. Clinging to the root of a nurs-ery tree in one of the great forests of the Pacific Northwest, his back on fire from the lash, his spirit had broken free—or been pulled, maybe. Hel had been waiting for him, that time.

Waiting to take him apart and put him back together in a new configura-tion, the old bits and pieces she had no use for torn free and discarded forev-er. The experience had been necessary, but necessity never made anything less terrifying or painful.

"I've walked between the worlds more than once," he said carefully. "I know the way to Helheim. I'll make an offering first and ask for Hel to grant me an audience."

And maybe I'll see Her again. He'd faced his goddess only once, and he couldn't precisely say it had been pleasant, but that sort of experience went beyond such simple concepts as pleasant or painful.

"I don't like it," Dan said. "But I don't see as we've got any other choice."

"Let's plan for tomorrow night. Sunset." Liminal times were always best for Journeying.

Taryn stretched like a cat; the ankh around her neck reflected the fire-light in a quick orange flash. "If that's decided, I'm going to bed. My teacher always said to get sleep when you could, because you never knew when you'd have to do without. The same with food, come to think of it."

"Good advice," Leif said. She gave him a sharp look, as if she expected sarcasm and was disconcerted not to find it.

Taryn left, her boots crunching through fallen leaves, the door squeaking to mark her passage. Once she was gone, Dan shuffled his chair close enough to lean against Leif. Pleasantly surprised, Leif draped his arm around his lover, drawing him closer.

"I'm sorry I haven't been very good company this evening," Dan said, unhappiness and guilt twisting the words.

Leif winced. The scene with Marlene had been...well, not as ugly as it could have been, all things considered. But Dan was still in pain. "I understand, baby."

Dan shook his head. "You've been more patient with me than I deserve. I used Marlene, and I was planning to lie about you. Think I'm such a nice guy now?"

"I told you I understood you couldn't be out with me."

"And did you understand about Marlene?"

I was hoping you wouldn't ask. "I was never comfortable with it," Leif admitted, because he'd already lied enough to Dan and never wanted to do it again. "I do think you owe her an apology. But you've been trying to give one all afternoon; the ball is in her court now. If she won't accept it, there's nothing more you can do."

Dan drained his beer. "Want to go to bed? Just to cuddle. I don't really feel up to more tonight. I'm sorry."

"There's nothing to be sorry for." Leif kissed him again. "It's not just about the sex, you know."

Dan's dark eyes softened, warm as melted chocolate. "No, it's not," he agreed.

CHAPTER 23

Breakfast the next morning was quiet, if you didn't count Taryn bitching about the lack of meat on the table. When the kids headed down to the bus stop, Taryn went into the living room and the pile of journals, hoping to find some clue Dan and Leif had both missed.

As for Leif, he'd skipped breakfast and instead gone out to the meditation rock, where he'd made an offering to Hel: dark beer, bittersweet chocolate, and his own blood. After, he would meditate and fast for the day, in preparation for his Walk.

Dan planned to do chores, before joining Taryn. Although he didn't really think they'd missed anything in the journals, the books represented their only hope other than Leif's Walk. *And if we find something, he won't have to go between worlds. He won't have to risk himself.*

The phone rang as he passed it. Automatically, he picked it up. "Hoary Oak Hill Farm, Dan speaking."

"Dan." Bea's voice, filled with tears.

"What's wrong?" A thousand scenarios jumped to mind: the bus had driven off the side of the road into a ravine, or someone had kidnapped Bea and Virgil both, or—

"Th-the mailbox…"

The mailbox? "What about it?"

Virgil's voice came across, strong and angry, as if he'd grabbed the phone away from his big sister. "Somebody hit it with a baseball bat and painted 'fag' on it. Happy?"

No. It wasn't anything he hadn't expected in theory, and yet the reality settled in his belly like a heavy stone. Marlene had talked, probably to every customer at the store last night. And in a small community like Ransom Gap, once a scandal started to spread, there was no stopping it.

"I see," Dan said. His lips felt numb.

Bea took back the phone. "I'm sorry, Dan."

"I'm the one who ought to apologize." He hadn't said anything about the incident yesterday, naïvely hoping to protect the kids from any fallout. "I probably should have let you know something like this might happen. Marlene came over yesterday and caught Leif and me making out." It had been considerably more than that, but he surely wasn't going into details with his sister. "She was pretty upset."

"Oh." Bea was quiet for a minute. "You don't think...I mean, she wouldn't do this, would she?"

"Probably not. But if she told someone else, and they told someone. Things spread. I'm sorry. I probably should've warned you, but I was hoping it wouldn't affect you guys. Pretty dumb of me."

"The bus is coming."

Hecate's bitches, he hated to hear the unhappy note in her voice. "All right. We'll talk after school. I love you, baby girl."

"Love you, too."

After she hung up, he stared at the phone for a few minutes without really seeing it. It wasn't fair. He'd spent years in the closet, trying to protect Bea and Virgil from shit like this, and all it took was one afternoon to make the whole effort meaningless.

He hung up the phone and went outside, telling himself there were chores as needed doing, whether he felt like working or not. Instead of going straight to the barn, though, he veered in the direction of the meditation rock, stopping a short distance away from it.

Leif sat cross-legged on the stone, his fair hair shining in the morning sun. His long-fingered hands rested lightly on the knees of his black jeans, and his back was straight, shoulders relaxed. The acrid scent of burning hung on the air, and a small pile of ashes lay on the rock in front of him. A used scalpel blade lay to one side, and he sported a fresh Band-Aid on his wrist.

He was handsome, strong, calm and contained. How could anyone hate him, without even knowing the first thing about him?

Dan must have made some small sound without realizing it, because Leif turned to look at him. His brows snapped together instantly in concern. "What's the matter?"

"Nothing. I didn't mean to disturb you."

"It's all right." Leif climbed to his feet and crossed the lawn. "And don't tell me nothing is wrong, when I can tell from the look on your face."

They hadn't known each other for long, and already Leif could read him like a book. "You're right. Bea called from the bottom of the drive."

Leif frowned as Dan told him about the mailbox. "Fuckers. Have you called the police yet?"

"No. Don't see much point, really. Mailboxes get bashed in all the time out here."

"They have to investigate. This is a hate crime."

"Not in North Carolina."

Leif swore, and his eyes darkened with anger.

"I'm sorry," Dan said unhappily. "You're supposed to be meditating, and here I am, distracting you with this shit."

Leif's hands closed around his shoulders, the fingers warm and strong through the fabric of his shirt. "You're not a distraction, baby. You're never a distraction."

"I could take my shirt off," Dan said, with a half-hearted smile at the lame joke.

It got Leif to smile, though, which was what he'd hoped to do. "Not the kind of distraction I meant. I only meant that-that you're important to me."

He tried not to read too much into Leif's words, but he couldn't deny it gave him a little thrill to hear them. "Thanks, but this is important, too."

"Yeah," Leif agreed with a sigh. His gaze lingered on Dan's lips, as if wanting to kiss him. But Dan knew Leif's fast wasn't just of food, but of anything else able to ground him too closely in his physical body, which meant anything sexual was off the menu. "I should get back to it. Just let me know if anything else happens. You shouldn't have to deal with this alone."

"We shouldn't have to deal with it at all." Dan didn't bother to keep the bitterness out of the words.

Leif winced. "Yeah."

The next phone call was from the preacher at the First Baptist Church. Dan let the machine get it, opting instead to stand by the fridge and listen, fighting the urge to punch something all the while.

"I had a long talk with Marlene Stoddard last night," the parson said, his voice pitched to indicate deep concern. "She's very worried about you. She feels you may have fallen in with the wrong crowd. Outside influences—" meaning Leif, no doubt "—may seem exciting and new, but it's good old-fashioned values as get us through the hard times. I'd like to invite you and your family to services on Sunday—"

"And I'd like for you to mind your fucking business," Dan snarled at the answering machine, before storming out of the room and back to the barn. At least he couldn't hear the phone ring out there.

Unfortunately, the next call he couldn't ignore. It was from Virgil's principal.

"What were you thinking?" Dan demanded, as he climbed into the truck. Virgil was already slouched on the passenger side, his backpack on the floor between his feet. "You know better than this."

Virgil shrugged and stared out the window, glaring at the school as if he could burn it down with his anger alone. There was a dark bruise under his left eye and scrapes on the knuckles of his right hand, but fortunately there hadn't been any real damage. According to the principal, teachers had separated the boys before things got too serious. Both were suspended for five days.

Dan threw the truck into gear and tried a different tactic. "The principal said you were fighting with Freddie."

"What's it matter to you?" Virgil didn't look at him, just kept staring out the window as they rolled out of the parking lot.

"I just thought the two of you were friends, that's all."

"We were—until he found out you're a fag!"

Shit. Dan's hands tightened on the steering wheel, bracing for an impact totally emotional instead of physical. "Why the fight?" He kept his voice deliberately light. "Figured it would give you more to talk about, not less."

"Screw you, Danny! I told him it wasn't any of his fucking business. But he started talking shit, started saying I must be a fag, too, and-and other stuff, awful stuff, and I just—I couldn't—I had to make him shut up. I hit him, and he hit me, and-and why do you have to be like this, *why?*"

Virgil's voice rose into a hoarse cry of misery on the last word, his fist hitting the dashboard again and again in fury, even as tears slid down his face. Horrified, Dan pulled off onto the berm, unsnapped his seatbelt, and slid over to put his arms around his little brother.

"Hey," he said. "Hey, Virge, it's okay."

"No it's not." Virgil was tense, as if torn between the desire to accept comfort and to shove Dan away. At least he hadn't thrown another punch. "Why, Dan? Why?"

Dan's heart was a lump of lead in his chest. "It's just the way things are."

"Y-You care more about your homo boyfriend than about Bea and me. You're going to leave us, just like Mom left us!"

Dan sat back, as stunned as if Virgil had hit him. "What?"

Virgil folded his arms over his chest and stared out the windshield, sniffling. "She cared more about haint-work than about us. And you care more about your boyfriend than about us."

Crawling in the dark, the mud, the rain, reaching out desperately even as everything got colder and colder...

"Mom didn't want to die," Dan grated out. *I failed her.* "She fought to come back to us down to her last breath."

"Yeah? Did she? *Did she, Dan?* Because she was the one who walked out the door and left us behind! And if that wasn't bad enough, you came back and-and killed Dad!"

Dan closed his eyes for a moment, but all he could see was the haint in

the lightning-struck oak. Just as Virgil likely could only see the body sway-
ing there in the breeze.

But the stab of guilt was less sharp now, even though sadness settled
over his shoulders like a waterlogged blanket. Maybe talking it out with Leif
had changed something in him, altered the way he thought about it.

"I didn't," he said quietly. "Dad left us, Virgil, and I don't know why. I
don't know why we weren't enough to make him stay, but we weren't. It's
just the way things are. And I've spent every day since trying to take his
place, but I can't. I just can't."

The taste of ashes filled his mouth, bitter and stringent. The taste of
truth, and maybe it was why people found honesty hard to swallow, because
sometimes it had no flavor but that of failure.

Virgil stared down at his hands. "I didn't mean..."

"I've done my best, and maybe it's not enough," Dan said, when Virgil
didn't continue. "But it'll be enough to get you out of Ransom Gap, if that's
what you want. Leif will be gone in a couple of days. Folks will move on to
the next bit of gossip. You've only got a few years of high school left, and I
know it seems like forever right now, but you've got to hang in and graduate.
Once you're done, you can leave and never see me again unless you want
to."

For a moment, Virgil looked like he might say something. Then he
shrugged sullenly and stared back down at his feet. Dan put the truck back
into gear, and they drove the rest of the way home in silence.

"Are you sure about this?" Dan asked as he unlocked the door to the
root cellar.

Night had fallen, and the wind blowing down from the mountain tasted
like frost and forgotten things. The stars were bright and hard, Orion striding
up the horizon, declaring winter was on its way. The breeze scattered leaves
across the yard, sounding as though a thousand little animals scurried around
them in the darkness.

"I'm not exactly thrilled with it," Leif said. "But we've exhausted our
options in the world of the living. That just leaves the realm of the dead."

Dan swung open the root cellar doors, revealing a set of wooden steps
descending into the earth. The cellar had been hacked out of the rocky hillside generations ago, and had always been used for two things: storing food
and Walking to the Underworld.

There was no electricity in the cellar. Dan switched on the camping
lantern he'd brought and led the way down the steps. Shelves of the pre-
served fruits and vegetables he and Bea had put away for the winter lined the
walls of the cellar. Bags of potatoes and onions lay on the floor, along with a
few crates of apples.

"Help me move this stuff," he said, grabbing one of the sacks of pota-toes and pulling it to the side.

With a little effort, they cleared the center of the room. His great-grand-father—Jedediah's grandson—had paved the floor with flat stones and carved a perfect circle into them, creating a ritual space. While Taryn put down a couple of old blankets to sit on, Dan went around the room lighting candles, and Leif sank to the floor in the center of the circle.

Dan had brought Mom's old drum with him, its deer hide surface paint-ed with symbols of the upper and under worlds. Bones and hooves hung from the frame, clattering together. The tempo he set would help carry Leif's consciousness into the underworld and act as a line to bring him back.

The responsibility was terrifying. *I couldn't help Mom; I couldn't save Dad. What if I mess this up? What if I fail and Leif can't find his way back?*

But Leif was an experienced Walker, not an apprentice taking his first tentative steps out of his body. Even if Dan fucked up, he'd find his way home again.

Right?

Dan settled on one of the blankets and put the drum in front of him. Taryn sank down on the other blanket, a rattle in her hands. She was a better psychic than Dan and would be able to sense if anything went wrong.

Although the plan for the Journey was simply to ask for information, when world-walking there was always the chance of running into something nasty that saw you as an enemy, an opportunity—or as food. If things went horribly wrong and Leif found himself in a situation he couldn't handle, the two of them would be able to pull him back.

Unless Hel decided to keep him. There was no rescuing anyone from Death.

That won't happen. There was no reason for it to happen. But Dan couldn't stop worrying about it, just like he couldn't stop worrying about any of the other things that could go wrong.

"Ready?" Leif asked. He sat with his legs folded and his hands in his lap, palms upturned. His sword lay to one side of him, his staff to the other. The silver on his belt and boots gleamed in the candlelight, along with the metal in his ears and face. His flaxen hair was pulled back and folded into a club at the back of his head, tied with a bit of black ribbon.

He's gorgeous. Gods, just looking at him made Dan's heart feel like it was stretched too full of emotion to contain. Sexy and brave, and if anything happened to him...

"Ready when you are," Taryn said.

Dan took a deep breath to calm his thumping heart. Doubt and fear had their place, but right now they were just distractions. *Focus and get the job done.*

"On your signal," he said.

Leif nodded. "Let's do it."

In silent harmony, they all centered, grounded, and shielded. Following a prompt from deep inside, Dan began to drum. The taut skin resounded under his fingers, slowly at first, but rapidly growing faster. As he slid into a light trance, the world became oddly distorted at the edges of his vision, as if there was more to be seen than what his eyes could quite perceive.

Since he wasn't leaving his body for the astral plane, he concentrated on maintaining an in-between state. A quick glance at Taryn revealed she sat by him with her eyes closed, her aura flaring around her. In this state, he could easily see a thin golden cord trailing out from the base of her skull, seeming to vanish a few feet out from her body. It was the psychic link between herself and her teacher; quiescent for now, but always there.

There would be no cord on his spine, not anymore, and a small flash of grief went through him at the thought. How different would all this have been if Mom had been alive to help them?

But she wasn't here, and it was up to him to help Leif. He turned his focus on the other man, just in time to hear Taryn's gasp of horror.

Leif sat in the center of the circle, his head slumped slightly forward, his blue eyes shut. A silver cord trailed out from his abdomen; at the other end would be his astral self, in whatever world he had journeyed to.

It should have been the only cord attached to him. After all, Leif had left Rúnar. If he'd thought about it at all, Dan would have assumed the link between them had been severed somehow.

He would've been wrong. Horribly, horribly wrong.

This link was no delicate thing of gold, no gentle connection between teacher and student, forged by trust and affection to be called upon in times of greatest need. This cord was flushed deep purple as a bruise, pulsing and thick, rammed into the base of Leif's skull in what could only be described as a profound violation. It crawled with the dark sheen of dirty oil, pulsing and throbbing like a live thing. Little rootlets arched away from the main point of connection, writhing amidst Leif's pale hair and gripping the skin of his neck.

Bile rose in Dan's throat just looking at it. "Fuck, what *is* that?"

Leif's head snapped back and his eyes opened. They were no longer the pale blue of a winter sky; rather, they crawled with the same greasy iridescence as the psychic link.

"I see you," Leif said, his voice deeper than it should have been, the words tinged with an unfamiliar accent. "You've interfered in something not your business. You think you can take my Leif away from me. But I will not allow it."

Snatching the sword up from where it lay beside him on the ground, the thing in Leif's body lunged straight at Dan.

CHAPTER 24

T he transition was sudden. One moment, Leif sat on the floor of the root cellar; the next, he was in a controlled fall through space. Wind roared around him, and he beheld a titanic tree. The smallest fold of its bark was the size of a mountain range, the veins in its leaves bigger than rivers. It was a tree meant to hold worlds.

Yggdrasil.

Helheim. He pictured his destination clearly, exerting his will, and the tree flashed past and was gone.

Leif found himself beneath the eternal twilight sky of Helheim, a place he glimpsed each time he laid a spirit to rest, but had Walked to only twice before. A quick inventory showed his astral self was dressed in t-shirt and jeans, with his sword and staff in their accustomed places.

Ahead of him lay a great river, rushing through a deep cleft in the black rocks: wild and cold and utterly impassable. The sole bridge stretched before him: thatched in gold and paved with knives. The Gjallarbrú, it was called, spanning the river Gjöll. On the far side, Mordgud's tower reared up like a warning finger.

Even though the Gjallarbrú was paved with knives, they didn't cut him as he strode onto the bridge without flinching. He took it as a good sign; if Hel had been put out with him, they *would* have sliced his astral self, no question about it. He walked across quickly, stopping at the other end, a respectful distance from the giantess who awaited him.

Even from a distance, her presence was palpable: strength and determination, partnered with compassion and a sort of wry humor. Her shining black armor gleamed in the darkness, and her long fair hair hung in two braids. Her face was battered, the nose crooked from an old break: the face of a warrior.

Most would have called her ugly, but Leif had always found her beautiful, from the first time he'd glimpsed her. She was strength embodied, but with the gallows humor of someone who had seen more than her share of battles.

"Hail Mighty Mordgud, Guardian of the Gjallarbrú, She-etin of the Sharp Road, Lady of the Lost Way," he said, bowing deeply.

He felt her attention on him; not as vast as that of the goddess they both served, but greater than anything mortal. "Your poetry needs work, death-walker," she said, but there was amusement in the words rather than reproach.

"I'm not very good at it," he agreed, straightening and looking at her directly, one warrior to another. "I'm here because Rúnar is disturbing the dead. I'm trying to stop him, but I need to know where he will go, and I can't find the information among the living. I humbly ask if Jedediah Van Horn, whom Rúnar troubled, would be willing to come and speak with me."

He didn't ask for the audience with Hel. If Hel had granted it, Mordgud would already know. If She hadn't, there was no point bringing it up.

Mordgud studied him closely, with eyes whose color shifted between the shiny black of the obsidian rocks around them and the gray-brown of the velvety shadows. He held himself calmly, concentrating on respect for her and for Hel, compassion for the dead Rúnar had tormented, and his desire to set things right.

"Not today," she said, in a voice broken from shouting battlefield orders. "You have other matters to see to first."

Disappointment cut him, accompanied by a flash of fear. If he went back empty-handed, he truly did not know what more they could do.

Even though he knew better than to argue, he couldn't stop himself from trying. "I'm sorry if I've offended—"

She cut him off with a laugh. "There's been no offense. As I said, you have other problems at the moment. Turn around and look behind you."

Confused, he obediently did as she ordered. He had a fleeting impression of black tendrils, just before the writhing mass enveloped him.

Dan barely had time to roll out of the way as Leif's sword swung through the space he'd occupied an instant before. His drum went flying; the steel blade smashed the wooden frame to bits and struck sparks from the floor.

"Leif!" he shouted—but it wasn't Leif, was it? It was Rúnar, who had turned the psychic link between student and teacher into an assault. Who used it to do gods-knew-what to Leif over the years.

Taryn was on her feet, her lips drawn back from her teeth and her knives in her hands. "That's not Leif," she said.

A cracked laugh broke from Leif's lips, and the greasy stain swam across his eyes. He straightened, but his movements were jerky and clumsy, nothing at all like his usual thoughtless grace. "Of course it is. After all, Leif is nothing but what I made him. He has no words, no thoughts, but what I put into him first."

Utter loathing twisted Dan's gut. Until that moment, he hadn't ever really hated anyone enough to want them dead, but now...

If I have to drag Rúnar to Hecate with my bare hands, I'll do it.

"It's still Leif's body," Dan said to Taryn. "Don't hurt him."

"I'm not going to let him carve us up. Easier for you to find a new boyfriend than a new head."

"Don't intend to let it come to that," Dan said, his whole body tensing.

Leif charged him again, a meat puppet clutching a sword sharp enough to be deadly, even if the puppeteer didn't have the finest control. Dan waited until the last instant before dropping to his knees, the sword passing close enough to stir his hair.

Leif ran full-tilt into him. Dan wrapped his arms around Leif's legs and fell to the side, letting gravity take them to the floor. The sword hit the flagstones and went caroming off into one corner.

Rúnar wasn't done yet. Leif went wild, thrashing and struggling. Taryn flung herself into their midst, grabbing Leif's wrists and yanking them back long enough for Dan to pin the other man beneath him. Leif bucked under him like a mad thing, hips almost heaving him off. His head jerked suddenly forward, smashing into Dan's chin hard enough to make him taste blood and see stars.

But he didn't let go; couldn't let go. "Leif!" he shouted urgently, but there was no recognition in the infected eyes. Leif's lips pulled back from his teeth in a grimace of hate and effort; he was all but foaming at the mouth, and a spike of terror went through Dan.

"We've got to do something!" he cried, desperate and wild, and for a moment all he could see was the man he loved slipping away from him.

"We will." The grim determination in Taryn's voice surprised him. She crouched at Leif's head, her knives back in their sheaths, her eyes narrowed in thought as she studied the turgid, pulsing cord twisting out of the base of Leif's skull. "We're going to rip that thing out by the roots."

Which didn't sound good. "Can't you just cut through it with your knives?"

She shook her head, while Leif growled and snapped at her like a mad thing. "No. I don't want it growing back. We get it all out, and we get it out now."

It scared him to fucking death. The drum had been smashed, and in the back of his head a little voice screamed how Leif was probably lost somewhere, unable to find his way home again without the connection. What if tearing out the psychic link damaged him—killed him? But what if leaving it in would be worse?

Leif's body convulsed against his, fighting to break free, and he knew they didn't have a choice. *Oh gods, sweetheart, I'm sorry.* "What do you need me to do?"

The golden cord linking Taryn to her teacher had grown brighter, stronger, as she pulled on his power. "Your job is to hold him down while I work," she said, and her calm tone took the edge off Dan's panic. "He'll do anything he can to get free. Don't let him."

"Don't listen to her," Leif said hoarsely. "She hates me. She's trying to hurt me!"

Dan shifted his grip, grimly pinning Leif's wrists to the floor. The cuff had come off during the struggle, exposing the band of binding runes. "Shut up, Rúnar," Dan said. "Don't you use his mouth to spout your filth."

A sly look crossed over Leif's face, and the tumescent cord flushed darker. "Let go of me, and I'll use his mouth for other things."

Hot anger spilled across Dan's veins, tinting his vision red. But Rúnar only laughed softly. "I know," he taunted. "My darling knows how to use his tongue, doesn't he? Tell me, does he beg you to fuck him, the way he begged me?"

"Shut up!"

"Don't let him get to you," Taryn said harshly. "And get ready."

She took a series of deep, centering breaths, the golden cord from her teacher glowing like fire. Her aura snapped into a shield, hard and slick as a beetle's carapace. White light formed around her fingers, shifting to the nails and curving into long, grasping claws.

She reached out, those hooked, ethereal claws passing through Leif's skull as she gripped the cord at its base with both hands and began to pull.

Leif instinctively brought up his astral sword, but it was too late. The dark, oily tendrils had already wrapped around him, ensnaring his arms and legs. He fell to the ground, struggling wildly, but beneath the cold, greasy surface they were strong as iron.

Too slow, too slow, if I'd just turned around the instant she told me to—

Pain arced through his head, flaring from the base of his skull. Something crawled there, thrashing, and he realized with horror it wasn't a matter of being too slow at all.

The tendrils hadn't leapt on him—they'd already been inside.

A tide of anger rushed over him, but it seemed curiously separate, as if he felt it from one remove. *The anger doesn't belong to me. It belongs to...*

No.

"*No!*" he screamed aloud, thrashing madly against the slick, pulsing grip of the psychic tendrils. *Oh gods, it's Rúnar, it's the link, he's been watching me, been* inside *me all this time.* Leif's stomach clenched, and he gagged, but there was nothing to vomit, not here, not in this place.

A soft laugh scraped the inside of his soul. "Oh yes," Rúnar crooned, and one of the tendrils slipped over Leif's face in a parody of a caress. The tip wriggled worm-like at the corner of his lips, seeking entrance. "Do you think I would leave you to face the world alone? What sort of teacher would I be, to abandon you?"

No. No, this wasn't happening; this was a nightmare. He'd escaped; he turned away; he'd tried to redeem himself. *And all this time, he's had a direct link into my mind. When I thought I was alone, when I was trying to find him, when I was with Dan—*

The tendrils tightened suddenly, like the coils of a boa constrictor. "You are mine. He can't have you!"

He could still see Alice's body, sprawled in his apartment, pieces everywhere. She'd been a warning: this was what Rúnar would do to anyone who came between them.

"And what I will do to your lover," Rúnar whispered in his ear. The tendrils squirmed beneath his clothing, slithering over his skin.

No, not Dan. Not Dan, whom he'd loved since—

"You are not to think of him!" The tendrils tightened, cutting off what passed for breath in the spirit worlds. Leif's convulsions had rolled them to the very edge of the Bridge of Knives; the roar of the Gjöll vibrated up through the rock beneath them and thundered in Leif's ears.

Dan—

"You'll never be his. Never. You're mine, now and forever."

It was true, Leif realized, and the shriveling of hope felt like a physical thing here in the Underworld, like a flower blighted by the latest of frosts. Rúnar had made him, had taken the raw clay of a teenaged whore and reshaped him into everything he was today. There was nothing in him that remained uncorrupted, untainted.

He would never escape, because there was nowhere to run. Better to admit it now. Better to accept his fate and return in defeat to the only place he would ever have to go.

Then Mordgud was there, a dark shape of iron and spikes against the twilight sky of Helheim. "Is this the best you can do?" she roared at him in the voice of a giantess: loud and hard as the breaking of bone. *"Fight!* There are others fighting for you even now, but they cannot do all of the work!"

He blinked, dazed, and in the echoes of Mordgud's voice the insidious little whisper, which spoke always of doubt and deceit fell silent just long enough for him to realize it didn't belong to him at all.

Oh, you cunning bastard.

He was utterly entwined by the tendrils; there was no getting to his feet. With a strangled howl of effort and rage, Leif heaved his body and rolled them both onto the Bridge of Knives.

~ * ~

Leif screamed and thrashed, almost bucking Dan off. Dan clung grimly, his hands locked around Leif's wrists hard enough for his fingers to go numb. His jaw ached where Leif had hit him, and a bruise bloomed on Leif's pale forehead.

Taryn let out a low growl of effort, every muscle in her arms tensing with the strain. The cord thrashed in her grip, slick and alive. But this was no physical battle, even though sweat stood out on her forehead.

For an endless time, nothing seemed to change. But, gradually, he thought Taryn might be getting somewhere. A few shorter tendrils popped free, curling and thrashing like tiny worms, seeking to burrow back in but unable to reach Leif's skin.

Hecate, Queen of Ghosts, Lady of the Crossroads, give us the strength to do Your work!

Leif—or what possessed him—stopped struggling. His lips twisted into a manic grin, utterly unlike anything Dan had ever seen on the real Leif's face.

"I'm only using you," he sneered contemptuously. Was there a glint of blue through the greasy corruption behind his corneas? "Or did you really think I'd be interested in an ignorant redneck?"

Dan swallowed against the tightness in his throat. This was Rúnar talking, not Leif, and if he was saying things Dan had feared, that still didn't make them true.

"Shut up," he snarled.

The thing in Leif's body laughed. "You know it's true," he mocked slyly.

"I said shut up!"

"Dan!" Taryn shouted. Sweat slicked her face, and her aura blazed with energy as she struggled with the cord. "Forget that fucker! Talk to Leif! Call him!"

She's right, she's right, stop wasting time, stop playing his games! Mom had taught him better than to listen to something that didn't have anyone's good in mind, and if he fell for a cheap trick like this, she'd come back from the Underworld and kick his ass herself.

Dan closed his eyes and took a deep breath, pulling Leif's scent of cedar and musk into his lungs and holding it there. He remembered the night in the woods, when he'd given into desire and kissed Leif; remembered, too, how surprised he'd been when Leif had kissed him back. He clung to the memory of the night in Asheville: the rain and Leif's tears, the sweetness of the strawberries and the greater sweetness of their bodies coming together. Other moments bubbled up: the kisses, the smiles over breakfast, the way Leif had just held him last night, gentle and solid and there in whatever way he needed.

"Fight this," Dan whispered haggardly. "Fight this bastard, Leif, please. I can't stand to lose you. I-I love you."

"No!" Rúnar said, Leif's features distorting horribly under his influence. "You will never have him!"

Agony exploded through Leif's head, wiping out all thought. The pain went on and on, red waves beating against his psyche, and all he could do was cling to consciousness and breathe. Surely his skull had broken open; surely he was going to die.

Fuck, Dan, I'm sorry. I didn't want it to be this way.

The thought of Dan lessened the pain, like a buffer. And hadn't the frequency of his headaches decreased when he'd spent the night in Dan's arms? Hadn't the whispering voice tearing him down been muffled?

He could almost feel Dan holding him, almost hear him calling. *"There are others fighting for you even now,"* Mordgud had said.

Leif opened eyes he had shut against the pain. The tendrils around him were loosened, and he felt a slick ichor leaking from them onto his skin. Grinning savagely, he rolled them farther onto the Gjallarbrú. Onto the Bridge of Knives.

Knives which wouldn't cut those who were there at Hel's invitation, such as Leif. But a necromancer who tormented the dead? Oh no, Rúnar was not at all welcome here, and neither was anything of his.

The knives sliced into the tendrils. Some of the smaller were severed outright and fell away, wriggling as they dissolved into black ichor. The others were lacerated, their hold weakening until Leif was able to free his arms and stagger to his feet.

Now it's my turn.

He slashed with the blade made of nothing but his will and intent made manifest in this place. The sword erupted in a stream of white light, burning away the tendrils everywhere it touched. They flinched away, retracting, or else fell in severed strands around him. Some tried to regain their hold, but he kept hacking, bitterly determined not to stop until all trace of contamination was gone.

One way or another, this would end here.

A curious lightness filled him as the tendrils dropped away, as if he'd been carrying a heavy burden for years and never even realized until he'd set it aside. Energized, he sliced more, until the larger ones were gone. Dropping the sword, he ripped the rest out with his bare hands. It hurt, as if they were covered with tiny, barbed hooks, tearing as he wrenched them free, but he didn't care about the pain anymore. Nothing mattered but to get Rúnar's psychic tendrils out and away from him, even if what was left behind had no more substance than tattered cheesecloth.

It was exhausting work, ripping each tendril free and sealing his aura against its return. As the last one popped out with a hideous, sucking sound, he heard a distant scream of rage. The writhing, dripping mass of tendrils surged at him in a frenzy—before they suddenly retracted, retreated, and vanished, as if something else had yanked them into another world.

He blinked, not sure it was really over. His knees felt weak, as if they might dump him onto the road at any second, and his very psyche ached, excoriated and laid open by the fight.

Is there anything left of me?

Mordgud's armor clanked behind him. "Foolish question," she said, and her grin was fierce when he turned wearily to face her. "You are more than you think, or you would not be standing here. It was a good fight."

Her approval warmed him. "Now what?"

"Now you go home and rest, world-walker." At her words, Helheim dissolved around him, and there was only chaos and wind.

And Dan's voice, calling him home.

CHAPTER 25

L eif's body arched under Dan's, nearly flinging him off. Leif's eyes rolled up, and spittle foamed at the corner of his mouth as a seizure rolled through him.

"Taryn!" Dan shouted, "Rúnar's using the link to kill him! Do something!"

Taryn's cry of effort spiraled up into a higher and higher register. The cord snapped free, as if it had been forcibly ejected. Dan got a horrifying glimpse of a score of tendrils on the end, like tiny rootlets burrowing deep into Leif's psyche, pumping gods-knew-what poison into him.

An instant later, it was gone, back to the man who had sent it. Taryn pitched back onto her rear with a curse.

Leif went limp. Was he even breathing? "Leif!" Dan whispered frantically, and oh gods, what if it had all been for nothing, what if Leif couldn't find his way back without the drum, even with the silver cord intact?

Dan pressed a kiss to his forehead, caressing his face, the skin pale as death. "Sweetheart, please, come back. Please. I can't do this without you."

Leif didn't respond. The world was falling out from under Dan again, a hole opening in his chest. It couldn't end like this, with Leif lost to the world and nothing but loneliness and despair in the place he'd been.

Taryn sat up gingerly. She looked utterly exhausted, her eyes bruised. "Tug on the cord," she whispered.

Dan seized the silver cord linking Leif to his body. There was something oddly intimate about touching it, and warmth filled him as he wrapped his hand around it and tugged. "Hecate, Lady of the Torches, You Who lead Persephone in safety through the darkness, You Who light the way, please, bring him back, I beg You. Come back to me, Leif. I love you."

Leif's breathing deepened. His brows quirked slightly, and he let out a faint moan.

The silver cord vanished as they all dropped fully back into the normal world. Leif opened eyes of untainted blue, like the highest arch of a winter's sky.

Oh goddesses. Thank You, Hecate. Thank You, Hel. Thank You.

"Dan," Leif whispered. His voice sounded faint and cracked, and shivers wracked his slender body.

Taryn climbed to her feet as if her very bones ached. "After that shit, we've got to get him grounded and all the way back in this world," she said.

Dan glanced up fearfully. "He's cold."

"Cleansing bath will help."

Dan nodded. While Taryn went up the stairs, he stroked Leif's face with his fingers. "Sweetheart? Can you stand?"

Leif swallowed. His eyes were only half-open and didn't entirely seem to focus on anything in this world. "I dunno," he mumbled, the words slurred. "I'll try."

"Never mind," Dan said. Sliding his arms around Leif's shoulders and under his legs, he said a quick prayer and surged to his feet.

Leif was taller, but heron-thin. Even though it wasn't easy, Dan managed to carry him out of the root cellar. Leif's head slumped against his neck, breath warm on his skin, and he took courage from the tangible sign of life.

He was halfway to the house when Bea ran out, her face pale. "Goddess's grace, is he going to be all right?"

"Yes," Dan said firmly, not letting his fear show. "Help me."

It was easier to manage with Bea to take some of Leif's weight. Between the two of them, they wrestled him into the house. Virgil stood in the living room, staring with wide, scared eyes, seeming at a loss.

"He needs food, to help ground him in his body," Dan said, once Bea had helped haul Leif up the stairs to the bathroom. Taryn was inside already, running a hot bath, into which she dumped sea salt mixed with sage and rosemary. "We still have some stew in the freezer—nuke it, and bring it up with a thick slice of bread."

Bea nodded and took off back downstairs. While Taryn fiddled with the bath, Dan gently helped Leif out of his clothes. Leif's skin felt ice-cold, and he shivered violently by the time he was naked.

There was a time and a place for modesty, but this surely wasn't it. Taryn lent a helping hand, and between them, they got Leif safely into the deep, claw-footed tub. The warmth of the water drew color back into his skin, and his shivering eased somewhat.

"I'll leave the rest to you," Taryn said, with a nod at Leif. "For now, I'm going to make sure nothing decides to come knocking. I know you've got wards up, but—"

"I'd feel better if you reinforced them," Dan agreed quickly. Both of them were spooked by what happened, not least because Rúnar must know exactly where to find Leif he if wanted to. "Thanks, Taryn. You really came through tonight. I owe you. Name a favor, and it's yours."

It was a big promise, considering the sort of danger a Walker might need help with, but it was the only thing he could think of that seemed adequate. Her eyes widened slightly, before she smiled, the old humor flashing across her face. "Don't worry about it. After what we saw tonight, any decent Walker would've done the same." She shivered visibly, despite the warm steam filling the bathroom.

"It was pretty bad."

"It was a fucking abomination. I never even thought about how lucky you and I were, to have teachers who did right by us. Makes you realize how vulnerable apprentices really are. The thought of living with it day in and day out, for years on end...shit, I don't even want to think about it." She glanced at Leif, her look one of grudging respect. "Your boy's got spine, is all I'm saying. And maybe I was a little too fast to rush to judgment."

She left, shutting the door behind her. Leif sat in the tub, his knees drawn up to his chest, his arms wrapped around them, staring into nothing.

Dan crouched down by the tub. "Sweetheart?"

Leif blinked sluggishly. "I heard you calling."

Merciful goddess, he still sounded awfully weak. "I'm going to take care of you, okay? You just relax."

Leif nodded and closed his pale eyes, taking a deep breath, drawing the herb-scented steam into his lungs. Dan found the lavender soap kept for just such circumstances and lathered it up.

He washed Leif's skin gently, paying special attention to the spot where the spine joined the skull. There was a bruise on Leif's forehead, and more bruises in the shape of Dan's fingers encircled his wrists.

He'd never meant to hurt Leif, not ever. There hadn't been a choice, but his heart still twisted painfully at the sight.

Gradually, Leif stopped shivering, and some of the color came back into his skin. When the bath was done, Dan pressed a kiss to Leif's temple. "Wait here a minute while I get some clothes for you."

Leif nodded, his eyes finally focusing on Dan. "Thank you."

"I'll be right back."

He dug out a pair of Leif's boxers and the worn, cotton pants he usually wore while practicing his sword forms. But none of Leif's shirts seemed heavy enough; instead, Dan grabbed one of his own flannels and a pair of his thick, winter socks.

Once Leif was dressed, Dan helped him into the bed and propped him up on some pillows. Bea brought up a steaming bowl of stew, a cup of tea, and a thick slab of bread. She sat on the edge of the bed, watching Leif eat with a look of concern.

The food seemed to do the trick; after a few mouthfuls, Leif's grip on the bowl strengthened, and his gaze lost its unfocused quality and fixed on the here-and-now. As he was mopping up the last of the stew with the bread, Taryn appeared in the doorway, leaning against the frame with her arms crossed.

"How are you feeling?" she asked, without the belligerent edge she had previously used with Leif.

He glanced up at her. "Better. But I failed. I wasn't able to talk to the dead."

"Don't worry about it, sweetheart," Dan said quickly.

"I didn't get any farther than the Gjallarbrú—the bridge over the river guarding the entrance to Helheim." He lowered his gaze, as if ashamed. "Rúnar..."

"We know. The psychic link was still in place."

Leif's eyes were dark with misery and shame. "I didn't know. I swear! I thought; I mean, I assumed..."

"You didn't really ever think about it at all, did you?" Taryn asked, but there was only rueful understanding in her words rather than accusation.

Leif blanched anyway, as if she had slapped him. "I didn't..." he trailed off and shook his head. "No. Sweet death, *why* didn't I realize it would be a vulnerability? I'm sorry, I—"

"You didn't realize, because Rúnar was manipulating you through the link," Taryn said bluntly. "You *couldn't* have thought of it. He made sure of it."

The color drained out of Leif's face. "Surely it wasn't that bad, was it?"

"You didn't see what the link had become. If you had, you wouldn't have to ask."

"He was able to take over your body," Dan said, not wanting to cause Leif more pain but needing him to understand. "He tried to fight us. I had to hold you down while Taryn yanked out the cord. I'm sorry, sweetheart."

"If you were fighting him in the Otherworld at the same time, it explains why the cord came free as easy as it did," Taryn mused. "You chucked him out where he'd wormed in deep, and I was able to pull up the shallow roots."

"I see." Leif set aside the now-empty bowl, his face carefully composed, except for the utter lack of color. "You've done this sort of thing before?" He sounded almost hopeful, like maybe he could pretend it wasn't a big deal.

Taryn shook her head. "Not exactly. I've taken care of a few cases of spirit possession, where a ghost had got some psychic tendrils wormed in and was making somebody crazy. Teacher says I've got a knack for it. This was similar enough that I knew what to do, but about a thousand times worse."

"Why?" Bea asked, wide-eyed.

How to explain something like this to her? "Because it wasn't just an attack from the outside, which is bad enough. When you're an apprentice, you have to trust your teacher, not just with your life, but with everything. Your very self, all the way to the center of your being. To take that trust and turn it into an assault is about as wrong as it gets. You can't get away, even in your own mind, because the abuser's there, in your thoughts and your feelings and-and everything."

Bea went almost as pale as Leif. "Oh," she said in a small voice.

Leif buried his face in his hands. "I've been a spy in our midst. No wonder he found me in Asheville. No wonder he got to the Festival ahead of us and left the *draugr* for us to find."

The self-accusatory tone in his voice made Dan wince. "Leif, no, you can't blame yourself. None of us do. We *saw* what he'd done to you."

"The man speaks the truth." Taryn peeled herself away from the door. "I'm going to make another patrol. Bea, you get ready for bed."

"I want to make sure Leif's okay," Bea said.

"You leave him to your brother, girl."

"I'm fine," Leif said, reaching out to touch Bea's hand. "Just tired."

Bea gave him a narrow look, but nodded. Gathering the dishes, she left the room, Taryn sweeping after her.

Dan shut the door behind them, trusting Taryn to keep watch as she'd promised. When he turned to the bed again, he saw Leif curled up on his side, his back to Dan and his arms wrapped around himself.

"Sweetie?" Dan pulled off his boots, before lying down beside Leif and sliding an arm around his waist.

Leif shuddered. "How can you stand to touch me?" he whispered. "Knowing the corruption I've carried inside me? How can you bear to think about all the times we-we..."

Dan pressed his face against Leif's hair and tightened his grip, trying to convey through words all the things making his chest ache and his eyes burn with unshed tears. "Because you aren't corrupt, or wrong, or tainted, or whatever else is going through your head," he whispered. "It was all him. And he never had any place in what's between us."

Leif sniffled. "It w-was always better when you were near. I can see it now, when he isn't in me anymore, distorting my perceptions. Something about you..."

"Because I'm another Walker, maybe."

"Maybe. Or maybe because," Leif hesitated, as if censoring what he'd been about to say. "When you called me back, you said..."

He trailed off, as if he couldn't bring himself to speak the words. Or wanted to give Dan an out, maybe.

"I said I love you." He pressed his lips against Leif's hair, still damp from the bath and smelling of lavender. "We haven't known each other for long, but I know how I feel. I love you, Leif Helsvin."

Leif let out a choked sob and rolled blindly to face him. They held each other, Leif's face buried against his chest, tears soaking through his shirt. "Shh," Dan murmured, stroking his hair. "It's all right. I've got you."

Eventually, the tears stopped, and Leif's grip became slightly less desperate. He drew back, eyeliner smeared, eyes reddened, but with a tremulous smile on his mouth. "Yeah. You do have me. All of me, for as long as you want."

And, gods, Dan couldn't help the wave of joy sweeping through him, all the way to his toes. Leif touched the corner of his mouth lightly, tracing the contours.

"You have the most beautiful smile," he whispered, just before Dan kissed him.

Dan tried to keep the kiss tender rather than passionate, but Leif deepened it, pressing against him. When they broke apart, Leif framed his face with his long hands, fingers threading through Dan's hair.

"Make love to me," Leif begged, voice throaty and raw with need.

Dan's skin tingled in response, and his cock stirred. Still, he hesitated. Sex could help ground someone who'd been through an intense out-of-body experience like Leif had, but sex had also been a component of what Rúnar had done to him.

"Are you sure?" Dan asked, pulling back to study Leif's face. "You've been through a lot. If you just want to cuddle…"

"I need to know you still want me. And I want to show you how I feel. Please, baby?"

It wasn't fair; he couldn't resist a plea like that. He kissed Leif again, more passionately this time, and was rewarded with a soft moan against his mouth. He reached for the buttons on the flannel shirt he'd fastened not very long before and started working them free again.

"I like wearing your shirt," Leif whispered. "I like having your scent on me."

Dan pushed the fabric back and kissed Leif's chest above his heart, tasting his skin. Dan traced the lines of the tattoo with his tongue, nipping and sucking at each nipple, getting a thrust of Leif's hips in response. Leif's fingers tangled in his hair, tugging deliciously.

He didn't remove the flannel shirt altogether, although he did pull Leif's pants and boxers off and toss them onto the floor. Leif's cock bobbed invitingly against his flat stomach, and Dan's mouth practically watered with the desire to taste him without anything in between. But it wasn't going to happen until Leif got tested, which meant, with him leaving in a couple of days, it wasn't going to happen at all.

Don't think about it. Not now. Better to enjoy this while it lasted and worry about the future when it arrived.

Dan stripped hurriedly out of his own clothing. He stretched out on top of his lover, their cocks rubbing together. Their pre-come slicked each other, and he wrapped one hand loosely around their lengths, rocking his hips to provide friction.

Leif arched against him, eager to offer some friction of his own. "Feels good," he whispered into Dan's ear, low and sexy and panting with need.

"Yeah," Dan grunted, which was about all he could manage. Leif's cock burned against his from base to tip, balls warm and tight against his own. Fingers dug into his shoulders, Leif clinging to him like a drowning man. His body arched and twisted and writhed frantically under Dan's, before suddenly stilling as hot spunk spilled between them.

Dan closed his eyes and thrust against Leif, biting back a moan as his balls tightened and pleasure convulsed his body, leaving him limp and wrung-out as a warm cloth.

He sighed contentedly and eased off Leif, stretching out by him. Leif rolled to face him, arms and legs tangling, softening cocks pressed together and their mingled come sticky against their bellies.

"Love you," Leif murmured. He looked better, except for the bruising on his forehead and wrists. His eyes were sleepy but sated, and the expression in them was fully present once again.

Dan pressed his lips tenderly against Leif's forehead, careful to avoid the bruise. "Try to get some sleep."

"Not a problem," Leif mumbled, his eyes already sliding closed. Within minutes, his breathing was soft and deep.

I wish... But there was no point in wishing they could fall asleep like this every night and wake up together every morning. Dan propped himself up on his elbow and studied his lover's face in silence, memorizing every line and freckle against the loneliness to come.

CHAPTER 26

Dan walked down to the mailbox, carrying a can of paint and some brushes. He only had haint-blue on hand, not the black of the mailbox, which meant the whole thing would have to get another coat eventually.

The mailbox was heavily dented, the flag bent and broken off. "Fag" was spray-painted in white on one side, and "burn in hell" on the other.

Fuckers. There wasn't anything wrong with him being in love with Leif. Anyone would be lucky to find somebody as special. At least the cowards had just hit the mailbox, instead of showing up at the front door with a set of brass knuckles. Or a gun.

I hate this. He'd never dealt with this sort of shit before, but the dread of it had hung over him since he was a kid, when he'd realized he wasn't like the other boys.

Leif would've come down to help if he had asked. But Leif had already dealt with more than his share of pain; there was no reason for him to face this, too. It wouldn't take long to repair the physical damage. The emotional fallout? That was a different story.

Before heading down to take care of the mailbox, Taryn and Dan had wracked their brains and desperately searched through the journals one last time while Leif slept away most of the morning. Frustrated, Taryn finally decided to drive to the library, in case they had some record Dan and Leif had missed. The thought of her grilling the poor librarian almost made him smile.

Leif came downstairs while she was gone. The suspended Virgil sulked in his room, the door shut, ostensibly keeping up with his schoolwork. Dan kept pouring over the journals, looking up to find Leif leaning against the doorway, watching him.

"Hey."

"Hey, yourself. You're looking better."

"I'm feeling better." Leif's eyes softened. "You take such good care of me."

"I love you."

Leif crossed the room and touched his face gently. "Love you, too, baby."

It still didn't seem possible. Why would somebody like Leif fall for a poor country haint-worker?

But he did. Maybe the why of it didn't matter. And surely the opinion of the dickheads who'd vandalized the mailbox didn't matter. The thought gave him the strength to shove aside his anger and open the can of paint.

He heard the low growl of a car engine coming up the road. Dan paused, half-ashamed to be seen fixing the damage, half defiant. He expected the car to pass, but the familiar sedan instead slowed, turned into the drive, and stopped.

Shit.

The door opened, and Corey stepped out. He still wore his tie and shirtsleeves from work. He closed the car door and nodded at the mailbox. "Need a hand with that?"

Dan watched him warily for a moment, but the man was offering to help, and he couldn't throw it back in his face. "I'd appreciate it."

Dan had brought two different sizes of brush down, not sure which might be better for the job. Corey picked one up, dipped it in the paint, and started in on the other side.

They painted in silence for a few minutes, until Corey said, "This why you been distant these last few years?"

"Yeah." Dan bent to the paint can again. "I hated lying to you, and the only way to avoid it was to avoid you."

"I figured it was a race thing."

"Shit, Corey!" Dan stood with his brush in mid-air, slowly dripping paint onto the ground. "You were my best friend in high school."

Corey shrugged, his eyes still on the mailbox as he carefully laid a coat of paint over the hateful words. "Yeah, well. Fellow goes off for a while, comes back changed. I wasn't sure what sort of crowd you'd fallen in with while you were gone."

"Well, I'm powerful sorry you thought that," Dan said at last, with a little shake of his head.

"Yeah, well, I'm sorry you thought you had to lie to me. Although I can't say as I blame you, seeing as how folks have taken it," Corey added with a wry nod at the battered mailbox.

Dan set his brush back to the metal, trying to focus on it instead of the nervousness coiled in his belly. "You're okay with me being gay?"

"I don't see as it's any business of mine who you're sleeping with." Corey shrugged. "But seeing how friends are supposed to butt in whether it's their business or not: this Leif your boyfriend?"

Corey thought they could still be friends. It lightened Dan's heart, brought a small smile to his face that wasn't just due to the mention of Leif. "Yeah."

"Huh. Well, I guess I don't really know what to make of the eyeliner and nail polish, but he seems like an all-right guy."

"The best."

Corey snorted. "Sounds like you got it bad."

Dan grinned. Even though some awful things had come from being out-ed, at least this had gone right. "Yeah. I guess I do."

Corey just shook his head, and they finished painting the mailbox to-gether in comfortable silence.

Taryn laid her kit on the kitchen table where Leif sat. He'd heard the door slam behind her a few minutes ago when she returned from the library, so he watched warily as she dropped into the chair across from him, pulled out a whetstone and oil, and began to sharpen her knives.

She'd been almost nice to him last night, but he wasn't sure if she'd sat with him now because she wanted a target for her frustration, or just needed the table space.

Neither, as it turned out. "How are you holding up?" she asked gruffly as she ran the whetstone along the edge of the gleaming blade.

"Fine." Which was a lie. He still felt as if a thin layer of greasy dirt cov-ered his body, something reeking of sickness, the last exudation from a plague-ridden corpse. He'd showered in near-scalding water after waking, scrubbing with every cleansing soap in the bathroom. It had helped, but he couldn't shake the sense of having been tainted. Violated.

She nodded, not pushing any further. "I should've trusted Dan when he said you were on our side."

"Why?" he asked, not quite able to keep a trace of bitterness from the word. "You were right—I was working for Rúnar. I just didn't know it."

The whetstone paused while she shot him a glare. "Listen, motherfuck-er, I'm trying to apologize here. Shut up and let me."

The front door opened, and Dan came in, followed by one of the men Leif had met his first night here. Corey, was it?

"Corey's coming to dinner," Dan said, with a nod at his friend.

"Just let me call Nakesha and let her know, or she'll skin me alive," Corey said, flashing them a grin.

He went to the phone. Leif cast Dan a questioning look, got a small nod and a smile in return. At least not everyone in Ransom Gap was a bigot, it seemed.

"You remember Taryn," Dan said, when Corey got off the phone with his wife.

She tested the edge of her knife by shaving off the fine hairs on her fore-arm in a single, quick motion. "Good to see you again," she said neutrally.

Corey had started to extend his hand; he withdrew it with alacrity. "Er, same here."

"Hi, Corey," Leif said, taking pity on him.

Corey's handshake was firm and dry. "Thanks again for helping out with that haint of Zach's. And sorry to hear about your recent troubles."

Dan tapped Taryn on the shoulder. "Clean off the table so we can eat like civilized people."

"You haven't even started cooking yet."

"Well, I'm about to."

"Nag, nag, nag," she muttered, gathering her things. "Fine, I'll take it in the living room. Happy?"

Dan rolled his eyes and tossed her a beer from the fridge. Taryn caught it almost without looking. He passed a couple of beers to Corey and Leif as well, before pulling out ingredients to make dinner.

"I'm going to grab a quick smoke in the yard," Corey said. "Leif? You smoke?"

The invitation surprised him. "Not anymore, but I'll keep you company."

They went out into the yard together. Corey went almost automatically to the oak, leaning against its bulk while he lit up. Leif wondered how many times he'd done this very thing, when he and Dan were younger.

The sun had set, and the only light came from inside the farmhouse. The wind rose, shaking the dry, dead leaves in the tree and scattering those already fallen. They sounded like the scrabble of bony fingers, and Leif suppressed the urge to look around in paranoia.

"Where are you from?" Corey asked.

Leif suppressed a grin. *Making sure I'm good enough to date your friend?* "Chicago, originally. All over, recently."

"What do your folks think about all your traveling?"

Subtle. "Don't know. I came up in foster care." And the less said about his past, the better. "I'm not a rootless wanderer by choice, but circumstance. If you're worried I'm going to break Dan's heart by haring off the first time the wind blows, don't be."

Corey laughed ruefully. "I don't know what to think, to be honest. I just know this family's had more than its share of troubles."

Leif's eyes were drawn irresistibly to the oak above them. "I know. It was never my intention to add to them, believe me. Dan doesn't deserve it. None of them do."

"Trouble finds us all, the saints and the sinners. According to my grand-ma, anyway. Depending on her mood, she'd add you might as well be a sinner and enjoy it."

Leif started to laugh. The sound died, though, as his skin unexpectedly went to goose bumps.

The night around them fell utterly silent, except for the sigh of the breeze and the skitter of dry leaves. He wracked his brain, trying to remember if there had been any sound of insects or frogs before, or if the evening was too cold for them.

"Damn, that's a frosty wind," Corey said, hunching his shoulders for warmth. Or protection.

"Shh." Leif held up his hand, and to his credit, Corey fell silent instantly. Leif scanned the backyard around them, his Walker eyes piercing the gloom.

The skittering grew louder, and with a sudden sinking sensation, Leif realized it wasn't just leaves on grass. There were wards around the property, but wards were only effective against the dead. The living could slip in and disrupt or destroy the wards with impunity, leaving the way open for anything else that wanted to come in.

Fuck, fuck, fuck. Rúnar had been here, had been close, creeping around while Leif slept earlier, sly enough to go unnoticed because he wasn't trying to get any further than the boundaries.

Leif motioned to Corey. "Get behind me and head for the house."

Corey did as he asked without argument. "What is it?"

Leif was spared answering when the *draugr* stumbled out of the darkness.

It was tall and rangy. Greasy rags of flesh clung unnaturally to a skeletal frame, barely covering the brown, rotting bone. It wore the dirt-encrusted remains of a Confederate uniform, and the white, burning light of the dead glowed in its bulging, maggot-ridden eyes.

"Run!" Leif shouted, throwing himself between Corey and the *draugr*.

"Dan!" Corey bellowed, bolting for the house. "Taryn!"

Leif grounded and drew hard on his shields as the *draugr* closed. His sword was in the house, but he still had his boot knife. The *draugr* swung at his off side, and he grabbed its decaying arm, felt the cold, slippery flesh cave in beneath his grip. The stench of rot burst forth in a nauseating wave. With startling speed, the *draugr* spun and snapped its dry teeth. Leif flung up his other forearm to block.

His thick jacket foiled most of the bite, but it still hurt—and worse, kept him pinned while broken fingernails clawed at him. He twisted in an unsuccessful attempt to break free, aura flaring with astral fire, and the *draugr* let out a low moan of animal pain—

"Leave him alone!"

Dan's wand smashed down in a vicious arc, spearing through the *draugr's* rotting skull, releasing a slurry of putrefaction. "Hecate, Lady of Torches, light the way!" Dan shouted, and Leif felt the pulse of energy as he shoved the uprooted spirit back to the Underworld.

"You all right?" Dan demanded as the corrupted ectoplasm dissolved back into the ground.

Leif nodded, despite his aching forearm. "Yes. Thanks to your timely rescue."

"Corey came in shouting about a haint attacking you," Taryn said from a few feet behind Dan.

"Rúnar sent it," Leif answered, tight and angry. "After last night, he couldn't chance me getting away. I should have left—"

"It wouldn't have made a difference," Dan said. "Besides, we've got bigger problems."

Leif turned and stared out across the rolling land. At first, he thought the moving shadows were nothing but the wind-tossed branches of trees or grass.

Then he realized it had gotten cold enough for him to see his breath, and the reek of the grave rode the breeze.

"How many, do you think?" Taryn asked.

Dan shook his head. "Three coming up on this side of the house. Probably more we can't see."

"Well, shit."

The growls grew louder, and the *draugar* broke into a lurching run.

"Fuck! Into the house!" Dan shouted.

Leif didn't need to be told twice. He bolted through the back door, Dan and Taryn on his heels.

The tang of thyme and cumin filled the air, both starting to char in the pan on the stove where Dan had abandoned dinner. Bea and Virgil stood just inside with Corey, no doubt summoned downstairs by the commotion.

"Get away from the doors and windows!" Leif ordered, pushing them ahead of him into the living room. His sword lay on the coffee table; he slung on the baldric and drew the blade.

"What's going on?" Virgil demanded. He tried to sound tough, but his voice cracked with fear.

"We're under attack," Dan said. The door slammed behind Taryn, who was the last one into the house. "Do as Leif said and get out of the way!"

"Come on, kids," Corey said, shepherding them to the relative safety of the stairwell.

"Under attack?" Virgil's voice hit a higher register. "From what? Why? What's going on?"

"Hush," Bea said, although she sounded terrified herself. "Don't worry—they won't let anything happen to us."

Leif's fingers twitched around the hilt of his sword. *Civilians in the mid-*

dle of a fight. Hel Half-dead, don't embrace them yet, please.

"What protection have we got?" Leif asked.

"Sigils buried at each corner of the house, wind chimes, and the haint blue door," Dan rattled off.

"That it?" Taryn asked, sounding annoyed.

"It isn't like haints wander up every day," Dan snapped back. "It's good enough to keep most things out, and small enough not to scare the church-going folk into running us out of town on a rail."

"It would be enough for one *draugr*," Leif added in Dan's defense. "Who the fuck expects to be attacked by more than one at a time?"

Taryn swore at him. Something heavy hit the door, and she shifted her invective toward it instead.

The house groaned, its wards straining under the assault. Leif wished they'd had the chance to lay salt along the windows and doors, but there was nothing for it now. It was only a matter of time before something gave.

The porch creaked under the trod of multiple feet. From the direction of the kitchen, dry, skeletal fingers scrabbled against the window. The knob on the backdoor rattled ominously at the same time, and Leif spared an instant to be glad Taryn had thought to lock it.

"Shit, how many are there?" Dan wondered aloud.

Leif shook his head. "Doesn't matter. I'll take the front window and door. Taryn, you've got the living room window. Dan: kitchen and mudroom."

"Got it," Dan said; Taryn only nodded and strode to the window, her knives gleaming in her hands.

The front window looking out onto the porch burst inward in a shower of glass. Leif was ready; his sword swung down, impacting with the dead arms reaching through.

The blade severed both near the elbow; a gush of black ichor burst from the stumps, accompanied by the familiar charnel-house reek. He thought Corey let out a cry of horror and disgust, but couldn't spare the attention.

The *draugr* made the mistake of sticking its head in next, as it dragged itself through the window on oozing stumps. Only a few scraps of flesh clung to the brown bone, accompanied by an incongruous mane of matted hair. It was at a disadvantage, unable to use its speed or strength while in such a vulnerable position, and a moment later its head joined its severed arms and Mordgud took the spirit.

Even as it dissolved into corrupted ectoplasm, two more began to climb in over it. Silently cursing the old house with its big windows, Leif slashed at the nearest before it could come through.

Bea let out a strangled cry. "Leif, don't! That's Mr. Polk! He was my math teacher!"

Bea's shout jarred him, honed reflexes angling the sword just to one side, even as his senses scrambled to sort out the living from the dead.

"Mr. Polk died in a car wreck last year, Bea!" Virgil shouted back, hysteria edging his voice.

Silently cursing, Leif tried to correct, but he'd lost his momentum. Mr. Polk, his body bloated with decay beneath his cheap suit, reached out with inhumanly strong hands, seeking to crush or strangle. Fortunately, the shattered frame of the window dug into his rotting belly, the wood tearing open an unheeded gash, spearing him in place. The sound of at least one person vomiting came from the stairwell.

The other *draugr* took the advantage and clambered in over Mr. Polk's flailing corpse. The empty white glow in its sockets fixed on Leif. Its jaw was half-torn free from its face, giving it the horrifying illusion of a smile as it leapt for him.

Leif managed to catch it on his sword, the length of the blade spearing it through the chest as it came down on him. Its weight shoved him to the floor, even as it began to dissolve. "Mighty Mordgud, gate-guardian, let these lost ones find their feet on the path to Hel's hall!" he chanted.

Mr. Polk had freed himself in the meantime and made for Taryn's unprotected back. Another *draugr* had broken through the living room window; she dispatched it quickly, the hilt of one knife used to punch its head back, the blade of the second slicing through its now-exposed throat.

"Taryn! Behind you!" Leif shouted, jumping over the couch.

Polk hit her hard, even as she began to turn. Rotting hands closed around her throat. She smashed him in the face with one knife, knocking aside the toupee he'd been buried in.

"Fuck!" Dan shouted, turning from his own fight at the broken-in backdoor.

The kitchen window shattered inwards. A bony hand flailed inside, tangling with the white curtains. The curtain rod tore free and fell with a crash, dropping the cloth directly onto the stove, where dinner sat forgotten on a hot burner.

The curtains burst into flame with shocking speed. Even as Dan drove the antler point of his wand into Polk's skull, Leif ran to the kitchen, his only thought to do something to put out the rapidly-growing fire.

The *draugr,* still tangled in the curtains, stumbled to its feet. Its preternatural flesh burned as it thrashed about, trailing fire where it went. Leif shied back, even as Dan let out a strangled cry of horror and rushed toward the kitchen. Leif grabbed him by the arm. "It's too late! We have to get out of the house!"

"No!"

"Move!" Taryn yelled behind them. "Dan, get your ass over here, in case there are more of them in the yard! I need you to help protect the fucking civvies!"

That snapped Dan out of his shock. Smoke was already billowing out from the fire, making it hard to see. Leif let go of him, and they hurried back through the living room. Taryn bailed out the front door, Corey, Bea, and Virgil behind her.

Dan went out next, Leif on his heels. To his vast relief, there were no more *draugr* to be seen. Conjuring even six of them had been a prodigious work. How long had Rúnar been planning this?

They stumbled out into the yard. Corey frantically tried to get a signal on his cell phone to call the fire department. "The animals—" Leif said.

"The barn's far enough away—they should be okay." Flames were dancing behind the windows of the house by now. "Shit, I'll get the hose, try to put it out—"

Bea ran past them and onto the porch.

"Bea!" Dan shouted in horror. "Get back!"

For a moment, she was framed in the smoke and flames of the open door, before she disappeared inside.

CHAPTER 27

"Fuck!" Leif ran into the burning house after Bea, Dan right behind him.

Inside, everything was heat and foul black smoke. Coughing, Leif held his jacket sleeve up to his mouth. Dan grabbed him by the arm, and together they ran up the stairs.

The fire had spread with unbelievable speed. Smoke poured up through the floorboards as the ceiling below caught. *If the flames eat through, we'll fall into an inferno.*

"Bea!" Dan shouted, coughing heavily. "Where are you?"

"I'm in here!" came her voice, interspersed by coughing. Smoke stung Leif's eyes as he followed the sound to her room.

She was on her knees by the bed, something hugged tight to her chest. Dan flung an arm around her and pulled her up.

"We can't go back the way we came," Leif said. He shut the door, hoping to keep back some of the noxious black smoke for at least a few seconds more.

"The window." Dan helped Bea to the window, while Leif flung it open it. A quick kick knocked loose the screen, and Leif stuck out his head.

To his relief, Bea's window overlooked a row of overgrown bushes. Hollies, unfortunately, but at least they were thick.

"We can lower Bea by her arms," Leif suggested between racking coughs.

Dan nodded. "Come on, Bea."

Her face pale, she peered out the window, then tossed out whatever she had risked her life to retrieve, before Leif had a chance to see what it was. She scrambled onto the windowsill, her legs dangling out, with a frightened look at them both.

"I'm sorry—"

"Later," Dan said, grabbing her by one arm.

Leif took the other; between the two of them, they were able to lower her the length of her body before letting go. She dropped to the holly bushes with a loud crack of branches, but fortunately no snap of bones. A moment later, she staggered free, scooped something off the ground, and turned to look up at them.

"You next," Leif said.

Dan cast him a worried look. "No, I'll—"

The house groaned like a live thing, and to his horror, Leif saw the door beginning to smolder, along with the floor. "Move your ass, Dan Miller, or I'll throw you out the window myself!"

Dan swore at him but went. Gripping the windowsill, he gingerly lowered himself over, while Leif held onto his wrists for as long as he could.

Dan dropped safely to the hollies as well. The heat in the room was now intense, and Leif heard the breaking of glass as other windows blew out. Not giving himself time to think about it, he followed Dan's example, trying to lower his body over the sill while clinging with his fingers. It wasn't easy, and the moment most of his weight was on his hands, his grip slipped and he was falling—

He struck something warm and firm in the midst of the springy holly branches. "Got you," Dan grunted.

The leaves tore at their skin and clothes, but Leif barely noticed the scratches as they stumbled away from the burning house. The sound of sirens wailed in the night, and headlights cut the darkness as some of the neighbors pulled up, either to gawk or to help, Leif wasn't sure. Corey's sedan threw gravel out behind it as he roared up the drive; he was out of the car almost before it had stopped. "I drove down to the Little's place and called the fire department," he explained.

Taryn swept Bea up in her arms, hugging the girl tight. Still clinging to whatever she'd rescued from the fire, Bea burst into tears, wailing against the other woman's shoulder.

Leif turned to Dan as the first fire trucks pulled up. Dan stood absolutely still, his eyes fixed on the burning house. His skin was smeared with soot, his eyes red from the smoke and his skin scratched from the hollies.

"Baby?" Leif said uncertainly. "Are you all right?"

The old farmhouse was nothing but a tower of flame. The firefighters might be able to keep the sparks from spreading farther, but the intense heat had already set alight the oak. The dry leaves on the tree went up, turning it into a living torch.

The flames reflected in Dan's eyes, masking his expression. "No," he said. "I'm really not."

Taryn took Dan's wand and Leif's sword, stowing the weapons in her car before anyone could ask about them. Firefighters ran hoses across the yard, turning jets of water on what remained of the house. EMTs ushered Leif to sit in the back of one ambulance while they checked him out, and Dan and Bea to another.

Dan sat there numbly: answering questions, letting them treat him with oxygen, listening to their chatter back and forth. He felt as if a thick, gray fog had wrapped around him, cutting him off from everything except for loss.

Their home was gone, and he didn't know how they were going to replace it. All their clothes were ashes now, along with photo albums, the old journals, grandma's jewelry, and the rocking horse Dad had carved for Bea. Everything they owned, everything handed down to them from past generations, just...gone.

The EMTs finished up with them; no one needed to go to the hospital, at least. Bea clung to Dan's arm as they left the ambulance. The yard was a whirlwind of rushing people, flashing lights, and deep shadows, blinding even a Walker's ability to make out anything clearly.

A sheriff's deputy appeared at Dan's elbow. "Mr. Miller? I'm sorry, but I need you to answer some questions for the report. Can you tell me how the fire started?"

"The curtain rod fell," Dan said; at least that much of the truth could be told. "I was cooking dinner, and the curtains touched the hot eye."

The questions went on: who had been in the house, was he certain everyone had gotten out all right, on and on. Dan answered them all on autopilot.

Eventually, the deputy handed over his card and left. Corey had been hovering nearby; now he came up and put an awkward hand to Dan's arm. "If you need somewhere to stay, you're welcome to sleep at our place," he offered. "I can't promise more than a fold-out couch in the basement, but at least it's better than nothing."

Gratitude all but melted Dan's bones. "Just for tonight—I don't want to put you out—but yes, thank you, Corey."

"You'll stay for as long as you need to," Corey said firmly. "Come on. No sense waiting around here."

Dan glanced one last time at the burned-out husk, which had been the only home he'd ever known. Firefighters still milled around the smoking ruin, aiming streams of water at smoldering patches of embers. All that remained were a few charred beams and a huge pile of ashes. Even the great oak was nothing but a fire-hollowed stump.

It's all gone.

Taryn appeared out of the dark like a ghost materializing. "No more haints, at least," she said. "You okay, Dan? Bea?"

"Okay as we're going to be," Dan said. Bea gave a little nod and a sniffle. "Corey's offered us a place to stay. We just need to grab Leif and Virgil."

Taryn frowned slightly. "I thought Virgil went with you to call for help," she said to Corey.

Corey shook his head. "He didn't come with me. I thought he was with you."

"Maybe he's with Leif," Dan suggested.

"Where's Leif?" Taryn asked.

"The EMTs were taking a look at him, last I saw."

"Not anymore," she said with a nod in the direction of the remaining ambulance. "The other left—no sirens—and this one's just hanging around in case one of the firefighters need them."

Everything had been confusing: firefighters rushing around, neighbors gawking, flashing lights, sirens, the groan and crash as the upper story of the house collapsed into the lower. But surely nothing could have happened. Not right under their noses.

"Maybe they went to Leif's car," Dan said, trying not to let any fear show in his voice.

Leif's Porsche was still parked where it had sat since his return from Asheville. As they came up on it, Dan saw deep lines scratched into the hood, forming a series of runes similar to the ones encircling Leif's left wrist.

No. Oh no.

"Dan?" Bea asked, her voice high and cracking with fear. "What's it mean?"

"I don't know." But he could guess.

Taryn dropped to her knees and picked something up from the ground. "What's this?"

The last time Dan had seen the blade, it had sailed past him to bury itself in a haint's forehead in Asheville. "Leif's boot knife. He always carried it concealed. In case he got caught somewhere without his sword."

"He got in a fight?" Corey asked.

"No. We would've noticed a fight, no matter how many other people were running around," Dan said. Taryn only looked annoyed, as if she thought Corey had deliberately insulted her. "Somebody grabbed him. They knew he carried the knife, and where, took it from him, and used it on his car."

"'They?'"

Dan felt Bea's horrified gaze on him, but he couldn't look away from the knife, couldn't move, couldn't do anything but speak.

"He. Rúnar. He has Leif and Virgil."

Dawn, and Dan hadn't slept a single moment of the night. He sat on the edge of the foldout couch in Corey's basement, his face buried in his hands.

The hot water heater in the corner hissed softly as it struggled to replenish what had gone into showers for Bea and him, to wash off the soot. In the other corner, a washer and dryer hummed and rumbled, the only clothes they now owned tumbling about inside.

Great Mother, help me. Help us all, please.

He didn't know what to do. Rúnar had made off with Virgil and Leif, and there was no way to know where he had taken them. As for what he might do to them...

Dan shuddered, remembering the twisted perversion Rúnar had made of the psychic link between himself and Leif. Leif had escaped once, but would Rúnar use the power from the Harrow to force something even worse on him?

And Virgil...Dan couldn't stand to even think what might happen to his brother. Virgil, who'd never wanted any contact with the Otherworld, who'd hated Walkers and everything to do with them since Mom died.

Leif had used blood as an offering. And Rúnar used blood to call up the haints and bind them. If he wanted to use the place of power for something truly spectacular, surely he'd need blood to do it.

Virgil would be the sacrifice. And if that much blood wasn't needed, Rúnar would surely kill him out of hand when he'd taken what he wanted. Just as he'd killed Kristian, for no reason other than to hurt Leif.

I've failed everyone. Virgil was going to die, and Leif would end up possessed or enslaved. Bea was homeless, without even a roof over her head.

He'd let down everyone who'd ever depended on him, just like he'd let down Mom that dark night on the mountainside. He'd tried to feed her energy and strength, he'd tried to get home in time to save her, but none of it had been enough.

Nothing he'd done had ever been enough.

Maybe if he'd held to his promise to stay out of haint-work, if he'd told Leif to hit the road the first day they'd met, none of this would've happened. Rúnar wouldn't have had reason to send haints to the house, or to notice Virgil's existence. Leif would never have found out about the Eye of the Uktena, or the Harrow, or any of it.

But no, Dan had to be selfish, didn't he? He had to go back to haint-work, when he'd sworn he wouldn't. He had to help the beautiful man who turned up on his doorstep, because he was lonely.

Hadn't he learned his lesson, when he'd come back to the farm and found Dad lost to booze and his siblings hungry and cold? Hadn't he learned to put others first, not just follow his own whims?

Apparently not. And this is what came of it: everything lost, everyone lost, and no hope of making things right.

A soft knock sounded on the half-open door. Raising his head, he saw

Bea, looking scared and uncertain. The dark circles under her eyes said she hadn't gotten any more sleep than he had. Taryn lurked behind her on the stairs, a dark, protective shape.

"Hey, Bea," he said, trying to keep his voice from cracking on unshed tears. He had to stay strong for her. At least he could manage that much.

"Dan, I have something I need to tell you," she said tremulously. Her eyes were wide and worried, and she clutched something to her chest.

He patted the foldout bed beside him. As Bea sat down, Dan shot Taryn a questioning look. The other Walker responded with a shrug. She didn't come all the way into the room, but leaned her shoulder against the doorframe, her hands loose and ready near the knives at her belt.

"I'm sorry, Dan," Bea said in a small voice. She lowered her arms, revealing a bundle wrapped in an old feed bag. The acrid stench of their burning home rose from it; this must be what she'd rescued from under her bed.

He rested a hand on her back, hoping she'd find some comfort in it. "You've got nothing to apologize for."

"Hear me out before you say that." She leaned against his shoulder though, the bundle on her lap. "When you went back to haint-work, I was scared, Danny. After Mom and Dad, we couldn't lose you. We just couldn't. And I saw Leif made you happy, and I liked him, and I didn't want anything bad to happen to him either."

It was hard to talk past the knot in his throat. "I know. I'm sorry, Bea. I shouldn't have—"

"Let me finish," she said, blinking rapidly against tears. "I thought maybe, if you couldn't find the place Rúnar was after, he'd just go away. And you and Leif would both be safe, and maybe Leif would stay with us, and, Goddess, it sounds *stupid* now. I didn't say anything, and I-I'm s-sorry."

"I don't understand, Bea."

She handed him the burlap-wrapped package. "Here."

Perplexed, he took it from her and unwrapped it. Inside lay a simple book, bound in brown and black leather, with a latch shaped like a silver skull. And though it had been years since he'd seen it, he knew it immediately, even before he caught sight of the familiar handwriting inside.

"What is it?" Taryn asked, confused.

Dan shook his head slowly, barely able to believe his eyes. "It's Mom's Book of Shadows."

Leif blinked sluggishly back to wakefulness. His head ached, and his mouth tasted like the bottom of a shoe, and for a confused minute he wondered if he'd drunk too much and passed out somewhere other than his bed. But the surface under him was cold, hard, and damp; surely Dan wouldn't have let him sleep it off just anywhere.

Dan. The fire. The house.

Leif opened his eyes, trying to roll to his feet at the same moment. But his arms and legs were both tied; the movement only succeeded in tumbling him onto his side. His head swam with agony, even as bile pooled in the back of his throat.

He swallowed it and struggled to take stock of his surroundings. He lay on his side in what looked like a cave, the stone smooth and shaped by the water dripping slowly from the ceiling. A narrow opening led up and away from the small room; the wall opposite it was suspiciously smooth when contrasted with the rest of the cave. The stone pressing against his cheek exuded a damp odor along with something else, some breath of cold darkness that had never seen the light of the sun.

What the fuck?

He followed the fragile thread of memory, fighting to understand where he was and how he'd gotten there. *The draugar...the fire...Bea...sitting in the back of the ambulance while the EMTs checked me out...*

Everything after was a blank.

"Leif? Are you awake?" Virgil's voice, made almost unrecognizable by fear.

Oh shit. "Virgil?" he whispered, lifting his aching head and casting about.

The teen sat facing him, bound hand and foot, and lashed to a stalagmite for good measure. He must have heard Leif's movements, because the cave would be utterly black to his non-Walker eyes.

Leif's heart sank and fear clawed at the back of his throat. Still, he forced his breathing to steady and his voice to remain calm. "Are you all right?"

Virgil nodded, his throat working visibly. "I-I'm okay."

"Do you know where we are?"

"N-No. He grabbed me—Corey went down to use the Little's phone to call the fire department, and Taryn was looking for more haints and trying to decide if she needed to run in the house, and-and he grabbed me. I didn't even have time to yell for help. He was too strong, and he had a knife, and-and he put me in the trunk of his car. I tried to get out, but he tied me up. I didn't even know he had you, too, until we got here. Is Bea okay?"

"She's fine. The man who brought us here—what did he look like?"

There came the sound of boots against stone from the direction of the entrance. Virgil fell silent, his eyes going wide with terror as the steps grew closer. The glint of reflected light showed on the slick stone, growing stronger, until their captor strolled into view, a camping lantern held loosely in one hand.

Rúnar.

CHAPTER 28

Rúnar had changed little in the years since Leif had last seen him: tall and well built, his long hair a fall of sleek silver over his broad shoulders. He wore a long, wool coat against the chill, along with a dark sweater and exquisitely-tailored slacks. The hilt of his two-handed sword jutted up over his right shoulder, gleaming in the artificial light of the lantern.

Ignoring Virgil, Rúnar came to stand over Leif, steel-gray eyes as sharp as his sword, dissecting Leif right down to his bloody core. His hawk-fierce features were painfully familiar: the tiny scar above one eye, given to him by a *draugr* in his youth, the curving lips Leif had kissed, the little line between his brows that deepened when he came. Despite everything, Leif's heart beat a little faster, his body remembering what had seemed good at the time.

"Leif." The deep voice was like an electric shock. How many times had he heard it teaching him, praising him, moaning with passion for him?

There seemed nothing to say—pleas would surely get him nowhere. He settled for glowering instead. The corner of his teacher's mouth twitched down in disapproval. "Don't act like a petulant child."

Absurdly, the words stung. "What should I say?" Leif asked. "Should I rant? Cry? Beg? What were you expecting?"

Rúnar crouched down. With a quick movement, he pulled Leif into a sitting position and straddled him. Leif's body responded, blindly Pavlovian, as the scent of lotus and musk surrounded him.

"I expected your rebellious phase to end before now," Rúnar replied. His eyes bored into Leif's soul, like a pin thrust through a butterfly. "You wish to assert your independence? You wish to make my life more difficult? Fine. The impulse is not strange to young men. But to do *this*—"

Fast as a striking snake, he wound one hand around Leif's hair, right at the nape of his neck. His fingers curled into a fist, pulling harshly, but Leif refused to acknowledge the pain.

"To sever our connection?" Rúnar's breath ghosted across his cheek, drawing forth a shiver of mixed revulsion and delight. "This I will not tolerate."

A half-hysterical laugh cracked Leif's throat. "Do you truly think that's all this has been about? Asserting my independence?"

Rúnar let go of his hair. His fingers slid to cup Leif's chin, thumb lightly stroking across his lips. "Of course it is. I created you. You do not exist without me—you cannot."

"I'm not your puppet!"

"Don't be a fool," Rúnar said, with an air of infinite patience, like some Zen master tutoring his errant student. "I took the husk of a junkie whore and grew you inside. There is nothing in you I did not make, did not guide, did not shape." The hand tightened on Leif's jaw, until he felt the bone creak. "And you were content until the bitch tried to take you from me."

"Don't you fucking call her that," Leif said, and would have spat in Rúnar's face, if the grip on his jaw had let him. "You murdered her!"

"She interfered where she had no right. She tried to take what was mine, and for that she had to pay."

"And Kristian? What did he do? Or were you seriously threatened by a college student who was only looking for a good time?"

The barb failed to hit home; even after all these years, he couldn't win an argument. "He was a message to you, nothing more. But these other Walkers have done far worse than even the harlot Alice."

No. Leif tried for a casual shrug, even though his heart hammered with terror. "They're nothing. Just the means to an end."

"Don't try to fool me," Rúnar said disgustedly. "I've watched through your eyes. It was always more difficult to see when this *lover* of yours was nearby. His influence on you was strong. Still, I might have forgiven it, until he severed you from me. The woman helped, but he was the one who inspired you. For this, he will suffer, as will his kin. Starting with the boy."

Virgil let out a soft whimper. "Leave Dan and his family alone," Leif said, hoping he sounded steadier than he felt. "They have no part in this."

Rúnar's eyes narrowed. "Haven't you been listening? Everyone who has tried to take you from me is part of this. 'This' has never been about anything other than you and me." His grip shifted into a caress, slid down Leif's throat to his chest, and gave one nipple a vicious tweak through the soot-stained t-shirt. Leif bit his lip hard, his mind recoiling even as his body longed to lean closer.

"But after tonight, none of it will matter, my dear. With the power of this place behind me, everyone who ever dared oppose me will fall. And you will be mine forever." Rúnar smiled in a parody of tenderness. "Whether you wish it or not."

~ * ~

"I don't understand," Dan said, staring down at the book in his hands. He ran his thumb across the binding, the familiar feel of the worn leather a visceral tug in his gut. "H-How did you get this?"

Because this book shouldn't even exist anymore; it should have burned along with Mom, its ashes scattered over the mountainside.

Bea huddled in on herself. "When Mom died, it felt like-like Dad wanted to erase her. He took her clothes to Goodwill, and stored all the photos, and-and when he told you he was putting her Book of Shadows to rest with her...I don't know. She wouldn't have cared about the other stuff, but she wouldn't have wanted that. When we were getting ready to leave after the viewing, I told Dad I wanted to say goodbye alone. I went in and-and took it out of her coffin."

Bea was crying now, silent tears running down her face. "It's okay," Dan managed to say, though he wanted to cry too, whether from grief or hope he didn't even know. "I think you did what she would've wanted. But why didn't you say anything to me?"

"B-Because I don't want you to die!" She hiccupped on a sob, her thin shoulders shaking. "After Dad passed, I was scared something would happen to you! I hid the book and never said anything about it. When Leif showed up, and you got back into haint-work, and Rúnar...I was scared, Dan. I was scared you'd go the same way as Mom, and I didn't say anything, even though I knew you needed the book. But now he's got Virgil and Leif, and we've got to get them back; we've got to!"

Dan set the book aside and put his arms around Bea, pulling her close. "Shh. It's okay, Bea. We don't even know if the book will help."

"I do. I looked. Danny, it's the haint that killed Mom!"

Her words didn't make any sense. "We aren't looking for a haint, Bea. We're looking for a place."

"I know, but—oh, just read the book! Mom found it! There's a haint in the Harrow, and it killed her, and it might kill Virgil and Leif too!"

Ice flooded his veins. The memory of cold and pain, of a rain-soaked night, of a long crawl up a steep slope, momentarily blocked out everything else. "Oh, shit. Are you sure?"

"L-Look for yourself."

His hands shook, badly enough he almost dropped the book. Taryn came over and sat down by him, her dark fingers folding over his pale ones, steadying him silently. He flipped to the final pages with writing on them, barely two-thirds of the way through the journal.

She expected to live so much longer. But didn't everyone?

It was there, just like Bea said. Although he skimmed quickly over the words, it seemed as if Mom had been trying to locate the Harrow for a while.

She'd spent the months since he'd left for college piecing together the clues.

But not to get power, not like Rúnar. *"Everything points to the haint being a powerful necromancer when he was alive,"* she'd written. *"Van Horn was scared enough to murder him. But all things must have their season, and in this case, Samhain is the weak point.*

"The amulet is lost, thank Hecate, but there is still a crack in the seal starting at sundown on Samhain. There hasn't been any trouble out of Ezekiel in recent years, but there's been talk of putting a subdivision right on top of where I calculate the cave to be."

The housing bubble had collapsed, and even that much prosperity had passed by Ransom County. Mom hadn't had any way of knowing what would happen, of course. She would've worried about folks moving in right on top of a powerfully evil haint. How many of them would have gone mad, or become mired in silent misery, or otherwise fallen victim, had the original plans gone through?

She'd gone out to lay the haint on the one day she knew she could reach it, when the gateway would open by a sliver.

Why didn't she call me? Why didn't she ask me to come home?

Did she know I would fail, when it came down to it?

A sob tore its way out of him, and he curled up, pressing his face against his knees. "Dan?" Bea asked anxiously. When he couldn't answer, she put her arms around him, as did Taryn.

"Shh," Taryn murmured. "We know where to go now. We're going to kick this motherfucker's ass."

"Yes." He took a deep breath, struggling for control. "We are."

Thanks, Mom.

"All right," Dan said, a few hours later, "this is the plan."

Samhain began at sundown, going by the old Celtic calendar, which meant they didn't have much time left to make their move.

"Corey, before we leave, we'll seal the house. *Don't* step outside until we give the all-clear. Or until sunrise—and take a good look around before you do." Because if they didn't come back by dawn, chances were they weren't coming back at all.

Corey nodded. His brown face was set into serious lines, and he seemed to have aged years in less than a day. *Guess that makes two of us.* "Got it."

"Taryn and I will head up to Old Litch Creek Road," Dan went on. "Rúnar will probably be waiting for us. We're going to try to get the amulet away from him before he has the chance to open the Harrow."

"You'll get them back, right?" Bea asked. "Virgil and Leif."

Gods, she looked scared. Scared, and young, and looking at maybe losing the last of the family she had, if he and Taryn couldn't put a stop to things. Because, having seen Rúnar's depravity during those awful minutes when the necromancer had possessed Leif, Dan didn't doubt he'd kill them all before letting them walk away.

"We're going to try, Bea," he said, unable to lie to her, even though he knew that's what she wanted right now.

"C-Come back, Dan. Promise me."

Shit. He wrapped his arms around her, pulling her close. "I can't, baby girl. But I promise I'll try."

She was crying now, and tears burned his eyes, too, although he fought them back. "Don't leave us like Dad did."

"I won't." He pulled back and caught her gently under the chin, tilting her head back to look into his eyes and see the truth for herself. "I won't pretend to know what was going through Dad's head. But I'm not him. You and Virgil are the most important things in the world to me, and I swear by my breath and blood I'll always take care of you, as long as my heart beats. I'm going to do everything I can to save Virgil, and I'm going to fight with everything I got in me to bring us both back here to you."

She swallowed, her face slick with snot and tears. "L-Leif, too."

Oh, gods, Leif. He'd been trying not to think about what Rúnar might do to Leif during the long hours before sunset. "Leif, too."

Bea nodded and wiped her eyes. Dan released her, and Taryn took his place, hugging Bea and murmuring something to her.

"I'll look after her like she was my own," Corey promised quietly.

"Thanks, Corey," Dan said, holding out his hand. "I don't know how I'm going to repay you for all you've done for us."

Corey ignored the hand and pulled Dan into a rough, if quick, hug. "Just do your thing and bring Virgil back. And I won't say I entirely know what to make of him, but Leif seems like a decent sort, the way he ran into the burning house after Bea."

"Yeah. He is."

"Come on, Danny-boy," Taryn said, having finished with Bea. "Let's gear up."

Dan nodded. "I figure we'll take everything we've got, since we don't know what's waiting for us. Including Leif's sword and boot knife."

"Want to borrow our shotgun?" Corey asked.

Dan shook his head. "Keep it here with you. Just in case. Pack it with rock salt instead of shot—it'll do more damage against the dead." Not that it would do anything but slow them down, but sometimes a few seconds was enough.

Corey didn't look happy. "Do you think we'll need it?"

"I surely hope not."

Dan and Taryn went around and sealed all the doors and windows with salt and rosemary, then went outside and repeated the entire process, just in case. Taryn even marked little hex signs on the dryer vent and heat pump with blue and white chalk. Even though he wanted to hurry, aware of every minute slipping away, Dan made himself work slowly and thoroughly. If he couldn't stay here to protect them, he could at least do everything in his power to make sure nothing could easily reach them.

Corey opened a window and watched him through the screen. "That's it," Dan said. Taryn was already striding toward her car.

"Good luck," Corey said.

"Dan!" Taryn yelled from the driveway. "Move your ass!"

"I've got to go. Bye, Corey. Thanks for everything."

"Stay safe, Dan."

Dan laughed without humor as he went to join Taryn. "Staying safe is definitely not part of the plan."

CHAPTER 29

Sunset was coming.

Deep within the cave, cut off from the sky or any clock, Leif knew it only by instinct. The stones around him seemed to vibrate in tune with some faint, far-off sound, growing stronger and stronger as the sun slipped down the sky. He half-wished he couldn't sense it, that he was as ignorant to how little time remained as poor Virgil.

Mercifully, Rúnar hadn't taken the opportunity to torment him any further. Instead, he'd spent the day meditating and gathering his power, sitting cross-legged with his sword across his lap in the pose he'd taught Leif.

Sweet death, it all felt terribly familiar. How many times had he and Rúnar sat together, before attempting some tomb or ancient ruin?

After, once they'd gotten what they needed, there had been sweat-sticky skin, triumphant laughter, and Rúnar's strong hands holding Leif's hips in place while fucking him.

Today, of course, Leif had spent the hours tied securely, his hands and feet asleep and his ass gone numb against the cold stone. As for later, well. With the power of the Harrow behind him, Rúnar would no doubt be able to reestablish their psychic link despite everything Leif could do to keep him out. Once that was done...

Rúnar had already shown himself willing to possess Leif. With an excess of power to draw on, he'd use the link to force Leif to do whatever pleased him, which would doubtless include sex.

And after?

It didn't bear contemplating. At best, Rúnar would take him back to New York or Chicago, and forget about Ransom Gap and everyone in it. In reality, Leif knew better.

"It is almost time." Rúnar rose smoothly to his feet. Instead of going to the blank wall in the back of the cave, however, he strode past them toward the entrance.

"Are you all right?" Leif asked, as soon as Rúnar was gone.

"Yeah," Virgil said, but his voice shook on the words.

Leif swallowed. "Listen, I'm going to try to distract him, or bargain with him, or something. The instant you see an opportunity, you have to run."

"I won't be able to see! It's dark in here!"

He'd forgotten for a moment. "Do your best. The cave isn't very deep. Keep following one wall with your hand, and you'll end up at the entrance eventually."

"You'll help me, though, if I get lost, right?"

Shit. He didn't want to scare the kid, but a comforting lie could mean Virgil's death.

"I won't be leaving here," he said, and was glad his voice remained steady. "Not alive, or at least, not under my own will. I can't beat him in a one-on-one fight. I'm going to buy you as much time as I possibly can, but you have to run and not wait for me."

Virgil let out a strangled sob. "You're going to have to be brave," Leif went on. "But I know you can do this. You can."

The echo of returning footsteps interrupted. A few moments later, Rúnar stepped back into sight, a satisfied smile on his face. Pulling a heavy knife from his belt, he went to Virgil and knelt near the boy's feet.

"I'm going to free your ankles," he said conversationally. "But if you get any silly ideas about running, my servant will stop you."

Something shuffled into the cave, to be revealed in the lantern light. Virgil let out a cry of terror, his face going chalk-white and his eyes round with fear.

The *draugr* hadn't died easily. It wore a cheap polyester suit, and its mangled corpse seemed mostly held together by the thick stitches of the morticians. The putrescence of rot and embalming fluid rolled out from it in a wave, barely muffled by the icy cold surrounding it. The white light of the dead burned hatefully in its eyes, and bloody runes decorated its sunken cheeks.

"Try to escape, and it will tear you limb from limb," Rúnar went on, without the slightest inflection to indicate there was anything horrible about his words.

Fuck me. Oh, this is not good. A distraction wouldn't work against a draugr. That only left bargaining.

Rúnar left Virgil and came to cut through the bindings on Leif's feet. "Be careful," Rúnar said, and solicitously helped him up with a firm hand beneath his elbow. "I wouldn't want you to get hurt."

"Let the boy go, Rúnar," Leif said, even though bile burned his throat. "Let him go, and I'll do whatever you want."

Rúnar paused and looked down at him. The familiar planes of his features were close enough to trace the lightly-engraved lines, the tiny scar to one side of the mouth which had traced every inch of Leif's skin when he was barely older than Virgil.

"You will do whatever I want anyway," Rúnar said simply.

Leif swallowed hard. "But you'll always know I'm not willing. Not really. This way, I'll do anything you ask, of my own free will. I'll be your slave for the rest of my life, in whatever way you wish. Just let Virgil go, promise to leave the Miller family alone, and I'm yours."

Rúnar's eyes grew hooded. Leif recognized the thoughtful look. *Please, oh please. I'm out of options here. Just do what I want, just this one time.*

Rúnar traced Leif's lips with his thumb. Leif felt the heat of his body, smelled the lotus-and-musk cologne, and the old tangle of emotion threatened to cut off his breath. *Savior, father, lover, enemy.*

"How could I trust you to keep your word?" Rúnar asked.

Leif's tongue tried to balk, but he choked the oath out. "I swear it on Hel's left hand."

For a long moment, Rúnar said nothing. Then he shook his head. "Your mistake, Leif, is believing you have any will of your own to offer. But you are *mine*. Despite your handsome offer, we shall do this my way."

Taryn's Camaro roared up Old Litch Creek Road, skidding around corners and sending gravel flying, every horse under the hood stampeding up the steep ridge. A huge plume of dust fanned out behind the car, and the wind screamed in through the open windows, whipping their hair into their eyes. Dan clung to the dashboard, leaning forward to peer out the windshield, as if he could somehow get them there faster if he just willed it hard enough.

The sun set low on the horizon, and shadows striped the gravel road. Trees blazed in the late light, their golden leaves turned blood red by the dying of the day. Bare rock faces loomed on the mountainside, where the bones of the earth had been blasted apart to create the road. On the other side, the drop into the ravine cut by Old Litch Creek flashed by, getting steeper with every mile falling away under the Camaro's fat tires.

"You remember where this place was?" Taryn shouted above the roar of the wind and the engine.

I couldn't forget it if I wanted to. This was where Mom had died, six years ago tonight. And even though he'd never set foot on the steep slope, he knew every inch of rock she'd dragged her dying body over, every grove of rhododendron and mountain laurel watered by her blood.

I couldn't save her. What makes me think I can possibly save Virgil and Leif?

"Right around this corner," he said, and braced himself to bail out of the car the second it came to a halt.

The Camaro fishtailed as Taryn took the curve too fast. There was a small turnout just past the bend, and she had to slam on the brakes to keep from rear-ending the silver Bentley already parked there. The strap of the seatbelt went tight across Dan's chest, cutting into his shoulder; if he hadn't been wearing it, Taryn's violent braking would have launched him straight through the windshield.

He didn't complain, just unsnapped the seatbelt the second the pressure eased and flung open the door handle. He was out of the car almost before it had finished moving, his wand in his hand, his aura tight and hard as a carapace around him. Taryn pulled Leif's sword from the back seat and followed suit a few seconds later. He heard the scrape of gravel under her boots as she pivoted in a crouch, looking for trouble.

Nothing moved, either in the car, on the road, or in the woods around them. In fact, an eerie silence hung between the trees: no birds fluttered or chirped, no squirrels chattered in alarm, nothing.

Not good.

Dan slowly rose out of his crouch, every nerve taut with anticipation. Taryn did the same, exchanging a quick glance with him over the Camaro's hood, before settling Leif's sword on her back and drawing her knives. Without speaking, they both glided toward the sedan.

Its shining paint was coated in a layer of dust from the road. The doors were locked and all the windows up. Dan started to wipe the dust away to peer inside, but Taryn simply reversed one of her knives and smashed the glass out of the driver's side window with the handle.

"What?" she asked, in response to his look. "It must belong to Rúnar, and I plan to do a lot worse to him than break his toys."

"It might have had an alarm on it!"

She shrugged. "He's kidnapped two people. You think he wants the police poking around because a raccoon climbed on his hood and set the fucking alarm off?"

"Point. Although you didn't know that for sure," he grumbled, as she reached inside and unlocked the doors.

The front seats were spotlessly clean, with only a few long, silver hairs to show anyone had been in the car. The back was a different story. An irregularly-shaped dark stain about the size of a quarter showed on the tan leather upholstery.

Blood. Even though it was only a small amount, fear froze Dan in place. Taryn leaned in from the other side, practically pressing her face into the leather, until she spotted what she was looking for. "Leif," she said, holding up a long, blond hair. "I'm guessing we'll find Virgil's hair in the trunk."

"Yeah," he said, taking a step back and slamming the door shut. "I—"

The back of his neck prickled, cutting off his words. The air had grown steadily colder as the sun went down, but now a deeper chill gusted out of the dark, tangled wood behind him, accompanied by the unmistakable stink of rot.

"We've got company," he said casually, even as his pulse ratcheted up a notch. The charms on his wand rattled a warning as he turned to face the shadowed ravine.

"I guess Rúnar didn't want us to get lonely up here," Taryn replied, falling in beside him. Her knives gleamed in the last sunlight. "Back-to-back, or straight ahead?"

The haints staggered up out of the deep ravine, their rotting shoes sliding on the slick surface of new-fallen leaves. A putrid wind blew up from the depths, masking the wholesome scents of autumn and dust, and transforming the gorge into an open grave.

"Straight fucking ahead," he said.

She shot him a feral grin, her teeth white in her dark face. "My kind of plan."

Then the haints were on them, and there was no more time for talk.

"Stand there, Leif," Rúnar said. "I dislike resorting to crude threats, but allow me to remind you—you have no weapons and no tools."

Except my will. But Rúnar's willpower was hardly weak. *And he has a sword. And at least one draugr.*

Not that he would kill Leif at this point. But hurt him? Of course.

It didn't matter. Leif's life was over; he'd come to accept it during the long hours of the day. But Virgil...

I can't let him die here. I can't. It would destroy Dan.

Dan. The memory of his brilliant smile made Leif ache with grief. *I'm sorry, baby. I wish this could all have been different.*

But it hadn't been. Maybe it *couldn't* have been. There was no fairytale end in store for Leif Helsvin, not after everything he'd done. No fairy godmother to free him; no handsome prince to kiss him awake from the nightmare.

Just let me save Virgil. That's all I ask. But Hel had no pity to spare for the living, and no other deity had reason to care about Leif's desperate prayers. He was on his own.

Sunset was coming on fast; he felt the tension in the ancient spell, the ward growing thinner and thinner, the very stones of the mountain seeming to tremble beneath his feet. Rúnar stepped up to the blank stone wall in the back of the cave. From his pocket, he drew out what could only be the Eye of the Uktena.

The amulet didn't look like much to normal sight, but Leif's Walker eyes were almost blinded by the brilliant energy pouring out of it. A crude gold setting cradled a crystal clear as water—some kind of quartz, perhaps, although he didn't know much about minerals. The whole was attached to a rough gold chain, no doubt welded together by the local blacksmith instead of any jeweler. A faint sound seemed to come from the amulet, like distant music, and he wondered if the miser had been sensitive enough to hear it, or if the gold alone had lured him to snatch it up in lieu of other payment.

Van Horn's ward went taut and began to fray at the edges. A dark crack appeared in the stone of the blank wall, like a rip in the universe. In the center of the crack was a deeper hollow the precise shape and size of the amulet.

Smiling in grim triumph, Rúnar stepped up to the wall and set the amulet into the hole like a key in a lock. The crystal flashed, and the crack began to widen, stone turning into sand and falling to the ground with a soft hiss, until the doorway into the Witches Harrow stood open.

The final haint dissolved into a slick of goo beneath Taryn's knives. "Anubis, Lord of the Sacred Land, throw wide the doors!"

Dan took a deep breath, despite the reeking air. Both of them were splattered with ichor. He didn't know if this batch of haints had been raised and set to guard against casual passers-by, or if they were meant to slow down Dan and Taryn in particular. *Neither of which would be a good thing.*

If the intention had been to slow them down, it had worked. The sun had slid below the mountain, plunging the ravine into night and leaving precious little light on the road. They didn't need it to see, but once the sun was truly down, Rúnar would make his move. And if he had all the power of the Harrow behind him when they faced him...

We're fucked.

"We've got to move," he said, even though every doubt he'd ever had screamed they were already too late.

"Well, gee, and here I was lollygagging around," Taryn snapped. "Tell me something I don't fucking know!"

"Sorry."

"We're doing the best we can." She flicked a spatter of ichor off her knives and onto the gravel shoulder. Her dark eyes narrowed and her full lips pursed with determination as she studied the shadowy hillside falling sharply away in front of them. "What do you bet these aren't the only surprises Rúnar left for us?"

"No bet there." Because even if Rúnar believed they had no idea where to find him, he seemed like the type to take precautions, especially when close to getting what he wanted.

Close to getting Leif.

"Lead the way," Taryn said.

Dan hesitated. This slope had featured in every one of his nightmares for six long years. And even though the skies were clear, for a moment all he could feel was the rain pounding down on exposed skin, numbing the red haze of agony even as it stole heat from a body without much more to lose. The taste of failure clung to his tongue, like sucking on a copper penny dipped in ashes.

Now he was back here, in the flesh this time, only it was Virgil and Leif depending on him. *I let Mom down. I couldn't find her in time. She died here alone in the dark, and it was my fault.*

If anything happens to Virgil or Leif, if I fail them, too…

"Come on," Dan said, and headed down into the waiting hollow.

CHAPTER 30

Rúnar tucked the amulet back into his coat pocket. Drawing his sword, he motioned to Leif. "I will allow you the honor of entering first, my wayward love."

Leif swallowed and glanced uneasily at Virgil. The chances of escape for either of them didn't look good, but maybe if he played along, Rúnar would let his guard down. It wasn't likely, but it was the only plan he had.

His bound hands left him off balance, as he walked to the now-open archway leading into darkness. Rúnar stepped smoothly back, too far away for Leif to lunge at him. The naked blade of his sword swung around to point at Leif, and Rúnar smiled a grim, bitter smile.

"Such a shame, to come to this. Today should have been our greatest triumph. You should have been here at my side, not at the end of my sword."

Leif ignored him; nothing he said now would make any difference. With the tip of Rúnar's sword pressed into his back, he stepped through the archway and into the Harrow.

Beyond, the mountain abruptly opened up into an enormous cavern, its stalactite-draped ceiling lost even to his enhanced sight. Water had sculpted the walls into a fantasia of stone curtains, draperies, and lace, which seemed almost to move when the light of Rúnar's lantern chased shadows across them.

But, magnificent as the cavern was, it wasn't what stole Leif's breath and made his heart thunder in his chest. *Power* filled the lacuna at the mountain's center, a great torrent, which made his hair stand on end and delicately twitched every nerve ending. For a moment, he couldn't make sense of it, any more than if he'd been dropped into a lake beneath a waterfall, or dumped into the most ferocious tangle of whitewater.

He took a deep breath, automatically grounding and centering. Ley lines crossed here, as they did at every place of power, but this churning rush of energy was like nothing he'd ever felt before. The breath and blood of the mountains themselves poured down in rivers, all of which swirled together here in a violent maelstrom of power. No wonder Rúnar had wanted to find this place, if he'd guessed even a fraction of what awaited him here. *And no wonder Jedediah was desperate to seal it away.*

A rough stone block stood at the center of the cavern, in the very heart of the vortex of energy. It looked old; far older than Jedediah's time, and he wondered if ten thousand years of shamans might not have stood here, long before any Europeans even dreamed this continent existed. Lines had been scratched in the floor all around the altar stone—and these felt and looked newer, somehow.

It didn't take long to realize why. A leathery shape lay to one side of the altar, dressed in tatters of clothing more than a century old. Curled in one bony hand was the hilt of a knife, its blade worn down to nothing more than a dull nub.

Ezekiel.

"Ah," Rúnar moaned; the sound was oddly sexual, and Leif shuddered involuntarily. "You feel it, don't you? Of course you do—even a mundane like the boy can probably sense this place is beyond the ordinary."

Leif deliberately didn't glance in Virgil's direction, not wanting to focus Rúnar's attention on him. "I feel it."

"A man with this at his command can do anything he chooses. *Have* anything he chooses. If the bitch hadn't turned you against me, this would have been yours as much as mine. Tell me you wish you hadn't listened to her, having felt this. With this power, no one would ever be able to hurt you again."

"No one but you," Leif said quietly. He raised his head and met Rúnar's iron gaze. "Is that what this is about? What it's always been about?"

He wasn't certain what made things slip into place at that moment; maybe it was simply being able to think clearly, without the interference of the psychic link. Or maybe Dan had helped him put aside enough of his own pain, allowing him to see beyond himself in a way not even Alice had taught him.

"You never spent the night with me," Leif said, parsing through a thousand clues he'd never considered before. "I thought you were being kind, giving me space all my own. But you never asked me into your bed to sleep, either. We even had separate tents in Siberia. Do you have nightmares? Were you afraid I'd see you in a moment of weakness? Afraid I'd find out what haunts your dreams? Why *did* you choose a drugged-out whore off the streets to remake in your own image? What battle are you fighting with your own fear, Rúnar?"

All the blood drained from Rúnar's face, and for a split second Leif saw something he'd never been allowed to glimpse before: vulnerability.

The shutters slammed back into place, and Rúnar's lips writhed back from his teeth in a snarl of pure rage. His left hand shot out and closed around Leif's throat.

Leif gagged at the pressure against his windpipe and tried to pull away. Rúnar's fingers dug savagely into the vulnerable flesh, holding him in place. A look of utter rage transformed Rúnar's face, and for a moment Leif thought the necromancer would actually kill him.

A figure stepped through the entrance to the cavern. It was covered with ichor and smeared with mud, but there was no mistaking the broad shoulders and shaggy hair, or the wand with its wicked antler hook.

"Get your fucking hands off him," Dan said.

Dan's heart thundered in his chest, and his hands shook, although thankfully the buzz and rattle of the charms on his wand covered his trembling. He reeked head-to-foot of rot, and his clothes clung to him where he'd gotten soaked falling in Litch Creek while fighting a particularly vicious haint.

But they'd made it through, Taryn and him, all the way down to the cave. His eyes flicked over the cavern as he came through the natural arch and into the Harrow. Virgil cowered to one side, his hands bound and his expression scared, but looking okay otherwise. A leathery corpse lay near the altar, which must have belonged to Ezekiel.

And there, directly in front of him, was Leif, being held by the throat by an enraged man who could only be Rúnar.

His first, insane thought was Rúnar looked nothing like Dan had imagined. If Leif was a Nordic supermodel, Rúnar was a fallen king. His long hair flowed in a silver mane over broad shoulders, and his face was a sculpture of high cheekbones and straight nose, honed by the years until everything unnecessary had been chipped away. He was even taller than Leif, his frame broad and powerful, like an aging lion.

And he's hurting Leif.

"Get your fucking hands off him," Dan ordered, his voice shaking with rage. His hand tightened on the wand; he'd never tried to harm a living person with it, but at the moment all he wanted to do was kill the man who'd dared hurt Leif.

Rúnar shoved Leif away, sending him sprawling onto the stone floor near Virgil. His cold eyes ran up and down Dan's form, judging—and clearly finding him wanting.

"Ah, my replacement," Rúnar said contemptuously, in the same accent which had warped Leif's voice when the necromancer had possessed him. "I thought I'd taught Leif to have better taste."

Dan was peripherally aware of Taryn slipping into the cavern behind him, but he didn't dare take his eyes off Rúnar. Instead, he casually moved in the opposite direction, away from Virgil and Leif, hoping to draw Rúnar's attention. "Well," he drawled, "I guess even a backwoods hick like me looks good compared to an evil maniac."

Rúnar's eyes narrowed. "You think to judge something far beyond your comprehension." His aura flared, oily black, which was the only warning Dan had before a haint lumbered out from among the stalagmites.

Dan spun, his wand held out ready before him, his shields snapping into place. Time seem to slow, and his eyes picked out the details of the bound haint: the cheap suit, the coarse stitches of the undertaker, meant to keep the body in one piece until it could be buried, the bloodless pallor of the flesh, spotted here and there with rot.

Even with all the marks of death, the face sent a bolt of agonized recognition through him.

"Jimmy!" he gasped.

The haint slammed into him, and they both went to the floor.

When Rúnar shoved him away, Leif managed to roll, saving himself from a hard impact with the stone floor. He kept rolling, using his momentum to put distance between them, in case Rúnar decided to use him as a hostage.

His back fetched up against a stalagmite near the edge of the cavern, almost knocking the breath out of him. Shaking it off, he struggled to his knees.

Dan and Rúnar circled each other a short distance from the center of the cavern, where the power flowed at its greatest concentration. And, sweet death, Dan looked magnificent: black eyes snapping defiantly, his mouth set in a grim line of determination, as if no power in any of the nine worlds could make him back down.

The *draugr* hovered near them, awaiting Rúnar's command. Closer to Dan, Virgil huddled against a stalagmite, his eyes wide and fixed on his older brother.

"Hold still," Taryn said, and Leif jumped. A moment later, he felt the rope around his hands part. He shook off the remains of the bindings and rubbed at his wrists.

Taryn's face was scraped and bruised on one side, her clothing covered with mud and ichor. Still, she had both her knives, and Leif's sword strapped to her back.

She tucked away one knife just long enough to unbuckle the baldric and pass the sword to him. "Get Virgil out of here," she said, as he unsheathed the sword with a hiss of steel. "I'll help Dan handle this bastard."

Leif shook his head, dreadful certainty settling in his gut. He'd been on this path since the day Alice had called out to him from a table at a sidewalk café. Or who knew: maybe since the night he'd taken shelter in a haunted warehouse.

Either way, every step had been bringing him here, now, to this night and this place and this moment.

"I know how Rúnar fights," he said, as she cut Virgil loose. "I'll have a better chance. You—"

Something dark moved in the entryway of the cavern, and twin points of white fire appeared as yet another *draugr* stumbled into view.

"Shit, how many of these things does he have?" Taryn muttered. "Fine. I'll take care of this one. You gut the bastard."

"Yeah," Leif said, and turned just in time to see the first *draugr* knock Dan to the floor.

Leif's heart jerked into overdrive, and he started to bolt to Dan's side, ready to help. But movement caught his attention, and he saw Rúnar hurrying to the altar in the center of the cavern.

Shit. For an instant, he wavered, torn between the urge to save one of the only two men he'd ever loved, and to kill the other.

But he hadn't been sent here to rescue Dan. He'd been sent to save both the dead and the living by the score, and one man's life didn't—couldn't—balance that. No matter how desperately Leif wanted it to.

Forgive me, Dan.

Firming his grip on his sword, Leif waded into the torrent of coruscating power surrounding the altar.

The fierce energy shoved at him, nudging his consciousness out of his body, and he let it take him. Half in the physical world, half in the astral, his vision shifted, revealing the golden fire of the ley lines, the power of the mountain's spines meeting in the empty space at the center of the cavern. The marks scratched onto the floor burned with reddish light, pulsing to no rhythm Leif could discern. He saw the golden cord connecting Taryn to her distant teacher, could even make out the thin, wispy linkage of shared blood binding Virgil and Dan together.

Rúnar's aura pulsed dark gray, mottled with patches of black and scabrous red, like something diseased. Bloated tendrils of power snaked away from him, binding the *draugr* he'd raised and now compelled. He'd paused at the verge of the scratched lines surrounding the altar, his head cocked to one side as he studied them.

He turned smoothly as Leif approached, drawing his own sword: a great, two-handed blade a lesser man would never be able to wield. Ethereal flames ran along the edges and lit his face from below, calling up orange sparks in the depths of his pale eyes.

"You would truly try to kill me?" he asked, and gods, if he didn't actually sound hurt.

And maybe he had reason. Leif was no cold-blooded killer, whatever else he might be. Rúnar had known him better than anyone else ever had, perhaps ever could. They'd lived and loved together for years, and some part of Leif would never entirely leave that behind.

But things had changed. He'd changed. He'd hung on Yggdrasil and kissed the left hand Death.

He *owed* Hel. And such a debt was always paid in blood and pain, one way or another.

"You've left me with no choice," Leif said, half-surprised his voice remained steady. "You won't stop. Therefore, I have to *make* you stop. And there's only one way I can do it."

Rúnar's eyes narrowed, and Leif saw in them a reflection of everything he felt: hate and love, anger and sorrow, revulsion and desire. For a moment, the world seemed balanced on a breath, and the mad thought came to him: perhaps Rúnar wouldn't force him to this after all. Maybe he would atone, repent, become whatever it was he might have been had his life not been twisted out of all recognition.

Cold pride clouded Rúnar's eyes, mingled with greed, and beneath both the fear engendering them: fear of losing control, of being victimized, of abandonment and pain and a thousand other things Leif understood far, far too well.

"If that's how you will have it, on your head be the consequences," Rúnar said. Contempt twisted his handsome features into a sneer. "I created you. I can destroy you just as easily."

"You can try."

"You know how this will end. I'm the better swordsman. I always have been."

"Prove it."

"You think I won't kill you? I will, and I'll drag you screaming back from Helheim and bind you to your corpse forever. I'll fuck your boyfriend while you watch, and cut his throat when I'm done."

Leif's gut clenched with fear, but he tamped down on it hard. Fear was weakness, in this place where intent was as much a weapon as the sword in his hand. "Say hello to Mordgud for me," he said instead.

Rúnar hissed and raised his sword, falling into a fighting stance. Leif did the same, and blue light wreathed his blade in his astral sight. For a minute, they stared at one another, poised with muscles tense, caught on the instant between readiness and action. Leif grinned.

"Bring it," he said.

They both moved at the same moment, the space between them vanishing with frightening speed. The heavy weight of Rúnar's sword deflected off the thinner line of steel in Leif's hands, the shock jolting all the way from wrists to shoulders. Then they were apart, circling, each looking for advantage, and in some strange way it was almost as if they were back sparring in the dojo.

Except this was no mock fight, no matter how earnest. This was a deadly battle not just of steel, but of sorcery.

Spikes shot out from Rúnar's aura, seeking to penetrate and control, but Leif was ready for that gambit. Indigo fire erupted across his aura, and the spikes fell into ash. "You're going to have to do better."

Rúnar didn't rise to the bait, instead feinting at Leif, testing his defenses with a quick exchange of steel-on-steel. Leif used momentum to twist the heavier blade aside. He flung out his left hand, a fiery whip erupting from his fingers and wrapping around Rúnar's wrists.

Rúnar snarled, snapping the binding apart with a quick flick. But it had held him up for a moment; encouraged, Leif pressed forward, blade-to-blade, forcing Rúnar back.

Can I do this? It wasn't something he'd let himself contemplate, not really. *Can I beat him?*

Rúnar's left foot touched the outermost ring of scratched symbols, where the greatest concentration of power lay. A lupine smile warped his mouth: it was all the warning Leif received.

Dropping the sword point-first to the ground, Rúnar held the weapon in place with his left hand while sliding his right up along the sharp edge of the blade. Blood dripped from his fingers, hanging suspended in the air as he sketched a quick series of runes, fueling his spellcraft with the power of the ley lines.

Shit!

Leif fell back, slashing the veins of his left arm hastily—but he was slow, too slow, and the bindrune he tried to draw with his blood was only half-complete when Rúnar's spell hit him.

Thick and sticky, the clotted magic closed around him, forcing its way into his mouth and nose, cutting off his breath. He tasted blood and rot; bile rose in his throat and was blocked, burning. His lungs heaved in panic.

No. Even without breath, he could find the center of himself, the core of calm filled with the silence of Helheim. Quiet and still, ready to do what must be done, it gave him the space to think without fear.

Rúnar isn't the only one who can use the power of this place.

The scorching fire of the crossing ley lines filled him, burning in his veins and turning Rúnar's spell to flaking red dust. Leif's own wound still oozed sluggishly; he dipped his fingers in the congealing blood, sketching one rune on the burning blade of his sword, another on the air. Sword runes, sharp runes, symbols with edges meant to cut through defenses both physical and astral.

Rúnar staggered slightly under the return assault. His brows drew together in rage and pain, and he let out a noise like a wounded bull right before charging.

Their swords came together again, steel ringing off steel, the cavern's echoes turning the sound into a scream of metallic anguish. Leif was younger, faster—and less experienced. Rúnar might be older and slower, but he'd battled other necromancers to the death more than once. The fact he'd survived meant he was very, very good at winning.

It wasn't long before Leif found himself fighting a purely defensive battle: steel-to-steel, spell-to-spell. The power of the Harrow blazed through them both, turning Rúnar into a figure of corrupted flame. As the heavier sword smashed into his defenses yet again, Leif's left wrist broke with the sound of a wet twig snapping under a boot.

Pain smashed up his arm, and he felt his grip slip away, leaving his sword in his right hand only, nothing but the strength of one arm to shield him from the next attack. He retreated an automatic step, heart smashing against his ribs even as time seemed to slow down. He had forever to watch realization bloom across Rúnar's face, to see one flicker of regret, followed by a smile of triumph.

Rúnar drove his sword point-first at Leif's torso. Leif tried to block, but his blade was turned aside by sheer power.

The steel tip of Rúnar's sword pierced him, and the hot slickness of blood gushed down his belly.

CHAPTER 31

*F*uck, oh fuck, oh fuck!

Pain jarred up Dan's spine as he hit the damp stone floor with all the terrible weight of the dead on top of him. Dry teeth snapped at his face, and he jerked to one side, felt them tangle with hair instead of flesh. The stench of decay boiled out of Jimmy's mouth, strong enough Dan wanted to vomit. He twisted under Jimmy's weight, trying and failing to get his wand into position to stab. His right arm was free, but his left arm and both legs were pinned under Jimmy's weight.

Jimmy bit at him again; Dan managed to catch his face between the prongs of antler, using the wand as a brace to hold his head back. The tips of antler dug into sloughing skin and flesh as the haint struggled against them.

Sorry, Jimmy.

Jimmy's right hand closed around Dan's throat. As the pressure cut off his airflow, Dan shifted his hips, trying to throw off the weight bearing down on him. But he had no leverage, and with his other arm trapped, the only thing he could do was push hard with the wand. Jimmy's neck bent back, but he didn't let go.

Dark spots began to dance in front of Dan's eyes. He heard the faint clash of metal-on-metal—*swords?*—and spared an instant to wonder where Taryn was, and if Virgil was okay. Whatever else was happening, it didn't look like anyone was coming to save him.

Shit. Time to get risky.

He yanked the wand to one side, an arc of decaying flesh and black ichor flying away with it.

Jimmy's head instantly snapped forward, teeth bared. Dan was ready for the attack, and smashed the heavy oak into Jimmy's head, deflecting it up and back. Jimmy let out a low snarl, opening his mouth to lunge and bite again.

Dan jammed the wand into Jimmy's open mouth. The tip of the antler hook dug into the soft palate, then snagged on bone. The second prong grated against the teeth of the lower jaw.

Jimmy thrashed, but his mouth was wedged open, unable to close. Silently praying the antler didn't snap from the pressure, Dan slid his fingers into Jimmy's mouth.

A slimy tongue prodded his fingers, and his nails scraped through tissue gone slick with decay. Gritting his teeth, Dan thrust his fingers beneath Jimmy's tongue, until they closed around a thin square of rune-marked wood. The wood was covered with putrefaction, and almost slipped out of his grip, but he managed to pull it free.

The effect was instantaneous: Jimmy went limp, weight crushing down on Dan, who couldn't even gasp out the words to send him back to the Otherworld. Black runnels appeared in the flesh as it collapsed in on itself, sloughing off the skeleton, before the bone turned spongy and went to goo, all of it soaking horribly into Dan's clothes.

But he was free, as was poor Jimmy. Whispering a prayer for his friend, Dan rolled to his side, just in time to see Rúnar run Leif through.

Everything went very, very still. Leif stood, his sword clutched in his right hand. Rúnar's blade pinned his t-shirt to his abdomen, the steel like a shaft of pure ice inside his body.

He did it. I was too slow, too weak. Just like he always said.

Rúnar wrenched the sword back out, and the pain hit.

Agony blazed below his ribs, white-hot and inescapable. It drove him to his knees on the cold stone, robbing him of breath, of movement, of everything but the animal instinct to freeze in place.

But Leif knew pain, just as he knew the hot blood pouring down his stomach and soaking into his jeans.

Hel Half-dead, Loki's Daughter, Lady of the Lost Way, accept the offering of my pain. Take this sacrifice, and give me the strength to do what must be done.

The agony didn't lessen—but somehow it became transmuted, sharpening every sense, settling his scattered thoughts into perfect clarity. He heard Dan scream his name, heard Taryn's shriek of rage and even Virgil's cry of grief. From his position on his knees, he saw Rúnar turn away from him, coat swirling lazily around his legs, ready to go to the altar and lay claim over all the dead of Ransom County.

It seemed to take an age, but Leif had all the time in the universe as he tilted his head back and firmed his grip on his sword. He felt the tensing of every muscle in his legs, followed by the release as they uncoiled, pushing him up and off the ground.

Something must have caught Rúnar's attention; he started to spin, realizing his mistake. His silver hair caught the glow of surging power, and the blue flames wreathing Leif's sword reflected for an instant in the very depths of his eyes.

Leif felt the tip of his sword hit cloth and stick a moment, before piercing skin. He shoved the blade all the way to the hilt, angled up beneath the ribs.

The last frantic spasm of Rúnar's heart transmitted itself down the sword. Leif met Rúnar's gaze, and for a moment it almost seemed as if none of this had ever happened.

Father, lover, savior, teacher.

"I'm sorry," Leif whispered.

He wrenched the sword back out the path it had made in Rúnar's body. Blood spurted out, drenching him and mingling with his own. Rúnar collapsed backward, sprawling across the altar for which he'd sacrificed everything.

Then Leif was falling as well, and it was almost a relief to feel the hard stone against his back, even as Dan screamed his name.

"Leif!" Something deep in Dan's throat ripped with the force of the cry, and he tasted blood, but it didn't matter. *Nothing* mattered, except the man he loved had collapsed to the stone floor, blood gushing out of the wound in his abdomen.

"Dan!" Taryn said urgently—but fuck that, *damn* that, Leif was hurt, was dying, no different from Mom, blood spilling out fast and thick.

Virgil lurched awkwardly from where he'd been hiding behind a stalagmite and pressed both hands to the wound in Leif's side. Leif let out a high--pitched moan and jerked away.

Dan shoved Virgil's hands back down. "No! Keep pressure on it, Virgil!"

"Dan!" Taryn called again.

Dan ignored her, bending over Leif. His heart pounded as though it would wrench its way out of his chest in an attempt to keep his lover's beating. "Leif? Sweetheart?"

Leif licked his lips and swallowed. "Thirsty," he mumbled. "Fuck. Dan?"

"Yeah. I'm here. It-it's going to be all right."

"Dan!" Taryn shouted, and the naked horror in her voice spun him around like a hand on his shoulder.

Rúnar's body lay sprawled across the altar. With the cessation of his heart, his blood dripped only sluggishly, flowing through the channels someone had cut in the rock.

No, not cut. Scratched, with the dull point of a knife as life ebbed away day after day, trapped in a cave with no food and only the moisture which could be licked off the damp walls.

No.

Even as Dan watched, the blood reached the leathery corpse lying to one side, clutching the nub of a knife.

Light sprang into being, almost blinding him. For a moment, it tied together the two bodies, one ancient and one recent.

Rúnar's eyes opened.

"Shit!" Taryn shouted, and one of her knives flew through the air as if impelled by her will alone.

Rúnar moved, faster than he should have been able to given the blood loss. The knife slammed home in his side, but only a few drops of crimson remained to creep out.

What the fuck?

Rúnar's head swung around, a ghastly grin on his face—and the burning light of the dead in his eyes.

"Ezekiel," Dan whispered, even though it wasn't possible. Mom had put Ezekiel down, sent him to his rest.

Hadn't she?

A low, evil laugh escaped Rúnar's bloodless lips. "Child of Jedediah," he whispered. "Oh, this is sweet, to find it is one of his blood who has freed me from this prison." He cocked his head, the motion stiff and inhuman, as if the thing possessing Rúnar's corpse only dimly recalled what it was like to have a body. "The same blood as came to put an end to me, not very long ago."

"No," Dan managed to say, even though his tongue felt made out of lead.

"She came with the moonrise, looking to reach through the crack in the barrier and banish me. But I reached back; even though the barrier was still in place, there was just enough space for me to call up the haint of a man who had drowned in the creek. She never expected to be attacked from behind."

No. This thing, this haint, this dead necromancer, had killed Mom.

Cold swept over him, as if he were on the mountainside with her again, blood draining inexorably from her wounds and taking all the warmth in the world with it.

"It's not possible," Taryn said. "The dead can't—you can't—"

The thing in Rúnar laughed. "I suppose this is impossible as well."

He waved a hand, and a dome of diseased green light sprang up from the circle scratched around the altar. Taryn let out a shrill cry, her remaining knife arcing through the air, before bouncing off the barrier as surely as if it were a solid wall.

Shit!

Ezekiel laughed, a hollow sound wrung from dead vocal cords, skin-crawling as nails on chalkboard. "Fools! Do you think I lay here dying over days, thanks to that coward Jedediah, and made no preparations? Do you think I haunted this cavern afterward, with nothing but time, and gave no thought to my revenge? I knew someone would eventually find the amulet and stumble in here, seeking power. I had intended to attach myself to him more subtly, but you've provided me with an empty body, and I intend to use it."

Dan felt as though the mountain had fallen out from under him, leaving him flailing. *A haint with all the power of a necromancer. How can we fight him?*

This thing killed Mom. Or sent the haint after her that did it.

He's had a hundred years to plot and plan. He isn't even human any-more, not really; he can't be.

And Leif... Great Goddess, he couldn't turn around, couldn't see if Leif had died, couldn't, couldn't—

The haint stepped up to the altar. Pulling Taryn's knife from his side without the slightest sign of pain, he wiped blood from the blade and used it to draw sigils on the stone altar. His hands outspread, he began to chant in Latin.

"Shit!" Taryn swore. "He's using the power of the Harrow to fuel his spell! He's raising the dead of Ransom County—*all* of them!"

Horror shuddered through the numbness of shock. Dan *felt* it on some level, whether because of his connection to the dead or because Hecate sent him a vision, he didn't know. Hundreds of haints, dragged back from the Otherworld, screaming in pain and confusion, as they appeared as a mist above their graves, before taking solid form. Driven by Ezekiel's madness, they would attack any of the living who happened to be nearby.

Oh fuck. Oh no. They couldn't fight that many haints; it would take a lit-eral army of Walkers to put them down. And in the meantime, the living would die and add to the ranks of the haints bent on killing everyone in Ran-som County.

"Dan!" Taryn shouted, and the fear in her voice reached him. "Don't zone out on me! We've got to *do* something!"

What? What can we do when we've already lost?

The cold of that night on the mountain came back to him. Mom had fought to come back to them, even though she had to know it was hopeless. She'd reached out to Dan through their psychic link, wanting him to save her. He'd failed her, and he'd fail now.

He couldn't free himself from the memory. Six years ago tonight, al-most to the hour, she'd died on the side of this mountain, and now it was his turn. His turn to crawl and to reach out, but there was no one to reach out too. No one to beg—

But no, that wasn't right. Mom had never begged for a thing in her life. She hadn't given up. She'd struggled to reach him, wanting him to…

That wasn't right, either. It wasn't what she'd said to him, as the life left her. He'd blocked out the last moment even at the time, because he'd known she was saying the one thing he couldn't stand to hear from her: good-bye.

He'd told himself she reached out for help, told himself there was still time to save her. Lied as much as he needed to get through the long hours of searching, clinging to hope because he wasn't ready to let go of her, not yet.

"I'm proud of you."

That was what she had told him, dying on the mountainside. The last thing she'd ever said to anyone in this world.

And she hadn't died alone, not really, had she? Because he'd been there with her, and she'd known it.

She'd known she wasn't alone.

"I'm proud of you."

And maybe there was no hope, and the living would die by the dozen at the hands of the bound dead. Maybe he'd die here in this cave, along with Virgil, and Leif, and Taryn. But there wasn't anything in Mom's lessons about giving up and going home. There wasn't anything about not doing your duty just because it was too hard, or too scary, or even impossible.

He'd given up and hid for six long years, because he figured he'd failed Mom and failed Dad and failed everybody. Because it was easier to hide, to keep his head down and never take a chance on anything, telling himself it was the responsible thing to do.

But he was a Walker-Between-Worlds. More: he was Simone Miller's apprentice. And if he'd fucking let her down in the last six years, he was going to make up for it right now, even if it was the last thing he ever did.

Dan firmed his grip on his wand and lifted it. "Yeah. We've got to do something. Let's start by taking this fucker down."

"Great idea. How are we supposed to do that?" Taryn asked.

Dan took a deep, centering breath. His astral vision sharpened, even though he was still mainly in his body: he could see the torrent of the ley lines, the sickly green barrier Ezekiel had erected, and the golden cord linking Taryn to her teacher. He deliberately didn't look behind him at Virgil and Leif; as long as he could believe Leif was still alive, he could fight to save and not to avenge him.

For the first time, Dan wished he knew something beyond the rudiments of necromancy. But this was far past anything he'd trained in; Jedediah might have been a sorcerer, but the tradition had died out of their line before Mom had been born, let alone him.

Which means we do this the hard way.

"We find a weak spot and fight our way through. Brute force."

"He's got all the power of the ley lines behind him!"

"Yeah. But so do we."

Taryn cursed at him, but he ignored it, instead fighting the push of the Harrow and dropping further into his body. His astral sight faded, and he concentrated on the lines crudely scratched into the floor.

Whatever Ezekiel might be now, when he'd made those marks, he'd been dying—and had known there was no escape. No matter how badly he'd wanted revenge, the certain knowledge of his slow, agonizing demise from thirst and hunger would have affected him. As the days had passed, he would have grown weaker, especially if he couldn't get enough water by licking the damp walls. His coordination would have begun to fail even before his strength started to give out.

Dan traced the scratched lines around the perimeter, trying to stay calm, trying not to remember how people might be dying with every passing second, because right now to hurry was to miss a detail, and that led to failure. If Ezekiel had set up the spell for his own resurrection first, and this defense as an afterthought, there would surely be some flaw.

There. It was tiny—even dying, the sorcerer had been meticulous. The gap between hacked lines was barely even a millimeter in width. But it was enough.

The circle wasn't complete. Which meant things could get out.

Or in.

"Here," he muttered to Taryn. "We can drive a wedge here."

She came to his side and nodded. "Got it."

She thrust her remaining dagger forward; it skittered along the impermeable shell of the barrier—then sank in, the edge finding the tiny gap and forcing it open farther. Snarling with effort, she pushed against it, her muscles tensing even though the effort wasn't physical.

He waited, watching now with astral sight, seeing the crack widen and spread, flaws opening up in the barrier like glass breaking but not yet shattering apart. At least, not until the right pressure was applied.

"On three," he said. "One."

He honed his will into a spike, concentrating on the point of antler on his wand with everything he had.

"Two."

Like a pitcher getting ready to throw a ball, he twisted his body away from the barrier, leg muscles bunching, arm drawn back, wand cocked.

"Three."

CHAPTER 32

Coiled tension exploded into movement, Dan's body swinging in an arc, bringing him up off his feet, the antler smashing down with all the of energy, psychic and kinetic, he could give it.

The flawed barrier exploded, shards falling into mist and ectoplasm, smearing the floor of the cavern.

The haint spun, an inhuman snarl distorting Rúnar's handsome features. A great web of black cords rose from the altar behind him, and some part of Dan's mind registered the bound dead were tied to the Harrow rather than Ezekiel. But it didn't matter at the moment—what mattered was the sorcerer heading for them with murder in his eyes: Ezekiel wrapped in the possessed flesh of Rúnar.

Dan dodged left and Taryn right, flanking Ezekiel as if they'd done this a hundred times before. Ezekiel went for Dan; Taryn came up behind him, her knife drawing a flash of congealing blood from his shoulder before he spun on her instead.

"Die," Ezekiel growled.

He drew his arms in, bowing his head. His aura flashed into a deep gray-black, tendrils forming, turning to spikes, and stabbing at them both. Icy cold gripped Dan's body as the spikes shredded his defenses, accompanied by the greasy, questing feel of Ezekiel's psychic touch.

Dan fell back, gasping, trying to center and ground, to rebuild his tattered aura. Ezekiel raised his head, the white points of his glowing eyes finding Dan's face, and a horrifying grin warped his mouth.

"Blood of Jedediah. Bow to me."

No. But he was colder than he'd ever been. Dan's entire body shuddered with the chill, muscles locking, and he found himself on his knees, curling up in desperation to preserve whatever warmth remained.

"Bow yourself, fucker!" Taryn screamed, and brought her knife down in a deadly arc, aimed straight for Ezekiel's skull.

He spun, faster than anything human, and his arm dashed aside her knife with all the strength of the dead. Unarmed, she kept fighting, kicking and punching, but the only effect it had was to stagger him slightly. Growling savagely, he closed his fingers around her throat to crush.

The spell faded slightly as Ezekiel focused his attack on Taryn, but Dan was still so fucking cold, his body wracked by chills. It would be easy to curl up and close his eyes, just for a minute.

Get up! Mom's voice in his head, so clear he would have sworn she was standing beside him instead of speaking from a distant memory. *Move or die, Danny!*

Every muscle throbbed, but Dan forced himself to his feet. It took both hands to keep the wand steady, but he lifted it high above his head.

It fell, with all the strength and weight of his body behind it. The antler point smashed into Ezekiel's skull, the freshly-dead bone snapping beneath the force.

"Hecate, Lady of the Keys, take this one and lock him far from the land of the living!" Dan cried hoarsely.

Ezekiel reared back, and for a horrified moment Dan thought it hadn't worked. Then the stolen corpse began to dissolve into corrupted ectoplasm, black ichor cutting runnels in the flesh. Ezekiel screamed, even as he stumbled away from Dan, flesh sloughing to leave behind an animate skeleton. Finally even the bones began to dissolve, and with a last moan Rúnar's corpse went to ichor.

The baying of hounds echoed in the cavern; Ezekiel was making Hecate's pack chase him down. But there was nowhere to flee, and within moments the barks faded into silence.

Dan collapsed to his knees. Taryn whimpered and rolled onto her side; injured but alive.

"G-good work," rasped a voice Dan barely recognized as Leif's.

He crawled across the rough stone to where Leif lay. Virgil still applied pressure to the wound, but Leif's color was horribly pale. Reaching out, Dan wrapped his fingers around Leif's, the chill of his lover's skin sending a frisson of fear through him.

"Save your strength, sweetheart," he said. "We'll get you to a hospital."

Leif smiled and shook his head. "No. Not until we're done here."

Dan cast a glance behind him, to where a slick, greasy puddle of black marked the remains of Rúnar and Ezekiel. "Taryn and I took care of it. Rúnar's dead, and Ezekiel's in the Otherworld."

"I know. But we've got one thing left to do. We have to lay the dead Ezekiel raised."

Dan swallowed hard against the grief clawing his throat. "Taryn and I will take care of it, okay? We'll get you to a hospital and we'll...we'll do what we've got to."

It would be the death of them both, no question. But at least Leif would have a chance. It wouldn't take long for word to spread, and other Walkers would come in and try to clean up. Leif, Virgil, and Bea might still escape, even if they had to abandon Ransom County to the haints.

Leif managed a tremulous smile. One bloodied hand lifted and touched Dan's face tenderly. "That isn't what I meant, baby. Sorcery raised the dead. Sorcery can lay them again. And lucky for you, you have a sorcerer right here."

A look of sheer terror crossed Dan's face, and Leif realized it was for his sake and nothing else. "No," Dan said. "You can't—you're bleeding—"

And, sweet death, it hurt. Leif clung to the pain, because he knew once he started to lose track of it, once the numbness set in, he'd go all the way into shock and be of no use to anyone. Right now, while he could still follow what was happening around him, still use his will to shape the world, now was the time to act.

Now was the only time he had left. But in a way, it always was.

"You can't fight them one at a time," he said. *Fuck, I'm thirsty.* "Someone has to do this. And unless Taryn forgot to mention she's a sorceress, I'm the only one who can."

Dan's fingers tightened convulsively on his. "But—"

Disheveled and bruised and covered with dirt and ichor, Dan was still as gorgeous as the day they'd met, with dark eyes and soft hair, and a heart big enough to love even someone like him.

"It's the only way," he said.

"He's right," Taryn agreed from over Dan's shoulder. "We'll keep the pressure on the wound, and you can support him, but he's right, Dan. He's our only hope."

Raw fear showed in Dan's eyes, and he leaned down, the ends of his hair brushing Leif's face. "I love you," he whispered.

And, despite everything, Leif smiled. "I love you, too, Dan Miller. More than anything else in this life.

"Now help me up."

It *hurt*—far more than the flogging he'd taken willingly, far more than the rapes by his foster father, far more than any of the thousand pains he'd endured in his life. Something inside his guts tore, as he struggled to his feet, and his vision turned black at the edges.

Hel, forgive me, but I can't even try for a proper chant now, just a prayer. You who tend the dead, who brew the mead in Elvidnir, who feed those who have starved in life, and love those who knew no love, give me the strength to do what must be done. Help me return these bound ones to Your hall.

It was the only thing he could ask for, the only thing She might give him. A part of him wanted to beg for Dan's life, and Virgil's, and Taryn's, and all those in Ransom County. But they weren't Her charges, and he belonged to no other goddess.

She answered him; the pain served to hone his will to iron hardness, and he made it to his feet despite the agony. His breath came in short pants, and he forced himself to control it, to draw air into his lungs and let it go only slowly. Virgil and Taryn clung to him, each pressing against one side of the terrible wound Rúnar's sword had made, fighting to keep him alive long enough to perform this final task.

A strong arm slipped around his shoulders, holding him up. Dan's soft lips brushed across his face; they felt made of fire, and a flicker of fear whispered it was because Leif had lost too much blood and was going into shock, his body instinctively hoarding warmth in its core, struggling to keep him alive just a little longer.

He would never have made it to the altar without their support. When he finally stood before it, he studied the sigils Ezekiel had left behind. Different than what Rúnar would have used, had he decided to raise the dead of Ransom Gap en masse, but similar enough Leif knew what to do.

"All right," he gasped, as much to himself as anyone else. "Let's do this."

Gathering some of the blood turning his shirt sodden, he wiped his hand across the altar, obliterating the signs drawn in sluggish, dead blood with his own. The black tendrils arcing off the altar became more tenuous...but not tenuous enough.

"Dan, Taryn, concentrate on Hecate and Anubis," he said, through the desert dryness gripping his mouth. "Concentrate on opening the way."

He thought they nodded, but most of his concentration was sharp and pointed, focused on the flood of power pouring into the Harrow. Until now, he'd clung to his body, praying not to be swept away by the torrent and into the Underworld.

No more.

Opening himself to all the power of the mountains, of the converging ley lines, he let go.

Instantly, he was swept into the astral. Yggdrasil towered before him, the nine worlds glowing like bonfires amidst its canopy, branches, trunk, and roots. Sharpening his concentration on this world, he zeroed in, felt the etheric distortion of all the *draugar* summoned forth into Ransom Gap. He saw the white corpse-candles of their eyes turning in his direction.

"Mordgud, lead them across the Gjallarbrú," he said. And sweet death, he felt almost a god himself, hovering above the world with all the ancient power of the mountains behind him. "Garm, let them pass unmolested. Hel, accept them into Elvidnir, and let them find peace!"

He had no sword in his hands to sever them from this world, so he made himself into a blade, everything in him honed to a single edge. And one by one, five by five, a dozen at a time, they dissolved into ichor, their souls freed.

They were gone, all of them. No *draugar,* no haints, remained anywhere in Ransom Gap.

He hovered above the earth, seeing it all with incredible clarity, even as his grip on his body faded. The power of the ley lines had been too great, had pushed him too far out of himself. Distantly, he was aware of his heart faltering, of someone he loved crying out his name.

Somehow, Ransom Gap became the Gjallarbrú, smoothly enough he barely noticed the transition. Mordgud stood there as always, and the look on her coarse features was one of approval. In front of her, overshadowing even the great strength of the giantess, waited Hel.

She was still as the dead, not even the whisper of breath to stir Her cloak. The fetor of rot wafted from Her, and an aura of cold touched him as She held out Her left hand, the one nothing more than sloughing flesh on bone.

Which struck him as odd; he'd always believed She offered Her dead hand to the living, but only Her living hand to the dead. But it didn't matter, not really; he went to one knee and kissed Her cold, lifeless fingers before pressing his forehead against them.

"My lady," he whispered, but in this realm, those simple words conveyed all the love and grief he had to give.

Her fingers stirred, cupping his face. *"Will you come with me? Or will you return?"*

It caught him off guard; he'd had no idea such a choice existed, even could exist. "I still have things to do."

"You have pleased me with your service. If you wish to come into my hall, you will be welcomed there."

Tears started in his eyes, because he'd never expected such mercy. He began to answer Her, but paused at the memory of dark eyes and strong hands, of love and belonging, of pain and healing.

"He will join you in the Otherworld, in his own time."

But until then, what? Dan had done everything for him. And he'd barely been able to repay even the smallest part.

"Forgive me, my lady, my goddess," Leif said through the grief clogging his throat. "If I truly have the choice, I choose to return. To serve You further...but because I want to be with him as well. I'm not ready to let go."

He thought the faintest hint of a smile might have touched Her impassive features, although he couldn't be certain it wasn't just a spasm from the dead side of Her face. *"It would hardly be a choice if I did not agree to send you back. Your life is a gift few are given, Leif Helsvin. Use it wisely."*

"In your service."

"As I said."

Leif felt the press of cold stone on his back, and blinked into consciousness. Something hot and wet burned against his face, and after a moment he realized it was Dan's tears.

"Hey," he whispered.

Dan's head jerked up, his eyes wide with wonder. "L-Leif?"

Leif managed a shaky grin. "I think I'd like that hospital now, if you don't mind. Just hold my hand, for as long as they let you?"

The smile transformed Dan's features, just as it had on their first night together. "Sure thing, sweetheart," he whispered, his fingers twining tightly with Leif's. "Sure thing."

CHAPTER 33

Dan walked slowly past the charred timbers and piles of ash, which were all that remained of the farmhouse. Spring wildflowers perfumed the air, and blades of green grass poked up from amidst the ashes. Overhead, a pair of Red-shouldered Hawks called to one another, promising new life.

Ransom Gap had mostly returned to normal in the months since that night in the Harrow. Thanks to Leif's quick action, the only victims of the raised dead had been an unfortunate group of teenagers spending the night in a cemetery. The newspapers had blamed their deaths on a bear attack, but most folks knew what had really happened, especially once Corey had quietly spread the word. The story of what Leif had done beneath the mountain had kept most of the bigots off their backs, although Dan still endured plenty of dark looks and nasty whispers every time he went into town.

They'd stayed in a rented house owned by one of Corey's cousins while Leif recovered. Bea and Virgil finished out the school year; Bea graduated just last week, and was already getting ready to move into an apartment near the university where she had a scholarship waiting for her.

Virgil still had a couple of years of high school to go, but he could finish up anywhere. Ever since the night in the Witches Harrow, his attitude had changed completely. Leif was his new hero, and he was more than happy to move anywhere Leif wanted.

Being the one who had actually lived outside of North Carolina, Leif had suggested several places where they might relocate. Dan noticed every state he mentioned was one where they could legally marry.

Dan paused at the crest of the hill and looked back. "Need some help?"

"I'm good," Leif called, flashing him an easy grin. As always, he dressed all in black, and eyeliner ringed his pale eyes. The ebony cane was a new addition, but would only last until he was able to get around without pain. And, fuck, it was a huge improvement over lying flat on his back in a hospital bed, or being on crutches.

Dan waited until Leif caught up to him, before slipping an arm around his lover's waist and leaning in for a soft kiss. After living with Leif for the last several months, not to mention seeing him through a painful recovery, he was honestly more in love than ever before.

"I should ask if you're all right," Leif said, once the kiss was finished. "You haven't been back here since the fire."

Dan shrugged awkwardly. "That's not strictly true. I came by to take care of the animals the first couple of days, until I could find someone to buy them. I didn't mention it at the time since you were still in intensive care. I thought I should take the chance to see the place one more time before we leave. Say good-bye. I'm not selling the land—it'll be here if Virgil or Bea ever decide they want it. But I'm not coming back."

"Do you want to look at the tree?"

"There's nothing to see, I reckon," Dan said. But he walked slowly with Leif around the ruin of the house anyway.

The great oak had burned with the house, and Dan expected only a charred stump. And indeed, as they rounded the remaining timbers, a stump was exactly what he saw.

A stump with green shoots springing forth.

Emotion clogged his throat. Seeming to sense it, Leif put an arm around him, pulling him close.

Everything came around. Mom and Dad had died, but they still lived on in their children. Bea would be fine, as would Virgil. With Leif beside him, so would Dan. Winter came, but spring always followed.

There were no guarantees in this new life. But maybe, just maybe, they could flourish, like new growth from an old tree. And there was one advantage they had over the stump, Dan thought, as he took Leif in his arms and kissed him tenderly among the ashes.

They had each other. And in the end, it was all that ever really mattered.

ABOUT THE AUTHOR

Jordan L. Hawk is a trans author from North Carolina. Childhood tales of mountain ghosts and mysterious creatures gave him a life-long love of things that go bump in the night. When he isn't writing, he brews his own beer and tries to keep the cats from destroying the house. His best-selling Whyborne & Griffin series (beginning with *Widdershins*) can be found in print, ebook, and audiobook.

If you're interested in receiving Jordan's newsletter and being the first to know when new books are released, please sign up at his website: http://www.jordanlhawk.com. Or join his Facebook reader group, Widdershins Knows Its Own.

Find Jordan online:

http://www.jordanlhawk.com

https://twitter.com/jordanlhawk

https://www.facebook.com/jordanlhawk

Made in the USA
Columbia, SC
19 April 2025

56829806R00150